the EQUINOX TOR

Also by David Doersch:

The Gathering Storm

The Fury

THE EQUINOX TOR

The Chronicles of the Raven
Book III

DAVID DOERSCH

CORVUS
Enterprises, LLC

THE EQUINOX TOR
The Chronicles of the Raven, Book IIi

ISBN 979-8-9879819-6-2

Published by Corvus Enterprises, LLC
125 S Lexington Ave., Suite 101, PMB 131
Asheville, NC 28801

The shiver of the "other"
Creeps up the stalwart spine.
The spirits quail and hand will fail
Against the bidden time.

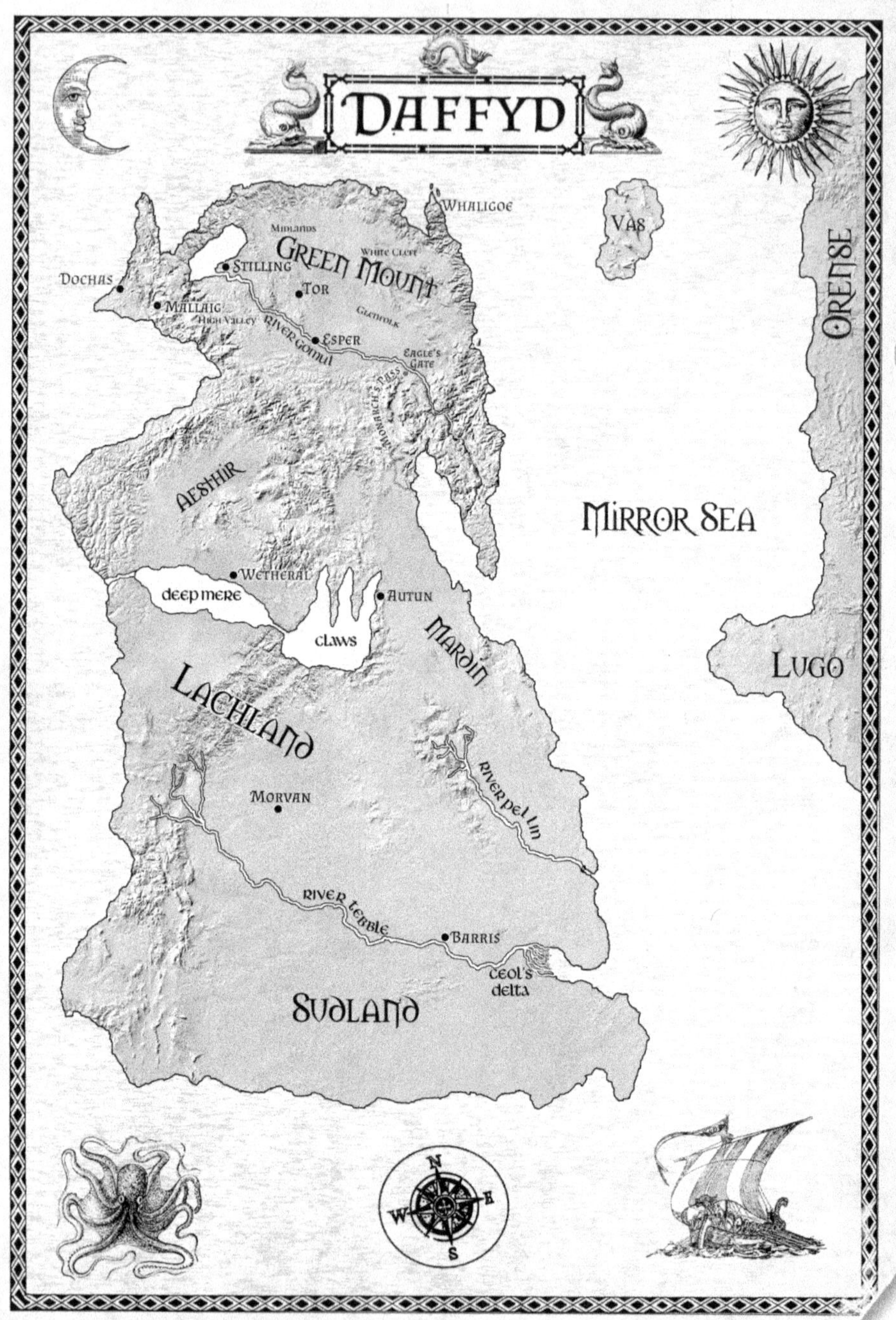

DAFFYD
WHALIGOE
VAS
ORENSE
MIDLANDS
GREEN MOUNT
WHITE CLEFF
DOCHAS
STILLING
TOR
GLENFOLK
MALLAIG
HIGH VALLEY
RIVER GOINUL
ESPER
EAGLE'S GATE
MONARCH'S PASS
AESHIR
MIRROR SEA
WETHERAL
deep mere
AUTUN
CLAWS
MAROIN
LACHLAND
LUGO
MORVAN
RIVER PELLIN
RIVER TEBBLE
BARRIS
CEOL'S DELTA
SUDLAND
N
E
W
S

KOHIMAA
FROSTED LANDS
FREE TERRITORIES
ORENSE
the steppe
VAS
DAFFYO
MIRROR SEA
GERESDLAR
LUGO
SEA OF SORROW
the shadow mountains
ANDUL RIVER
ANGOR
swamp
GREATER ANDUL
LESSER ANDUL
the BREAK
N
W E
S
the gemelos
CANTABRIA
TIPLAI
TABITH
JURUF
OUBANE
mt. noul
PALACE OF THE SILKEN EMPEROR
tivat
BUHAYRA SHIFA
ASLAND
JADIDATAN
SOUTHERN REACHES
ANTSIRABE
zwa miafwa
REEF OF SOULS
the horn
THE EASTERN LANDS
FOREVER ICE

The Story thus far...

In the time before time, the Six — the founding gods or beings that shaped the world of Hortus: Ilian, Manu, Feryn, Nuada, Cruim, and Duff — raised four Tors on separate continents. These four places of power are the Gates through which they transported ancient peoples from Earth to populate their world, operated by mystical tools called "Keys."

In time, Duff was corrupted by his studies, turning to the darkness and renaming himself "Fel." The other five, horrified by his betrayal, strove first to contain him and then ultimately to destroy him, but so great was his might that centuries of warfare and the sacrifice of countless heroes and heroines failed to stop him and his minions. The Five were eventually able to overthrow Fel, destroying his fortress and casting his spirit into the noxious swamps and hidden places of the world.

Though Fel has slept for millennia since, the darkness of his spirit inspired a group of twelve men to gain dreadful power through their vile blood sorcery. Known as the Angor Shamans, each member possesses unique sorcerous abilities. Seven of the shamans, led by one named Sangine, have allied themselves with the brutal Barbárs and bring their horrific powers to bear against our heroes.

Corvus Corax, the renowned warlord known as "the Raven," continues to train his beloved fyrd, a civilian force that he and his longtime comrade and friend, Yazid, have turned into a fearsome military unit. During one training session, he spots the Fool, Latrans, an unusual character that seems always to arrive before grave danger, offering good advice despite his obvious madness. The Fool, whom our heroes later come to suspect is actually Cruim the Clever, tells him that the dreaded and savage Barbárs are returning to attack the lands of the Green Mount again. As per the ancient accords, Corvus alerts the other kingdoms within the Green Mount to rally their forces and meet at Eagle's Gate, while he summons the fyrd.

In far-off Asland, Nabila Warad, a priestess of the Divine Halls of the Ancestors known to those around her as "Mama," is summoned to a mysterious midnight meeting in a remote area of the desert. There, she is greeted by her old love, Grandmaster Ashahl, Sword Master to the Silken Emperor, whom she hasn't seen in over thirty years. Ashahl gives her a strange staff and informs her that it is one of the Keys to the Gates and must find its way to the lands of the Green Mount in far-off Daffyd before the Autumn Equinox. She is to give it to his former student, Corvus Corax. She takes her three votaries, Yadira, Lupe, and Amina, with her, and together they set off on a seemingly hopeless search. Along the way, they find and rescue a child with mismatched eyes, Argant, who Mama senses has a critical destiny to fulfill. Eventually, they find their way to Eagle's Gate, where they meet Corvus just before the Barbár army arrives. Using her spiritual divinatory powers, Mama discovers the small group of Barbárs led by the Angor Shaman that has sneaked into the Green Mount via the Hidden Stair and is now headed for the Tor—and the Gate. Corvus sends Mama's group, along with his son Ligulf and Li's lover Piper—a fellow minstrel—and a small contingent of thirty warriors to intercept them, while Corvus and the gathering Green Mount armies stay behind to face the Barbár horde. Along their journey, Mama and her group are attacked by the shaman's assassins, who successfully abduct Argant. Mama uses her shape-shifting abilities to follow the assassins and, with the supernatural help of Athdar, Guardian of the Tor, they recover Argant and continue their journey toward the Tor, where they hope to find the Gate.

Empress Zsoka, former ruler of the Orensian people, continues to suffer as the captive of the shaman Blood-Tooth, who was sent to free her from her island prison by her former lover, Vajk, the father of her son and Grand Hadvezér of all the Barbárs. She has been horrified by the sanguinary acts and barbarity of the Angor Shaman, and suspects him of being a demon of some sort. She has been biding her time, trying not to anger the mercurial Blood-Tooth, but finally has enough when he abducts Argant and puts a child's life in danger. As Mama rescues the boy, Zsoka presents herself and Mama tells the Empress to come with her.

Darienne, now Queen Darienne I of Lachland after the death of her mother in the defense of Autun against the Barbárs, learns of the unexpected invasion in the south of the country by their erstwhile peaceful neighbor, Sudland. There is another attempt on her life when she is attacked in front of all her nobles, and Archbishop Mormand's role in a treacherous scheme against both her and her late mother is revealed. The archbishop flees with the help of the Church's Holy Knights. Darienne is only able to survive with the aid of her lady-in-waiting, Maddie, and her supernatural healing abilities. When the young Queen reappears the next day, tired but decidedly not dead, it spurs a surge of patriotic energy among the nobles, and she uses this sympathy to rally her country's forces to prepare to repel the invaders in Morvan—Lachland's former capital city.

Queen Darienne elevates both Justiniere and Zach to knighthood and she tasks each of them with vital new positions which will play a critical part in the defense of the country. Justiniere is raised to Knight Commander and sent to Autun to relieve Sir Reginald Bleiz, allowing him to assume command of the strike force which will launch a surprise attack on the

Sudlandese invaders in Morvan. Zach, meanwhile, is promoted into Justiniere's vacated position as sub-commander of the Lake Jacks, answering to Brigadier St. Fiacre. He and his wife take in the spirited child who accompanied them back from Autun on Mormand's yacht.

Mama and her votaries arrive at the base of the Tor, along with Ligulf, the minstrels, and some two dozen Adders, to find it already under Barbár control, though without the key, there is little Blood-Tooth can accomplish. They pause in the stillness of the night, unsure of how to advance, when a startling vision occurs. Under the harsh, silver light of a private star, Corvus Corax comes thundering into their campsite, his enchanted horse glowing golden. They are all relieved to see him, and he quickly takes command of the small unit as they prepare to take the Tor on the eve of the Equinox. They must get Argant to the temple atop it before the next morning's dawn if they are to have any hope of preventing the Gate from falling into the hands of their enemy.

The story continues…

Chapter 1

"When to fight? When not to fight? These are the most important questions."

—Anonymous

One day before the Autumn Equinox - 574 HR
The Road Near Ben Strath, Glenfolk Region of the Green Mount

Bradana

"Alright then, Nicol?" she asked softly.

"All clear to my eye, Bradana," Nicol replied with a quick wave.

Moving quietly, Bradana continued on to the next picket position. It was still a few hours before dawn. The night was cold, the sky cloudless and scattered with more stars than she could recall ever seeing. For five grueling days and nights, the allied force had held the Barbárs at bay, though at significant cost. After Corvus and Fergus had departed for the Tor, taking the White Cleft troops and three hundred of the fyrd with them, the enemy had held off for the day. Cailean had rearranged the Green Mount forces, keeping the Midlands troops in the center of the line, prepared to take the brunt should the enemy attempt another charge. Toren's archers had precious few arrows left, so there was no chance of a repeat of their earlier tactic of fouling the Barbárs' charge and peppering them with missiles. Anticipating that the enemy would attempt to charge around the narrow gap in the road where it rounded the shoulder of Ben Strath, Cailean moved all of the remaining Glenfolk soldiers into position between the road and the river. It was difficult terrain, steep and slippery, and they struggled to find reliable footing on which to make a stand. Scouts reported that the enemy was encamped about a mile down the road and seemed to have paused to tend their wounded and plot their next move. Cailean used the reprieve wisely, distributing the few shovels and tools they had in their baggage train to the Glenfolk soldiers and instructing them to dig into the hillside, creating terraces upon which to fight. He dispatched some three hundred of the fyrd to assist and give the Glenfolk soldiers a needed rest. By nightfall, the hillside down to the river had been carved into a series of four terraced banks, upon which the soldiers created separate shield walls. It wasn't perfect. Enemies on foot could, potentially, slip between the terraced banks, but not in any great number, and each cluster of soldiers on the downhill side was prepared for that possibility, their shield wall curving to face the uphill slope.

The attack had finally come that night. It had been a bloody business, and the Glenfolk soldiers had taken the worst of it. The Räubers had been tricked and fouled repeatedly by the Highlanders when making mounted attacks. So, that night, they did indeed come on foot. A contingent of around a hundred men spent the day stealthily climbing the rugged slopes of Ben Strath to position themselves above the archers, while the rest waited until the dark of night to creep along the river's edge directly before the Glenfolk terraces.

In the small hours of the night, the Highlanders were awakened by a bloodcurdling scream, followed by the roar of over a thousand Räubers. Seeing where the attack was focused,

Cailean had quickly sent Donella's troops scrambling down the slope to reinforce the Glenfolk nearest the raging Gomul, moving the remainder of the fyrd to the center defensive position on the road. It was then that the contingent on the mountainside struck, cutting through the archers on the slope and charging down to hit the south flank of the fyrd.

Toren

He had found himself suddenly surrounded by five Räubers on the steep mountainside, as the rest of the enemy assault surged down the slope. He put an arrow through the eye of the nearest one then, spinning, managed to drop another with a shaft through his throat. The third forced him to use his carved longbow as a staff, blocking an axe swing that would have decapitated him. He put his foot on his attacker's chest and shoved, casting the brute down the mountain in a series of painful tumbles and collisions with rocks and trees. The Räuber did not rise. Faster than his foes could react, Toren nocked and fired again, dropping the fourth man with a feathered shaft buried in his neck. The fifth man was more wary, hiding his bulk behind the trunk of a tree, a throwing axe in hand. Toren heard a scream from nearby and, taking his eyes off the Räuber, saw that young Aibne was being attacked. A brute held him by the neck against a rock and was about to split the boy's skull with a barbed sword. Toren pivoted and put an arrow in the man's back. Then, firing twice more, he wounded the leg of a Räuber who was creeping down the steep hillside toward Cailean's position and pierced the temple of a foe that had just stove in the skull of old Gus.

But Toren couldn't defend his archers and himself at the same time. Seeing him distracted, the Räuber behind the tree had leaned out and thrown his axe, burying it in the heart of Davonna's taciturn husband. The enemy had paid a heavy toll to take down the legendary archer, but his loss was an immeasurable blow to the Green Mount and the fyrd.

Bradana

Bradana had had barely enough time to reposition the shield wall, rushing the reserves into position to face the road, while the veterans quickly shifted to face the charge from the mountainside. Several of the rushing Räubers had managed to vault the shield wall during the confusion, hacking and slashing great holes in her troops before finally being put down. The stalwart Yazid had been enormously helpful, his spear twice taking vaulting Barbárs in mid-air. He had shouted bold encouragement to the troops, reminding them of their training and the importance of their spears. Then he, too, had fallen to a grievous wound—a leaping Räuber had grabbed the haft of his spear with his left hand, and the brute's axe had laid open Yazid's left breast. They had managed to drag him back out of the line, and get him to the healers, but the wound was severe and his survival was in doubt.

The fall of the burly Aslene had shaken the confidence of the fyrd. All had been trained by Yazid and Corvus, and with Corvus absent, their morale was largely pinned on the constancy of the big man and his flashing, deadly spear. Bradana had done all she could to rally them, pushing her way to the center of the line and screaming defiance at the gigantic charging madmen before them. Tearlach, the limping veteran to whom she had grown close, and upon whom she had come to rely for advice and camaraderie, had pushed his way to stand at her side, flashing her a quick, reassuring grin. Many of her friends had fallen that night. Too many, she thought, quickly stopping her mind from lingering on their faces and reciting their names. By the time they had managed to put down the assault from the mountainside, the attack by the river had turned ugly. The shield wall on the lowest terrace had folded and been overrun; several of the Glenfolk soldiers and more than a few of the supporting fyrd were shoved off the terrace to die in the river. Had it not been for Donella's troops rushing down the slope, the enemy would have turned all of the Glenfolk walls.

Having exacted a bloody toll and sensing that the battle would turn against them, the Barbárs then withdrew, leaving Cailean, Donella, and Bradana to assess their losses as the sky began to move from black to grey and the stars in the east made their exit in advance of the dawn.

That was five days ago now, and each day since had seen another devious stratagem and bloody assault by the enemy. Yesterday they had tried another mounted attack, nearly breaking through the Midlands line at the center of the road. The Highlanders had once more secured the trip rope, only to discover that a small dismounted group of the enemy had been lying in wait near the rise of the road. They had rushed forward and cut the line, just before the horses thundered up over the rise. How the dismounted men had managed to sneak so close to the Highlanders undetected was a mystery to them.

During that battle, the enemy commander—a fierce older man with grievous, weeping burns on the side of his face and a mangled ear—had ridden too close to the Highlanders, his sword taking its vicious toll among the front line of the Midlands' troops. Cailean had rushed forward from where he stood between the fyrd and Donella's men, his sword slashing a gaping wound in the man's leg. Two Räubers had immediately moved their mounts forward, cutting Cailean off from his intended prey, their blades hacking down at the young general's shield with breathtaking ferocity. The son of the Raven had managed to lash out with his blade, striking the face of one of the Barbár mounts, causing it to rear and pull back in a frenzy, its mouth a bloody ruin. Cailean barely got his rapidly disintegrating shield back up in time to catch another vicious chop from his other opponent, who had seen his comrade's horse get injured and expertly urged his own mount forward to fill the gap. Regardless of their wildness, the Barbárs had proved themselves to be skilled horsemen and clever warriors. The blow drove Cailean to his knees, and he struck at the only target available to him—the horse's stamping foreleg. His sword shattered the leg bone. With a scream the mount buckled and fell, the Räuber vaulting nimbly from its back before his leg could be trapped under the falling horse.

"Hold the line!" Bradana shouted at her men, curbing any impulse they might have to rush to Cailean's aid. If the wall fell into disarray, the mounted enemies would cut through them and all would be lost. The Highlanders stood watching helplessly as the tattooed brute raised his sword above the dazed son of Corvus. But, remarkably, just as the blow descended, Cailean shed his useless shield and rolled forward within the arc of his opponent's blade, coming up kneeling with his own sword buried in the chest of the Räuber. It was a move Bradana had seen Corvus execute more than once, his training evident now in his son. A roar of approval and pride went up from the Highland troops. Cailean turned just as another mounted enemy thundered toward him and with an acrobatic leap, the young general dived back toward the line, narrowly avoiding a wicked slash from the charging brute, whose momentum pulled him close to the Highlander wall. Before the Räuber could recover himself, two spears lanced out from the line, one stabbing the frothing mount in the shoulder and the other piercing the Räuber's side, just above his hip.

"My thanks, lads," Cailean had said, lightly, as though it had been nothing more serious than a mere stumble on a morning stroll. The moment had served to infuse the Highlanders with much-needed confidence and Bradana wondered if the young general had planned to take some bold risk to bolster the Highland troops' courage, knowing their morale was faltering.

She shook her head at the memory. Yesterday's battle had tested their dwindling line and though the enemy ranks were shrinking as well, the fierceness of each assault—and the speed and strength of the enemy's horses—seemed to be whittling away at the Highlanders more rapidly. A familiar knot settled in her stomach as she continued creeping from one picket position to the next. She dreaded to think what today might bring. Would the line hold? How many more friends would fall?

"Alright Gavenia?" she called softly.

"S'alright here, Bradana," the surly woman barked back with asperity. Gavenia's husband had died in the wall two days earlier, and a bitter fury had replaced the joy he had brought her. Bradana had pulled her out of the wall, moving her to stand among the few reserves remaining, worried that the woman would be reckless and unsteady—more apt to seek suicidal revenge rather than hold her place with discipline. But the move had only fueled Gavenia's rage and frustration. In another situation, Bradana would have sent her back to Esper with the stream of wounded being carted there daily. But their numbers had been thinned too badly. She needed every available sword left to her.

With a resigned sigh, Bradana moved on, stealthily making her way to the next picket.

The morning sun found her rushing through camp, cursing herself for her own stupidity. She was late for the meeting. After finishing her rounds, she had made the mistake of sitting against a tree by her campfire, thinking only to rest for a moment. But the exertions of the past days swept her into a deep sleep from which she had been startled awake hours later by the sounds of Kina, her campmate, making tea.

She burst into Cailean's command tent, nodding quickly to the general and Lady Donella. As she did, she noted an older veteran standing behind Cailean with a grizzled, red beard. He was dressed in Glenfolk colors. To her right, she was surprised to see Yazid propped up on a cot, his bare chest wrapped in a blood-stained bandage, his features sallow and wan.

"What're you doin' here, Yazid?" she asked, interrupting the discussion.

"There are important matters before us this morning, I think," he answered weakly, grimacing in pain at the effort the speech had cost him. "I did not wish to miss it."

"Sorry I'm late," she said, turning to Cailean, who flashed her an indulgent smile.

"I was just sayin'," the young general said, "that our rate of attrition is too high. We canna hold this position much longer."

"Yet if we march for Esper," Donella replied, "the enemy will run us down on the road. We'll have no defense."

"True, my lady," he responded. "However, Alasdair here has a clever plan that may just allow us the chance we need." He turned to the red-bearded veteran. "Care to explain?"

The older man took a step forward and cleared his throat. "As you're aware, the road from here to Esper follows the line between the mountains and the river. However, the river makes a sharp bend around Nuada's Rock, creating a pocket of land that faces the road. Perfectly formed for a defensive position."

"How far is that?" Bradana asked.

"It's a two-hour march," he replied. "And I've scouted the ground. The land in the bend of the river is not boggy nor rough. 'Twould be a bonnie place for a shield wall."

"Provided we could reach it before the enemy rode us down," Donella said dubiously. "What then? We make a stand by the river, and let the enemy ride past us on the road, with nothing to stop them 'twixt here and Esper or the villages beyond… or even Stilling itself?"

"No, milady," Alasdair continued. "The road there is quite narrow and lined with trees on the south side where the slope of the mountain is quite steep. Two days ago, I set a team to fellin' those trees, blocking the road. If we position ourselves in the land formed by the crook of the river, the enemy will have no way to pass without facing us in our stronger position. If they try to clear the road, their flank will be open to us."

"Our latest scout reports," Cailean interjected, "suggest the enemy numbers no more than five hundred."

"And our numbers?" Yazid asked weakly.

"We've suffered sorely," Cailean responded grimly. "The wounded now outnumber the hale. We can stand no more than a thousand in the wall, but that's with no one left to tend to and transport the wounded. If we allow for that, we'll be able to stand around six hundred. Though, in this new position, we won't be spread so thin and we'll have the river protecting us on three sides."

"Very well," Donella said cautiously. "How do we extract ourselves from here?"

"We'll take a page from Alasdair's book," Cailean said with a wry smile. "We'll fell trees from the slope, blocking the road at the shoulder of Ben Strath. Meanwhile, the Glenfolk soldiers will begin marching with the baggage train and wounded for Nuada's Rock, and the Midlands troops will replace them on the slope." Turning to Bradana, Cailean asked, "How much lamp oil d'ye suppose we have in our supplies?"

"No more than a hogshead or two, I'd wager," she responded. "We've used most of what we brought along, and we didn't bring much to begin with. Lady Donella's troops brought more, but I'm afraid it's largely burned through."

Cailean nodded thoughtfully.

"I see where your thoughts take you, I think," Yazid said, his eyes narrowing in appreciation. "You are your father's son, after all," he added, winking at the young general, who smiled in response.

"Two hours after the Glenfolk troops march, the fyrd will follow behind, double-time." He looked at Bradana, and she nodded in understanding. Then he turned to Donella. "Meanwhile, the Midlands troops will have spiked the slope from here to the river with sharpened stakes and broken spears—anything that will slow those blasted horses. An hour after the fyrd's departure, the Midlands troops will follow. Use the last of the oil to fire the roadblock, that'll force the bastards onto the slope, where treacherous footing and the spikes should slow their advance enough to allow you time to reach the rest of us, provided your men move with haste."

"It could work," Donella said approvingly. "If the Barbárs give us the time."

"Aye." He nodded grimly. "*If* we have the time."

The enemy had not attacked so far that morning. Bradana stood near the felled trees of the growing barrier, staring down the slope of the road toward the enemy camp. She had seen a group of enemy scouts, no doubt drawn by the sound of their axes. The scouts observed the Highlanders' activities for a time, then rode furiously back to the enemy camp. *It won't be long, now,* she thought.

The time was near for the fyrd to march. She had set them to breaking down camp hours earlier. By now, they should be ready to move. Grabbing her spear from where she'd left it leaning on a tree, she took one more look down the road and froze, her brow creased. The unmistakable cloud of dust told her their time was up. She turned and sprinted back, searching the area for Cailean, shouting an alarm as she ran.

"To arms! They're coming! To arms!"

Cailean

He was helping Yazid onto the last of the wagons when he heard Bradana's shouts. He patted the big man's hand, giving him a concerned look. Then to the driver, he called, "Get moving!"

He hailed Bradana from a distance and the two rushed toward one another.

"Cloud of dust on the road, Cai," she said quickly. "They're coming."

"Bugger!" he muttered under his breath. "Right, I'll fire the barrier, you gather the fyrd and start marching. Fast! Two hundred yards, then turn and make a wall. We'll leapfrog it all the way." She acknowledged the order and dashed off while Cai sprinted for the log barrier. It wasn't as high or as imposing as he had hoped, but it would have to do. As he ran, he saw a group of men standing by a felled tree, unsure whether to proceed with their labor.

"Get that tree on the barrier now!" he shouted. He rushed to the side of the makeshift wall that abutted the mountain. There, two small barrels of oil had been placed this morning, along with a pile of candle butts, tent canvas, and half-empty lanterns. Gathering some nearby Midlands soldiers to help him, he threw the candle butts and lanterns onto the barrier and draped the canvas from the tents over the top of the whole pile. They had to step aside for the men dragging the felled tree. It was a big pine, and from the look of it, full of pitch. He directed them to heave it on the top of the mound.

Checking the road again, he saw the Barbárs charging pell-mell toward him. The barrier was already high enough to block their easy passage, but he had to get the Midlands troops moving.

"Douse it with oil, lads," he told the men helping him. "Then fire it up! Quick like!" Turning to the Midlands positions on the slope, he shouted, "Donella! Donella!"

"Here, Cailean!" she shouted from down the slope where she was helping embed a spike.

"New plan! Get your troops ready to move!"

In short order, the Midlands troops were formed up on the road. Stepping up to Donella, Cailean spoke quickly. "We'll leapfrog it the whole way. Take your troops a hundred yards beyond the fyrd, then turn and make a wall. As soon as you're in position, they'll hop around you and so on."

She nodded, then issued her orders.

The barrier caught flame, rapidly growing into a massive wall of fire blocking his view. Down the slope, the Barbárs slowed into a milling mass as their eyes darted between the wall of flame and the slippery slope dotted with spearheads. He rounded up the last of the workers and sent them on, pausing only to remember this battlefield and briefly promise those Highlanders that had fallen that he would not let their deaths be in vain. Then he jogged after the departing troops.

When he reached the fyrd line, Bradana came forward to meet him.

"It'll take them at least an hour to work past the obstacles and spikes and re-form," he said. "We'll move as quickly as we can in the meantime."

Bradana turned and, dividing the fyrd in half, she sent them charging around the Midlands troops with orders to form up a hundred yards past their wall. Cai noted with pride how quickly the fyrd responded to the unusual orders—no confusion or milling about, just immediate, obedient response. *You've trained them well, Da,* he thought. Glancing back, he could now see a rank of Barbárs on foot, moving through the terraced defensive positions, pulling up stakes and spearheads to allow those behind to ride through unhindered. He jogged on. As he approached the Midlands wall, he gestured for them to split and continue along the road. They would have to move more cautiously once the Barbárs reached them, but until then, haste was critical.

They leapfrogged four more times before the Barbárs had finally worked their way around the flaming barrier and clustered together again. There seemed to be some confusion among them, which struck him as uncharacteristic. Over the past few days, the Barbárs had charged headlong after them whenever given the chance, heedless of whether the whole force was ready or not. Today, however, they seemed more cautious. Perhaps it was the fact that their numbers had been steadily reduced in the battles since they arrived at Monarch's Pass with over ten thousand warriors, and now they fielded just over five hundred. It was equally possible that they had gained a wary respect for the Highlanders and their seemingly unbreakable shield walls. Whatever the reason for their hesitancy, he was thankful for it and jogged on, urging his troops to leapfrog again and even once more.

Finally, the Barbárs came, but he noted that they came at a trot, not a mad gallop. They seemed to be watching with some interest as the Highlanders continued making their unusual maneuver. *They're drawing closer,* he thought. *They're counting how long it takes for the front wall to rush back to the protection of the one behind.* The enemy was still a half mile back as he approached the fyrd wall and waved a negating gesture to Bradana, pausing her order to move.

"Only fifty yards back this time!" he shouted, so all the troops could hear. "They'll charge the moment you split apart, so run like Fel himself is at your heels. Go, now! Go!"

The fyrd did not wait for Bradana's signal. The wall dissolved into a mass of men and women sprinting for the safety of the next wall, which seemed impossibly far. Cai was running with them when he glanced over his shoulder and saw the enemy spur their horses and give chase. *It'll be close!* he thought, panicked. Just then he saw a woman go down, badly. It looked like she'd twisted her ankle. Not pausing to think, he changed direction and scooped her up, throwing her roughly over his shoulder and running on for all he was worth. The added weight slowed him severely, and his legs were soon complaining, his chest heaving with the effort.

"Leave me, Cai!" the woman managed, as she bounced on his shoulder. He recognized the voice, but couldn't see her face. His mind worked furiously to summon her name as his legs pumped madly, chewing up the distance to the Midlands troops. *Too slow, Cai, you're moving too slow!*

"Give her to me!" a voice suddenly shouted, as a burly man—Donal, a blacksmith from Helmsdale—doubled back to relieve Cai's burden. Without slowing pace, they shifted the woman onto the big man's shoulder, and Donal charged on, seemingly heedless of the added weight. Cai didn't need to glance back to know how close the enemy was getting; he could hear the thundering hooves drawing near, and see the worry in the eyes of the Midland troops watching him race toward them.

He was still twenty yards from safety when he heard a shriek behind him. He ducked, slapping the ground with his hands momentarily as he felt the whoosh of a blade just over his head. The rider's mount passed him on the left. The enemy would have to veer aside as they approached the wall of shields and spears facing them. The road directly ahead was pitted and uneven, with a large puddle of mud just off to his right. The many days of his youth spent playing Touchball on the sodden field to the south of the village suddenly came flooding back. How many times had he scored the winning point by sliding across the line in the mud and into the try zone? He leapt for the puddle, his arms out before him like a diver entering the water. A blade clipped his side weakly just as he got himself airborne, his unexpected maneuver saving him from a serious wound. His chest hit the puddle hard, the air exploding out of him, but his momentum through the slippery ooze propelled him forward the final yards down the pebbled road into the Midlands wall. The shouting soldiers stepped aside momentarily as he scraped to a stop somewhere in their midst.

The Barbárs veered to either side of the shield wall, hoping to find an opening, but the wall curved around to keep them out, and all they got were jeers and occasional stabs with spears if they ventured too close.

Cai rose to his feet grinning, his face and whole body covered with mud and scrapes. He worked his way back through the Midlands troops, hands slapping his shoulders in congratulations as he went, as though he had scored the winning point of a festival tourney. When he reached the rear of the formation, he could see Bradana's wall only fifty yards back. *Well done*, he thought. *Now, if the bleedin' Barbárs will just…*

He didn't finish the thought, because at that moment, the Räubers began to dismount and form their own wall. The numbers of the enemy and the Midlands troops were roughly equal, but the Räubers had a distinct size advantage. No doubt they hoped to destroy this wall, then move on to the fyrd.

He waited until he saw the bulk of the enemy on foot, then shouted, "Now lads, fifty yards beyond. Run like the devil!"

The Midlanders' wall dissolved into a mass of sprinting soldiers, dashing back behind the fyrd wall. The Barbárs were momentarily caught flat-footed, and scrambled to round up and remount their horses. In the time it took them to prepare, Cai was able to reach the fyrd and send them dashing to form up beyond the Midlands wall yet again. He too reached the Midlands troops again, winded but safe. Donella intercepted him.

"At this rate, Cai," she said, breathing hard from the exertion, "it'll take us all day."

"Aye, it will," he agreed. "But if we stand and fight them, the cost will be terrible, even if we win. I'd rather pull back like this until we reach the stone and have our full force."

She sighed and wiped the sweat dripping from beneath her helmet with the back of her mailed hand. She looked him up and down with a wry smile. "You look like you've been wrestling pigs."

"Oh?" he said, looking down at the mud caked into his leather, as if surprised. "I likely smell like it, too." He flashed her a wink, then shouted to the troops. "Steady, lads! They canna breach the wall when mounted if you remain firm."

The mounted enemy was circling now, menacing the Midlands wall, looking for an opening. They were too close for the troops to try another leapfrog maneuver.

"One step at a time, now," Cai commanded. "We're goin' ta march our way to the fyrd together. Keep the wall tight!"

He nodded to a nearby sergeant to call the cadence, and the man proceeded to shout in an admirable battlefield voice, "Step! Step! Step!" Little by little, the Midlands wall inched its way toward the fyrd, the Barbárs riding in circles about them, menacing their every stride while staying just out of range of the deadly spears.

The enemy soon realized that they meant to join forces with the fyrd, doubling their strength, but clearly weren't sure how to prevent it. If they positioned their horses between the two walls, the fyrd could attack their rear as they faced the back of the Midlands formation. Bradana, seeming to read the situation, ordered the fyrd wall to begin advancing to meet the Midlands troops midway. The Barbárs hurled insults and jeered, walking their mounts alongside the retreating wall as the two Highland forces came toward one another. Ultimately, the invaders could do nothing to stop the two forces from merging into one, much larger force in a circular wall now some six hundred strong.

The Barbárs pulled back, and a single Räuber rode forward and dismounted some twenty yards from the Highland line.

Donella looked quizzically at Cailean. Taking a shield from a nearby soldier, Cai stepped out of the formation to meet the man.

Though large, as were all Räubers, this one had a more wiry build. Surprisingly, his hair was light brown—uncharacteristic for the Barbárs, who typically had a mop of unruly, near white-blonde hair. His jaw was covered with a rich, brown beard, also unlike their typical sparse and scraggly blonde beards. He wore leather breeches, much as his comrades wore, except that his bore red-fringed tassels along the sides. He stood some six or seven inches taller than Cai, yet his bare shoulders were narrower, the bones of his shoulders protruding. The muscles of his arms were sharply defined with pulsing veins bulging up the length. His skin was somewhat darker than that of his fellows, though it was covered in the same tattoos and his eyes bore the same battle madness. He strode toward Cai confidently.

Cai stopped with his sword and shield resting easily in his hands. He looked up at the Räuber with a relaxed, calm expression.

"And what are you about, ye great bruid?" he asked.

The Räuber smiled a feral grin, then spoke in a halting command of Sudlandese. "We fight... shield to shield." He gestured to indicate all present. "No more run. No more chase."

"What if just you and I fight?" Cai suggested. "Man to man."

The Räuber's eyes lit up at the possibility.

"If I win," Cai proposed, "you take your boggin' forces back to where you came from."

"And... I kill you?" the Räuber asked.

"Our troops step aside and let you pass," Cai answered, to which the Räuber smiled his hungry grin once again.

"You have fought well," the Räuber said, a note of admiration in his voice. "Highlanders very strong."

"I'll put that on your burial stone," Cai answered with grim determination.

Chapter 2

The boy must be ours. You must be prepared. Bend all your considerable skills to finding a way to secure that child. If the Empress proves too great an obstacle, perhaps a coup might solve that. Despite her military accomplishments, the Orensian court has never been happy being ruled by a female. As you know, her cousin, Count Eberardo of Celje, is a friend to the Church and stands ready to step forward should the throne of Orense become vacant. I say again, you must secure the boy.

*—Excerpt of a missive from Pentatarch Vella IV
to Archbishop Mormand, found among the papers seized
on the Archbishop's yacht.*

One day before the Autumn Equinox
Wetheral Castle, Lachland

Darienne

She was seated alone in the Queen's study above the great hall, the morning sun streaming through the east-facing window behind her. A fire had been stoked in the hearth to break the chill, and a fresh tea service sat steaming on the table before her. Though she had awakened early and enjoyed a stroll in the garden as the sun rose, she still felt weary from the long day before. The hours of pageantry and pomp that she had endured drained her more than even the most grueling training sessions with Kaiso ever did. Still, there were highlights that she would keep among her fondest memories. The look on Major Zachar's face—Sir Zachar, now, she reminded herself—upon being elevated to knighthood, and the tears of pride that rolled down his wife's cheeks, had truly touched her. The benediction given by Reverend Yanna at the conclusion of the funeral—so balanced, warm, and loving—had struck just the right tone, evoking vivid memories of the very best of Queen Isador. But nothing had fired her soul like the cheers the dinner guests had given in response to Darienne's speech and the chanting of her new nom de guerre, "Moonflower." Yes, it had been a good day. She sighed and stirred a dollop of cream into her tea.

The door to the chamber opened and Kaiso leaned his head in. "They're here, Majesty," he said. A slight smile played on her lips. She wasn't sure if she would ever get used to hearing herself referred to as "Majesty," especially by Kaiso.

"Show them in," she replied.

He pushed the door further open and ushered in the two newly minted knights, Justiniere and Zachar, before exiting the chamber and closing the door behind him. The two stepped forward and bowed almost in unison, though Zachar's injuries inhibited his stride. They were each dressed in the uniforms of their rank and unit, though devoid of weapons or armor.

"Gentlemen," she said, gesturing to the chairs on the opposite side of the hexagonal table. "Please sit." She was pleased to see Justiniere assist Zachar with the heavy chair before taking his own seat. "Help yourselves to tea."

The two murmured their gratitude but politely declined.

"Sir Pierrick," she said, using Justiniere's new title, "you are familiar with the plan as discussed yesterday?"

"I am, Majesty," he affirmed. "And stand ready to depart at once."

"It is unfortunate we have been delayed these two days," she said, a frown creasing her brow. "But there's nothing for it. Haste is critical. You are to board ship this afternoon and make all haste to Autun. Your orders will be delivered to the docks."

"Yes, Majesty," he said with an inclination of his head. "And may I say, I am deeply honored by the trust you place in me."

She waved her hand. "You have certainly earned it. Use this time, this coming winter, to prepare Autun for the attack we know will come in the spring. The Barbárs will return, and Autun must not fall."

"I understand, Your Majesty," he replied gravely.

"You no doubt have many details to which you must attend, if you are to sail in a matter of hours," she said, making it clear that he was dismissed.

"I thank you," Sir Pierrick responded, rising. "I will send word upon my arrival in Autun." Turning to Zachar, Justiniere extended his hand. "I wish you good fortune, sir." Zachar began to rise, but Sir Pierrick waved him down.

"And to you, sir," Zachar replied fervently, taking the proffered hand and shaking it firmly.

With that, Justiniere turned and strode from the chamber to take up his new command in Autun, and to direct Sir Reginald Bleiz onward to action in Morvan.

As she watched the door close behind him, Darienne thought of poor Maddie and said softly, "He shall be missed."

"I am sure he will, ma'am," Sir Zachar responded. "Though I have only just made his acquaintance, his presence and role here at Wetheral has been significant."

Darienne turned her attention to him now. "Tell me about the boy."

"The boy?" Zachar blinked, perplexed by the sudden change in subject. "Oh, Talon, Majesty?"

"Is that his name?" she replied. "The boy on Mormand's yacht, that I understand you and your wife have taken into your home."

"Indeed, Majesty," he answered. "I trust I have not overstepped in doing so?"

"Not at all," she answered quickly. Then leaning forward, added, "Though it would be uncharacteristic for Archbishop

Mormand to adopt a child. The more I learn of the man, through his actions and what we have found among his papers, the more apparent it becomes that his machinations run deep, with far-reaching consequence. Who is this boy?"

"I don't really know, Majesty," Zachar replied. "I know only that both his parents live far from Lachland. However, I have my suspicions."

"Go on."

"He has spirit," he said thoughtfully. "Defiance. Clearly not used to humble surroundings."

"Yes," she said, urging him to continue.

"On the ship, I witnessed a tense moment between him and Mormand, in which Mormand insisted the boy refer to him as 'my lord.' With any other child, I might dismiss the moment as merely educating him as to courtly etiquette."

"But with this boy?

"It felt… I'm not sure how to describe it, properly."

"Try," she said flatly.

He paused for a moment before speaking again, his eyes seeming to drift off in memory. "Years ago, I took Loeiza on a brief holiday to Morvan. I was stationed in the south at the time, and she had endured some hardship traveling in the baggage train."

"Your point?"

"She had never been to a city so large," he continued, flustered by her blunt and direct demeanor. "And besides the delights of shopping among the many market stalls, and mingling with so many people from different lands, I had hoped to show her something rare, something unforgettable. I heard tell in the barracks of a troupe of entertainers—jugglers, musicians, prestidigitators, and the like—that had set up on the outskirts of the city proper."

"Sir, I hope this fascinating tale is somehow relevant to our discussion of the boy," she said, struggling to stop some irritation creeping into her voice.

"I believe so, Your Majesty," he continued. "The central entertainment of the evening was a man who entered a great cage filled with lions and other terrible beasts, armed only with a whip and a prod. He was somehow able to make the fearsome creatures do all sorts of tricks—leaping over one another, perching upon platforms of various heights. It was quite remarkable."

"It sounds memorable, indeed..." she said, taking a deep breath..

"My point, Majesty," he said, focusing his penetrating eyes upon hers, "is that in that moment that Mormand insisted the boy call him 'my lord,' I perceived the same powerful defiance that the greatest of the lions exhibited toward its tamer. That boy is no ordinary waif. He has a powerful, indomitable, and imperious streak within him, despite his youth. I would stake my life that this child has a noble—perhaps even royal—pedigree of some sort."

"I see," she said, leaning forward, suddenly quite interested. "Do you have any sense of his origins?"

"Not as such, Your Majesty," he replied thoughtfully, "though some clues do present themselves. First, the boy is large for his age. Though not yet eight summers old, he could easily pass for a boy of ten or eleven. His shoulders are unusually thick for a child, and presage that he shall grow into a man of fearsome size. Add to that his shock of white-blonde hair..."

"A Barbár?"

"Most likely, Majesty," he said with a nod of affirmation. "Though he speaks with an Orensian accent, and has little command of our tongue."

"I see." She leaned back in her chair, her steepled fingers before her lips. "So, we may infer that he was only recently taken... or sent... from his homeland."

"A reasonable conclusion."

"Orensian accent. Imperious disposition and likely of Barbár blood... Could he be the bastard heir, perhaps?" Darienne's eyes widened even as she spoke the words. The torrid and scandalous rumors of how the Empress of the Steppes and the Grand Hadvezér of the Barbárs had together produced a child were infamous.

"That was my guess," he said hesitantly. "Though I certainly don't wish to jump to any conclusion prematurely. But, if my recollection is correct, that event happened some eight years past, did it not?"

"He would be the correct age," Darienne replied thoughtfully.

"My hope was to gain the boy's trust," Zachar continued. "School him in our language and, in time, learn of his past."

"I agree," she said. "But regardless of the boy's true parentage, we must proceed with the understanding that he is but a child. An innocent. I will not have him used or misled for political purposes."

"Of course, Majesty," Zachar said sincerely. "Though he has been with us but a day, Loeiza is already growing quite fond of him. And he seems to be warming to her as well, though he, understandably, is less than enthusiastic about her cooking. Loeiza is many wonderful things but, I am afraid, a cook she is not." He smiled ruefully, prompting a light laugh from Darienne.

"Well," she said, placing both hands upon the table, "let us see about changing your situation, shall we?"

"How so, Your Majesty?"

"You and your wife are to move into the north wing of the castle, at once," she said, finally arriving at the point of this interview. "You will take up your new duties here, replacing Sir Pierrick as the second in command of the Lake Jacks. You will answer directly to Brigadier St. Fiacre. I believe he is expecting you this forenoon."

"Your Majesty, I'm honored," he said with awe.

"Furthermore," she continued, "I should very much appreciate having Loeiza attend me as a lady-in-waiting. That is, when her duties with young Talon permit, of course."

Zach's mouth fell open in shock and he blinked in a moment of confusion and gratitude. When he did respond, he could only stammer, "Your… Majesty!"

"That will be all for now, Sir Zachar," she said, rising. "I look forward to observing you in your new position, and ask Loeiza to introduce young Talon to me when she feels the time is right, won't you?"

"Of course, of course," Zach said, rising with some difficulty. "Thank you, Your Majesty. I will endeavor to earn the trust you place in me."

"You already have, Sir Zachar," she replied, her eyes narrowing with intensity. "By serving my mother so faithfully."

Chapter 3

The path along the rise of the Tor is a magical thing indeed. Stands of birch, pine, oak, yew, holly and more. Each distinct. Who knows how these stands came to be? Who knows their provenance? An ancient well, dug long before the time of kings, still stands offering its fresh, clear waters to those who might make the journey. An ancient archway... Why? To what purpose?

—Oidhche MacAllan
Historian of the Tor

One day before the Autumn Equinox
The Tor, Green Mount

Corvus

He crouched next to a large hawthorn bush by the base of the Tor as the small company gathered around him. Once they had all arrived from their dash across the sward, he addressed them in a hushed voice.

"The trail zags and zigs its way up the Tor," he said. "At times, it's quite steep and narrow. Plenty of places for ambushes or traps. The darkness of the early hour works both for and against us. Move carefully and pay attention. Though there are only five of the buggers left, they'll have advantages. They will have chosen where to fight, using the terrain against us. And let's no' forget they have a dangerous wizard. If he's anything like the bastard I fought at Eagle's Gate, he'll hae the strength of ten men. Stay back from him, let me engage. Our priority is to protect the boy and the staff, and get them both to the top of the Tor… but we'll kill the bastards along the way."

The group absorbed his words with grim determination and prepared to move.

Corvus placed an affectionate hand on Li's shoulder, before nodding to Dallin and Lupe to join him as he moved off onto the broad trail that led up the Tor. The path started anticlockwise around the north of the Tor, beneath a canopy of trees and bushes that overhung it, making it feel at first like they were walking into a tunnel. Corvus was impressed with Lupe's stealth. Dressed in a black robe that was belted at the waist and a matching black veil, the sturdy young woman moved as silently as Toren himself. Twice as they advanced, Corvus had to turn to make sure she was still with him. He could hear the rest of the company creeping along at a distance behind them — the occasional snapped twig, or the faint clink of metal. But overall, he was pleased with the group's efforts at stealth.

He had only advanced some hundred yards onto the trail, when the boy started screaming.

Cursing, Corvus dashed back down the path, squeezing his way past the Adders to get to the rear. He found Mama's group crouched beside Argant, only a few feet onto the beginning of the trail. The boy was clutching his ears and yelling.

"Stop it! Stop it! You're too loud!" The boy's eyes were closed and he was shaking his head. Mama looked to Corvus, distress and worry on her face.

"What's happening?" Corvus demanded.

"I don't know," she replied in Aslene. "He just suddenly grabbed his ears and started to scream."

Corvus sheathed Raven's Tooth and knelt down to the boy, taking Argant's face in his hands. With the gentle firmness of a father who had raised two sons, he squeezed just hard enough to gain the boy's attention. The child's mismatched, jewel-like eyes blinked and he looked distraught.

"Argant," Corvus whispered urgently. "What's the matter, lad? What's doin'?"

"The Tor is really loud in my head," the boy said, tears blossoming in his eyes. "It suddenly started shouting the moment I stepped on the trail. Talking really fast and loud."

"What's it saying?" Corvus asked, not doubting the child for a moment.

Argant winced and shook his head, as though hearing Corvus' question through the din in his mind was a struggle. "The same thing as always," he replied eventually. "Owl, pine, heather, fox… He's just saying it really fast and loud all of a sudden. He keeps saying 'oak' and 'raven' a lot! Like they're important."

Corvus was confused and looked to Mama, who shrugged helplessly. When he looked back at Argant, the child's attention had turned inward once more.

"Argant, Argant!" But the boy ignored Corvus' voice until he shook him gently and he blinked, the mismatched eyes focusing on him again. "You have to be brave and quiet, no matter the pain. Can you do that for me?"

The boy sniffled, winced, and slowly nodded his head with a whimper. After a moment, he fell silent, grimacing and gripping his ears, still in obvious discomfort. Standing, Corvus glanced at Mama, then Ligulf.

"Try to keep him quiet as best you can," he said with resignation, then moved back up the trail to the front of the company. He shot a worried glance at Dallin as he once more drew his sword and led the way.

Some quarter mile on, the trail turned steeply uphill, climbing past a rocky outcrop before turning back in the direction they had come. They passed under the branches of a great yew, and through a stand of white birch, the trail weaving between the ghostly trees. Lupe and Dallin moved from bole to bole, bows at the ready. Pausing to listen, Corvus knelt down, trying to discern the faint trail in the near total blackness.

After a moment, they proceeded out from the copse. The trail here crossed a steep meadow, the tall grass soughing in the light breeze. Despite the cover of darkness, Corvus felt suddenly exposed, a chill of unease dashing up his spine. Ahead, the trail disappeared into a pine grove, the trees massive and full. He jogged across the meadow, ducking into the deep gloom beneath the pines, his feet crunching on dried needles. He paused to allow Lupe and Dallin to join him and realized that his left hand had unconsciously slipped into the pouch at his belt where he fingered the strange medallion that had lit his journey. He toyed with the idea of using it. Standing in the blackness beneath the trees, he realized how easily the company might lose their way. But, despite Argant's outcry, he was still hoping for some element of surprise, and hearing the Adders arrive noisily in the grove behind him, he decided it would be best to press on without the light — at least for now. Perforce he moved slowly, at times only inching along, his eyes struggling to perceive the outlines of a trail. The blanket of pine needles that covered everything made that task more challenging yet. Twice, he strayed from the path, misled by a tangle of roots and a jutting stone. Both times, Lupe's near silent hiss drew him up before he wandered too far.

They finally came to the far edge of the pine grove, a stone structure marking its end. It took him a moment to discern that it was a well, dug and placed here long ago for the comfort of those making the pilgrimage up the Tor. A plain, unmarked stone bench sat nearby, positioned to allow a weary traveler a moment's rest beneath the shade of the pine boughs, while affording them a no-doubt pleasant view of the countryside to the east.

Just past the well, the trail turned once more uphill, disappearing steeply between the prickly leaves of two holly trees. It was a perfect place for an ambush, as the trail narrowed between them, their dense and forbidding foliage preventing side coverage from bows. The company would be forced to slip through the gap single file. But looking right and left, he could perceive no alternative route, the ground being steep, rocky and overgrown. With a resigned sigh, he gestured to Lupe to follow directly behind him and, closing his eyes, slipped into Badger form, the world slowing in his perception. He eased forward into the gap, his ears alert for any sound. The hollies were thick and the passage deep before he felt, rather than saw, that he was emerging. The ground here was steep and the trail climbed directly upward, over a boulder, before cutting back to the right and disappearing over an open rise. The holly branches swayed slowly as they were brushed by the light wind.

It was only the faintest momentary glimmer — possibly a trick of the eyes in the dark — but he reacted with the lightning reflexes of Badger form, his blade sweeping up and to the right as he leaned suddenly to the left, his face scraping the barbed holly leaves. He felt the thrown dagger impact his sword, the telltale *ting* reverberating in the silence before the blade skittered harmlessly off under the trees. There was a gasp of alarm from behind him. With a rush, he dashed forward, scaling the rock, clearing the gap so that the two archers might pass through behind him. He crouched down and listened intently. A soft footfall from amongst the bramble of growth up the slope. Then another. The assassin was slipping quietly away into the woods. It would be a fool's errand to try to pursue. Directly uphill of the trail, the ground sloped sharply upward, into what he assumed — by its darkened shape — to be a tangle of hawthorn. *Was that wych elm towering above?* In this dark, he couldn't see so much as a game trail in the wall of underbrush.

The first of the Adders, MacLief, emerged through the gap behind him. Corvus waved him up to join him on the rock.

"Assassin amongst those trees," he whispered. "Be wary. Pass it on." Then, as MacLief turned to whisper to the Adder behind him, Corvus gestured to Lupe and Dallin to follow, and moved cautiously onward over the small rise.

An hour passed. The company made slow progress through thicket and bramble, across brief open meadows, scaling rocks and passing through dense copses of trees that were impossibly dark, as the trail wound its way back and forth up the steep side of the Tor.

Corvus paused near a wide turn in the trail. Another stone bench sat in a grassy clearing overlooking a vista that was probably quite stunning in the daylight, given how high they had climbed. The route had been particularly steep just prior, and looking out from the bench, he could just make out the tops of the tall pines on the path below. He waited until the company assembled in the grassy space, silently checking in with Li, and Piper. He glanced around in the darkness, but couldn't make out Argant at first. Finding Mama in alarm, she gestured to a shadowy figure near them. He leaned close and discovered it was Rhona, who was carrying the boy in her arms, fatigue on her face. He whispered to them all to rest there for a moment.

They still had some hours before dawn. After the opening in the pine trees up ahead, the trail turned up a steep incline then once more doubled back to the north, disappearing beneath the stout branches of a cluster of majestic oaks.

Rhona sat on the bench, Argant still in her arms. Piper sagged onto the seat beside her, the pallor of his skin making him nearly glow in the dim starlight. Corvus knelt before him, fishing in his pouch and producing the nub of the pain-killing root Shanna had given him back in Dóchas.

"Here, lad," he whispered to the bard, offering the root. "A bite of this will still the pain. Careful, though, too much and you'll stumble like a drunkard."

Piper thanked him and, taking the proffered root, sniffed it, then took an exploratory bite, grimacing at the bitter taste and immediate cottonmouth. Corvus patted the minstrel's leg, then with a gesture to the company that their rest was ended, climbed the steep bend in the trail and continued, sword drawn.

Mama

Just as Corvus disappeared up the trail, a raven croaked. She looked up in alarm, then closed her eyes and searched the breeze for warning. Argant whimpered on Rhona's shoulder. The company was slowly easing its way forward, the Adders following Corvus and the two archers. The trail ahead was wider, allowing the group to travel two or even three abreast.

"What does the wind tell you, sitti?" Yadira asked quietly.

"The creature is near." Mama shook her head in frustration. "But somehow he is masked from me. Almost as though he uses the Canon of Concealment."

Yadira put a hand to her breast in horror at the thought of the filthy blood-magic sorcerer having access to the sacred mysteries of the Sisterhood.

The last of the Adders made their way up the steep bend and onto the switchback, following Corvus. Mama nodded to her group with a sigh and, leaning heavily on the staff, moved toward the incline, pausing to allow Amina to go first, aided by Yadira. After Mama came Rhona, close behind, carrying the troubled Argant. She was followed by Zsoka, who reached over and wiped the boy's brow tenderly. Ligulf then supported Piper up the path, and they were followed by the three Adders bringing up the rear.

The group passed beneath the first of the oak branches, the path beneath littered with fallen leaves and acorn husks left behind by fattened squirrels. Mama grew concerned as their company seemed to be dividing. Corvus, the archers, and the bulk of the Adders had moved forward briskly, leaving her smaller group— Amina and Yadira, Rhona carrying Argant, Zsoka, Piper and Ligulf, and the three Adders—to follow behind. She stopped and gasped in alarm as a bright silver light suddenly streamed through the canopy of oak leaves. It seemed to be the same light that had accompanied Corvus to find them earlier that night, and it shone brilliantly, changing their world from black gloom to a series of wondrous spears of light stabbing down through the trees.

The raven croaked again from a branch ahead.

"I know!" Argant moaned. "Oak and raven, I know!"

Hearing this, Mama spun in a crouch, the staff out before her, and the others scattered in alarm, just as death dropped from the branches above.

Corvus

When it emerged from the oak trees, the path turned once more uphill, then passed through a crumbling stone archway. A long stone wall, some six feet high, abutted the arch on the downhill side. The base of the wall nearest the arch sat a good four feet above the trail below, as it exited the trees. Corvus paused. Again, they would be forced to pass one at a time. He leaned through the arch, peering uphill. He couldn't perceive much beyond the trail continuing up a steep grassy slope, dotted with small trees and shrubs. His hackles rose. It was another perfect place for an ambush. He estimated they had climbed over half the height of the Tor now. The enemy wouldn't wait for them to reach the top to attack. If he were them, this is the place he would choose. He turned and whispered instructions to the two archers, reaching into his pouch and producing the medallion. With a silent prayer that Nuada would guide Dallin's and Lupe's aim, he leaned once more partially through the arch, casting the metal star into the air, then quickly leaned back, anticipating thrown daggers. With a hum, the star flew from his hand, immediately bathing the entire area in a brilliant silver light. Anticipating his enemies' surprise, he dived through the arch, rolling nimbly and coming up to his feet. Lupe followed him through, quickly turning to the right to aim up the hill. Dallin rushed through right after her, tossing Brochy up onto the grassy slope, then drawing her bow, her eyes scanning the terrain.

Two men screamed a challenge and leapt down onto Corvus from behind a cluster of concealing shrubs, their short swords flashing in the light. A thrown knife narrowly missed Lupe's head, clinking off the archway just as MacLief dashed through.

"Bugger that!" he exclaimed.

The grass rustled with the movement of the badger as he growled and took off straight toward a stand of aspen, their fluttering leaves serving to mask the assassin hiding among them. Lupe sent an arrow into the stand in a vain effort to flush him out. Dallin was desperately trying to get a clear shot at one of the men attacking Corvus, but the three were moving so rapidly, changing positions, that she dared not release her shaft.

Corvus' blade flashed madly, deflecting and blocking the attacks from the two assassins, the silver light from the "star" reflecting off their blades. They were skilled, and their blade work was lightning fast. Raven's Tooth rang like a bell, its peal sounding defiantly up the hillside. Corvus slipped deftly between the other men, inverting the triangle of their position. Raven's Tooth nearly took the throat of the assassin to his right, but the man managed to parry at the last instant. The assassin spun away into a crouch, then riposted with a deadly low thrust. Having just blocked a slash to his hip from the left man, Corvus quickly bound the offending blade up and over, bringing it down to foul the incoming thrust from the man on the right, and throwing both assassins momentarily off-balance. He slipped back gracefully into the deep preparatory lunge of Eagle form just as a third assassin came charging down the trail from his left.

Voices shrieked in terror further down the Tor, but he didn't have time to investigate as an arrow slashed overhead, taking the latest charging assassin in the breast and propelling him backward. With a roar, Corvus sprung from his lunge, his rear leg sweeping up and around in a graceful spinning Eagle-form leap between his assailants. The left man slashed vainly at empty space as the power of Corvus' leap pulled his body into a horizontal plane in mid-air. At the apex of this jump, he slashed Raven's Tooth across the eyes of the man on the right who fell in a bloody, screaming ruin.

Further shrieks from down the hill finally demanded Corvus' attention and a thunderous boom rattled a shower of leaves from the oak trees on the far side of the wall. His remaining assailant turned to flee, only to drop dead as Dallin's powerful shot snapped his spine. Just then, a man's panicked shout came from up the slope, and the final assassin emerged from the aspen stand, slashing down at something harrying his leg. Lupe's shot took him in the shoulder, spinning him around before he fell. There was a rustle of fur and the man shrieked again, only to fall silent a moment later, Brochy savaging his throat. Corvus didn't wait to see more, dashing back toward the archway, shouting for the Adders to make way.

Ligulf

Li, along with Piper, Rhona, and Zsoka, had instinctively drawn quickly off to the side when Mama spun around, her staff at the ready. He looked about for danger and, for a moment, nothing happened. Then, suddenly, a strange, ill-featured bald man dropped from the branches above, spider-like, landing between two of the three Adders in the rear, a hand on each neck. They immediately dropped their weapons and began shrieking in agony, their knees buckling in submission. The skin where his hands touched seemed to boil and steam with black blisters appearing on their necks and faces all around his hands. Everyone was momentarily frozen in horror until the shaman, his sinews swelling with sudden strength and a madness in his eyes, smashed the heads of the two Adders together, breaking them open like melons. The third Adder—Jamie, Ligulf recalled—leapt forward, his spear lancing in rapid thrusts, high and low. Somehow the shaman avoided each one, moving with preternatural speed, his body shifting and pivoting until he suddenly grasped the spear near the head, and with an effortless twist, shattered the haft, then plunged the spearhead, dagger-like, into Jamie's chest with such force Li could hear ribs break.

Four more Adders ran back and pushed past Mama and her group. They quickly formed a disciplined line, shoulder to shoulder, their spears snaking out with deadly speed and accuracy. Li knew from having observed Yazid's training sessions with them that this formation was called "the Bear Trap," as the rapid thrusts from multiple spears could overwhelm and fell even a mighty bear. Again, the shaman moved with such unnatural speed, and insect-like angularity, that none of the thrusts landed. Instead, the shaman suddenly exploded forward into their midst, and the bodies of two Adders went flying. Before the other two could shift to face him, he lashed out with a clawed hand in each direction, his left taking the throat from one, and his right striking the other's face with such force it snapped his neck.

Li pushed Piper behind him and stood trembling, the thin blade of his puntina seeming wholly inadequate before this creature. The shaman snarled at Mama and looked around the clearing, his eyes lighting on Rhona, who gripped a terrified Argant to her chest. With a single bound, he crossed the thirty feet to her, grabbing her wrist and wrenching it toward him. Reacting instinctively, Li slashed at the shaman's hand with his razor-sharp blade. The creature howled and released her, looking at his now mostly severed wrist, the hand dangling from it at a sickening angle. With a snarl of fury, the shaman slashed at Li with his right claw. Li's training kicked in and he lunged deeply away from the blow, receiving only a glancing hit, rather than its lethal full force. Nonetheless, such was the strength of it that it sent him to the ground, his head ringing and his sword skittering away. Li's world dimmed to blackness.

Mama

When the creature attacked Li, Mama saw her moment and swung her staff, striking the shaman's back with a mighty blow. The characteristic boom echoed through the woods, and the shaman was propelled forward into the trunk of the oak near where Piper was crouched, with Zsoka beside him. The minstrel barely rolled out of the way in time, driving Zsoka further around the bole of the tree. Rhona stood some ten feet away, terror in her eyes. Her left arm seemed to have been injured by the shaman's grip, and she was having trouble supporting Argant's weight without it.

Impossibly, the shaman's head snapped around like an owl's might, rotating far beyond a human's normal range to face her. Argant screamed. Mama frowned in amazement. *That blow would have shattered the spine of an ox. How is he still moving?*

With a snarl, the shaman lunged once more for Rhona and Argant, but the creature was clearly damaged. His left leg didn't seem to be working quite right and Li had nearly severed his left hand. Yet the shaman still moved with incredible speed and strength. His right hand grasped Argant's shoulder, as though he would rip the boy from Rhona's failing grasp. Mama raised her staff to strike again but before she could, Zsoka leapt onto the shaman's back, shrieking in defiance and clawing at the monster's eyes with her nails.

"No! Leave him be!" she screamed as blood spurted from the shaman's right eye. With a snarl that was equal parts agony, frustration, and rage, the creature released Argant, and reached back to grasp Zsoka's neck, hurling her across the trail, where her body crashed against the trunk of a tree. She fell to the ground and lay still.

The shaman snarled defiantly at them, his right eye bloody and closed. He suddenly reeled back as a spear buried itself in his chest. Una, the young woman that had spoken so politely to Mama and Yadira in camp days earlier, had rushed ahead of her comrades and slid on her knees to strike a telling blow.

The shaman teetered, looking down at the spear haft in his chest. His claw-like hand reached for Una's face.

"Away!" Mama shouted, and Una rolled backward, abandoning her weapon. Mama's staff fell on the shaman's skull like a hammer blow from the heavens. Finally, the creature crumpled beneath the force, his head crushed. There was an enormous blast that threw them all to the ground, and when Mama finally sat up blinking and sore, she found a shadowed figure standing over her, panting, his blade drawn. It was Corvus, and in the dim, filtered starlight, she could see fury in his eyes.

Argant slipped away from Rhona and ran, crying, to Mama's side. She wrapped an arm around the boy and gave him a reassuring hug.

"Mama!" It was Amina's voice that called out to her now. She looked around, panicked that the girl might have suffered greater injury in the fight. She finally spotted her kneeling by Zsoka's limp form. Yadira helped Mama to her feet, and together they limped over to Amina with Argant at their side. Corvus joined them, blade still at the ready. Zsoka lived, though she was badly injured. Her eyes blinked and looked around in stunned confusion. Amina moved to the side to allow Mama room to kneel by the woman's head. She stroked Zsoka's cheek, wiping away a tear that trickled down.

"Very brave, Zsoka," she murmured to the stricken woman.

"He's just a boy," the Empress said, weakly. "Like my son, Talon." She slipped into unconsciousness. Corvus silently sheathed his sword.

Lupe and Dallin came running back breathlessly, the badger close behind, blood on his snout and claws.

"All clear?" Corvus asked them.

"Aye," Dallin replied grimly, to which he nodded quickly. Then, looking around, he spotted Li's prone form.

"Tend to her," he said to Mama, indicating Zsoka. "She's earned a place of trust with us." Then he moved to his son's side.

Li was just starting to come around. He startled suddenly, as though he remembered the danger, and tried to sit up. There was a livid bruise near his left temple, and he blinked furiously, as though trying to clear his vision.

"Easy now, Li" Corvus said, kneeling and supporting his son's efforts to sit up. "You took quite a blow."

Li blinked a few more times, then smiled at his father weakly. "Oh, I've had worse, Da." Then he passed out in Corvus' arms.

Chapter 4

Very little is known of the so-called powers of the Angor Shamans. Many believe them to have no supernatural gifts whatsoever. The mystique that has grown about them being perhaps entirely a product of myth and legend, and the whisperings of those with overactive imaginations. Perhaps we will never know, but I, for one, find many of the legends hard to credit, and feel that without strong proofs, we should assume the simplest possible answers. I suspect that as scholarly inquiry expands in this area, rather than a council of foul, immortal blood-wizards, we will find simply a collection of sinister men interested perhaps in the arcane, but lacking any supernatural gifts or understanding.

—*"The Mysteries of Angor, a Traveler's Guide"*
by Lady Gebrilda St. Germaine

One day before the Autumn Equinox
Atalaya de Locus, Cantabria

Bishop Galea

He was awakened by a pounding on his door. He rose groggily, flung on his robe, and opened the door, blinking at the torchlight from the hallway.

"What is it?" he demanded of the breathless guard at his door.

"The idolator," the guard answered, clearly uneasy speaking of the shaman. "He is screaming again."

Galea hung his head and sighed in resignation. "And no one but me, the Pentatarch's personal secretary, can deal with this?" His voice rose to a fevered pitch.

The guard shrugged helplessly, his face a mask of desperation.

"Never mind!" Galea hissed, and turned back into his chambers. Dressing quickly, he returned to the door a moment later, gesturing peremptorily for the guard to precede him.

Some minutes later, Bishop Galea stepped through the door to the captive shaman's cell, holding a candle aloft. The screaming had ceased—that, at least, was a blessing. However, it had been replaced by a pathetic whimpering, the source of which was difficult to pinpoint in the darkened room.

"Geminus," he called gently. "Are you in here?"

A muffled whine was the only answer. It seemed to come from the far side of the chamber, between the small bed and the wall. The bishop hugged the edge of the room until he could see the form of the shaman crumpled in the corner, an arm held protectively over his head.

"Geminus," he said again. "What news?"

"Blood-Tooth," the ghoul-like creature muttered through a mouth that seemed filled with too many teeth.

"What of him?" Galea asked, his voice soft, despite his rising impatience.

He detested this creature. Every time he was required to speak with him, his gorge rose. The foul smell that emanated from the shaman—a toxic blend of a pungent, moldy cheese, with gangrenous flesh and rotten meat thrown in, the brown teeth that dripped continuously with a viscous slime, the rheumy jaundiced eyes, the isolated shanks of wispy black hair that clung to his scabrous pate like tufts of grass on a swampy and pestilential hillock... He hated everything about him, and would gladly have seen him put to the sword— or worse. But it was clear they needed him still. His unique talent seemed to be to know the whereabouts and relative health of each of his brethren. Perhaps the foul thing had other skills; Galea didn't know, nor care. The Church's plans for unifying Daffyd depended upon the Barbárs—with the aid of the Angor Shamans—clearing out the territories of the Green Mount, and the creatures seemed all too glad to do so, due to some superstitious foolishness about a hill up there being a sacred Tor or some such nonsense. If allowing them to seize and keep that hill could inspire them to throw themselves against the formidable Highland defenders, so much the better. Galea found it more interesting that the shamans seemed to have convinced Vella of the importance of the Tor as well. That was very entertaining. He didn't for a moment believe that Vella understood why the Tor was important, nor that the Pentatarch's blunt mind was capable of penetrating the arcane legends of the Lost Keys. No, it was only that the Pentatarch found the story compelling and perhaps mysterious and, like a child hearing an interesting faerie story, wanted to hear more.

He sighed and shook his head in disgust. Back to the task at hand.

"Geminus," he said, more sharply. "Get up and tell me what has happened to Blood-Tooth."

"Dead," the shaman replied, hugging his knees to his chest and rocking back and forth. "Dead, dead, dead."

A cold dread poured over Galea. The Pentatarch would not take this well. Of the twelve Angor Shamans, the Church and the Barbárs were only able to convince seven to work with them. Of those seven, four were now dead. Four virtually immortal beings, hundreds of years old and possessing untold arcane knowledge and a memory of history far surpassing any living being… dead. *What a waste*, he thought.

"I am sorry for your pain," Galea said diplomatically.

"Pain?" the creature replied, finally pulling his head from his folded arms and looking at the bishop. "I feel no pain."

"Then…" Galea began, confused, "why are you screaming?"

The shaman looked at him as if seeing him for the first time.

"Fool," the creature said, though his voice was soft it was barely a whisper.

"What?"

"Fool," the shaman repeated, standing and pointing a trembling finger at Galea. "Fool, fool, fool!" His voice rose with each utterance.

"Now, now, Geminus," the bishop said, his tone calming as he made a placating gesture. "Let's not forget that you are our guest, and that we are paying you and your brethren rather generously."

"No!" the shaman shrieked as he leapt at Galea, his hand suddenly around the bishop's throat.

Galea blanched at the suddenness of the attack and the febrile intensity in the shaman's eyes and voice. He tried to back away, but quickly found himself against the wall of the cell.

"What are you doing, Geminus?" he croaked.

"You mistake everything, bishop," the shaman said, his words slow and careful as he worked around too many teeth to say them.

"What do you mean?"

"I do not mourn my brethren." The shaman's breath was fetid and smelled of rot. "I fear the consequence of their death."

"What consequence?" Galea gasped, straining to free himself from the grip of this foul creature.

"The princes have returned," he said, his eyes wandering as if he listened to some inner sound.

"Princes? What princes? What do you mean, you foul thing?"

"His commanders," the shaman answered. "Umbral and Timor."

"What is that? What is a Timor?" Galea strained against the shaman's wrist with both hands, to no avail. The creature had surprising strength. "I don't know what you're talking about!"

"The Shadow Lord's princes, fool," the shaman snapped. "They will know of my brethren's failures and will punish the rest of us." Then his eyes became imploring, and his grip on Galea's throat suddenly released. "You have no idea of the torments we will endure."

"We will protect you," the bishop replied, rubbing his throat and easing away from the shaman. "The Church will protect you."

The shaman's arms suddenly dropped limp at his sides, his head likewise dropping as if he suddenly looked to his feet. Then, his shoulders began to rise and fall rhythmically. The movement was so uncharacteristic that it took Galea some time to realize the shaman was laughing.

"You have… no idea… what you're saying," the shaman said through his laughter. "There will be a reckoning at the feet of Timor, the tormentor." He winced at the idea of this imagined torment. Then, once again, the shaman surged forward and seized the lapels of Galea's robes, his face mere inches from the bishop's.

"Unhand me at once!" Galea shouted, striking at the shaman's hands to no avail.

Suddenly, Geminus' eyes lit with a new fire. He stared into Galea's as though trying to discern some hidden depth within them.

"Perhaps…" the shaman hissed softly, one hand releasing the robe and stroking down the bishop's cheek instead.

"What are you…?"

"Perhaps I could." Geminus' eyes took on a feverish yet hopeful quality as he continued to stroke the horrified bishop's face. "Slip behind… Ride along… I could… He wouldn't know."

"Stop this! Guards!"

But, before the bishop could utter another cry of alarm, something happened — something obscene. Somehow, Geminus' consciousness shed his flesh and slipped behind the eyes of Bishop Xosep Galea. It did not displace the bishop himself, but its oily, putrid presence inserted itself alongside him, infecting the bishop's mind… His very soul.

Galea was only vaguely aware of the empty husk of the shaman's body falling dead to the ground, then withering with alarming speed, as though hundreds of years of deferred decay suddenly happened in moments. He stared in horror as the flesh shriveled and began to flake away into a grey dust. Within a matter of heartbeats, not even bones were left.

He glanced around the room, seeing the cell with a new perspective. He looked to his hands, suddenly vibrantly aware of the blood coursing through his veins, and yet nothing had changed, had it? He was still Xosep Galea, secretary to the Pentatarch — or was he Geminus, ancient and filled with lifetimes of memories? Perhaps both? The schemes and machinations that Galea had in place for his advancement within the Church, his manipulations of the Pentatarch and maneuvering of the mercenaries and sycophants of the court, suddenly seemed so paltry and unimportant as he — they — grasped the enormity of the conflict before them. Their thoughts dashed down one path after another, exploring the power and capabilities of the shaman, the awareness of his brethren, and the might of blood magic. *Such power!* Galea marveled. *Yet so very vulnerable if exposed.* Geminus wandered through Galea's thoughts and memories, marveling at the inner workings of the Church, its political maneuverings and hegemonic ambitions. How easily manipulated and vain the Pentatarch was.

A sly grin danced over their face as the shaman and the bishop began to understand how their merging could be wildly beneficial. The bishop sought a greater understanding of these names the shaman had voiced, Timor and Umbral. *Who are these two? Why do you fear them so?* Images and memories, generations old, of the two princes coursed through their minds. Neither could look away, such was their symbiosis.

Umbral, the master of shadows, was able to move between the world of light and dark, allowing him to appear anywhere at any time, invisible and unseen if he desired. But when visible, he was mighty in strength. Countless fell creatures of the darkness answered to him, when needed. He could appear soundlessly anywhere, or send minions to do so. The ultimate assassin.

Timor was fear incarnate, tormentor, excruciator. The abomination of the soul. He was the closest in spirit to the Shadow Lord himself. He was the more tainted of the two, the more damaged, and yet the more powerful by virtue of his closeness to their master.

These were the princes. Unyielding, irresistible, and unwavering in their dedication to the Shadow Lord, Fel. The very thought of Him left the Geminus portion of them trembling and silent, quivering and hiding behind the eyes of Galea.

Protect us, it implored. *Do not let them find us.*

I can, Galea responded in silent reassurance. *I will protect you.*

I will give you knowledge, Geminus offered in exchange.

Yes. Galea smiled. *Yes, together we shall do great things.*

Chapter 5

"Pride is both the armor and weakness of every warrior."
—Sebastian Trevisano, Third Shield to the Emperor

One day before the Autumn Equinox
The Road between Ben Strath and Nuada's Rock,
Glenfolk Region of the Green Mount

Cailean

"You told him what?!" Donella shouted indignantly. "Cai, how could you?"

Cailean sighed and continued unstrapping his padded leather vest. Mud had gotten caked between the vest and his undershirt, and besides being uncomfortable, it was limiting his movement. The Barbár commander had agreed to meet him on the field in one hour. He prayed it would be enough time. As soon as he had returned to his troops, he had sent a rider to Nuada's Rock to tell the Glenfolk troops to march back as quickly as possible to reinforce them here. He looked at the lay of the land and shook his head in frustration. *Weak defensive position,* he thought.

"Cai, answer me!" she pressed.

"Donella…" he began wearily. Then, seeing their proximity to the listening ears of the troops, he pulled her aside and continued quietly. "*Lady* Donella, you may no' have noticed, but we're in a bad spot. The ground here is too open. As long as the enemy remains mounted, we have to be in a circular formation and we canna hardly move."

She shook her head. "We should have stayed at Ben Strath."

"Perhaps," he said with a small nod. "But here we are now, and I'm playin' for time. Every minute I can delay these bastards with the theater of a champions' duel is a minute more I've bought for the Glenfolk troops to reinforce us."

"But you promised him we'd step aside if you lose," she said, looking horrified at the thought.

"And you're not bound to that," he said with a cajoling smirk. "No matter wha' happens out there between that hackit bastard and meself, you dinna let them pass. Once the Glenfolk arrive, you can anchor the left side of the wall on the bank of the river, well across toward the road, and attack for all you're worth before they have a chance to remount. Finish the bastards here and now."

"So," she began, "you never intended for us to stand down, should you lose?"

"Not for one second," he replied firmly.

"Your da wouldna approve," she said. "His word is like iron. He ne'er breaks it."

"And he can take me to task for it, should I live," Cai said, once more scraping mud from his jerkin. "As far as I can see, I have one responsibility here: to do everything in my power to stop those bastards from getting past us. We have to finish this, and I'm just buyin' time until the Glenfolk get back here."

She nodded her understanding, and started helping him refasten the buckles of his leather.

"You'll not wear chain?" she asked, concerned.

"Slows me down too much."

"He's not as big as some of the brutes, I suppose."

"Aye, that worries me," he said, looking over his shoulder to eye the enemy commander. He was standing in conference with a small group of Räubers, no doubt his chieftains. "He didna rise to command on his good looks. He's dangerous, and no doubt full of tricks."

"You're a brave man, Cailean," she said, seeming to resign herself to his plan.

The two of them walked back to the troops, who were watching him expectantly.

"Friends," Cai said, raising his voice to be heard. "I'm gon' tae step away for a bit and have a wee dance with yon bastard. I've sent for the Glenfolk troops to join us." Looks of encouragement flashed across the faces of the troops. "I'll drag this out as long as I can. But, regardless of the outcome, you be ready to fight the moment it's finished." Nervous nods answered him. "Keep the wall firm. Show them what it means to be a Highlander. Show them what the folk of the Green Mount are made of!"

A cheer went up, intermingled with cries of "The young Raven!" and "Son of Corvus!"

Turning back to face the Barbárs, Cai drew his longsword and muttered to himself, "'The young Raven,' eh? Nothin' like high expectations."

He casually rolled his sword across the back of his hand, reversing the grip momentarily before once more flipping the weapon back to a standard grip. It wasn't the two-handed great sword the Highlanders were famous for, but instead a solid, well-balanced single-hand longsword his father had given him years earlier — King Fergus had given it to Corvus to present to Cai on his thirteenth birthday. It was made of fine Cleftian steel, with golden brass inlay along the quillons. It was too long for use in the shield wall, but he found it an excellent pairing with a shield in single combat. He smiled down at the familiar feel of its leather-bound grip in his hand. *Sure and yer no Raven's Tooth, but yer a bonnie blade nonetheless.* Hefting his shield, he strode out alone to meet the challenge.

The enemy commander stood waiting, a curved sword in each hand and an expectant grin on his face. Seeing that Cai approached alone, he dismissed the two Räubers who stood with him, sending them back to his waiting troops, who were raucously gathered some fifty yards away. They had dismounted to watch the duel. They jeered and shouted, jockeying amongst themselves for the best position to see, their commanders struggling to keep them back at the agreed distance.

"What should I call you?" Cai asked as he approached.

"I am called Bence," the man said, twirling the blade in his left hand carelessly.

"Bence, eh?" Cai responded. "What's that mean?"

"You stall," the commander replied, shaking his head. "No more talk."

"Suit yourself," Cai said with a shrug. At the sight of the two swords in Bence's hands, Corvus' words echoed in his mind: *When disadvantaged in any way, always attack. Make him dance to your tune.* So, without waiting, he leapt to it.

His attack was a rapid testing maneuver. A quick feinting thrust high, then a roll of the wrist to cut low on the opposite side and a swipe with the metal edge of the shield, which pulled Cai into a spin—out of which he slashed the real attack at the enemy's right ankle. Bence parried and avoided each move expertly, his right foot lifting at the end as he anticipated the final slash. Faster than expected, he reversed momentum and came at Cai with a flurry of cuts and thrusts that the young general only barely managed to block and escape, employing both his shield and sword desperately as he spun away to regain breathing room. He nodded appreciatively to the Räuber as they circled. He understood how this man had risen to leadership among the Barbárs. He had blinding speed and excellent reflexes.

Well then, I guess I'll just have to be faster, won't I?

"We will destroy you, Highlander," Bence spat. "You cannot stop Barbárs."

"I'd say we've done a right fair job so far," Cai said with a grin. "You came with what, ten thousand men? Now look at ye." He gestured with his chin at the remaining Räuber force.

"We burn your cities," Bence taunted. "Rape your women. You cannot stop Barbárs!"

"So you said." And Cai attacked again, cutting first to Bence's left, he batted his own blade with the edge of his shield, reversing the momentum of the sword. A fluid roll of the wrist and his blade was suddenly on his opponent's right. His father called this move "the quick cut." It was one of the myriad fighting techniques and tricks Corvus had shown him over the years, the fluid roll of the wrist being unusual and unexpected with a longsword. Bence was clearly caught off guard by the rapid stroke of the blade, and barely got his parry up in time, staggering out of the way, off-balance. Cai pressed the momentary advantage with a quick low thrust, which drew his enemy's blades down to counter, just as he had hoped. Another quick roll of the wrist and suddenly Cai's sword was chopping down at the Räuber's face as the son of the Raven lunged forward deeply on the attack. With a gasp of effort, the Räuber wheeled out of the way, his left sword just barely rising in time to deflect the blow, as he staggered back, again off-balance. Cai held his elegant pose for a moment, feeling the solid connection to the ground beneath him. This was theater, played for the benefit of the watching troops on each side, and the contrast between his graceful, balanced posture and Bence's desperate, imbalanced escape would not be lost on them.

Balance is everything. His father's words again. *Feel the ground beneath your feet. Draw strength from it.*

Cai rose casually from his lunge. Bence's eyes flashed in confusion and anger. He clearly couldn't understand how Cai was able to move the longsword so quickly. Bence looked over his shoulder at the watching Räubers. *I've tweaked his pride,* Cai thought. *He has to regain their support. Now, he'll try something flashy to answer.*

The Räuber began twirling the blades at his sides as he circled Cai, considering. Suddenly, the Räuber launched into a flurry of cuts and thrusts, driving the Highlander back. Somewhere in the midst of the sequence, Bence spun and lashed out with his foot, hitting Cai's shield squarely and knocking him back a few feet.

Cai could imagine that move overbalancing other fighters, but he had spent countless hours sparring with his father, and a spin kick was a regular element in Corvus' arsenal. Cai had learned, long ago, to read the hips of his opponent and anticipate the kick, bracing the shield with his shoulder, leaning into it. Were it not for the Räuber's unusual power, Cai would have responded to the kick with a quick thrust to the groin before the enemy could settle his weight. Instead, the kick had driven him back two steps, out of the blade's reach.

All power comes from the hips, boy, his father would say. *You wound a man in the hip, and the game's up.*

Cai grinned. He knew the measure of the man. He settled into the "invitation" posture, his sword and shield held off to his left, exposing his right side. Bence accepted the invitation, attacking with another flurry—first a cut to the exposed right side, followed by a downward chop to Cai's head, then a quick thrust to the belly, followed by a powerful cut to Cai's left side.

It was essentially what Cai had expected. His blade flashed up to parry the first cut, while his shield rose to catch the second. Rolling his blade expertly in his hand, he switched to an inverted grip while he batted away the thrust to his belly with a downward sweep of the shield and turned to catch the final cut with his sword point down. The inverted grip enabled him to react to the final cut with a lightning backhand slash across Bence's face, opening a cut from lip to ear and sending the tall man reeling back. Again, Cai held his final pose as he casually rolled the weapon back to a standard grip.

Get your opponent to fight with rage, and you'll win every time.

Bence shook his head, sending blood droplets flying. The Räuber commander snarled and charged, his blades flashing. Cai shifted his weight to the right, then deftly spun to a kneeling position. Bence's charge passed him as the Räuber struggled to change the direction of his cut to follow the spinning Highlander. Cai's shield was high to take the awkward hit, while his sword slashed the back of Bence's leg, biting deep into the calf. Cai continued his spinning movement, rising and stepping away with a casual grace. The Räuber howled in surprise and staggered as his leg suddenly failed to support him.

The jeers from the Räubers had stilled now, replaced with a growing outrage. Cai would need to finish this soon, or the insult to their pride would drive the restive Barbárs to charge him. He glanced at his cheering troops, flashing them a quick smile. Beyond them, he could see the Glenfolk army, still some distance out. He turned back to the wounded enemy commander.

"We could stop now, if you like," he offered amiably. "You can take your smelly friends and leave the Highlands. We'll let you live."

"We are Räubers!" Bence growled through gritted teeth, his cheek streaming with blood. "We are Barbárs! The world bows to us!"

"Now, I think you've got that wrong, there," Cai said conversationally, his weapons casually at his side. "Y'see, we're the Highlanders of the Green Mount. And we bow to no one!"

As he finished speaking, he rushed forward into a rapid attack series. Bence's blades flashed in response, desperately trying to parry the blows while being driven back onto his wounded leg. Cai sensed the man's balance shift off as the Räuber blocked a powerful stroke with both blades. Cai punched the edge of his shield into Bence's raised swords, crashing them back into the Räuber's face and hurling the tall warrior onto his back. Faster than the man could regain his wits, Cai buried his sword in his foe's chest, releasing it momentarily and stepping clear, so the gathered Räubers might see the blade quivering in their commander's heart, the golden filigree flashing in the sunlight. He shrugged casually to the enraged Barbárs, as though the morning's effort was nothing much. He was answered with a collective howl of outrage, and, as one, the Räubers charged.

Pulling his weapon from Bence's body, he turned and sprinted back to his troops, who were spreading rapidly into a straight shield wall, ready to receive the enemy's undisciplined attack. The Glenfolk troops were beginning to arrive now, bolstering the rear of the line, and filling in on the right side. He grinned as he ran.

His ploy had been to humiliate the Räuber commander, tweaking their vaunted pride. It had worked, and now the Barbárs were charging pell mell, on foot, against a disciplined shield wall with twice their numbers.

This should be a good day, he thought.

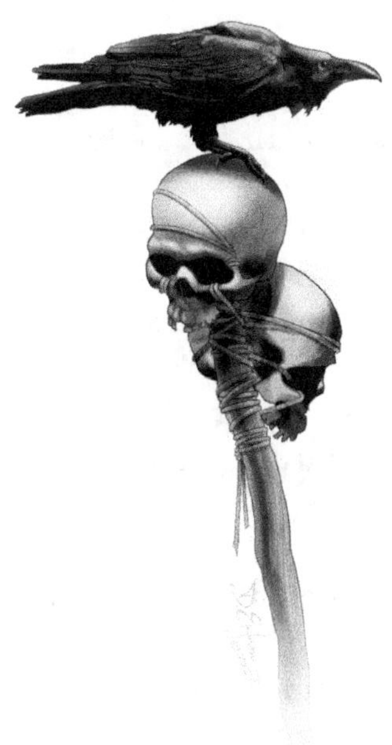

Chapter 6

Fear itself is usually more deadly than the thing we fear.

—Anonymous

One day before the Autumn Equinox - 574 HR.
The White Cleft, Green Mount

Sangine

The shaman crouched by the flame in the night. The camp was silent, save for the snores of the enormous Räubers, exhausted from their march. Though, even had the camp been a busy thoroughfare, he would likely have been unaware of it. He had been lost in communing for some time. It had begun as a standard connection with Torn Claw, the seventh member of his faction, from whom he received an update on his secret mission spying on the rebel shamans. But they were interrupted when Timor, the Prince of Terror, had shoved into his mind. Torn Claw had recoiled and fled promptly from the mental connection, as Timor turned his terrible countenance upon Sangine—a partially fleshed skull with hollow eye sockets in which swirled faint whorls of red mist. The few times he had ever been in his physical presence, Sangine had never heard Timor actually speak—the prince's skeletal visage lacked a tongue or lips—Timor's mind-voice now reverberated through Sangine's skull in a whisper-shriek at debilitating volume.

"The princes have returned, Sangine," he stated, the echoes of his voice continuing painfully for some seconds.

"We welcome your return," the shaman replied, wincing against the volume and timbre of the Prince of Terror's voice.

"I search for your brethren, and cannot sense Philaenus," Timor said, each word like the screech of metal on metal. "Where is he?"

"Philaenus is fallen," Sangine answered, knowing this was but the first piece of bad news he must confess. This conversation would not be a pleasant one.

Timor's skeletal face surged closer in his mind, the dead flesh that clung to the bone writhing with maggots and unseen worms as the red mist that served for eyes seemed to coalesce, gaining intensity and danger. "How?!"

"I do not know, Dread One," Sangine answered, knowing that the prince would tolerate neither excuses nor equivocation. "He leapt up the cliffs on the western coast as planned and was abruptly felled shortly thereafter."

"No battle?"

"No, my prince,"

"How is't possible?" Timor's voice seemed to take on a less strident shriek, becoming almost contemplative. "And Bone-Eye, what of him? I sense him not."

"Fallen also," Sangine replied, already wincing against the prince's coming response.

"HOW?!"

The shriek in his mind was soul-splitting, though worse was likely yet to come. There were no limits to the torments Timor could inflict.

"HOW? HOW? HOW?!" His whisper-shriek rose in intensity. "Answer me, wretch!"

"The champion of the Highlanders, the Raven, felled him in single combat," Sangine said with difficulty, as a soul-rending terror began to creep into him, his legs suddenly numb.

"Champion?" Timor seemed to consider for a moment. "Tell me what you know of him."

And Sangine did. He shared all of his knowledge of Corvus Corax with the dark prince at the speed of thought.

When he had finished, Timor was silent for a time, then the red whorls seemed to focus once more on Sangine. "And Blood-Tooth and Singer have likewise fallen?"

"They have," Sangine answered wearily, his strength failing rapidly. Communing was by its very nature draining, and communing with one of the princes was infinitely more so.

"HOW? HOW? HOW?!" The prince's howling voice sounded like metal scraping glass. "You fail us, cretin!" The pain from the shriek felt like Sangine's eyes were bursting in their sockets. He gritted his teeth against it.

"Singer died in battle against the army of Lachland," he reported, "while Blood-Tooth was greedy and thought to seize the Key for himself. He was crushed by the witch."

Another scream of rage and frustration. The shaman felt his head would burst. Then, abruptly, there was a long, merciful silence during which Sangine desperately gasped lungfuls of air.

"Geminus is masked from me," Timor said finally. "Though I sense he lives still."

"I..." was the only response Sangine could make as the terror that crept into his very bones combined with his stultifying weariness and rendered him almost mindless.

"More of that anon," the prince continued, seemingly oblivious to Sangine's helpless state. "I sense that you are nearing the Tor. I am across the sea and unable to reach you in time, but as you shall soon face that Champion and his fellows, I would give to you a gift." The torn flesh along the edges of his skeletal mouth pulled up in a horrific grin, the pressure of the tightening flesh forcing a maggot out through a small hole, the worm quickly falling away.

"My lord, I..." Sangine muttered, trying to break off the draining mind-sharing.

"I know, I know." Timor shook his head in disgust. "You are weaker than I recall, Sangine. Hard to conceive how you rose above your brethren."

"Yes, my prince."

"Feed. Regain strength!" Timor's shriek became urgent as the contact began to fade. "When you awake, you will have command of the Maelstrom Malefic. Use it well! Your failures disappoint!"

Chapter 7

"Oh, she is the darling of the sailors and merchants, she is. Any who ply the sea pray to Feryn for a sailor's luck—good weather, fair winds, an overflowing tankard, and a seat at the dice table once they arrive safely. Of course, there should be a smiling doxy beckoning from the stairway. Oh, the sailors love her, they do."

—Storyteller in Cape Nihr

One day before the Autumn Equinox
The Tor, Green Mount

Corvus

They carried the bodies of the dead Adders off the road, laying them among the roots of a great oak. After this was finished, should he live, Corvus would see to giving them a proper burial. He dragged the shaman's ruined corpse down to the observation bench and heaved it over the edge, watching it tumble down the steep cliffside. He then cleaned his hands of the smell of the creature and told the company to rest there until morning under the branches of the oak trees. The exhausted group needed no urging, the toll of their exertions weighing heavy upon them all.

It was nearing dawn, and there was frost in the air. He settled beside Li and leaned back against the thick bole of an oak.

He woke to the smell of cinnamon and looked up to find Yadira crouched beside him, a steaming mug of spiced tea in her hand.

"Here, Corvus," she said, handing him the mug and a small, wrapped bundle. He blinked and looked around, chilly with the cold. It was well past dawn now. Opening the bundle, he found a piece of Aslene travel bread, dripping with honey, and a small piece of goat's cheese.

"Wherever did you get this?" he asked her, amazed.

Her eyes crinkled in a mysterious smile behind her jimas, as she rose and walked back to their small fire. He shook his head in wonder and sniffed the cheese. It smelled heavenly and his mouth watered instantly. Until that moment, he hadn't realized just how hungry he was.

Li stirred and sat up, touching his head gingerly.

"How are you feelin', lad?" Corvus asked him softly.

"Like I was kicked in the head by a mule," Li answered with a light chuckle.

Corvus offered Li a bit of the travel bread and they sat and ate together, enjoying a few moments of peace before what he knew would be a difficult day. As they finished, he handed Li the puntina. He had found it half-buried in a pile of leaves nearby. Li sighed with relief and stood, slipping it into its sheath.

Corvus rose and called the company together. Fires were extinguished, and the troupe gathered, looking to him expectantly. He paused a moment to examine each face, silently reciting each person's name as he did. Many, if not all, would die this day. He bit down sharply on the sudden tightness in his throat, swallowing hard before speaking.

"I'll not lie to you," he began, "today will be a hard day."

Muted murmurs and apprehensive glances were exchanged.

"The enemy comes with over two hundred Räubers. They'll likely arrive sometime mid-day and storm this mount in an effort to kill us and seize the Key and Argant." He looked pointedly at the boy. "The White Cleft army and some three hundred of the fyrd should arrive by nightfall. That means we have to hold the Tor for at least six hours against an overwhelming force before help arrives. And even then, they'll keep pressing. Tomorrow's the Equinox. We have to hold the Tor and protect Argant until then. No matter the cost."

Silence fell among them as the gravity of their situation sank in. He paused to give them a moment before continuing.

"Now, as we've seen, there are a few choke points along the route, where a small force can hold a larger one at bay. But those will serve to *delay*, not stop, the enemy." He turned to Dallin and Lupe. "How many arrows do you each have left?"

"Some twenty or so for me," Dallin replied.

Lupe looked forlorn as she said quietly, "Ten. Only ten."

"Well…" He nodded grimly, accepting the information. "Make every shot count and try to recover arrows whenever possible." He gestured to Mama. "Mama, you and your group, along with Li, Piper, and Rhona, will continue to the top of the Tor. The Adders and I will head back to prepare a welcome for our unwanted guests. Una, Barclay, Jack, and Anna will go with you and help you get to the top safely." The four named Adders nodded, accepting their orders. "Now, let's get movin'. Time is pressing."

Li put his hand on Corvus' arm and looked at his father with tears welling in his eyes. Corvus patted his son's hand and offered a halfhearted smile.

"Go on, son," he said, his voice filled with emotion. "Protect the boy and live to tell the tale."

"I will, Da," Li replied, and wrapped his father in a fierce embrace, which Corvus returned heartily. As they pulled apart, something caught Li's eye to the east.

"Hang on," he said, turning to look out over the fields below. "What's that?"

Corvus followed his gaze and his heart sunk like a stone. In the distance, shadowing the lands of the White Cleft to the east of the Tor, unnatural black clouds roiled ominously. Unseasonal lightning played and flashed among them.

"He comes," Mama said, stepping up beside him. "And brings great evil."

"Alright!" Corvus shouted to the troupe with new urgency. "Let's move, now!"

He flagged Una for a quick conference before she could depart.

"Yes, Corvus?" she asked, responding quickly.

"As you accompany them to the top, keep your eye open for another good choke point that we can fall back to. It's been many a long year since I came to the Tor, but I seem to recall a steep climb between rocks near the top. Regardless, once they're safely to the ruins, return back here. Your spear will be needed."

"I will," she responded, then turned and jogged up the trail to catch up to the others.

"Adders, with me!" he barked and moved quickly down the trail into the pine grove. Turning off the trail amidst the trees, he worked his way to the edge of the slope. Below them, the trail cut back across some fifteen feet down.

"MacLief," he called.

"Sir?" The solid man stepped forward and planted the butt of his spear sharply.

"If I recall correctly," Corvus began, "you're a builder, from… Applecross, am I right?"

"Aye, sir," MacLief responded, his eyes widening in surprise that the Raven himself would recall such detail about him.

"Well, I need you to build me something, quickly," he said, then explained to both MacLief and the Adders what was needed. When he finished, the man nodded enthusiastically.

"I have some ideas that might work, sir."

"Take five of the Adders to help you. The rest of you, follow me." With that, he turned and strode quickly back to the trail, working his way around the bend and down the hill to the narrow opening between the holly bushes. Five Adders followed.

"This will be our first choke point," he said. "There should be ten of us to hold this gap. Bear Trap formation—five in front, five behind. As soon as a spear gets fouled or trapped in a body, an Adder from the back line steps in to take that spot. Five spears at all times." He waited to see if they understood his instructions before continuing. "Once they realize what we're doin', they'll rush the gap, trusting to their size and ferocity to overwhelm us, but they can only come through one at a time. At some point, they will drive us back or find their way around the gap. I'll call the retreat, and you lot make for the stone arch as fast as you're able. Once you're through, turn and set up again for Bear Trap. Understood?"

There were only a few clarifying questions, after which he placed his hand on the shoulder of the thick, stonemason from Mallaig, just over the mountain from Dóchas. He was a stout, reliable man with a shock of red hair.

"Cuddy, I have a separate task for you. Follow me."

Together, they jogged up the trail, through the pine grove. He checked on MacLief's progress as he passed. With the help of the other Adders, the young builder was in the midst of digging a sizable boulder out of the ground, but he looked up and gave an encouraging wave before returning to his labors. They continued up the slope, around the bend and through the oak trees. There was the steep curve in the trail that hooked back through the stone archway. The rugged hillside to the right of the arch was steep and impassable, made of soil that crumbled to the touch. The enemy would be unable to scale that once they were stalled at the arch. Some twenty feet above it, a rock ledge jutted out.

"I need you on that ledge," he said, pointing up. "I believe you can reach it from the trail above. Gather rocks, stones, whatever you can, and be ready to rain them down on the enemy when they reach this arch. Can you do that?"

"Aye, I can," the mason replied, a mischievous smile on his face.

"Good man," Corvus replied, patting him on the shoulder. "Off you go."

Cuddy hefted his spear and ran through the archway, up the trail. Corvus stepped after him through the arch and turned, surveying the place from their defensive position. The path just inside the arch was narrow. The trail was bounded on the right by the six-foot stone wall and on the left by a sharp two-foot-tall rise to the sward, with slippery grass overhanging it. Two spearmen could stand abreast on the trail. It wasn't ideal, but it should serve to slow the enemy, and their passage would be costly. Passing back through the arch, he smiled approvingly at the steep, curving hook in the path that led to the opening. The enemy would have to take that at a run, one man at a time, the tall Räubers ducking to pass through the low arch. Turning, he examined the wall from the downhill side. The base of it stood some four feet above the trail at the nearest point, climbing to over twenty feet further on as the hill sloped down away from it. The bank up to the wall was steep and covered in vines. Difficult, but not impossible to climb for a determined foe. Once the enemy realized they were choked at the arch, they would storm the wall.

He jogged back down the trail where he found all of the Adders working as a group to help MacLief in his efforts. He gathered them and explained how they should deploy once through the archway. When he was confident that the group understood the plan, he left them to their work and moved back up the trail, out of the pine grove to the wide grassy area with the bench, where the company had rested earlier. His eyes were drawn to the black clouds that fumed and boiled to the east. The formation was unusual, thickest at a point some fifteen or twenty miles from the Tor and spreading in all directions. He stared at the fields directly below the blackness. Daylight could not penetrate the dark clouds, and the lands beneath looked to be in the black of night. He gazed in wonder at the creeping shadow and imagined the shaman and the foul Barbárs accompanying it, marching inexorably closer to the Tor, spreading its crepuscular gloom. Death and suffering concomitant with their advance.

"What evil do you bring?" he whispered to himself, and a chill of dread ran up his spine.

Dallin

The two archers had taken the lead up the winding trail, leapfrogging their way — one covering while the other advanced. They encountered no one, however, and the final twists in the path had been difficult, the trail steep and rocky. With each bend, they recrossed a stream that cut down the face of the Tor, its progress making small waterfalls and cutting narrow gullies across the trail. As they neared their destination, Dallin caught glimpses of the blocky ruins atop the Tor. Two circular pillars fronted the structure. At some point in the distant past, their height had been sheared off, leaving only irregular, broken columns pointing to the sky. There were glimpses of more structures behind them, but her vision was obscured by the rocky overhang above her, on which the ruins perched. She wondered who in the world could ever have built such a thing in such a place. Trying to imagine the engineering required to hoist the stones up the Tor boggled her mind.

She paused to check the rest of the group's progress before climbing a steep bend in the trail. Lupe was some ten feet behind her, Rhona close behind, clutching her arm to her side. The shaman had wrenched it painfully, and though Yadira had soothed it with an ointment and a makeshift sling, the pallor of Rhona's skin and the clench of her teeth as she climbed suggested it was still quite tender. Behind her came Li supporting Piper, with the four Adders taking turns assisting the wounded minstrels in their progress. Argant, Amina, Mama, and Yadira brought up the rear.

"Oh, there you are."

A man's deep, cheerful voice startled her and she spun to find a one-armed man with ebony skin and gentle eyes smiling down at her from the top of the bend. She couldn't place his accent, though it sounded rich and elegant. She heard gasps of alarm from the group behind her, as she quickly took in the man's appearance. He was missing his right arm, and he held a tall, elegantly carved walking stick in his left, on which he leaned, his posture casual and relaxed. He wore rope sandals and was dressed in brightly colored bloused trousers, covered with intricate patterns in gold, black, and red. He wore a long vest in similar hues and patterns, with a red cotton shirt beneath it that matched the red in his trousers and vest. The shirt was open at the collar, revealing a rich necklace of amber, its generous oblong stones matching the startling amber color of his eyes, which stood out starkly against the warm dark of his skin.

Her bow was up in an instant and she asked in a faltering voice, "Excuse me, but who are you?"

"You found it," he said, admiring her bow. "I'm glad." With that, he began to work his way down the steep bend toward her.

"Hold it now, mister," she barked, drawing the string of her bow still further back. He paused and smiled once more, an indulgent, warm smile showing bright-white teeth.

"I left you a gift, Dallin," he said, gesturing with his chin to the ruins. Then, looking to Lupe, he added something in fluent Aslene. Presumably that he had left one for her too. He turned back to Dallin and added, "Use them well."

A chill coursed over her, bringing gooseflesh down the length of her arms. Yet, somehow, she sensed no danger from this man. She lowered her bow. With another quick grin, he looked down at his feet, carefully placing his walking stick as he eased his way past her down the path. She watched him pass back through the group, each person making way for him as he stepped jauntily down the trail. He paused before Argant, staring deeply into the boy's eyes for a long moment. Finally, he nodded his head, as though in approval, and continued on his way. Dallin noted the deep, reverent bow Mama made as he passed. Yadira and Amina followed suit, with Lupe bowing tardily afterward.

"Excuse me, sir!" Dallin shouted after him just before he rounded the next bend. He paused and looked back up to her. "There's danger down the Tor. It isna safe for you."

He smiled up at her in response, an air of paternal pride in his expression. She thought she heard him say, "You'll do just fine," then he turned and sauntered on down the trail, disappearing from view.

Exchanging a brief look of confused wonder with Li, Dallin turned to finish the climb. Slinging her bow, she scampered up the bend before her, needing both hands to help her progress. The trail proceeded some twenty feet more before angling left, where verdant bushes covered steep stone on her right, and there was a vertical drop-off her left, from which she looked down on treetops and scattered rock fall below.

As she reached the end of the trail, she turned and gazed up at ruins above. A narrow, almost vertical defile marked the end of their journey. The stream bubbled down its center, its source somewhere above, within the ruins. Grasping jutting stones on either side, she hoisted herself up the final ten feet, crawling out onto the smooth stone floor of the ruined temple, then turning to reach a hand back to Lupe. The two marveled at the structure around them.

More broken pillars were now visible, lining the back of the structure. An ornate stone dish filled with water sat on a plinth at the center of the floor, the underside of it carved to resemble the blossom of a flower of some sort. A piece of the dish directly in front of her had been broken off at some point. A steady flow of water issued from the crack—the source of the stream they had crossed and recrossed on their climb. Two great rectangular blocks of stone lay broken on the floor; one lay diagonally across the back right corner of the space, the other in the center of what would have been the left wall. Only half of that block remained, however, the other half having broken off and tumbled down the Tor long ago. The temple itself was not large, defining a rectangle some sixty feet wide by thirty deep. Dallin was struck with how ancient it all felt and she stared at the elegant columns, wondering how tall they might once have been. Lupe's touch on her arm brought her attention back to the present moment. The veiled woman was pointing to three small barrels tucked behind the cracked stone block on her right. The two moved over to the barrels as their companions worked their way up into the temple behind them.

Cracking open the first of the casks, Dallin gasped in wonder. "Arrows!" she cried in amazement. "Dozens of them!"

She drew one out and examined it, her mouth agape. It was the finest she had ever held. Its perfectly straight shaft was intricately carved with designs similar to those on the bow staff. The fletching was of black feathers, perfectly attached and cut with a master's hand. Unlike the rough iron arrowheads she was accustomed to, these ones were not metal. They seemed to be crafted from some smooth black stone. Touching the tip, she gasped and jerked her hand back, sucking at the small dot of blood the arrowhead had drawn from her fingertip.

Lupe had cracked another barrel open to discover it was filled with smaller, thicker shafts like those she used with her recurved bow. She held one up, marveling at the design and craftsmanship. The two women exchanged a meaningful glance, filled suddenly with renewed hope and grim determination.

"The Räubers will pay a dear price to take this temple," Dallin said grimly.

Yadira

She rounded the penultimate bend in the steep trail up the Tor, her eyes focused on her footing as she struggled to control her breathing. To her left was a vertical, rocky wall, with a stone overhang some fifteen feet up. To her right, the trail was bounded by a sloped ledge, overgrown with shrubs and ivy. As was her practice, she scanned the bushes, looking for any that might have medicinal or nutritious value. She noted a redcurrant bush tucked between two large junipers. Sadly, it was too late in the season for there to be currants, however the juniper branches sagged with ripe, blue berries. She excused herself from Mama's side, and opening her satchel, knelt by the bushes to harvest the fruit. A tincture from the berries made an excellent antiseptic. Plucking a handful, she suddenly felt someone walk past her on the trail, which struck her as strange since she was bringing up the rear of the group. Glancing over her shoulder, she saw a woman standing where the path ended, over by the entrance to the ruins. Her back was to Yadira, but she was dressed in rich clothing that seemed very out of place in such a rugged locale: a lush maroon skirt that shimmered in the light, an embroidered bodice of royal blue with maroon highlights that matched her skirt, and a royal-blue satin blouse with bejeweled cuffs. Her black hair was long and wavy, with an ornate sterling hair clip in the back. Even her shoes seemed out of place. They were delicate and narrow at the toe, of the type worn in southern climes by rich merchant women, decorated with large silver buckles. Despite the richness of her attire, something about the woman's physique and stride suggested she was no stranger to swordplay or perhaps, the heaving deck of a ship. The woman looked over her shoulder at Yadira, a sapphire bindi sparkling in the center of her forehead, and suddenly a memory overtook the eldest votary.

She was once more the gangly adolescent beggar sneaking into the gambling house in Saddaq to watch the games of chance. She felt a strange, warm tingling sensation as she looked down at her dirty hands, resting on the soft green top of the dice table. She pulled her hands away, knowing the croupier would beat her if she soiled the felt.

"Crowns or crests, little one," the woman asked softly, her voice possessed of a faint echo. Yadira looked up to see the woman with the bindi smiling down at her in her memory.

"Crowns," Yadira answered, staring into the woman's deep-brown eyes and marveling anew at the expert way the woman painted her face—her lashes long and lush, kohl lining her almond-shaped eyes, her lips red and ripe against her olive skin.

The woman smiled and tossed a coin into the air with a carefree expertise. It landed before Yadira on the dice table, the ringing sound muffled by the felt as it finished its spin and settled, crown side up. Yadira smiled. It meant she could keep it, that she would eat today. She scooped up the precious coin, noting from its weight that it was silver. She would eat for a month!

She smiled up at the woman as the strange glamour of the memory faded, leaving her once more her adult self, kneeling among the junipers on the Tor. The woman was no longer there, but behind where she had been standing, Yadira saw the broad gold-and-speckled-red leaves of a plant that should not be here. It was a Hanging Lantern bush. She blinked in wonder at the unexpected sight. The plant was not hardy, and favored sunny, dry climes, withering at any hint of frost. She rose and moved over to it, feeling something in her hand. She opened her fist, and there in her palm was a silver coin, crown side up. She paused to stare in wonder at it, then glanced around, searching the area for any sign of the strange woman. Seeing none, she turned back and knelt before the out-of-place bush.

The curled and heavy leaves, fiery in color, gave the plant its name. She lifted them, searching for the coveted seed pods. After a moment, she was rewarded with three large woody pods, each filled with the tiny grain-like seeds. She gasped at the unexpected bounty. Hanging Lantern seeds were a powerful stimulant—though addictive if overused—and a small dose could keep an exhausted soldier marching all night, arriving fresh for battle the next day, or help a drover stay alert for wolves after a long, sweaty day tending her flock. The peril came when the drug wore off, leaving the user spent, sometimes even comatose.

She quickly slipped the pods into her satchel, marveling at the luck of her discovery—though something told her it wasn't truly *luck*. It was a gift, and she bowed her head, touching her brow with her clasped hands in gratitude.

Chapter 8

"But you're so brave," the little girl said to the warrior before her. "You're never afraid."

"Oh, yes, I am." The fierce woman smiled down, adjusting her shield so that she might kneel before the child. "I'm often afraid. You see, being brave doesn't mean you're not afraid. It means we feel the fear, but we still stand up for what's right in spite of it."

"That sounds hard," the child replied, awe in her voice.

The woman nodded. "Sometimes," she said, "it is the hardest thing in the world."

—*"The Kaaranaamon,"*
as translated by Wilhelmina van der Blodt

One day before the Autumn Equinox
The Tor, Green Mount

Corvus

He watched the black clouds approach, slowly blotting out the sky and the sunshine. As the angry darkness covered the Tor, daylight dimmed to a bitter twilight, and a cold, creeping dread came over him. This was an ancient evil, from a time of legend, awakened once more to bring its spite and vengeance to the world. His heart sank as he felt the endless, raw malice wash over him. What chance had they against such might?

He looked down the trail at the Adders laboring among the trees without proper tools or ropes and imagined hundreds of savage Räubers storming up the trail, fueled by the power and might of this darkness. The Adders would all die, and it would be his fault. Who was he to stand against such malevolence? He thought of the rest of the party, struggling their way up the Tor. Weak, infirm, wounded, and trying to hold up a child against such power… A child! It was ludicrous and hopeless. For perhaps the first time since Greer's death, he knew true despair and sagged heavily onto the stone bench as though he'd been pushed down onto it, his shoulders drooping under the burden of his failure. His thoughts turned to Ligulf. Trusting, true-hearted Ligulf, so willing to follow and obey his father, so filled with joy and love and song. Corvus' throat tightened. He had utterly failed his son and brought him, and all the rest, to ruin.

A raven croaked urgently from a nearby tree. He ignored the sound, submerged in despondency. It croaked again and again, but so thick was the miasma in which he struggled, he barely noticed. Finally, the bird flew to him, its wings battering his head, its claw scratching his cheek as it croaked loudly in his face. His hands came up instinctively to fend off the bird, and it ceased its attack, settling on the bench beside him. He stared at it, blinking, as the fumes in his mind cleared momentarily. What had he been thinking about? Ligulf. A warm, familiar spark flared in his heart at the thought of his precious, trusting son, and the spark drove the darkness back a touch. Now countless dear memories flashed before him, of Li and Cai growing up, their triumphs, discoveries, joys, and sorrows — the purity of their desire to please him and be good sons. He remembered Cai's first word; it had been "Da," and the boy's open face had sparkled with discovery. Then Corvus smiled, recalling Li's first word: "Cai." Greer had thrown her hands up in mock frustration that neither had said "Mama," smacking Corvus' shoulder when he'd laughed out loud at her disappointment. He thought of Li practicing his cittern with his obsessive passion. He saw his son's eyes filled with tears, as they had said farewell earlier that day. He looked up toward the top of the Tor. Li was up there, depending on Corvus to protect him. Li *needed* him!

The spark of warmth in his heart roared into a flame, the despair and hopelessness melting from its heat, becoming no more than a mere memory. He couldn't fail Li. He couldn't fail them. They all needed him, now more than ever. He stood and shook his head to clear it, his lips curling in defiance as he acknowledged the diabolic nature of this dread. *You thought to overwhelm me, you bastard? You misjudged! You've only redoubled my resolve, you foul fiend!* He looked to the Adders once again. Their efforts to resist the enemy may indeed be paltry compared to the power facing them, but they would stand nonetheless. They would delay the enemy. They would make their foe pay for every foot he advanced up the Tor. He touched his cheek, running his finger over the scratch the raven had given him, and looked to the bird, which still perched on the bench, its black eyes watching him intently.

"I thank you," he said with a raw fervency to his voice. "You've reminded me of who I am, and" —he flashed another glance up the Tor—"what's at stake."

With renewed purpose, he moved quickly down the trail, his eyes squinting in the failing light to find MacLief and the crew of Adders. After a few moments, he came upon them, stalled in their efforts, sitting against the trees with their heads in their hands—gripped by the same despair he had known moments earlier. Instinctively, he withdrew the medallion from his pouch and cast it into the air. Once more, its silver beams shone down like the bright light from a star, washing away the gloom, melting the cold despair that locked the men in hopelessness, and holding the stygian vapors at bay. The Adders blinked and stirred, as though waking from a deep and troubled slumber.

"The enemy seeks to sap our will with foul sorcery," Corvus said loudly. "But he willna prevail in this, nor in his efforts to take this hill." The Adders stared at him, eyes wide and hopeful, drinking up his words like precious rain falling on those who were parched and suffering. "We are all that stands between the

Green Mount and that darkness you felt. If we fail, our land, our homes, our people, will fall into that same pit. Will you allow that? Or will you stand with me to defy the beast and say to him, 'You canna pass, for we are Highlanders and we will no' allow it!'"

MacLief stood, wiping his eyes. He shook his head and took a deep breath, defiance on his face.

"Get up, you lot!" the builder barked to the others. "Remember who we are. We're the Adders of the fyrd! Not some wayward band of hopeless amateurs. Are we to lie down in despair and fail our leader, the great Raven? Up, I say! We have work to do!"

With that, the men scrambled to their feet, muttering apologies and returning to their efforts.

Corvus took a moment to shake each man's hand and look him in the face, calling them all by name and letting them see the fierce resolve in his eyes. Like a candle lighting another, he sensed the heat of the flame burning within him pass to each man, as their spines stiffened, heads raised, and eyes narrowed with purpose.

A powerful, cold wind suddenly blew from the east, the trees thrashing. He thought he felt the very ground beneath him shudder, and he nodded grimly.

"They come," he said quietly.

Piper

He winced as he moved his shoulder, testing the wound as he paced restlessly. They had bid farewell to Una as she rushed back down the Tor to help Corvus below. Barclay, Anna, and Jack, the three remaining Adders, discussed defensive positions.

The climb up the Tor had been grueling, and several times Piper had stumbled, his arm instinctively reaching out to catch him, provoking lancing pain that left him breathless and weak. Ligulf would quickly be by his side, supporting, comforting, encouraging. Precious Li. Piper felt that there was nothing he couldn't accomplish, so long as he had Li by his side.

He paused in his pacing near the edge of the temple platform, and gazed to the east, watching with trepidation as the boiling black clouds advanced, their shadow plunging the lands below into darkness. Mama came up beside him for a moment, likewise watching the approaching gloom. Then she turned and addressed the group matter-of-factly.

"Dark magic comes," she said. "Everyone must wash face from fountain, and sit in circle." Her votaries and Argant moved promptly to obey. Piper, Dallin, and Li exchanged a quick glance before accepting Mama's instructions. The three Adders looked bemused and uncomfortable with the request. At a gesture from Li, however, they complied and queued up by the fountain.

The water was cold and clear as it splashed Piper's face, and he gasped involuntarily at its icy touch. Something about the cold, clear water seemed to open his heart unexpectedly, as if it had removed some film of dirt or grime that had allowed his spirit to slumber. Wiping his face on his sleeve, he stepped away from the fountain and found a seat with Li on his left and Rhona to his right. Argant sat next to Li, his legs folded and his little face serene. Next to him sat Amina, then Dallin, Lupe, Mama, and Yadira. The three Adders filled in the circle.

Mama spoke to Yadira in Aslene, and the tall votary translated for the group.

"The coming clouds bring despair," Yadira said, her voice soft but resonant. "The enemy seeks to sap our will, divide us from the strength we give one another, and leave each of us alone, a victim to our fears."

Nervous glances passed among the group as Mama spoke again to her eldest votary.

"We must draw strength from one another," Yadira continued. "There is no failure, unless we allow it."

At a word of instruction from Mama, she and the three votaries began to chant quietly, eyes closed, hands resting on their knees with their palms up. Argant imitated their actions, closing his eyes and moving his lips, though he clearly didn't know the actual words of the recitation.

Piper instinctively felt that the women were working to create some type of protection for the group, but worried that the six Highlanders would not be contributing to the effort. He glanced at the sky. The black clouds roiled toward them with unnatural speed. Something was niggling at the back of his mind, something pertinent to their situation that he couldn't quite recall. He returned to the ballad of Athdar, vaguely recalling an earlier passage that spoke of black clouds… What was it?

The women seemed to have found their rhythm in the chant, their soft voices syncing together in their recitation. Closing his eyes to try to recall the ballad, he sensed a warmth on his face, as though a small campfire were in their midst; the icy water with which he had washed left his face more sensitive to the subtle glow. The sensation cheered him and he visualized a small fire, even to the point of seeing the flicker of the flames on his eyelids and hearing the crackling of the wood. He smiled at the comfortable image, its warmth suffusing him and easing his worries. He sighed and felt his body relax. Suddenly the pertinent verses popped into his mind.

> Then mounted he his great white steed
> And drew his sword, intent to bleed
> The life from out the drui so fell
> That plagued the land o'er hill and dell.
>
> But the cursèd drui sensed his plan
> And sent foul humors o'er the land,
> Despair and fear their ruinous rain
> To bury the will in gloom and pain.
>
> When Athdar felt the rising fear
> He drew no blade, nor lance, nor spear,
> But to the faery's harp he turned,
> A tune of hope from her he'd learned.

As vapors black and foul did fall
Despair beset the people all,
But Athdar's song, like break of day,
Shone forth to hold the gloom at bay.

Piper opened his eyes with triumph, turning to share his epiphany with Li. He opened his mouth to speak, but just then, the world went very dark.

A wave of futility and hopelessness hit him like a physical force as the dark shadow covered the Tor. He blinked and looked around their circle. The chanting of the Aslene women continued, though he noted Mama's brow was furrowed with increased effort, and the volume of her recitation had grown. Argant's little shoulders drooped, and he put his head in his hands and began to quietly sob. Brochy whined a pitiful sound from somewhere. Amina looked stricken, a grimace of pain or effort on her gaunt face as she struggled to continue the chant. The three Adders were looking around the temple as though desperately seeking some escape, panic written on their features. Rhona's face was carved with sadness, tears streaming down her cheeks, her head shaking, as though watching the loss of all she loved. Li's jaw was clenched, his closed eyes wincing in furious concentration. Only Dallin seemed unmoved, her eyes open, her face writ with a grim and defiant determination—as though this pit of despair was familiar territory, and she a weary but unflagging traveler therein. A gasping sob escaped Piper as he looked over this pathetic little band and felt the sheer enormity of what faced them all. How could they ever hope to stand in the face of malice so vast? How could any of them make a difference? The warmth from Mama's chanting was helping, but the little hope it offered was rapidly dwindling in the face of the bitter darkness swallowing them.

He saw Amina falter and finally stop her recitation, her head sinking in failure, tears falling into her lap as her slender frame bent and failed beneath the weight of the oppression. The flame of hope dwindled with her exit, as Yadira, Mama, and Lupe raised their voices still louder, struggling all the harder against the gloom that was rapidly overtaking them all. Piper grasped Li's hand in a fierce grip that was returned with desperate strength, their knuckles white, as their clasped hands shook with the effort. A baleful roaring was growing in Piper's ears, though he couldn't tell if it was real or imagined. He felt increasingly like a stranded waif, alone in the teeth of the bitterest of winter's winds—no shelter, no hope, strength fading. Just a failing man, so very small against a monstrous vastness beyond his ken. Tears streamed down his cheeks, and he glanced from face to face, desperate for some tinge of hope.

His eyes lighted again on Dallin, seeing her iron-like intransigence. Her face had paled, the livid scars now a deep purple, her brow was set and unwavering as she stared forward, her eyes unfocused, grim, and fierce. Something in that unbreakable aspect beckoned him. It was the tiniest spark of hope, but it was fanned by the mysterious power of Mama's chanting. It was like a thin, fragile rope cast to guide him out of his despondency, though the distance he needed to travel seemed too far for his frail strength. He focused on Dallin's eyes, drawing from them the strength he needed to think, to hope. There had been an epiphany he'd wanted to share. Something that might help. *What was it*

A flash of insight washed over him. His desperate mind clung to it like a drowning man clinging to a passing piece of driftwood in a gale. With a monumental effort, he released Li's hand and reaching behind him to clutch his satchel, ripping it open with single-minded effort. The roaring in his ears had increased to a deafening pitch and he winced in pain as the sound threatened to submerge him. His searching hand found the long, wooden tube for which he searched, his fingertips tingling at the contact. He drew forth an old, battered flute, the wood weathered and scarred. Grimacing with pain, he moved his wounded arm so that he might grip the instrument with both hands and bring it to his lips. The roar, already unbearably loud in his ears, crescendoed in response, like a living creature infuriated by his temerity. His hands shook and his eyes closed, and he almost dropped the instrument. But he fixed the image of Dallin's coldly defiant stare in his mind, and somehow, impossibly, he found the strength to begin playing the pipe.

The notes faltered and were uncertain at first, but even that fragile sound somehow heartened him, giving him the strength to continue playing with increasing boldness. The melody was hopeful and sweet, like a gentle summer breeze scented with the rich aroma of the forest near his mountain cabin and the blooms that filled the meadows in the springtime. The roaring receded, pushed back like the darkness when a candle is lit. He found his rhythm. This, he understood. He was, after all, a seasoned performer, with a lifetime of experience playing music in distracting and noisy environments. His body and his heart knew what to do, and his fingers deftly danced across the flute, its warm tone filling the temple as the candle in his mind grew to become a campfire, merging with that of Mama and the votaries. He sensed, rather than saw or heard, tension release from the others in the circle as the chanting continued, but with less evident strain. He felt the heat of Li's hand on his knee, support and gratitude flowing through that touch. Piper smiled inwardly, his confidence growing with each note as he poured his heart into the intricate, beautiful melody.

He played for Li, the man he loved, who had brought him such joy. And Li's eyes stared at him with tears of gratitude and pride. He played for Argant, the innocent child being buffeted unfairly by powers so far beyond him. The boy lifted his head in response, a fragile hope kindling in his mismatched eyes. He played for Amina, buttressing her wounded and frail form against the massive weight bearing down on her, and watched as the youngest votary's posture straightened. She took a deep, calming breath, and once more closed her eyes, rejoining the chanting.

Piper stood without pausing his melody. Seeing the result of the music, he felt a boldness, a strength, that he couldn't explain. He moved around the circle, playing to each individual, gazing at them with strength and resilience—willing them to draw those things from him. No longer did he feel overwhelmed by the gloom. Instead, he felt an abundance of strength, of determination, of hope. He moved with clarity and purpose around the circle, sharing his newfound tenacity and fortitude and watched as, one by one, each member of their small group was drawn back from the brink, emboldened, enlivened. The inner flame he perceived, which had merged with the flame of the women's chanting, grew to become a raging bonfire, driving back the darkness beyond the walls of the temple. The sound of the instrument now overtook the rapidly diminishing roar, its sweet notes echoing down the Tor. He played more loudly still, standing at the edge of the platform, defiantly facing east toward the source of the cloud, a mad joy welling up within him as he faced the malignant darkness and knew it could not touch them. He played like never before, the melody growing with new invention and ornamentation as his heart swelled. This. This was his purpose.

Soon, he felt a hand on his back as Li joined him, raising his voice to join with the flute, harmonizing wordlessly. A thrill went through him as Rhona stepped to his other side, her hand also on his back, while her skilled voice found yet another harmony. The beauty and power of the music of the three minstrels sailed out over the Tor.

Piper felt invigorated by the effort, his strength and stamina growing rather than diminishing. He could keep this up as long as the enemy rained dread upon them, he was sure. He sensed that both Li and Rhona shared this feeling, as their voices grew stronger, more joyful, by the minute.

In a lifetime of learning and playing music, sharing his talents with grateful and adoring audiences—bringing tears and laughter to so many and feeling the ineffable satisfaction in knowing his truest self through the priceless gift of music—never had he experienced anything close to the transcendent joy and effulgent power he now felt.

He stood atop the Tor, holding the dread storm at bay, together with those he loved. His heart soared, his spirit at one with all things good and wholesome.

He felt another hand on his back and heard Mama's voice continuing her chant close behind him, its rhythm augmenting his melody with a contrapuntal and complex beauty. Three more hands touched him as Yadira, Lupe, and Amina joined the cluster. Soon he felt Argant's little hand on his leg as the boy squeezed between Mama and him.

The enemy had sent a dread clamor to drain and defeat them, yet together they stood, contumaciously facing that arrogant and malicious foe. They replied with sublime and heartfelt beauty, somehow shattering the wave of malice where it touched them like brittle and bitter ice and scattering the iniquity like noxious fumes before the bold winds of summer's joy.

Chapter 9

"Victory, my son, so often relies more on terrain than numbers, bravery or skill."

—"The Epistles of the Mountain Fox"
by Field Marshal Lucian Aleghieri

One day before the Autumn Equinox
The Tor, Green Mount

Corvus

The first of the Räubers to rush through the gap between the holly trees fell quickly, simultaneously speared above and below his shield—in his neck from the right, and his inner thigh from the left. The Adder whose spear had taken him in the neck had been quick to retract his weapon before the falling Barbár's body could collapse and trap the blade momentarily. Unfortunately, Ramsay—whose spear took the Räuber in the leg—was not as quick, and his spear got tangled in the falling man's limbs, ripping it from his hands. Rather than scramble for his weapon and potentially get in the way of the other Adders, he'd quickly stepped back out of their lineup, allowing Pherson in the second row to step into his place while he recovered it.

The second and third Räubers to rush through met a similar fate, two spears each from either side, felling them quickly. The path up to the gap was steep just before the holly trees, making it difficult—though not impossible—for the enemy to cluster and charge through in groups. The Adders stood to either side of the opening, four men to a side: two in a front rank and two offset behind, ready to step in. Corvus had positioned himself to the right of the opening, furthest from the gap. Should any Räuber make it past the initial thrust of spears, he stood ready with Raven's Tooth.

After the first three, there was a pause. The next man was clearly able to see the bodies of his comrades on the ground and hesitated. while an animated discussion in the guttural tongue of the Barbárs took place on the other side. A deep, harsh voice further back from the gap was shouting commands, while the man nearest the gap was arguing in response. Soon, other voices joined in, jeering and yelling.

"Be ready, lads," Corvus said softly. The Adders crouched lower in their stances.

With a defiant scream, two Räubers burst through the gap, the one behind hugging close to the man in front, whose sword was sweeping frantically in an effort to bat away the spears. Quick as the serpent from which they drew their names, two Adders' spears struck and withdrew, followed lightning fast by two more, then two more. The Räubers fell on top of one another. Corvus smiled with grim pride. *Yazid would be proud.*

Another argument ensued on the other side of the gap, the deep, commanding voice harsh and full of disdain, while more men shouted encouragement and ridicule from further back. The argument became a discussion—they were plotting some kind of new tactic. While the fullness of the holly trees prevented the Räubers from seeing the positions of the Adders, and thus knowledge that they faced only nine men, it also prevented Corvus from seeing what the enemy was doing to overcome the bottleneck.

A moment later, he had his answer. Four men rushed through the gap in quick succession. The one in front dived over the bodies of his slain fellows, while the second tried to turn immediately to the left, shield high, while hacking down with a hand axe. The third also tried to dive through, but his way was partially blocked by the second man, making for an graceless belly flop onto the corpses. Two spears immediately took him in the back. The fourth Räuber—the broadest of them—bulled his way forward shieldless, his two swords flashing.

Corvus had instructed the Adders not to pursue anyone who was able to pass their gauntlet, but to instead maintain their position and focus on the next man through. The first Räuber's dive had successfully gotten him past their spears, his body flying through the gap low and horizontal. He tucked and rolled, his barbed sword slashing blindly out as he rose from his leap. Corvus came at him from the side, Raven's Tooth neatly removing his head in a single stroke.

A cry came from Pherson as the hand axe from the second brute broke his collarbone. The Räuber had a spear buried in his gut and a nasty gash on his face, but was still pushing forward into the Adders on the right, tangling their efforts as his body was shoved by the broader man behind. Corvus leapt directly toward the gap, chopping deeply into the weapon arm of the man with the axe, then lashing out with a vicious kick to the broader man's knee, shattering it and folding it backward. As that man fell with a scream, the spears took him.

"Pherson," Corvus shouted, holding his ground before the center of the gap. "Fall back! Head on up the hill!" He couldn't look to check if the wounded Adder obeyed the order, because more men were forcing their way through the gap and Raven's Tooth had work to do.

Spears flashed, blades clashed, men screamed and died in the frenzy, but no Räubers were able to break through. Finally there was another pause, with intense discussion and plotting heard from the far side of the trees. The respite allowing Corvus and the Adders to catch their breath and survey the mound of dead Räubers piled before the gap. A quick rough count told him that some fifteen men had fallen so far, and the Adders quickly dispatched any wounded enemies. Ahead, Corvus spotted Pherson staggering his way up the trail, holding his useless arm.

There was a rustling on the far side of the overgrowth, followed by the sound of axes on wood. Several men were working to take down the offending bushes, allowing more of the brutes to rush them at once. He had anticipated this. No one else would charge the gap until the path had been broadened. With a quick hiss, he gestured for all of the Adders to group to the left of the gap, out of sight.

"Your work here is done, lads," he said in a low voice. "Make your way to the next position quickly, and help Pherson along should you catch up to him." Nods of understanding from the Adders were followed by the men slipping away up the steep bend in the trail toward the pine grove to assist MacLief's crew. Corvus remained at the gap alone, in case any foolhardy Räuber decided to chance his luck while his fellows were busy hacking at the trees.

The hollies were already thinning noticeably, and he knew he had only a few moments more before the enemy would see that only one man now resisted them. As a huge branch was cleared from the tree on the left, his eyes met those of the Räuber wielding the axe. A look of discovery flashed across his face and he shouted something to his fellows. Knowing a rush through the gap was now imminent, Corvus slipped into the crouch of Badger form, the world immediately slowing around him.

A stream of Räubers charged up the trail, the first falling as Raven's Tooth took out his throat, and the second losing the hand that gripped his sword, while the man behind him took a painful thrust in the hip, slowing him and clogging the charge. Corvus turned and sprinted up the trail.

"MacLief!" he shouted as he ran. "Now, lad!"

There was movement among the pine trees that overlooked the gap, and an avalanche of stones, boulders, and logs rained down on the unfortunate Räubers crowding through the holly trees, trying to step over and past their fallen comrades. The height from the trees down to the gap was a little over fifteen feet, so the barrage likely wouldn't be lethal, but the Adders had managed to gather a large enough pile that it would slow the enemy's advance, injuring some and tangling the rest, buying the Highlanders critical moments.

As Corvus rushed along the trail through the pine grove, the floating light tracked his progress and the Adders fell in behind him. They passed the bench and rounded the steep curve up the trail to the path through the oaks, screams and shouts of rage and defiance echoing up the hillside from behind them.

Cuddy

Following Corvus' earlier instructions, Cuddy had climbed along the trail, working his way out to the stone ledge that overlooked the archway some twenty feet below. He had watched the approach of the black clouds with trepidation as he gathered stones to hurl down from his vantage. Just a short distance from his ledge, he had discovered a sizable outcropping of slate from which he was busy hewing large, jagged slabs. When the wave of despair had overtaken the Tor, he had stopped his labors, collapsing to his knees, his pile still far from sufficient. Cuddy was a solid, reliable man, a stoneworker with a family back home, quiet and hardworking—he was not a man who was prone to showing much emotion. But with the arrival of the cloud, he had found himself weeping uncontrollably, the futility of the paltry pile of rocks at his side only adding to his despair.

He wasn't sure how long he remained there, trapped in his despondency before a strange, lilting melody drifted down the Tor, its strains first cracking then melting away his torpor like steaming water poured over a sheet of ice. He had gulped in a lungful of air, like a swimmer breaking the surface after a long, deep dive. Looking around with fresh eyes of hope, he returned to his labors, redoubling his efforts and hacking away at the slate while cursing his period of inaction. All the while, the sweet song drifted and echoed down from above, redounding him with renewed fervor.

He would be ready. He wouldn't fail the others.

Corvus

Una's breathless form almost collided with him as he charged through the stone arch, a dozen Adders rushing through behind him.

"Position yourselves along the wall here," he barked at them quickly. "They'll not be willing to face another bottleneck. They'll scale the wall. Two ranks, six and six. Second rank back up to the edge of the slope. The bastards will leap from the wall top to try to get behind the nearest spears." Turning back to Una, he asked quickly, "Did you find another spot where we can hold them?"

"Only at the ruins, really," she responded, still breathing heavily from her jog. "But that's a bonnie spot… Defensible."

"Well that'll be where we make our final stand, then," he replied. "We should be able to hold them here for a time. Position yourself on the slope just uphill of the arch there. It'll give you a height advantage. You and Liam, hold the opening."

"Right, Corvus," she responded, then climbed up onto the slope and took her position, spear held high.

"They're coming!" Cuddy yelled down from the ledge.

"Cuddy, you'll be our eyes," Corvus shouted. "Alert the lads when you see them scaling the wall."

"Aye, I will!" he responded sharply.

Then the first of the Räubers ducked through the low archway and was impaled on Liam's spear. The man fell on his right, his body partially blocking the entrance, causing the next man to slow his charge and simultaneously duck his head below the arch of the opening to step over his fallen comrade. Una's spear took him in the side of the neck, dropping him like a bull hit with a pithing rod, his body serving to further occlude the opening. The next man paused before the arch, seeing the danger. The man behind him collided with his back as he scampered up the steep bend in the trail and a cluster of the enemy quickly formed behind them at the base of the rise. Their comrades shouted impatiently at the two stalled at the opening, but their cries were interrupted when a heavy chunk of slate, two feet across, crashed into their midst, crushing the skull of a man at the base of the rise. Threats and cries of defiance were hurled up at Cuddy as the Räubers scrambled to raise their shields amidst the crowding. Another stone followed, splintering a shield and caroming into the back of another man. But the enemy could do little to avoid this new danger—the pressure from the Räubers charging up the trail from behind served to trap the growing cluster at the bend.

The man who was stalled at the archway was forced to dive through, hoping to avoid the spears and clear the corpses. His awkward leap served only to tumble him to Corvus' feet. Raven's Tooth flashed out, spearing him through the chest, while the man behind him also rushed through, taking Liam's thrust on his shield but falling quickly to Una's thrust to his back. Cuddy hurled another stone from above, deftly aiming this rounded rock at the base of the rise in the trail, where it rebounded and crashed into the unprotected legs of the men crouched beneath their shields. Cries of pain echoed up to him as a Räuber fell back, clutching his ruined knee, and another staggered away, also injured.

There was a booming shout of command from somewhere further back, followed by the sound of movement on the far side of the wall.

"They're moving on the wall!" Cuddy shouted, then grunted as he hurled a jagged hunk of slate down from the ledge, shattering a shield with a satisfying crunch. "They're spreading down the length."

Corvus nodded grimly, visualizing the enemy's actions. They would climb the embankment nearest the arch, where the rising trail below was only some four feet from the base of the wall. Then each man would move down the length of the stone barrier, making room for more to follow behind him. Once they were positioned all along it, they would scale it together. He tried to estimate how many might top the wall at once, based on its length.

"They'll come ten or twelve at a time," he shouted. "Be ready!"

Another Barbár shout of command came from further back, and hands suddenly appeared all along the top of the wall, followed quickly by savage faces beneath ragged mops of flaxen hair. Spears flashed, taking some of them, but there were too many. Corvus marveled at the almost inhuman speed of the Räubers. The second rank of spears flashed forward, and more of the enemy fell, but still not enough. Five Räubers successfully cleared the wall, leaping down amidst the Adders, drawing their weapons as they landed.

A rush of men hit the archway one at a time, as the cluster below charged up the curved incline, timing their attack to synchronize with those scaling the wall. Corvus was suddenly very busy helping Una and Liam stem that tide, the mound of corpses in the archway growing. Shouts and chaos broke out behind him, as the Adders struggled to fell the Räubers in their midst. More hands appeared atop the wall and another wave prepared to scale it.

They were being overwhelmed. The enemy was simply coming too fast. There were too many of them.

An arrow slashed through the air from somewhere above, then another. He looked up to find Dallin standing next to Cuddy on the rock ledge, drawing and firing with breathtaking speed, her face flushed with the effort of drawing her powerful bow. He glanced over his shoulder and discovered that all five of the Räubers who had cleared the wall were dead—a single arrow buried in each man's chest, neck, or skull. Further consideration of her deadly accuracy was interrupted, however, as a fresh rush of men came through the archway, demanding his attention. Raven's Tooth flashed as the Adders' spears snaked in and out, all striking with deadly efficiency. Arrows continued to fly overhead.

Soon the pile of bodies at the arch had become its own barricade, and the Räubers were hesitant to even try the opening. To clear the corpses, they would have to dive through, and given the steepness and sharp bend in the trail leading up to the archway—not to mention the occasional rock or arrow that fell from above—there was no good launching point for such a dive. The arch had become an impassable death trap.

There was a lull in the attacks as the enemy paused to rethink their strategy. Finally able to breathe and look about to check on the Adders behind him guarding the wall. Of the twelve, only seven remained standing—however, given the furious assault they had weathered, he was surprised there were that many. He was even more amazed to discover no less than thirty dead Räubers littering the trail on this side of it, not to mention an untold number that had been wounded or killed and fallen back down the far side. Many, if not most of the downed enemy had arrows buried deep in their bodies, regardless of whether they bore a shield or not. And, looking about, he realized he couldn't see a single arrow stuck in or lying on the ground. *She never missed a shot?!* He marveled anew. *And where did all the bleedin' arrows come from?*

Despite the protective and clarifying silver light shining down from the floating star, a wave of weariness threatened to overwhelm him and, judging from the way the Adders sagged and leaned on their spears, he wasn't the only one. The sun could not be seen through the thick mass of dark clouds, but he estimated it to be early afternoon. Fergus' troops should arrive by nightfall, and with any luck, they'd press on up the Tor without pause—unless they were overwhelmed by the dark clouds so oppressing them all. Still, that meant that he and the Adders would have to hold this wall for at least another four hours , probably more.

"Get a drink while you can," he called to the spearmen who dutifully reached for their waterskins, several draining the last drops from theirs.

"Alright, Cuddy? Dallin?" he shouted up to the ledge. They both waved that they were unharmed. But Cuddy indicated with gestures that he had exhausted his pile of ammunition. Appreciating the man's use of silent battlefield gestures, Corvus indicated that he should come down and help defend the wall with his spear. Then, catching Dallin's eye, he merely shook his head in awe at her accomplishment. Even from that distance, he could see her cheeks flush bright red in response to his unspoken praise. She wiped the sweat from her brow with her sleeve. He would have many questions for her later, should they live. For now, he was simply grateful to have her and her bow on that ledge.

Turning quickly to Una and Liam he said, "Pile the bodies as high as you can. Block that opening." Then he turned and jogged over to the other Adders.

"Grand work, all of you," he said, his voice low and intense. He singled out a wounded man, who was busy binding a nasty gash on his right arm with aid from MacLief. The rest of the man seemed unhurt, and his eyes were bright and energetic.

"Paton, isn't it?" Corvus asked. The man nodded sheepishly, as though embarrassed by his wound. "Are you well enough to walk?"

"Sure and I am, Corvus," Paton replied, an intensity in his eyes.

"You would be a great help to your comrades," Corvus said, "if you'd gather up the empty waterskins, and seek out a place to fill them up the trail. We crossed a stream earlier whose source seemed to be further up the Tor. Can you do that?"

"Happily!" he replied and, patting MacLief's shoulder in thanks, rose and quickly started gathering the empty skins, draping their straps over his unwounded shoulder. He was clearly glad to have something to contribute, despite his injury.

Cuddy came jogging down the trail and Corvus addressed him quickly.

"Good lad, Cuddy. Recover as many of these arrows as you can and get them back up to Dallin. Then hurry back, you'll be needed."

Acknowledging the order, the stoneworker bent to the grisly task of extracting the arrows from the bodies of the fallen Räubers. Corvus watched the man swallow hard as he gingerly pulled an arrow from the neck of a corpse, grimacing in disgust at the sucking sound the arrow made as it exited the wound.

"Quick now, Cuddy," Corvus said softly.

"Aye, Corvus," the stoneworker responded, then puffed out his cheeks, steeling himself to the bloody task as he moved on to the next body.

For the first time, Corvus noticed what he thought was music on the wind. He strained to listen, but it was faint, just a suggestion of voices and a flute coming from further up the Tor. The sound was distant and vague, but nonetheless, somehow heartening, like a glimmer of sunshine on a dreary day. Glancing up the trail, he was surprised to see Barclay jogging down toward him, passing Cuddy who was dashing back up to deliver the recovered arrows.

"Barclay," he called, walking to meet him. "What's doin', lad?"

"Yadira sends this," Barclay said, handing him a small cloth bundle. "She said to tell you only two for each person. No more!" He seemed confused by the instructions he was relaying and waited to see that Corvus understood before bending to help Alan—an Adder who had a badly injured leg and was struggling to make his way up the trail toward the temple, leaning heavily on a broken spear haft for support.

Curious, Corvus untied the small packet, discovering a handful of grey seeds with a distinctive fold to their form. They looked familiar, but he struggled to place them. A distant memory stirred from his time studying with Ashahl in Asland. When the time of his imprisonment and ordeal before the Emperor's son had come, Ashahl had visited him in his cell, giving him last minute instructions and handing him a single seed—with the same distinctive dark-grey creases folding in on themselves. *A seed of the Hanging Lantern plant,* his teacher had explained in his deep, elegant voice. *It carries great energy within it. It can fortify a man against terrible travails. Chew it thoroughly just before you enter the arena. But know that its strength will not last forever, and when it leaves you, you will have nothing but your own spirit on which to call.*

He remembered the powerful rush of energy, and unparalleled mental acuity that one seed had given him. It had felt like he was galloping on a crazed war steed, while those he faced were dismounted. The energy had helped him to last through the battering of so many of the emperor's elite guards, as he continued to rise again and again to face another round of the ordeal, despite multiple injuries. But when the stimulant within the seed wore off, he'd collapsed in the sand at a critical moment, leaving him at the mercy of the giant eunuch with nothing but his own stubbornness to fall back upon. *Where in the world did Yadira get these?* It was a timely gift, as the next assault would likely be more intense, and the Adders were already exhausted. They were dreadfully outnumbered, and had hours more of travail to endure.

"Adders, gather round," he barked quickly. As they collected together, he handed each person two seeds, instructing them to eat one—and chew it thoroughly—when the enemy attacked. "Not a moment before!" He then told them to keep the second one someplace readily accessible, and only to reach for it when the first one wore off.

"Now, careful," he adjured them. "This is a powerful med'cin that will stand you up when you feel you can no longer stand. You'll think you have the strength of ten men, but ye'll bleed just the same as always, so be wise. Dinna let it make you foolhardy, or take undue risk. But let it give ye the strength to keep upright when all the world tells you to fall."

The Adders accepted the seeds solemnly, then returned to their positions and prepared for the next assault.

Paton and Cuddy came jogging back down the trail, weighed down by heavy, sloshing waterskins, the stoneworker having detoured to help his wounded comrade with the heavy load. They distributed them quickly to the Adders, handing one to Corvus on the way. Cuddy picked up his spear and took his place along the wall, while Paton waved a quick farewell and headed up the trail again, toward the temple.

Just then, a horrible agonized shrieking began further down the Tor. It sounded like the very souls of men being ripped from their flesh. At first, the sounds were like those a rugged man might make in extremity, but as the screams continued, they became increasingly pitiful, rising in pitch until they sounded more like the helpless squealing of a trapped and tormented animal, weakening by the second. It raised gooseflesh on all of the Highlanders, and a chill of dread ran up Corvus' spine. The shaman was at work.

"They'll redouble their efforts when they come this time," Corvus said loudly to the group, hoping to snap the Adders out of their shocked horror with the firmness of his tone. "We've blocked the archway with their dead, so my guess is they'll focus entirely on scaling the wall, in overwhelming numbers. Stick to your training, be sharp. But when I call for a retreat, get yourselves up the trail as fast as humanly possible. Dinna stop till you reach the temple. D'ye ken?"

Their shout of understanding was staggered, atypical of the uniform responses that had been drilled into them, reflecting how much the sounds of terror had unnerved them. He prayed silently that these ordinary folk of the fyrd might find the extraordinary courage that they would need. He had already asked so much of them. How could he possibly ask more? And yet, if the Green Mount was to stand, this small band of shepherds, potters, weavers, and carpenters would have to become the dam that held back this foul flood. He was heartened to see several of the Adders pat the shoulder of those nearest them as they encouraged one another and prepared for the unknown trials to come.

"Corvus!" Dallin cried from the ledge above. "They're coming!"

"Right then," he called out, holding up a single seed to show them. "One seed only."

They all mirrored his action, each putting a seed on their tongue and chewing its woody husk.

Several sets of large hands appeared along the length of the wall just as Corvus felt the surge of energy. All fatigue was suddenly banished and his mind took on a razor-sharp acuity. His eyes flicked down the wall as, one by one, ten Räubers appeared along the top of the structure. He called a warning to the Adders to look sharp, and then just as the Barbárs leapt over, he noted ten more sets of hands preparing to climb.

Una

She chewed the strange seed, wrinkling her nose at the dusty, soil-like flavor. She looked over to Corvus, about to ask how long would it take for the seed to work, when her ears started ringing and her face flushed, suddenly hot. She was dimly aware of her heart racing, but what caught her interest more keenly was the feeling in her hands and arms. She started flexing her fists. First left, then right. She released her spear with one hand and flexed her grip, feeling the energy vibrating and powerful in her arms and fists, like she had somehow consumed lightning. She had never felt so… alive, so ready, so capable.

A shadow moved above her and she looked up just in time to see a Räuber in the act of leaping off the wall toward her, axe raised high. Without thinking, she executed the dayiri step, a graceful, circular sweeping movement with her back leg that pivoted her out of harm's way and left her behind where the her opponent had fruitlessly landed. Yazid had spent countless frustrating hours trying to drill this step into her, insisting it was the foundational element for excellence in fighting. Una had never gained any real facility with the move. While she had some limited success over the years executing it in training, she had never implemented it in sparring and certainly not in her limited experience actually fighting. Yet, suddenly, here she was, perfectly balanced and looking at the back of the hulking brute that had leapt down to kill her. Her spear snaked out and found the base of the Räuber's skull. She was vaguely aware of a crunching sound as she began an elaborate spin beneath her weapon, which was still stuck in the skull of her opponent, to face the wall. Her eyes found the top of the stone structure, where another Räuber was preparing to leap.

With a surge forward, she shoved her left shoulder into the haft of her spear. It bent and flexed, the tip still wedged into the skull of the brute behind her as she pressed forward. With unusual strength and clarity of purpose, she pulled down on the haft as she pressed forward with her shoulder, causing the spear tip to rip free of the Räuber's skull and fling itself forward and up, leaping spring-like out of her grip and burying itself in the torso of the enemy atop the wall.

Surprised, the man looked down at his abdomen, seeing the weapon protruding from his belly and the entire spearhead buried deep within his flesh. In the moment it took for his injury to register on his confused face, Una leapt up and grabbed the haft with both hands, her feet planted firmly on the wall some four feet off the ground. With a shout, she pushed off and propelled herself into a backflip, ripping the spear from the man's belly, causing his legs to buckle beneath him. This gymnastic maneuver would have been unthinkable prior to eating the seed. The Räuber's feet slipped forward as he tumbled down, hitting his lower back on the crest of the wall before rebounding forward and landing face down beside Liam, just as the young Adder was finishing a Räuber who had unwisely chosen to try to climb over the pile of corpses in the archway. He deftly sidestepped the man dropped by Una and, without hesitation, ripped his spear from the throat of the man he had just killed in the archway, twirled the weapon, and buried its head in the back of the newly fallen enemy.

Una peered right just in time to see MacLief finish a man with a powerful horizontal slash of his spear. However, unknown to MacLief, another Räuber had gained the wall behind him and was preparing to throw his hand axe at the Adder's unguarded back. With a circular leap, Una shifted her grip to long form and spun into a reaching thrust that found Hand Axe's cheek just below his right eye before he could release his weapon. The Räuber flinched and jerked away, fouling his throw. In that moment, MacLief arched his back in as beautiful a display of Sky Prayer—a virtually unattainable posture for her—as she'd ever seen. From this position, he thrust his spear up into the Räuber's unprotected nethers, the spear stopping only when it encountered the bone of his pelvis.

The sound the wounded Räuber made was deeply gratifying, and she would have liked to take a moment to revel in having reduced the big barbarian to a whimpering heap, but just then there was a sound like a deep growl from the section of wall nearest the arch, directly behind Liam. She turned to face it just as it exploded inward, sending blocks of stone flying, crushing Liam, and propelling her violently back.

Chapter 10

"Will you remain what cruelty has made you? Or will you lay down the burden of your pain, your woundedness, and choose to walk forward into life as something new? We are never truly free of the scars of our life, but we can choose—choose—not to dwell upon them, to cast our eyes up unto the heavens instead of down to the damaged clay of our bodies and hearts. And so I ask you again, will you remain what cruelty has made you?"

—Priestess Nura of the White Temple

The day before the Autumn Equinox
The Tor, Green Mount

Yadira

She knelt by the wounded man who had made his way up the Tor from the fighting below. Jack, Anna, and Barclay stood nearby, concern written on their faces. Jack shifted his feet nervously, wringing his hands, a mixture of worry and fear playing over his boyish features. Despite the combined calming and encouraging effect of the music from the three minstrels, coupled with the subtle encouragement provided by Mama's chanting, Jack seemed to be wrestling with himself, trying to stave off panic. He needed something to do. The three Adders had rushed down the path when they saw their comrade, Pherson, struggling up the trail. Together, they had given him water, and helped him the rest of the way, the final climb up the steep defile into the temple proving the most difficult. He had collapsed with a pained groan onto the temple floor.

Now, following Yadira's instructions, Anna and Barclay lifted him gingerly and moved him to the rear of the temple, where Jack positioned his bag to be a serviceable pillow. Yadira examined the wound. A blade had chopped through his collarbone—most likely an axe, based on the shape of the injury—cutting into the chest, though only shallowly. It was a painful wound no doubt, but the break looked to be a clean one, and given time, it should heal, provided she could keep it clean and stave off infection.

"I need a small fire just there" she said to Jack, pointing to the triangular area behind the collapsed block of stone. He nodded, seeming grateful to have another task, then dashed off to find fuel. Looking to the other two, she added, "The night will be cold. Perhaps you should help Jack collect firewood to last us."

Barclay looked to Anna, who was the senior Adder present. She seemed to weigh the thought, as though reluctant to leave. They had been charged with protecting Argant and the group in the temple, in case the enemy managed to get past Corvus and the others. But without a fire, the night would be miserable.

"C'mon, Barclay," she said, after a few moments. "She's right. A fire'll be welcome."

Hefting their spears, the two climbed down the defile and headed back down the trail at a jog.

Yadira examined the man's wound, gently picking out bits of dirt and cloth from the cut. She had seen so many injuries and so much death in her life. Anna had told her this wounded man's name was Pherson, which surprised her and called forth a sharp memory from her childhood she had thought locked away forever.

When she was only a skinny little girl of eight or nine, her father had died from a pox brought to their city by sailors. So many had died. The frightened townsfolk had shunned anyone from a household where sickness had resided. Unable to buy food or medicine for them, her mother had weakened and the evil pox returned to claim both her and Yadira's sister, Naila. Yadira had fallen sick as well, tossing with fever on her bed for what seemed an eternity, unaware that her mother and sister lay dead nearby. Somehow, she had survived the disease, eventually crawling feebly out of that house of death to dig in the trash for scraps of food, drinking from puddles in the street, her cheeks and neck forever scarred by the cruel blisters of the pox. But she had survived, just barely. And, in time, despite innumerable cruelties suffered and spite heaped upon her by people who saw her as no better than the trash in which she rummaged, she grew into a wily and clever urchin, her light fingers deftly relieving passersby of the weight of their purses or jewelry.

There was a man, Firson—a name similar to the injured Adder's—who was a merchant from the far north and sold brass goods at the market. He was a large, frightening man, always cruel and quick to dole out blows to the beggar children to discourage their thieving ways and keep them from his shop. He had beaten Yadira's young friend, Cyra, almost to death for trying to steal a small incense bowl. Firson was the first man Yadira had ever killed, slipping a deadly mixture of white sanicle and nightshade into his tea. Seeing him thrash and foam at the mouth, his eyes leaking tears of blood, she had felt no remorse. On the contrary, it had given her a remarkable sense of power.

She had always been clever—much smarter than her fellow beggar children—and by the time she was entering adolescence, she had become something of a leader among the urchins, plotting their thefts, nursing their wounds, finding them precious food when none seemed available. The polyglot of tongues that daily filled the market proved to be a mental playground for her, as she learned to tease out meaning from the various dialects she heard. Copying sounds, words, and phrases until she was conversational in at least a half-dozen languages.

She was always careful to mask her cleverness from the adults, finding them far more likely to reveal their secrets if they thought her a dullard. She always had a talent for plants and herbs, so when she discovered Hyat, the elderly herbalist whose small shop sat just behind Omphalos—the gambling den and center of town—the adolescent Yadira had set about earning the woman's trust. She had been amazed at the riches of knowledge and rare medicinal herbs the woman possessed, but Hyat had been slow to accept Yadira's help around the shop, at first seeing her as merely another urchin, as likely to steal from her as help her out. But the girl was single-minded in her earnest efforts to win the woman over, and Hyat lived alone with no offspring or apprentice to assist her. Lifting heavy jars and grinding seeds to powder with the weighty pestle were beginning to prove too much for her gnarled hands and crooked back. In time, she had allowed Yadira to assist her for a few hours each day, in exchange for a meager but tasty meal. Hyat had been miserly in sharing her knowledge with Yadira, but the girl was clever, and absorbed every morsel of information she could glean from the old woman's mutterings, asking occasional but insightful questions as to why this proportion or that combination. Despite her misgivings, Hyat had seemed inwardly pleased at Yadira's inquisitiveness. Soon, she began to share her knowledge more readily. Yadira drank up every bit of information, cataloguing it in her impressive young mind, unsure how this knowledge might be used later, but certain of its value.

True to the woman's fears, Yadira had stolen from her, though never taking coin nor food. Instead, she had carefully slipped small packets of powdered herbs into her ragged clothing, careful not to take so much as might arouse suspicion. At first, she had focused on healing herbs and antiseptic ointments to treat the sores and cuts of the other urchins, helping them fend off infection. But in time, driven by the cruelties inflicted on the children by the merchants, soldiers, and sailors in the port, she began fantasizing about exacting revenge—fantasies that soon blossomed into the full flower of reality.

Firson had been her first kill, but not her last. In the month that followed his death, no fewer than six other men had died horribly from her poisons. She remembered each one vividly, recalling their names as each face flashed now in her mind, a tear slipping down her scarred cheek as she tended to the wounded man before her, whose name had innocently conjured such memories.

There was Khalil, the foul-smelling, one-eyed doorman for the brothel, who delighted in abducting girls from the street and dragging them to his lice-ridden bed. Rayan, the fat sergeant of the local constabulary, who had laughed in her face and driven her from his office with his crop when she had shown the temerity to come to him for help, begging him to stop Khalil's depredations. Old Marwan, the knife merchant, who gleefully cut off the hands of children accused of stealing. Captain Qasim, the slave-trader that regularly rounded up the male urchins, marching them off to his ship in shackles to a lifetime of misery. Suleil, the seemingly benign beggar, who would sit by his basket a bland smile on his face, occasionally sharing a copper with one or another of the urchins, only to then lure the child down an alley and strangle them like a stray cat. It was said that the shopkeepers in the vicinity paid him a small bounty for each urchin disposed of in this manner. Three coppers for the life of a child.

Though each man had deserved his fate, Yadira had been too eager to inflict punishment, the sense of empowerment making her reckless. The killings all happened within the span of a single moon. Fear and suspicion spread through the marketplace, and soon every eye seemed filled with mistrust. Hyat had discovered Yadira's thefts and cast her out with shrill denunciations and curses. The girl had been forced to flee the dockside market, pursued by an angry mob intent on punishing the murderous child who had visited such terror upon them. She ran until exhaustion and fear had finally overcome her and she collapsed behind a pile of refuse in a neighboring town. She had been forced to abandon the other urchins and for weeks she wept in abject misery and worry over the fate of her circle of followers who had become so dependent upon her and followed her so willingly. In time, word had reached her that the angry mob, unable to catch Yadira, had turned their fury upon the other poor children, capturing and killing most of them. Those few that weren't captured had run off into the hills, where they had no doubt also perished. They had looked to her as their leader, and her recklessness had gotten them all killed.

She shook her head to banish the unwanted memories. She hadn't thought of those days in years. Why did she do so now? Long ago, she had changed her life—Mama had changed her life—and she had dedicated herself to the pursuit of learning and healing. She had embraced the life of a votary, sworn to the Path of the Divine Halls of the Ancestors, and immersed herself in the mysteries of that order. That was twenty years ago now. She glanced up at her teacher, chanting steadily beside the group of minstrels, helping to hold back the weight of those menacing clouds with such selfless steadfastness. Twenty years of service to this remarkable woman, and still Yadira was haunted by her past. Twice over the years, Mama had recommended that Yadira be elevated to priestess, eligible to take on her own votaries and begin her own ministry. She had declined the elevation each time, refusing to explain to her teacher her reasoning, unable to share how haunted she was by the memories of those children she had failed. They had followed her, listened to her, accepted her guidance. And she had abandoned them to their brutal fates. Worse still, she had caused their deaths. How could she ever again take on followers, seeing the trust in their eyes and knowing that at any time, she might again fail them? The thought terrified her on a deep level, though the tumult of emotions it stirred seemed inchoate, and her ordered mind struggled to organize them.

She shook her head, blinking away the tears and leaned once more over Pherson's injury. She gently daubed the blood from his chest, and the wounded man moaned in discomfort. Here, in service to Mama, despite their current circumstances, she found a certain peace and simplicity. She didn't bear the weight of decisions, nor did she have to face the horror of failing those who might follow her. Instead, she merely served. It was the easier path, and one that assuaged her long-held guilt. This Pherson she would tend and heal, unlike the other.

"Argant," Yadira called to the child, who—though clutching Mama's leg—was staring at Pherson's wound fearfully. "I need your help."

Without hesitation, the boy detached himself from Mama and came to her, his jewel-like eyes sparkling with an open willingness that stung her.

"Bring my satchel over here, please," she said, turning from his expression and focusing once more on picking dirt from the still-streaming wound. The child moved off, returning a moment later, straining to carry the bag.

"Set it just there, thank you," she said, her eyes crinkling in restrained gratitude above her jimas. "While I tend to Pherson,"can you please bring water for Miss Zsoka?" None of their party chose to use the woman's grandiose title.

The boy nodded, happy to be of some assistance, and Yadira busied herself mixing a poultice from healing herbs and a small dollop of lard from her satchel. When Argant returned once again, ready for a new task, she handed him a small towel.

"Wet this in the fountain for me," she instructed, then rummaged through the bag as he quickly obeyed. When he returned with the dripping fabric, she pulled out a small sachet made of waxed cloth. She took the towel and carefully wiped the wound, delicately removing still more bits of dirt and grime. She handed the reddened towel back to the boy with instructions to rinse it clean in the flowing water, not in the fountain's basin. She then undid the knot on the sachet and dropped a pinch of the powdered contents onto the cut, gently working it into the savaged flesh with her fingers. Pherson groaned and winced in discomfort. When Argant returned a moment later, she once more took the sodden fabric and squeezed the water into the cut, dissolving the powder. She waited a few minutes for the antiseptic powder to take effect, noting the grimace on poor Pherson's face. She knew how the powder stung, but nothing prevented infection as well as Angel's Root. After an appropriate time had passed, she applied the poultice, which would help slow the bleeding and prevent further infection. Sadly, she would have to wait until a fire was built before she could make a medicinal tea that would let the poor man sleep. Only then did she notice that Argant was shivering, the sleeves of his shirt soaked with the ice-cold water.

"Here." She indicated he should kneel beside her, biting back more unwanted memories of shivering children that threatened to engulf her. She hugged him close, letting him draw warmth from her, though even to her the gesture felt forced, lacking in any real comfort. She was too restrained in her affections.

Jack returned shortly after, panting with effort, carrying an armload of kindling and small branches. He arranged the pile of twigs, then left to gather more. Yadira looked at Argant meaningfully.

"Do you remember how Mama and I light the fire with our spirit?" she asked him, softly. The boy nodded earnestly. "She told me that she believes you have that same gift. Do you think you can try? I must stay by Pherson's side, and the others are busy." She indicated the minstrels who were continuing their song, holding the darkness at bay, while Mama, Lupe, and Amina chanted at their side, feeding them strength and courage despite their obvious and growing fatigue.

Argant looked worried.

"What if I can't do it?" he asked, his brow creased.

"You can, Argant," Yadira assured him with a cold confidence. She tried to infuse her voice with as much warmth and encouragement as she could, but she knew it had fallen far short of the nurturing tone that came so naturally to Mama. Again, it felt forced, and she scolded herself silently for her inability to truly open up to this boy, whose trusting expression so mirrored those of her young cohort long ago. She silently cursed the scars that bound her heart. *Will your past forever bind your future?* Mama had challenged her once, when Yadira had first refused elevation. *Will you remain what cruelty has made you? Or shall you become something else? Something of your choosing?*

She tried again, smiling once more at the boy, this time succeeding in conveying more warmth.

"Won't you try, child?" she asked softly. "It would be a help. The sooner I can make the tea, the sooner poor Pherson can sleep."

"I'll… try," Argant said, unsure, and moved toward the pile of kindling nervously.

"Wait." She stopped him as he started to move away, unsure of what she wanted to say, but knowing that the child deserved her compassion. Like her, cruel circumstance had orphaned him, and he had struggled to toughen his little heart, trying so hard to be brave despite the dangers and horrors that beset them. She beckoned him back, recalling suddenly the day Mama had found her. She had looked upon Yadira with eyes that seemed to know her past, yet held no judgment nor condemnation. Only compassion. She had spoken to the girl with love and warmth in her eyes, offering her hope and a way out of her misery. It had been the first kindness Yadira had felt from an adult in too many years, and the girl had mistrusted it. It couldn't be real. But each day, Mama had returned to sit with her, clean her hands, and eat a meal with her. She spoke of many things, of kindness and caring, about what life as a votary might be like. The girl was not interested and tried repeatedly to rebuff the priestess, occasionally hurling angry or hurtful words at her in an effort to drive her away, to stop tormenting her with forlorn hope. But each day, Mama had returned, understanding in her eyes and food in her basket. Yadira had finally suggested that they toss a coin—crowns or crests—the simple gambling game she had mastered years before. If Yadira won, Mama would leave her to her life on the streets, but if Mama won, Yadira would agree to come and study with her. The older woman had agreed, handing the child a silver coin to toss, a crown emblem embossed on one side, a royal crest on the other. Yadira had smiled inwardly, confident in the sleight of hand skills she had honed so effectively as a thief. She held the coin with a look of smug defiance on her face and called crowns on the toss, as had always been her habit. She caught the coin deftly and slapped it onto the back of her other hand. When her hands parted, revealing the unexpected emblem of the crest, she had been dumbstruck. She *always* won this game. She was too good to have lost. She looked up into Mama's knowing smile and everything had changed forever.

Will you remain what cruelty has made you?

The boy's innocent, mismatched eyes stared at her with a woundedness she hadn't noticed before. Had it always been there, and she had just been too closed off to notice? Or had she seen it and turned away because it reminded her of too much she wanted to forget? Her eyes suddenly stung and she reached out to take Argant's shoulders. With a sigh, she caressed them gently, blinking back tears, then pulled him softly into a genuine embrace. She held him for a time, her heart aching for his pain and vulnerability—aching, perhaps for the first time in her memory, for someone else's pain. She pulled back, cupping his face in her long, thin hands.

"I have something to show you," she said, and reached down into the pouch at her side, producing the coin she had won in her vision of the strange woman. The boy's eyes widened in confusion. "This is a blessed coin, Argant. See, here on one side is a crown, and on the other, a crest." The child stared, mesmerized by it. "I'm going to flip the coin," she continued, " and you tell me if it will be crowns or crests before I catch it. If you're right, then the blessing falls on you and you may keep the coin."

He looked at her in wonder. This bit of silver was likely more money than the child had ever seen, and the thought of the small game, no matter how trivial or simple, seemed to have captured his young spirit—as is always the way with children—allowing him to forget, for just a moment, the consequential and frightening things happening around him.

"Ready? Call out while the coin is in the air." she said, then flipped it expertly.

"Crown!" Argant called.

She caught the coin and slapped it onto the back of her hand. She was surprised at how readily the sleight of hand, so long unused, returned to her. Argant didn't notice anything untoward, and when she lifted her hand, revealing the coin, she smiled at the look of wonder in his eyes as he stared down at the crown emblem shining up at him.

"The coin is yours," she said, and placed it in his little hand, folding his fingers over it. "As is the blessing."

"Thank you, Yadira," he responded, almost awestruck.

"I know you can light the fire," she said with a wink. "The blessing is with you."

Argant

He climbed over the fallen block and hopped down beside the pile of kindling, eyeing it warily as though it were a serpent poised to strike him. He fingered the blessed coin Yadira had given him, then clutched it tightly. He couldn't understand why the thought of trying to light the fire frightened him so. He had only tried it the one time, weeks ago, shortly after Mama and the women had found him hiding under the hawthorn bush after his family was killed. His mind suddenly filled with unwanted memories. He tried to picture happier times with his family, the way Mama had taught him to chase away the bad memories with good ones—his father playfully dousing him with a bucket of water during one of their rare playtimes together, his sister yelling in mock outrage and chasing him when he'd stolen her hairbrush, his mother tucking him in to his little truckle bed, her soft voice singing the familiar lullaby. But then, the image of their burning house and ravaged corpses flashed before him, provoking a gasp. He closed his eyes and tried desperately to push the memory aside, chanting the calming words Mama had taught him. His racing heart slowed. He had experienced so many things since that awful time, learned so much from the kind women who had taken him in. He had met so many new people who cared for him and wanted to protect him: Ligulf with his kind eyes and beautiful voice, Dallin with her jagged teeth and funny accent, Corvus who could look scary but was always kind and protective to him. So much had happened. He had started visiting the old man in his dreams, who told him of the Tor and its history and how Argant was supposed to be the new Gatekeeper. There was so much!

It suddenly occurred to him that he didn't know the man's name. Strange to have had so many conversations with the mysterious man on his cobwebbed throne and not know his name. He knew that very important things were all happening. Tomorrow was the Equinox, the day Argant was somehow supposed to take the man's place, which terrified him. He wasn't sure he wanted that. It seemed too big, too scary. He was just a little boy. It wasn't fair that everything was going to rest on his shoulders. It wasn't fair that his family was murdered. None of it was fair!

He sniffed and wiped away a tear. Pherson moaned in pain. The Adder had been injured trying to hold off the bad men, trying to protect everyone here… trying to protect him. Yadira needed to make the special tea that would let him sleep, and to do that, she needed Argant to light the fire the way Mama had showed him. The bad people would be here soon, and all the adults would be too busy to make a fire. Maybe he could do this one thing. He rubbed the blessed coin with his thumb, feeling its embossed surface. After all, the blessing had fallen on him and he had felt something last time — at least he thought he had. Maybe he could try. He closed his eyes and reached his hand out toward the pile of sticks.

Suddenly, he was sitting in front of the man on the throne.

"Oh good, you're back," the old man said with a wheeze. His voice sounded older, dustier than usual.

"Yadira wants me to light the fire the way Mama showed me," Argant said in a small voice.

"Yes, pyrokinesis," the man replied.

"What?" he asked, confused.

"It's a very big word for a very small thing," the man said with a gentle smile.

"But I don't know how," Argant complained.

"Do you remember when the grass and vines covered and hid you, Argant?"

"Yes," the boy said. "That was really strange."

"You see," the old man explained, "they did that because I asked them to."

"Oh." He wasn't sure if he should thank the man or try harder to understand what was clearly another lesson. "What do you mean?" he asked, deciding on the latter.

"Within all things"—the old man's eyes drifted away from Argant as he spoke—"there exists a spark of life, waiting to take action. Do you understand?

"I… think so," Argant replied, unsure if he did understand.

"The trick, you see, is not to tell the grass to grow, nor is it to order the wood to burn. Instead, you merely find that spark that's waiting to spring to life and ask it to come forth."

"Oh…" Argant thought about this for a moment. "Like Mama said, you feel the heat waiting to happen inside the wood, and call to it to come out."

"Exactly!" The man smiled. "We mustn't speak for long right now. Your friends need you. But we will speak again later. Tomorrow is an important day, and I still have much to explain, but I confess I am weary."

"Okay." Argant's brow furrowed in worry.

"You needn't fear, little one," the man said, seeing the concern on the boy's face. "You are up to the tasks that face you. There is great power in you."

Argant nodded uncertainly and started to turn away, then stopped himself. "What's your name, anyway?" he asked the old man suddenly.

The man's eyes fluttered and he stirred. He had already dozed off in the few seconds since he finished speaking.

"Oh, yes," he said absently. "I am Athdar."

"Like the man in Piper's song?"

"Yes," he said, a fond smile wisping over his lips. "Just the same."

"And you did all those things in the song?"

"Some of them, yes," the man said with a slight nod. "Though the balladeers have taken some liberties over the years. But yes, that song is about me and how I came to be here." His gnarled hand gestured weakly to indicate the throne.

"Wow," the boy said with wonder.

"Off you go, now," Athdar urged gently. "Yadira needs that fire."

The throne faded away and he was once more seated in the temple before the firewood, eyes still closed, hand outstretched toward the wood. His brow creased in concentration. He tried to feel the spark within the wood, as Athdar had explained.

Nothing. He was aware of the minstrels singing behind him and the injured man moaning as Yadira tended his wound. Mama, Lupe, and Amina were still chanting, and outside the temple he could feel the glowering clouds pressing in, trying to reach through the protection his friends afforded him—to crush him again in hopelessness. He sighed in frustration and squinched his eyes more tightly shut.

"Please," he asked the wood. "Please, I don't know how to do this."

He gasped when he felt the tiniest tingle in the palm of his hand. He concentrated on that tingle, trying to picture it. He saw only blackness until… There it was, the smallest thread of light. He focused on it until he could see the thread more clearly, his awareness of the rest of the world drifting away from him. Soon, the thread filled his mind and he followed it, seeing where it split into several strands, each touching a piece of wood or kindling before him. Where the thread touched each piece, there was a tiny spark flickering, barely perceptible. He stared at one and felt something… It felt alive. It felt just like the time he had discovered a litter of kittens under their barn. They were shy and fearful at first, but with patience and a small bit of string to lure it forth, he had eventually coaxed one out of its hiding place. He remembered the words he had said to it.

"C'mon," he said, gently. "You can come out." The spark glowed a little brighter, though it didn't move. "C'mon," he said again. "It's okay. You can come and play. It'll be fun." The spark flared, drawing toward his hand, growing in brightness. "You'll be so glad to be a big roaring fire, keeping everybody warm. You can do that."

The spark's glow fluttered for a moment, as if in indecision, then suddenly leapt to Argant's palm, flaring brightly as it did. With a yelp, he opened his eyes in shock, his hand stinging where the spark had touched him. Before him, the pile of kindling was burning with a bright, merry blaze. His mouth fell open and he stared at it, feeling equal parts shock and pride. He looked back at Yadira, whose eyes crinkled in gentle acknowledgment of his accomplishment.

Within short order, Yadira was able to make the medicinal tea for the wounded Adder. Jack, Anna, and Barclay had returned with more wood, but very quickly had to pick up their spears and rush out of the temple. Yadira handed something to Barclay and instructed him to deliver it to Corvus as quickly as possible, meanwhile Anna and Jack moved to position themselves down the trail, near the final bend. They looked worried, though Argant didn't really understand what they said.

With nothing to do now, Argant tended his small fire proudly, occasionally feeding it with more wood, though Anna had stressed that what they brought had to last them through the night, so he had to be sparing. He sat enjoying the warmth of the fire and poking at it from time to time with a small stick. His eyes drifted around the temple, examining the intricate carvings and spiral decorations on the columns. The carvings seemed to be very similar on each of the pillars, and he entertained himself by trying to match the details on them. The floral element near the base was repeated on each one, though in a slightly different position. The braided wreath midway up the nearest pillar was repeated as well, though the braiding was subtly different. In fact, every decorative element seemed to be repeated on each column, with one exception. A circular motif on the east face of the column directly behind the fountain wasn't to be found on any of the other pillars.

He crossed to it and stared up at the unique carving, reaching up with his stick to tap the design. Six strands of rope were interwoven into what looked like a wreath. In the center of the design was a smaller circle, divided cleanly by a horizontal line. The top half looked to be a sun, either rising or setting with half its shape hidden by the horizon, while around the half that was visible were carved jagged lines of light streaming from it. The lower half of the circle seemed to be a night sky, complete with a crescent moon and stars etched into the stone. He found it curious that this symbol would only be present on this single column, and he carefully walked around each of the other pillars to see if perhaps the carving might be found on the outside surface, or maybe higher or lower, but his searched confirmed it was nowhere else.

His gaze drifted to the floor of the temple. It was made up of a series of two-foot-square tiles. Dirt had accumulated over the centuries, masking any details and mostly filling in the gaps between them, creating the sense that the floor was a single smooth surface. But near the pillars he could still make out the straight grooves between the tiles. Standing once more before the column with the strange design, he began to trace one of the gaps at his feet with his stick, digging away the dirt that encrusted it. Within a short time, with the single-mindedness of the young, he had dug out the straight line all the way from the pillar to the fountain. He then began work scratching out the horizontal gaps around it. It was a mindless exercise that kept him busy and, in some way, entertained him as the big world around him became too consequential for someone so small to consider.

As he dug away at a particular tile, located midway between the column and the fountain, he noticed something strange about its surface. A small portion of its face was exposed, revealing the corner of some design or carving on it. Setting aside his stick, he used both hands to try to brush it clean, but the accumulated dirt was too dry and crusty, and his hands soon became red and sore. Fetching a cup, he filled it with water from the fountain and poured it over the tile then, using his eating knife, he was able to chisel away at the encrustation, revealing the same, singular design from the pillar. An unexplained chill crawled over him as he stared at it in surprise. He couldn't explain why he felt the way he did, but for some reason, he *knew* this was important. He glanced about to see if there was anyone with whom he could share his discovery. Just then, Zsoka limped over to the fire, flashing a pained smile at him.

"What do you do there?" she asked, wincing and holding her shoulder as she sat carefully onto the fallen block of stone by the fire.

Pointing to the crest on the tile, he explained his discovery to her, and was surprised when the woman that called herself "Empress"—though he wasn't quite sure what that meant, only that it sounded important—gingerly knelt down beside him with a small stick in her hand and, despite her injury, began to help him dig out the accumulated mud.

The two of them worked at the tile in companionable silence. An empress and an orphan, a mother and a child, a woman of power and a boy of destiny.

Yadira

Mama's eldest votary stretched and arched her back, which was cramping from kneeling and leaning over Pherson. She glanced over to check on Argant and was shocked to see the wounded Zsoka kneeling stiffly beside him, a stick in her hand. The two were intently digging at something on the floor, talking animatedly with one another.

Yadira found her opinion of the so-called "Empress" softening a bit. Should they live through these tumultuous events, she might like to learn Zsoka's story. She imagined it would be quite interesting. She watched the woman's carefree and naturally warm engagement with Argant, so very different from her own strained efforts. Whatever Zsoka had experienced and endured, of one thing Yadira was certain: Zsoka was a *mother*. There was no concealing that. A stone of regret fell in Yadira's stomach. She might never know such compassion.

Chapter 11

No matter how aligned our purposes may be... should you injure those from my tribe, I will confound you.

—Tuxo'o aphorism

One day before the Autumn Equinox
Atalaya de Locus, Cantabria

Farric

"So," the field marshal asked dubiously, refilling his madeira, "this clandestine organization exists merely to bring to light corruption and graft? An effort to reform the Church?"

"Just so," Briguglio replied, accepting the bottle and topping off his own glass.

"You expect me to believe there is no ulterior motive?" Farric asked, disbelief dripping from his words. "Purely altruistic, and only focused upon the Church?"

"Oh, I wouldn't go that far," the scribe replied, setting down his glass. "Many of us, myself included, are driven by far more base motivations, and our order's goals extend well beyond the Church."

"Base motivations?" Farric asked. "Such as?"

"Vengeance," the scribe replied with a tone that suggested a story that Farric suddenly wanted to hear, and, consequently, a deep and abiding hatred of the Church.

"Tell me," he said encouragingly.

"Another time," the scribe replied, leaning back from the table. "We have spoken long this evening, and I have told you much."

"But not enough," the field marshal replied.

"Enough to find myself on an excruciating rack, should my words find the wrong ears."

Farric feigned woundedness. "You don't trust me?"

"We are far beyond questions of trust, you and I," Briguglio responded. "However, I do not have an entire mercenary army at my beck and call to defend me from the Church's inquisitors."

"Fair enough," Farric replied with a light laugh. "What news from the Court of Vella?"

"Ah," Briguglio said, clearly relieved at the change of subject. "It appears that more of the shamans have died."

"Oh?" Farric sat forward, interested. "The Pentatarch can't be happy about that."

"Oh, he isn't," the scribe said with a smirk, "I can assure you."

"The grand plan moves ahead, regardless, I assume?"

"Yes," the scribe affirmed. "Vella is so invested in the scheme—financially and otherwise—that nothing short of complete disaster will dissuade him. Already the Church is so deeply financially invested that should Vella's desired outcome not come to pass... Well." He ended on a dismissive shrug, suggesting complete ruin would engulf the Church.

"So, we march on Lachland?" the field marshal asked.

"All of Daffyd must yield to him," Briguglio confirmed. "Lachland, Aesthir, and the Green Mount."

"The Green Mount..." Farric said after a moment's pause. "Tell me about them. How are they proving such a thorn in

Vella's side? Explain to me how in the Five Depths they are holding off the Barbárs and killing shamans?"

Briguglio smiled knowingly. "That, my friend, is a long tale. Do you have more of this excellent madeira?" He held up the empty bottle, to which Farric laughed and rose, striding over to an elaborate wine rack near the hearth to fetch another.

Hours later, his curiosity sated, at least for now, Farric bade the scribe farewell and closed his door. Briguglio had given him much to consider. History, fact, legend. The scribe was remarkably well informed, and had an almost encyclopedic knowledge of the history of the past few hundred years. Farric shook his head and shrugged in resignation. How one person could acquire so much knowledge was beyond him. He had noticed one interesting detail about Briguglio that he wasn't sure the scribe had meant to reveal: The man wore a pendant beneath his robe. Small, unassuming. It was the triangle of Cruim, representing knowledge. There was nothing damning in this alone — people were, of course, allowed to show a preference for any one of the Five. But for a scribe of the Church not to wear the Orbit, and instead wear the triangle... Well, that could be an issue, were it revealed. But did Briguglio let him see it intentionally? Or was it an inadvertent revelation? The man was remarkably intelligent. It was hard to imagine him making a blunder like that unintentionally.

He crossed to the nighttime window and gazed out past his own reflection, seeking to penetrate the darkness of the square beyond. He was sure spies were watching. Still, he had set a squad of his best men to conduct the scribe to and from his chambers; while not as deadly or as feared as his Nizari assassins, these men were loyal, effective and discreet. He was confident Briguglio's movements this evening would escape the notice of the Church's spies — and if it did not, there would likely be fewer of the Church's spies come morning. Farric could not be seen to act against the Church directly — but a knife in the back in a dark alley, or a shadowed rooftop? Who was to say who was the culprit?

He downed the last of his drink, and set the glass on the mantel of the fireplace. The scribe had shared much information. Abhorrent and hypocritical actions the Church had taken over the years. Things Vella himself had done as he had clawed his way to the pinnacle of power. Reprehensible things. The scribe had revealed secrets of the Holy Knights and the Boreal Watchtower itself—Secrets held so closely, the punishment for disclosure would be a lifetime of torment and madness. Yet the scribe had shared them openly, as though there were no risk—as though he could trust Farric. As though the field marshal were not a venal mercenary, happy to sell out anyone for money. How could a man so intelligent misjudge the situation so completely?

It must be that the damning evidence Briguglio had shared so freely offended the scribe's sense of justice and integrity so much that he had projected that same sense of honor onto Farric. As though the mercenary commander would likewise be offended by such breaches in ethics. *Foolish assumption.* The field marshal shook his head and swirled the financial possibilities exposing the scribe would present around in his mind, much as he had swirled the expensive madeira in his glass earlier. So many ways to capitalize on this—partial revelation, full exposure… He knew the Church would pay exceedingly well for any information about the Ludicra Veritas, and perhaps the Ludicra might pay equally well *not* to be exposed. From everything the scribe had shared, it was clear he was a high-ranking member, if the group even had ranks.

And yet… something the scribe had said stuck in his mind, somehow deeper than all the other drivel about integrity, justice, and whatnot. It was the Church's ongoing effort to exterminate the people of the Tuxo'o, his mother's people. *His* people, perhaps. He hadn't been raised among them, but his mother had, and she had loved them. She had honored their ways and insisted her son learn to honor them from an early age. Primary among the principles of the Tuxo'o was the sense of tribe—of a *people*—and that the tribe would always come first. After her death, he had transferred that value to his membership in the Blades, despite their many cruelties and shortcomings. But something in

Briguglio's words had reignited his mother's original intent: that her son know of and value his connection to his people, though he had never lived among them.

He had already taken steps to delay the Pentatarch's ambitions in Daffyd, but was that enough? Was he honoring his mother's memory sufficiently if he was still working with the man who'd had her killed?

He knelt before the hearth, following his thoughts into the depths of the fire. But a scratching at the window soon drew him back to the darkened panes. Once more, a raven clung to the too-small ledge and croaked in irritation at him.

"Well, hello, again," Farric said, opening the window. Without hesitation, the raven fluttered into his chamber and alighted on his desk. "Yes, by all means, come in," the field marshal chuckled. "Make yourself at home."

The raven croaked and walked over to his empty madeira glass, tipping it quite intentionally onto the floor, where it shattered.

"Here, now," Farric said with irritation.

The raven croaked again, then turned its full attention on Farric. As their eyes met, the field marshal was swept into a dream or vision.

He stood in a tribal community, among a series of rustic longhouses, some twenty feet long and twenty feet high. People dressed in animal-skin clothing — buckskin trews with feathers in their hair — moved about the central fire pit, fetching water and disappearing back into the longhouses. He couldn't explain it, but he felt a deep affection for these people, like he knew them and trusted them. He *loved* them. Women carried babes on their hips as they performed their morning chores, men worked in the fields, weeding and harvesting from their large farm plots. He looked down at his hands and feet, and saw that they were the limbs of a young girl child. He was about to ask someone what was going on, when the sound of galloping horses turned his attention to the path into the village. A contingent of Holy Knights, accompanied by a fervent company of torch-bearing civilian settlers, came thundering into their midst. Before he could protest, torches were thrown, longhouses were engulfed in flame, Tuxo'o defenders were slaughtered—including one particular older man with kind eyes who had rushed over to protect him… To protect his mother, he now realized. This was her memory!

"Remember, little doe," the man had said, kneeling before her, despite the danger. "Remember us. Do not…" He winced in pain and his voice cut off as he arched his back in agony, a spear piercing him. "Do not… forget your people."

Farric was suddenly back in his chambers. The raven croaked once more, then fluttered to the window and perched on the sill.

The field marshal didn't move for some hours, but stood blinking in the growing dark as his candles and lamps burned out one by one, leaving only the red glow from the embers of the fire. His lips repeated the last words of the man he could only assume was his great-grandfather.

"Do not forget your people."

The raven croaked again and flew out the open window into the misty night.

Chapter 12

"The Adders, though they were but common folk—men and women, shepherds, masons, farmers—from the villages of the High Valley, stood firm and brave against the savage enemy, and would have held them long past the fateful hour, had the worst not happened..."

—Rhona the Bard, "The Tale of the Tor"

One day before the Autumn Equinox
The Tor, Green Mount

Una

Perhaps because of the heady rush she felt from the unusual seed Corvus had given them, events unfolded slowly to Una's eyes. A six-foot section of the wall burst inward, as though struck by a great force. The stones knocked Liam to the ground, dazed and bleeding, while shattering fragments struck Una's head and chest, throwing her back onto the hillside across from the wall. But there was no immediate mass rush of enemy through the new opening as she expected. At first she heard nothing, and her sight was blocked by a sheet of blood flowing freely from the laceration on her forehead. She reached up to wipe her vision clear, just in time to see two gargantuan Räubers step through the opening.

Räubers were all large, but these two were of monstrous proportions—over eight feet tall with shoulders as broad as a wagon axle, and arms thicker than the thighs of the mightiest Highlander. Their black eyes dripped with some vile, dark ichor, the veins in their arms bulged to the point that it looked like the skin would burst, and a web of dark lines over their bodies. Una had never beheld nor imagined such behemoths. Their eyes flashed with malice and their faces were contorted, teeth gritted as if in a rictus of intense pain. The giant on the left bore a great hammer—no doubt the instrument of the wall's destruction— while the other hefted a mighty double-bladed axe. Neither bore a shield.

Several things now happened at once. With an alacrity that surprised her, she sprang up from the grass, leaping onto the small retaining wall, then pivoted from her elevated position, lashing out with her spear at Hammer's face in an effort to drive him back so she might reach Liam. Corvus shouted at her to stay back, causing her to pause for a breath. Axe, moving with unnatural speed, knelt and buried his weapon in Liam's spine. With a cry of defiance, she leapt at Axe. Hammer's massive hand intercepted her, catching the shaft of Una's spear, arresting her leap in mid-air, the tip only inches from Axe's face and Una's feet dangling as she still clutched her weapon. With a disdainful shove, he hurled her across the trail, where she crashed painfully into the bank of the slope with a crunching sound as things within her broke. Despite the acuity and energy the seed granted, she found she suddenly couldn't move. Her limbs disobeyed her mental instructions. White stars of pain filled her vision and she found that she was having trouble drawing breath. She heard Corvus shout again, and was vaguely aware of movement toward her. The last thing she saw was the hammer descending.

Sangine

Some minutes earlier:

The communing was difficult this time, like trying to swim upstream against a strong current. The spiritual energies eddied and flowed around him with unusual strength, but rather than carry him along, they buffeted him, throwing him off course. He was reaching for the mind of Torn Claw, but for some reason, he couldn't reach him. He was there, he could feel him, but the torrent of dark magic swirling about the Tor clogged the pathways of their connection with fierce energies it was impossible to reach through. He would need additional blood. He gazed down the path to the area where wounded Räubers were being tended. Just as he stood to move down the hill, a swirl of shadows seemed to coalesce beneath the dense boughs of a nearby yew. He stepped closer to examine the unusual movement, and promptly dropped to his knees at the sight of the smooth black skin, black eyes, and jet-black teeth that greeted him.

"My prince."

"Hello, Sangine," Prince Umbral said softly, his tone habitually lighthearted.

"Why…?"

"Simply put," the Shadow Prince began, "Timor is furious with you. I had to convince him not to flay your mind to ragged bits. Your failures are mounting and are quite inexcusable."

"Yes, my prince," Sangine said. "But now that *you* are here…"

"Oh, I'm not here to fight," the prince replied. "We are still in the process of reconstituting, and must be very careful what we do. I tried to visit a library a few days past, and the whole damned thing collapsed, bringing part of a mountain down with it. The pain was unlike anything I've felt for ages. I cannot engage with the material world yet. If we make contact directly before our spirits have completely settled, we could destroy the Tor and possibly ourselves—and then where would we be?"

"I… understand, my lord."

"I very much doubt that," Umbral replied. "Anyway, we are watching as you and your lot bumble along. We can't have any more failures, old man, so I'm giving you this." A small, shiny black stone fell at Sangine's feet.

"What is it?"

"Nephellem," was the only answer, then Prince Umbral dissolved into a swirl of shadows that seemed to slip and slither away through the loam beneath the tree. Sangine stared at the stone with wonder and hunger in his eyes.

Vajk

The Grand Hadvezér shoved his way back through his clustered men, Barnat and Farkas—his First and Second Stone-Bearers—close behind. He moved quickly through the oaks down the trail to the stone bench, where he found Sangine kneeling over the corpse of a Räuber that had been wounded in the recent action. The shaman's hand still gripped the man's blistered face, blood streaming from a dozen places on the dead warrior.

"You dare torment one of my men?!?" Vajk spat, grabbing the surprisingly muscular arm of the shaman and pulling him to stand before him. Faster than thought, Sangine's clawed fingers lashed out and gripped the Grand Hadvezér's throat with vice-like strength. Barnat and Farkas surged forward to protect their leader, but the shaman shifted backward quickly, yanking the taller Vajk along by the throat like a dog worrying a child's doll.

"Tell your hounds to be still, or your time here is ended!" the shaman hissed in his face, spittle flying from his black lips.

Vajk raised his hands to hold back his men. Barnat pulled up seething, his great hammer poised to strike from Vajk's right, while Farkas—somewhat older and a little slower, but nonetheless fearsome — paused a step behind, his double-headed axe ready to swing from the left.

The shaman's eyes flashed from Vajk to his men then back to the Grand Hadvezér, whom he released with a hungry smile. Vajk staggered away from the creature, rubbing his bruised throat and gasping for breath.

"We have little time left to take the Tor," the shaman said quickly. "My masters grow impatient with your efforts."

"We will take this hill," Vajk rasped, but the shaman cut him off.

"Might I remind you, *Grand Hadvezér*," Sangine said with a feral intensity, "that an army follows close behind us, and will storm this Tor within hours. We cannot afford the losses this Raven is costing us. Your men must hold that army back until dawn. When the sun rises tomorrow, it must find us in possession of the temple and with me holding the Key, or this entire venture fails… and I assure you, the princes will not smile upon failure."

"The Räubers will not fail," Vajk growled with menace.

"No, and with the help of these two" — Sangine gestured to Barnat and Farkas — "we will exterminate the vermin above us."

Vajk's eyes widened in surprise.

"Explain, shaman."

"Prince Umbral has sent a dark gift," he said, holding up the dark stone before them, "which I will bestow upon these, your trusted seconds. They will clear the way to the temple, and finish this Raven and his witch."

The objection Vajk was about to voice died in his throat as Sangine slapped his hands together, somehow crushing the stone in his palms. A sulfurous odor mixed with the foulness of an abattoir suddenly overcame him. Gagging against the overwhelming infernal miasma, he blinked away tears to see black smoke — or perhaps clustered shadows that looked like smoke — begin to roil down the length of the shaman's arms, coalescing around his hands like a living thing, curling and twining through his fingers with a disturbing ophidian grace. Sangine's eyes lost their bloodshot and jaundiced tone, becoming darker, as though filling from within with the foul vapors, until they became like the stone he had crushed, obsidian set within the sallow mask of his face. The shaman moved so quickly he was but a blur, his claws grasping the weapon arms of Barnat and Farkas.

"No!" Vajk cried and surged forward to try to shove the shaman back, away from his advisors, but it was like trying to move a bronze statue secured to the earth. The Grand Hadvezér, among the greatest and most powerful warriors of all the Barbárs, rebounded, dazed from his impact with the shaman, like a child having run headlong into a stone wall.

With deep groans, the stone-bearers dropped to their knees, their faces contorted in agony. The black smoke writhed and wound quickly up their arms like a knot of serpents. Vajk watched in horror as the foul vapors reached their faces, slipping up their nostrils and into their mouths, passing between their gritted teeth, while other strands flowed past streaming tears of pain into their very eyes. The men shook and growled in a growing paroxysm of torment, veins bulging on their throats and faces, the muscles of their arms and chests surging and enlarging with a sound like bursting fruit. Trickles of blood appeared in various places as their skin was stretched beyond its capacity by their quickly burgeoning anatomies. Vajk tried again in vain to dislodge the shaman and save his men, screaming with effort as he flailed his fists against Sangine's immovable form, finally sinking back in exhausted failure, his knuckles bloody and bruised. No mark showed on the shaman.

The furor of the torment continued for a long moment as he watched helplessly, vaguely aware of nearby men rushing to help, weapons raised.

A burst of black energy suddenly radiated from the shaman, knocking Vajk and all of those rushing forward off their feet. The Grand Hadvezér hit the ground hard, the stones of the path digging painfully into his back. Sangine released his grip and stepped away from the two men with a satisfied smile, his eyes once more assuming their yellowed tint as the smoke that had suffused his arms slipped away in vanishing wisps, like shadows disappearing before a flickering torch's advance.

"Rise, great ones," he said, his voice little more than a sibilant whisper. "My Nephellem!"

Lifting his head, Vajk watched in horror as the two stone-bearers, no longer shaking in torment yet still grimacing in obvious ongoing pain, rose to standing, their now gargantuan forms towering over the shaman.

"Go, and kill them all," the shaman instructed simply, gesturing up the trail. Barnat and Farkas turned their heads as one to look up the Tor, their black eyes dripping some profane grey slime. They hoisted their weapons and moved quickly up the trail, their steps heavy and thunderous, despite their speed.

"What have you done?" Vajk asked, his voice thick with revulsion.

"As I said," Sangine responded in a silky voice, "a gift from Prince Umbral to clear the path. Now, I suggest you organize your men to hold the trail behind us. The White Cleft army will arrive soon."

Corvus

He watched in horror as the two giants stepped through the wall, dispatching Liam and Una in rapid succession. The rest of the Adders, newly empowered by the Hanging Lantern seeds, rushed forward, heedless of the danger.

"Fall back! Fall back!" he screamed, arresting their charge.

"But Una and Liam…" MacLief responded in horror.

"It's too late for them," Corvus barked. "Get to the temple, now!"

The Adders paused, trembling, caught between their fierce, energized desire for vengeance and the need to obey the Raven. Had it been anyone other than Corvus himself telling them to fall back, they probably would have ignored the order, but the long years of training under this man and fighting at his side had ingrained in them an instinctive trust and obedience.

"Adders, that's an order! Move, now!" he shouted once more, as the two behemoths turned to face the group.

With a bitter nod, MacLief pivoted and led his fellows up the trail at a quick jog, tears streaming down his face for their fallen comrades. Corvus faced the two giants alone, as the five remaining Adders flowed around and past him.

"You're a couple o' right handsome fellas, aren't ye?" he said as his eyes quickly scanned the terrain. Betting that, given their size, they would be overconfident, he placed himself in the center of the path, just where the trail turned steeply to continue upward toward the temple. Behind him was the natural barrier of a sheer drop-off, over a hundred feet straight down to the tops of tall trees and jagged rocks below. He also guessed that their size meant they would be unlikely to demonstrate the nimbleness needed to leap up onto the grassy slope to his left to flank him, though anything was possible. With the wall to his right, the drop off behind and the bank at the base of the slope to his left, the trail here narrowed enough to force the behemoths to come at him singly. *Best to face them one at a time, if I can.*

The two giants stalked toward him, their black eyes grim and dripping strange grey tears that oozed down their cheeks, their teeth gritted, as though they suffered some constant torment.

One of Dallin's arrows suddenly buried itself in the back of Hammer's neck. The creature grunted and turned to look up at where she stood on her shale ledge. Corvus gaped in disbelief. The arrow was buried nearly to the fletching, directly in the spine of the giant, yet the creature seemed unfazed. Hammer bent, and with his free hand lifted a massive chunk of the rubble from the shattered wall, the stone easily weighing as much as a man.

"Dallin, move!" Corvus shouted, a moment before the giant could hurl the debris.

Hammer heaved the rock right as Dallin threw herself into the bushes just uphill of the ledge. The chunk of rubble struck the thick shale on which she had been standing and it exploded into a shower of debris. The ledge shattered and fell onto the trail below. A tense moment passed in which Corvus scanned the rough terrain for any sign of Dallin.

A moment later, her head popped out from behind a tangle of hawthorn, eyes wide in a mixture of wonder and fear.

"Run, lass!" Corvus shouted. "Get to the temple!"

Then he pulled his attention back to the Räubers to find that Hammer had turned once more toward him, falling in behind Axe.

His shield would be useless. A single hit from either of these brutes would pulverize it and likely break the arm holding it. He cast it aside and instead used his left hand to draw his long knife. He would begin in Mountain form, though that could be problematic.

Mountain is a powerful defense, Ashahl had said so long ago. *But you cannot win on defense.*

Nonetheless, given the size of these mammoth warriors, he couldn't afford to take a single blow without the preternatural immovability the form offered. He settled into the stance, his arms before him, one hand resting atop the other in the form's characteristic hoop, and his eyelids drooped as he turned his thoughts inward and began to draw strength from the land—the very Tor itself.

The mountain is immovable... Its roots are deep and ancient, reaching to the very core of the world...

Axe stepped closer, raising the fearsome double-headed weapon, the veins on his massive arm nearly bursting.

In its majesty is peace...

He felt his heart rate slow. His breathing eased as he was suffused with the welcome solidity of the mountain.

In its immensity, strength...

The creature swung. Corvus shifted forward just far enough to step inside the attack while maintaining the form. The blade of the axe missed him, its handle striking his shoulder with the force of a battering ram. The weapon rebounded several inches while the impact of the blow reverberated up the behemoth's arm.

Corvus was unmoved.

Axe's brow furrowed in momentary confusion, at which point Corvus released Mountain form and lashed out with his long knife, burying it hilt-deep in the creature's chest. With surprising speed, the giant struck him in the torso with the fist of his left hand. Corvus was thrown backward like he'd been struck by a thunderbolt. He curled and rolled, dissipating much of the force of the hit, coming up to a crouch as he continued skidding back toward the cliff. With his now-empty left hand—his knife still buried in the chest of the giant—he managed to grip a rocky protuberance in the trail, arresting his slide. He quickly rose to his feet, rubbed his chest gingerly, and began backing away up the sloping trail. The two behemoths pursued steadily.

Neither blade nor bow harms these creatures, he marveled. *And such strength!*

His mind raced through options. Una had said there was no good bottleneck on the trail above, except for a narrow point just before the temple itself. As he backed further up the steep trail, Axe rounded the bend below, his left foot mere feet from the drop-off. Corvus attempted to drop into Ocean form, but having never tried it on such steep terrain, he found that he couldn't connect with its power. The form relied heavily on the semicircular steps and a shifting balance that the steep terrain denied him. Given the giant's progress, he knew it would take too long for him to adjust to the declivitous trail. But he saw another possibility. Due to the sharp rise in the path, Corvus now stood at Axe's head height.

Nothing for it, he thought. *It's time to fly.*

He drew his right foot back until its raised heel just touched the shin of his left leg, his arms flaring down and out to his sides, Raven's Tooth pointing to the ground. With a shout, he leapt, springing off his poised right foot, his left swinging around to propel him into the signature arcing leap of Eagle form. If he could wrap the creature's neck as he passed, his momentum might just be able to overbalance the giant, toppling him backward off the cliff.

But before he reached that point, the giant punched upward with the head of his axe, catching Corvus in mid-air. The breath exploded from his lungs as the heavy weapon's blunt eye struck him in the chest. Once more, Corvus found himself hurled back like a rag doll. The steep incline meant he had no chance to roll out of it. He slammed into the Tor, sliding several feet further uphill. Stars danced in his vision as he gasped for air, his ribs aching from the two blows.

The giants pressed on up the trail toward him, and he knew that in their inexorable stride and merciless, dripping eyes, death itself approached.

Chapter 13

"The creatures from the Pit, beyond the shadowed veil, roil in endless, venomous masses, awaiting the call to come through. But each one costs the Shadow Lord—both in pain and in a diminishing of His spirit. He must spend that coin carefully. This is why He so favors the shamans and his princes. Their spirits pay part of the cost."

—Horace of Angor

One day before the Autumn Equinox
The Tor, Green Mount

Lupe

The stout votary shifted nervously as she stood and chanted dutifully beside Mama, her hand touching Piper's back as the minstrel continued to play his flute. She was amazed at the minstrels' stamina. They'd been at it for hours, the soaring flute intermingling with the others' voices and somehow holding back the sense of despondency the roiling black clouds brought. She could feel the darkness lurking just above the temple, like a hungry predator snarling at the perimeter, eager to be let in. She shifted her weight again, uneasy at this prolonged inactivity. Perhaps it was her own fatigue catching up to her. The group had

had little sleep the night before and only a brief rest during the climb of the Tor. Even now, Amina looked pale and withered, like she might collapse at Mama's side at any moment. Meanwhile, Mama stood with her eyes closed, focused, stalwart, and reliable as the rocks of this strange hill, her brow furrowed in deep concentration. No sign of fatigue or indecision on her face. The woman was a wonder.

Lupe glanced at Yadira, noting the obvious fatigue in the slump of her shoulders, her eyes drooping as she tended the three wounded Adders who had made their way up the Tor. Each of the votaries had unique skills that had served the group well on their journey: Amina's remarkable talent for fully recalling any text read or map viewed in minute and accurate detail; Yadira's healing talents and knowledge of plants and herbs, both for their medicinal value and the daily miracles she managed with their meals; and Lupe's own fighting skills, archery, and natural stealth. She understood that the Path of the Divine Halls was both spiritual and physical—teaching the body and spirit to be in harmony — but, to Mama's constant frustration, Lupe had always been a poor student of the abstruse spiritual practices of the sisterhood, preferring anything active. She shifted her balance again, restlessly. She really should be concentrating on the chant, but she felt like she needed to be doing something more than just chanting.

Men and women were fighting and dying down below. She should be there with them, not here uselessly mouthing these words. She understood the need for her to remain behind when the clouds first arrived and the only thing resisting the despair had been the women's chanting. They had all been needed then, though the darkness had still pressed in, threatening to overwhelm them. But now that the minstrels had added the power of their music, Lupe's contribution was minimal.

Mama's eyes opened a slit, catching Lupe looking around. The young woman looked down, shamefaced at her lack of concentration. Mama tapped her arm and Lupe looked up, expecting stern disapproval. Instead, Mama's eyes winked in indulgent understanding. With a slight jerk of her head, she indicated that Lupe should go. The young votary's eyes widened in surprise. Mama nodded again, then closed her eyes and resumed her chant.

Lupe separated from the group, giving a reassuring pat to Piper's back as she left. She scooped up her bow and a quiver of arrows and started to move toward the temple exit.

"Lupe, wait," Yadira called softly. She turned to face the older votary, who rose slowly and crossed to her.

"Sister," Lupe said in soft greeting as Yadira approached.

She was surprised when the older woman reached out and took her hand, holding it in both of hers for a moment. Lupe's eyes widened at this uncharacteristic gesture of warmth. Something had changed in Yadira. Something seemed to have softened in her face, as if the woman had experienced something insightful.

"Here," Yadira said, placing a small seed in Lupe's hands. "Chew this thoroughly. It will give you strength for a time."

"Thank you, sister," Lupe responded solemnly, placing the seed in her mouth.

"And Lupe…" For a moment, Yadira seemed unsure of what words to choose. "Be safe. We need you."

"I will, Yadira," Lupe responded, then squeezed the older woman's shoulder warmly before turning and dashing out of the temple, through the defile, and down the trail.

The energy of the seed hit her all at once. The world shimmered with bright colors despite the overcast, gloomy sky. She felt suddenly powerful, energized, and remarkably alert. Her hearing seemed to be sharper as well, as she detected the sound of footsteps advancing up the trail. She quickly crouched behind a large rock at a turn in the path and readied her bow. A moment later, she spotted five Adders running vigorously up the hill. She lowered her bow and shouted a greeting. The leader of the group waved to her, though his face was twisted with grief.

"Corvus?" she asked as they neared.

She wasn't sure she understood everything the man said in response, but she gathered that Corvus was still alive, and standing alone against something terrible.

Just then, Dallin rounded the bend in the trail below. She looked worried and kept glancing over her shoulder, as if she expected pursuit. Lupe thanked the Adders and headed down to meet her.

"Dallin," Lupe called out. "Where Corvus?"

Dallin looked up at her, stricken. Worry and grief had replaced her typical cheerfulness. "Turn back, Lupe," she said, careful to speak slowly so the Aslene votary would understand. "You can be of no help to him."

"What? Why?" Lupe asked, confused.

"Giants," Dallin said with despair. "He's fightin' giants."

Lupe was unfamiliar with the word, but sensed the danger from the tone of her voice.

"Our arrows don't hurt them," Dallin continued. "They canna be killed."

"Blade? Spear?" Lupe asked helplessly, to which Dallin merely shook her head.

"Like the Nephellem." Amina's voice startled her and she turned.

"What are you doing here, Amina?" Lupe demanded.

"I was worried about you," she answered in a matter-of-fact monotone.

Lupe frowned in surprise. "Amina..." she began, struggling to find words.

"I want to see," Amina said, before Lupe could finish her thought.

Lupe stared at the younger votary for a long moment. "Alright, but you have to leave when I say so. No arguing." Amina shrugged as if to say, "Of course." Lupe searched her eyes a moment longer before reluctantly nodding her acceptance.

"Both of you need to go back," Dallin interrupted. "There's no help to be given. Corvus will be here shortly, I'm sure." Her tone indicated she didn't believe her own words.

"You go back," Lupe told Dallin. "Guard temple. We go on."

Dallin stared at her fellow archer, concern writ on her features. She studied Lupe's eyes, searching for any uncertainty.

Seeming to find none, Dallin nodded and placed a hand on the stout votary's shoulder.

"Be careful," she said sincerely.

Lupe gripped her arm, then gestured to Amina to follow before setting off down the trail. Dallin turned resignedly, and headed up the hill.

The two votaries moved cautiously down the steep bend, the sounds of conflict from below adding a grim counterpoint to the soaring music cascading down the Tor. Rounding the second bend, Lupe gasped as she caught sight of Corvus and his opponents. The two assailants were indeed giants, their legs thick as tree trunks, their arms like corded wood, eyes black as jet. She watched as the fearsome weapons flashed, faster than one could imagine. Corvus danced and spun nimbly between them, his curved blade striking the creatures' grey skin again and again. A boulder exploded beneath one giant's hammer as Corvus executed an impossible maneuver, diving between the monster's legs at the last possible instant and slashing his blade across them in what should have been a disabling, even killing, stroke. The behemoth was unbothered by the cut, and turned and swung his mighty hammer in a rising sweep at Corvus' face. Lupe gasped in horror. The attack was too sudden, too fast for anyone to possibly avoid. Her eyes widened in amazement as the Raven arched his back in a classic display of Willow form, the hammer missing his chin by the merest gap.

Lupe staring in fascination as the battle continued and Corvus utilized one martial form after another, with only short pauses between them for his mind to shift to the next one—but even those short pauses nearly got him killed more than once. She knew from her exposure to the martial masters that shifting between forms like that was extremely taxing and dangerous, usually requiring a three-to-five-second pause. Corvus was shaving that as close as possible, finding positions and moments for the transitions, but she knew his good fortune wouldn't last. Still, he was a marvel to watch. His blade spun and flashed, cutting, thrusting, parrying, as he dodged, leapt, countered, and continually repositioned himself so he only faced one giant at a time. The man was brilliant! She had caught glimpses of his fighting prowess before now, but nothing had prepared her for this display of martial mastery. She had never seen the like. Even the most celebrated combatants in the annual tournaments of the Greening Festival did not compare.

A thought occurred to her, and Lupe suddenly registered what Amina had first said.

"Nephellem?" she asked urgently. She vaguely recalled the children's tales of the giants that had once ravaged the land.

"Men possessed by evil spirits that turn them into giants," the girl responded. "They can't be harmed by any weapon."

Lupe wracked her memories, trying to recall the tales her father had told her about the Nephellem when she was young. They were two warriors, possessed by twin demons who had risen from a poisoned well, and afterward they had set off on a rampage of destruction. It was said no weapon could harm them, and that their strength was terrible. She seemed to recall a tale of a fateful battle in which the Nephellem had slain thousands… or was that the Giant Eagle of Silwan? Frustrated, she turned back to Amina.

"How do we kill them?" she asked, trying not to raise her voice and rattle Amina, despite the urgency boiling inside her.

"You can't," Amina responded calmly.

"There has to be a way!" Lupe responded, more sharply than she wanted. Amina winced and recoiled.

"The Nephellem are possessed by demons," the girl said, suddenly shy, looking down at the ground.

"Yes, but in the story," Lupe pressed more gently, "how were they beaten?"

"The demons were banished with a talisman," Amina replied quietly. "When they fled, the warriors changed back, and the soldiers of the sheik slew them and chopped them into bits, which were then burned."

Lupe's mind raced through the possibilities, finally latching on to an idea.

"Go fetch Mama, quickly," she told Amina.

"But she's busy chanting."

"Amina," Lupe said, her voice firm and resolved. "You have to get her, as quickly as possible. Corvus can't last much longer. If he falls, I will try to delay them, but you *must* get Mama right away. Tell her of the Nephellem. She'll understand."

Amina nodded simply, then trotted up the trail as quickly as the difficult terrain allowed.

Lupe looked back to the pitched fighting below. The energy of the seed burned in her limbs and heart, calling her to action, yet some rational part of her looked at the frightful beings fighting Corvus below and quailed, somewhat tempering the urge to leap into the fray. *If Corvus' blade is of no use, how can I hope to make a difference?*

She gasped as the giant with the axe swung a particularly vicious cut at Corvus, which he somehow—impossibly—managed to just avoid, his blade flashing out in what should have been a lethal response across the giant's neck. But the cut had no visible effect, and the Nephellem responded with a snarl and an unbelievably fast counterattack. The frightful speed and malice of the giant's movement sent a cold chill down her spine. *Hurry, Mama, hurry!*

Corvus

He was tiring. The energy from the seed had kept him going this long, but he knew that was a finite resource. He had tried everything he could. Mountain, Willow, Badger, Eagle... all to no avail. He had even thrown in some of the light, quick footwork of Sparrow form, scoring multiple thrusting hits into the creatures. Nothing worked. It was a miracle he had escaped injury this long. The power and speed of the giants was unlike any foe he had ever faced, and were it not for the quickness of thought and body granted by the seed, he would have fallen long before. He had to delay them, try to maneuver them into a position where he might be able to pitch one off the trail, though he doubted the fall from the cliff would kill it. It would, however, buy them time. And every moment he lasted, was a moment that Fergus' army and the fyrd elements drew nearer.

He rolled to his right just as the axe descended in a blow that would have split his body in half had Raven's Tooth not lashed out in a brutal cut that should have severed the wrist wielding it. As before, though the blade bit deeply into the monster's arm, the wound seemed to simply reseal, healing instantly. The giant swung a fist at Corvus' head, his body reacting as quick as thought, ducking the vicious blow and then charging forward. He slammed into the giant, momentarily trapping the creature's arm against its chest, tipping its balance backward. The maneuver bought him a precious second. He spun and leapt out of range of the fearsome axe, his feet sliding down the steep trail. He swore as the realization hit him. This was the position he didn't want. He was now downhill of the monsters, with nothing between them and the temple. His only hope was in blocking and delaying them, which he couldn't do from down here.

"Come and get me, you bastards!" he taunted, hoping he might draw them back down the trail. That hope died when the two giants, as one, turned their backs on him and began striding up the path.

"No!" he shouted, then dashed after them, his heart sinking, seeing no way to get in front of them on the steep, narrow path. He scanned the bends up ahead madly, trying to find anywhere he could cut them off, but the giants were moving so quickly, he wasn't sure he could even catch up to them, much less get ahead of them.

He had failed, and now Ligulf, Argant, and the others would pay the price! All of the Green Mount would pay.

Lupe

She saw the Nephellem turn away from Corvus and start moving up the trail toward the temple. Toward her! She had scrabbled off the path to a rocky outcrop that overlooked a bend in the trail to better observe the battle, and now she realized with a shock that she was all that stood between these monsters and the rest of the group—and they were coming at her quickly.. She could see Corvus scrambling desperately behind as he strove to find a way to once more get in front of them. But she could see his efforts would be fruitless. It would be up to her.

She knew she couldn't hope to defeat the creatures. But with the energy from that seed, she felt she could at least slow them long enough for Corvus to get around them. A determined grin spread beneath her jimas as she set aside her bow and drew the long, curved hunting knife she carried. She crouched in readiness, planning her attack and waiting for the first giant to approach. From her elevated position, she would be above it as they wound their way up the serpentine trail.

Setting down the blade, she wiped her sweat-moistened hands on her robes, quietly intoning the Canon of Peace, seeking focus and calm. The giant wielding the hammer rounded the bend just below her position. He was close enough now for her to see the strange grey slime that oozed from his eyes and dripped tear-like down his cheeks. His mouth was pulled in a continual rictus of pain, teeth gritted.

She scooped up a small handful of dirt and rubbed it between her palms, then wiped her hands on her robes again. Finally, she picked up her knife and muttered a soft prayer to the Ancestors.

Just a little further, monster, she thought. She knew her fighting skills could never compare to the mastery that Corvus had demonstrated, but there was no one else to try to slow the giants' advance. If she could time her leap just right, she might be able to—

"Lupe, no!" Corvus shouted, spotting her from further down the trail and realizing her intent.

The monster stepped into range, and she leapt.

Mama

She hurried down the trail as fast as she could, cursing herself every step for allowing her body to grow fat, her legs weakened with age. She had chosen to leave the staff behind in the temple. If what Amina had told her were true—that these were indeed Nephellem—the chances were good that she'd not return, and she couldn't risk losing the Key so close to the Equinox.

Faster, old woman! she thought, as she hopped down a rocky incline in the trail and landing unsteadily at its base. Looking around to get her bearings, she spotted Lupe some twenty yards further down the mount, perched on an outcropping above a curve in the winding path. What was the girl doing? Her knife was drawn, and from her stance…

"No!" Mama shouted, just as Lupe leapt onto the back of the first giant, who appeared around a bend in the trail. Despite the urgency of the moment, Mama stood transfixed, watching her votary's attack.

The sturdy young woman's body struck the giant's shoulders, her right hand encircling his neck, while her left reached around and plunged the long knife into the creature's left eye. There was an explosion of grey ichor from the ruined socket and Mama heard Lupe cry out in pain, though she couldn't see what had injured her. The giant stumbled, the edge of the trail crumbling from beneath his foot as his left hand flashed up to try to dislodge his attacker. Heedless of the massive hand grasping for her, Lupe withdrew the knife and struck again, this time sinking the blade to the hilt into the other eye. Another burst of the grey liquid splashed onto Lupe's arm, just as the Nephellem's hand closed on her neck, wrenching her from his back and hurling her onto the trail before him. Somehow Lupe managed to roll out of the savage throw, dissipating most of the shock, but it was clear she was hurt as she was slow to recover, clenching her left arm tightly against her. Her blade was gone and her breath came in ragged gasps. But she had a moment as the giant struggled to maintain his balance, the trail's edge falling away beneath his massive foot. There was a flash of a blade from the path below and the Nephellem staggered, which could only mean that Corvus was still alive and rushing to catch the creatures from behind. The snaking path of the trail meant that he could barely reach the wounded giant, but he was trying to buy Lupe time by hacking at the creature's ankle. The giant toppled off the path, falling to the switchback some eight or ten feet below. The second giant was now only moments away from Lupe, his steady stride up the path unslowed.

Mama resumed her own journey down the treacherous incline, desperate to reach Lupe before the axe-wielding giant did. But before she could even get to the next bend in the trail, Lupe gave a defiant, ululating battle cry and charged the Nephellem.

"Child! No!" Mama shouted in horror as her votary launched a flying sidekick down the hill, striking the giant solidly in the chest. Lupe had timed the attack just as the approaching Nephellem was navigating a steep spot in the trail. Her powerful kick tipped him back just enough that gravity did the rest, sending the creature tumbling back down the path. Mama had seen Lupe deliver this technique dozens of times, and the girl always managed to land in a battle crouch after the hit. This time, however, the votary fell to the ground hard, collapsing in a heap onto the rocky trail. The giant was simply too massive. No doubt kicking into him had been like hurling her body at a solid wall. Even at this distance, she could hear Lupe's gasp of pain. Mama redoubled her pace, as the clash of blades from below indicated that Corvus had re-engaged the Nephellem—though which one he was battling, she could not tell. Her foot slid on a loose stone, and her hand lashed out to find purchase and prevent a fall. She hissed in frustration as the skin of her arm and hand was abraded by the rough rocks.

Hurry, Nabila! she scolded herself. *Lupe needs you!*

She pushed herself up and hopped the next few feet to the flat rock at the bend in the trail below. Ignoring the protest in her legs from the jarring landing, she pivoted and tucked into a roll, propelling herself down the trail to the bend just uphill of Lupe's position, the rocks digging into her back. The axe-wielding giant had somehow arrested his backward tumble, regained his feet, and resumed his climb, his black eyes staring death at Lupe. Remarkably, the stout young woman was once more rising to her feet to meet him, shaking her head and muttering in defiance.

Closer now, Mama could see smoke rising from Lupe's injured left arm, which she clutched to her side. The giant raised his axe. Mama felt like she was pushing through water trying to reach Lupe's side. The young woman raised her fists and set her body in a fighting stance. But before the votary could charge forward, the giant threw the double-headed axe at her. The blade flashed faster than an arrow in flight. Lupe tried to pivot out of the way, a highly improbable feat even in the best of circumstances. She moved a fraction too late, and the axe took her in the chest, propelling her suddenly limp body back up the trail.

Mama froze, horrified. *Lupe! Ancestors, no!*

She rushed to the girl's side, heedless of the pain as she skidded to a stop on her knees in the loose gravel, her trembling hands cupping the fallen votary's cheeks. The girl's eyes stared up at her, glassy, lifeless.

Lupe was gone.

Chapter 14

One day before the Autumn Equinox
The Tor, Green Mount

Mama

The world stopped moving. There was no wind in the trees, no birds called, and no stream burbled. Nothing. Only Lupe's dead eyes staring up between Mama's shaking hands. Carefully, she removed the girl's jimas, stroking the young woman's cheek fondly. In that instant, she recalled the short, stocky, eager child who had come to meet her years before, standing between her parents, a hand in each of theirs. It was at the Greening Festival, twelve or thirteen years earlier. Mama had been there as senior judge of the mulakima contestants. Lupe's father had written to her weeks before — a formal request that they might present their daughter to her for consideration as a possible votary.

Though she received many such requests each year, she rarely accepted a new charge, being very particular as to whom she would take into her care. She preferred not to have more than two votaries at a time, and the child had to show a strong aptitude in all areas — physical skills, an eagerness for learning her letters, and a seriousness of spirit. The demands of the sisterhood were great, and no frivolous child would succeed. Only those who truly understood the rigors of the calling would last beyond the first few months, most being sent back to their parents because they lacked the concentration or the dedication to succeed. It always broke her heart to send a child back, knowing they would carry that failure with them. Far better to turn them away at the assessment than to burden them with the shame of failure later on.

Lupe hadn't been a promising candidate at first. She had little knowledge of letters — her writing was hasty, cramped, and sloppy, and she had little patience for such niceties as spelling or grammar. When Mama had questioned the girl about the three pillars of the faith — the Nabiuni Hikma (the wisdom of the prophets), the Alkhudue l Hikma (the wisdom of strength), and the Aeshabi Hikma (the wisdom of healing) — the girl had only been able to name the Alkhudue I Hikma, though her enthusiasm for that had been evident as she rattled off the names of all twenty-five forms of the first five degrees of attainment, in order! Even in that very first meeting, Mama had noted the scuffs and scabs on the girl's hands: training marks. The father explained that he had fashioned a punching dummy out of burlap, straw, and sand, and that the child spent hours each day punching and kicking it, often at the expense of her chores. In the end, the earnestness of the girl's desire to learn mulakima had won Mama over. Having recently promoted a votary to priestess, Mama had only Yadira with her at the time, who showed almost no interest in martial training. Perhaps this child's eagerness in that area would help Yadira bridge that gap, while the older votary's strengths in the other pillars would be of help teaching a new young one. And, despite the child's shortcomings in knowledge of letters and faith, Mama agreed to take her in.

Lupe was a restless child, always in motion. Perfectly happy to herd or milk the goats, fetch water, gather dung for the fire, run errands, or endure long hours of martial training. But try to get her to memorize the Canons, or sit still through the teachings of the prophets, and you would think you were inflicting physical torture on her. Mama remembered the girl's bouncing knee as she tried to sit still during her lessons. *Always in motion.* Mama's hope that Yadira's seriousness would be a good influence on the boisterous child came to nothing. The stern, older votary had shown only coldness and disapproval toward the girl, assisting her instruction out of obedience and duty, but never affection or compassion.

Still, when Lupe had first entered into the pre-trials for the Greening Festival, she had performed the five forms of third rank with remarkable precision and power, and the judges had advanced her to the formal competition without question—despite the fact that at only ten years of age, she would be two to three years younger than the other competitors at her rank, and would therefore have a significant size disadvantage.

Mama remembered the look of pride on the girl's bloody face when she had earned the trophy at the festival, standing before the crowd as the best of the third rank.

By the next year's pre-trials, Lupe had remarkably advanced to fourth rank, a rare achievement for an eleven-year-old, but the judges had denied her the chance to compete at the festival, citing worries for her safety as her opponents would be four and five years her senior. As the girl's teacher, Mama had no official say in such decisions, due to the long-standing tradition of impartial judging that prevented her from ruling on or advancing her own votary. The girl had been heartbroken at being denied her chance at the arena, and against her better judgment, Mama had quietly petitioned the judges to reconsider, citing Lupe's inherent stoutness and strength, and the unusual power demonstrated in her forms. The judges eventually relented, allowing Lupe to compete. The girl had not won, though she had learned important lessons about how to fight someone much larger and stronger than herself.

I wish those lessons had helped you more today, child.

With a shuddering sigh, Mama closed Lupe's dead eyes, silently reciting the Prayer of Passage, supplicating the Ancestors to accept the girl's spirit into their company.

A heavy thud nearby stirred her from her recitation, and she looked up to see Corvus tumbling across the trail. It took her a moment to understand that the giant he had been fighting on the path below must have somehow cast him up the Tor. She suddenly recalled the imminent danger in which she knelt. The memories had washed over her so completely she had lost precious moments. The giant responsible for Lupe's death was moving steadily toward her up the steep trail, its black implacable eyes flashing malice. Mama stared into those eyes, a powerful mix of emotions washing over her — a fierce maternal fury that this creature had killed her beloved charge; pity for the tormented soul of the man trapped in that flesh hidden behind those obsidian eyes; an urgent worry for Amina, Yadira, Argant, and the others should these monsters get past them; and concern for the bruised and battered Corvus, struggling to continue the fight.

Even as her thoughts turned to him, he rose shakily to his feet, clearly hurt, his strength faltering. She saw him slip another seed into his mouth as he struggled to clear his head, his eyes focused on the fast-approaching Nephellem. Corvus readied his blade, positioning himself between the oncoming creature and Mama.

"Corvus, no," Mama said, rising to her feet, a sense of calm and clarity of purpose coming over her. He glanced at her quickly, his brow creasing in grief as he finally took in the sight of Lupe's dead body. The Nephellem cleared a steep rock and broke into a run, its huge empty hands reaching for him.

With a movement born from years of martial training, Mama slid sideways into Corvus, shoving him aside and placing herself in the giant's path just as the huge hand closed on her shoulder and she was yanked into the air, the giant readying his other fist for a killing blow. She grimaced in agony as her shoulder was pulled from its socket. With a sharp inhalation, she focused past the pain, seeing the imminent danger of the fist.

Before the giant could strike, she slapped an open palm to his forehead. "Peace!" she said aloud, and immediately began intoning the Canon of Banishment.

The giant's fist froze in mid-strike, its eyebrows suddenly working in surprise and agony as the skin beneath her hand began to smoke with a foul, sulfuric stench. She heard guttural screams from somewhere and couldn't tell if they were the Nephellem's or hers or someone else's. She thought she heard the sounds of renewed conflict around her, but her concentration did not waver.

The Ancestors' command is absolute and cannot be denied: "Begone from this flesh. Begone from this land. Begone from this time, for they are not yours and you do not belong." Holy is the sacred arc of the Hall of the Ancestors. Holy is their immutable word. No darkness may exist before the Divine Light.

The palm of her hand burned, but she pressed it more firmly against the Nephellem's forehead. The creature dropped her as he fell to his knees, the jarring landing momentarily jostling her away from the giant, who snarled and moved to rise once more. Despite the burning pain in her shoulder, Mama lunged forward, once more slapping her hand against its head.

The Ancestors' command is absolute and cannot be denied: "Begone from this flesh. Begone from this land. Begone from this time, for they are not yours and you do not belong." Holy is the sacred arc of the Hall of the Ancestors. Holy is their immutable word. No darkness may exist before the Divine Light.

Though her eyes were closed in concentration, a savage face that looked to be carved of ebony flashed before her, lips pulled back in a ferocious grin, yellow teeth pointed and dripping, red eyes blazing with hunger.

"You cannot harm me, witch!" the face snarled, its echoing voice like the sound of hot embers scraping against one another. "I was ancient and mighty long before your furthest ancestor crept out of the mud. Your paltry spell cannot touch me!"

Mama quailed momentarily before the unbridled malice and timeless age of the demon. A moment of hopelessness washed over her, and she almost pulled away in defeat. But from some hidden reserve, she somehow drew strength. Perhaps it was the thought of those she loved, clustered above in the temple. Perhaps it was the image of Lupe's lifeless body, sacrificed so bravely to delay this demon's advance. Perhaps it was the assuredness born of a lifetime of dedicated service to the Ancestors. Whatever its source, a calm confidence came over her in this contest of wills with this ancient malevolence. She persisted in her recitation, the words of the canon echoing ever more loudly in her mind.

The Ancestors' command is absolute and cannot be denied…

The jet-black tone of the demon's face shifted to a sickly, mottled grey for a moment, its brow creasing in agony, before the foul being once more asserted control over its image. Its skin shifted again to smooth obsidian, a blood-red pointed tongue lashing out at her hungrily. She scrunched her eyes more tightly shut and continued her recitation.

"Begone from this flesh. Begone from this land. Begone from this time, for they are not yours and you do not belong."

The being's head tilted back in agony, its eyes closed. It uttered a prolonged wail of torment as its skin continued to shift between jet black and sickly grey, streaked with bloody rips and rents.

Holy is the sacred arc of the Hall of the Ancestors. Holy is their immutable word.

In her mind's eye, she held up her hand. She saw it limned in a blinding white light, which seemed to terrify the demon, its eyes suddenly open and frantic. She pushed the glowing hand toward the demon's shifting face, feeling resistance in the space between, like a thickness in the air.

"You… cannot… touch me… witch!" the creature growled through gritted teeth, its face tormented and straining.

The resistance strengthened, and she leaned her will into it, forcing her imagined hand forward. The thickness held her back at first, then seemed to yield slightly, Then, with a rush, it collapsed, allowing her to push forward and touch the fiend's mottled and ragged face.

She smiled triumphantly as her spirit hand contacted the demon's skin, producing blood-red sparks as from a smithy's forge. The white light grew, coruscating about her hand, auroral wisps of multicolored radiance blossoming and drifting upward.

"No!" the demon snarled defiantly, though its voice was strained and weakening. "Nooooo!"

No darkness may exist before the Divine Light!

The white light swelled still more, subsuming everything until only it existed. There was a piercing scream that seemed to diminish as quickly as it started, until all sound was gone, and she knew she was once more alone in her mind.

Opening her eyes, she staggered back, the pain in her shoulder once more asserting its presence. Before her, in place of a grey-skinned giant, lay the lacerated body of a rapidly dying Räuber. The cuts and wounds from Corvus' blade that had healed while the body was possessed, suddenly reopened, releasing the man's lifeblood in scarlet ribbons.

She heard a clash of weaponry and, blinking, looked down the trail to where Corvus bravely strove against the other giant, keeping the creature away from her, buying her the necessary time to affect the exorcism.

Her hands trembled from exhaustion and the agony of her shoulder, yet she knew she could not rest. Not yet. She quickly fetched a seed from the pouch at her waist and, praying for strength, popped it into her mouth. She gasped a moment later as the infusion of energy washed over her, the pain in her shoulder suddenly diminishing. She surged to her feet, her lips pulled tight in grim determination, and she stepped toward the second giant.

Yadira

The eldest votary stood at the front edge of the temple platform, gazing down the Tor. The inhuman screams and cries coming from below made her skin crawl in terror. Mama and Lupe were down there engaged with those things, whatever they were. She felt helpless as her eyes vainly searched for any sight of the conflict, hidden by the twists and turns of the steep trail below.

She heard a soft whimper behind her and turned to see Argant clutching Amina's leg, while the young votary stroked his head reassuringly. Amina's eyes were full of concern as she returned Yadira's gaze.

They need me to remain calm and be strong, Yadira thought. *Whatever happens, I must give them strength in Mama's absence.*

She smiled at Amina reassuringly, then crossed toward them.

"Argant," she said softly. "Could you see to the fire? We mustn't let it die."

With a sniffle, the boy looked at her, then timidly nodded his head.

"Perhaps Amina will help you," Yadira offered gently, and the two of them moved off to see to their task.

Just then, the screaming resumed below, though it sounded like a different voice. She sighed and hugged herself, then returned to the wounded Adders, quietly reciting the Canon of Peace as she checked Pherson's sleeping brow for fever.

Corvus

With a grunt of effort, he deflected a wild backswing from the hammer, Raven's Tooth ringing from the jarring blow. The diverted hammer arced just over Mama as she approached, clutching a useless arm to her side. He spun, planting a powerful back kick into the forward knee of the giant. The joint buckled momentarily, then quickly snapped back into place, the injury healed as suddenly as it had happened. He had become accustomed to the futility of this struggle, his most devastating attacks yielding no result as these creatures healed almost instantly from all physical trauma. Yet, somehow, Mama had overcome the other one. It had clearly come at great cost as he watched her hobble forward, her left arm limp, her skin pale, her febrile eyes filled with the hollow vibrancy of the seed. But still she came on, despite it all. Shaking his head, he prepared for another attack from the giant. If this stalwart woman could soldier on despite injury and grief, so could he.

Movement behind him. He spun again, avoiding yet another smashing blow from the hammer, Raven's Tooth lancing upward to spear the giant's cheek. The wound healed instantly again. The creature glared in his direction with milky grey eyes that seemed unable to clearly focus on him. The only injuries inflicted on these creatures that hadn't healed completely and immediately had been the damage Lupe had inflicted on this one's eyes. While the orbs had reformed, they were no longer jet black, seemingly filled instead with the same grey ichor that dripped down the monster's cheeks. Surprisingly, the giant's vision also seemed to be affected by the wounds, as the hammer blows—fearsome and frightening though they were—were no longer aimed with the same deadly accuracy. It seemed as though the creature flailed at figures in a fog. Yet its attacks had increased in tempo and were far less predictable, as if the giant were striking out madly due to its impaired vision.

"Get behind me" he warned Mama as she continued forward, apparently heedless of the danger. He was in the midst of switching to Mountain form, and hoped he had allowed enough time for the shift in concentration. Mama stepped adroitly behind him only a split second before she would have been felled by another bone-crushing hammer blow. The hammer fell on Corvus instead, as he had intended, yet it somehow bouncing harmlessly off his shoulder. Mama gasped at the ferocity the blow and the unexpected recoil of the weapon.

The giant roared its defiance and readied a two-handed overhead strike directly at Mama. Cursing in frustration, Corvus shoved her toward the giant, inside the arc of the blow, while he knelt beneath the strike, sword raised high, reinforcing what he knew to be a futile parry with a hand on the blade of Raven's Tooth. The shock of that strike would destroy his arms, he knew, but there was nothing for it. He didn't have time to roll out of the way or try to re-engage Mountain form. He clenched his eyes shut in anticipation of the shattering pain he knew would follow. But the blow never landed.

When he opened his eyes again, the giant was writhing in agony with the hammer hanging from its limp grip, Mama's hand on the giant's chest—as high as she could reach—with a sickly grey-green smoke curling out from where she touched its skin. The hammer dropped and the creature's knees buckled. Then, perhaps the most unexpected thing happened. This vast, muscular monster—terrible in its might and malice—whimpered like a wounded animal. Fresh gouts of ichor streamed from its milky eyes and its brow lifted in fear and defeat.

Mama's voice rose as her recitation continued unabated. The giant's head thrashed from side to side as if it railed against some unseen bonds.

Corvus staggered to his feet, backing away from the sight, as the creature gnashed its teeth in defiance, snarling and spitting its venom, but apparently unable to break away from whatever hold she had on it.

He watched this great contest of wills play out. At one point, Mama's knees buckled and she almost swooned. Corvus dashed forward to support her, but before he could arrive, she recovered herself and her voice reasserted its commanding quality, a fresh gout of smoke rising from her hand. Then, with a tone of finality, she shouted the final phrase of the banishment.

"No darkness may exist before the Divine Light!"

A piercing shriek rived the hillside, dropping Corvus to his knees, his eyes clenched shut and his hands clutching his ears desperately against the sound as Raven's Tooth fell to the ground beside him.

When, at last, he could open his eyes and look around, he saw Mama standing before the bloody body of a fallen Räuber. No longer a giant, but merely a gashed, broken, and blinded man, rapidly bleeding out. Corvus saw that Mama was teetering on the steep path, about to collapse. He lunged forward and grabbed her, evincing a sharp gasp as he inadvertently clutched her dislocated shoulder. With a hurried apology, he shifted his grip, easing her to a seated position on the rocky trail. Her body was drenched in sweat, her face pallid and wan, yet, after a moment, she still managed to smile up at him weakly.

"Now that," he said with a weary, wry smile, "is how you settle a giant, I'd say."

"That was… hard," she replied.

"Oh, ye think?" he answered, his eyes twinkling merrily. "You made it look so easy, I thought you could handle two or three o' those fellas before breakfast."

She searched his face, as if she wasn't entirely sure what he said, then her plump cheeks pushed up into a grin and she patted his chest affectionately. Then she folded into his arms, burying her face in his chest and wept, great sobs racking her body. Corvus held her silently, knowing that nothing he might say could lessen her grief. All he could do was be there and hold her as this strong woman—so accustomed to being the surety upon which others built their confidence—mourned the loss of one so dear.

A light breeze gusted by, chasing the brown leaves toward the setting sun in the unseen currents and eddies of its passing, while a warrior of the body comforted a warrior of the spirit in a grief as deep as her boundless compassion.

Chapter 15

"Thanks for the lift," the curious cat said as he hopped down off the back of the wagon.

"No trouble at all," the goose said with a wave, and watched the cat turn to look down each road at the crossroads, scratching his head in confusion.

"Which way didja say I should go, now?" he asked.

"Well, thataway," the goose answered, pointing east with a beautiful wing, "is filled with lions, alleygators, and all manner of other dangers."

"Oh!" The cat recoiled from the eastern road.

"And thataway," the goose continued, pointing west, "is filled with serpents and scorpions. And if they don't getcha, the wasps and hornets will sting you dead."

"Oh." The cat recoiled from the western road.

"And thataway"—the goose's wing pointed north—"is all ice and snow, blizzards and winds that'll blind you and leave you to freeze to death."

"Oh..." The cat recoiled from the northern road. "And what about that way?" He pointed back south, feeling a bit embarrassed.

"That's the way we came," the goose said. "And where I'm headed back to."

"I see," the cat replied.

"So, you know which'n way you'll be headed?" the goose asked.

"If it's all the same to you," the little cat replied, climbing back into the wagon, "I'll just hitch a ride back with you."

—The fable of "The Curious Cat and the Goose"

One day before the Autumn Equinox
Atalaya de Locus, Cantabria

Farric

Pentatarch Vella was going to great lengths to try to intimidate Farric. He had summoned the field marshal to the grand receiving hall, rather than his working chamber with his maps and papers, where they usually met. The receiving hall was lined with Holy Knights and scribes, including Briguglio, who sat attentively waiting to copy down each word that might drop from the holy lips. No courtiers were present, nor were there any of the dozens of annoying people that daily plagued the Pentatarch's receiving chamber in hopes of receiving some boon or other. No, this special audience was just for Farric. *I should feel honored,* he thought. *Strange that somehow I don't.*

Vella himself had entered after keeping Farric waiting—kneeling, as per protocol—for some twenty minutes. The Pentatarch's entrance was heralded by a man ringing a bell while a hidden choir somewhere in a choir loft sang his praises. Unlike his usual robes, which were rich and ostentatious by any standard, today he wore his formal robes of office: white satin trimmed with gold and enough jewels to make a monarch blush. He sat upon his gilded throne, high atop a platform, which itself sat upon a dais. It was all a bit much. Theatre, intended to impress. Farric understood why Vella was going to such lengths, but far from having the desired effect, it all made him feel like laughing. All this pomp and self-importance from an individual as depraved as Vella. Ridiculous.

The man with the bell stepped before the elevated throne and rang his instrument thrice more, its brass peals echoing through the vast chamber, then called out in a loud voice, "His Everlasting

Radiance, Pentatarch Nichola Vella II, Oscuridado, Keeper of the Holy Orbit, Explainer to the Downward Watchtower, Blessed Didact of the Meridional Watchtower, Guardian of the Boreal Watchtower, Provider to the Eventide Watchtower, and Oathkeeper to the Locus Watchtower. May his name be revered for all time. So is."

"So is," intoned the knights and the few priests scattered about the chamber.

"So will be," the herald added.

"So will be," the attendants echoed dutifully.

His task completed, the bell-toting herald turned sharply and stepped to the side of the dais, tucking himself against a pillar, as though trying to become as unnoticeable as possible.

Farric watched in mild amusement as the ceremony played itself out. Then Bishop Galea stepped forward and read from a scroll.

"Field marshal Farric of the Blades of Sebastian…" He paused for effect. "You are charged with—"

"Let's hold it right there," Farric interrupted, sauntering a few feet to his left.

"You will be silent and hear the charges against you!" Galea snapped.

"I would, Xosep," the field marshal replied with a regretful gesture, "except that it is in our charter agreement with the Church and the principality of Cantabria, that the Blades recognize no authority but their own. We are not subject to Church laws or governance, nor can civil authorities pass laws which affect us. We are the Blades of Sebastian." He looked up at the Pentatarch and shrugged apologetically. "So, I'm afraid all of this theatre was for nothing." He waved his hands to encompass the entire room and all of the proceedings before adding to the Pentatarch, "Nice robes, though."

The world exploded in stars and he collapsed, suddenly quite confused as to why his legs weren't working anymore. The pain in his skull should have been an indicator that one of the Knights had punched him from behind with a mailed fist.

Oh, that'll hurt tomorrow, he thought as he gently shook his head to try to regain his senses.

"That's enough!" He heard Vella's voice, but couldn't pinpoint its location. The room was still spinning and the voice was emanating from somewhere in that merry-go-bout. "Help him up, give him water."

Rough hands lifted him under his arms—too many hands. *Not one Knight, then. Two? Three?* A cup of water sloshed against his face, the clay clinking against his teeth. He grimaced and sipped from it, the coolness of the water helping to still the spinning room.

"Farric." Vella's voice was impatient. "Are you restored?"

Unable to reply verbally, the field marshal waved a hand and forced a smile, blinking all the while to try to get his world to settle into some sort of order.

"You took payment from us," the Pentatarch continued. "With the understanding that your troops would sail not later than the spring. Then, I hear that you have instructed the Blades not to be ready until the second harvest, one year from now."

"Whoever you heard that from," Farric managed to say with a ghost of his usual nonchalance, "will be dead by morning."

"Are you denying it?" the Pentatarch asked like a hunter caging his prey.

"Not at all," the field marshal replied.

"You dare admit this betrayal?" Bishop Galea shouted indignantly.

"Now, hold on," Farric snapped, his temper helping to pull him out of his daze. "In every contract for the services of the Blades, there are three elements: first, an agreement as to the overall goals of the mission; second, the size of the unit being contracted—a squad, a platoon, an entire company, or, in this case, the full legion; and finally, a *desired* timeline—with the understanding that the exigencies and challenges of military logistics and combat may cause changes to the proposed timeline without warning and at the sole discretion of the commander of the Blades of Sebastian... In other words, me."

"This delay has nothing to do with combat exigencies," Vella snapped.

"Perhaps," Farric replied, stepping away from the three Knights clustered around him, and looking up at the Pentatarch. "But it certainly has to do with the unprecedented logistical demands of your request."

"If you couldn't meet the timeline"—Galea stepped forward, not unlike a prosecutor pursuing his case—"you should never have accepted the charge."

"Ah, there you are mistaken, my good bishop," Farric said, snapping his finger and pointing at Galea. "Answer me this: What are the Blades of Sebastian? Hmmm?"

"An untrustworthy company of mercenaries," Galea hissed.

"Mercenaries…" Farric mused aloud. "And can you define that word for me, bishop?"

"This is not some classroom exercise," Galea spat, his heightened emotions making his wide-set eyes goggle comically.

"No, but on the definition of that word hangs my very argument. A mercenary is an individual hired for money to serve in a military fashion. You see, *money* is at the core of our purpose. Not loyalty, not faith, not any cause greater than our purse. So, of course, I accepted the charge. I made you no oath of fealty in doing so. I merely took your money, and according to our charter and the contract that exists between us, I have the freedom to change the delivery date at my discretion."

"You should have been a solicitor, Farric," Vella said, weariness writ upon his face. "Instead, you'll be a chorister."

"A chorister?" Farric asked.

A slight upward tick of the Pentatarch's lips lifted the jowls on one side of his face. "As each inch of flesh is peeled from your body," he said ominously, "you will sing in a loud, clear voice."

There was a click and the unmistakable sound of an arrow striking armor, then a blinding flash of light. Farric turned to see one of the three Holy Knights standing nearby, a crossbow bolt in his hand and a gaping hole in his armor. As one, he and his two companions drew their blades and looked about the chamber for the threat. Seeing none, they directed their swords at Farric. He remained calm and relaxed. He bore no weapons, nor did he look even slightly concerned by the array of blades pointed at him.

"You dare strike the Church?" Galea screamed in alarm, spittle flying from his lips.

"No," Farric said. "My men are not attacking the Church, they are defending the independence of the Blades of Sebastian against an overreaching Pentatarch. We are not your vassals, we are not your private army. Our contract, that you approved, details our independence quite clearly. There are blades and bolts aimed at your holy personage and all of your Knights. There is no exit. Your Knights will fall quickly enough but, more importantly, Your Effulgence, *you* will not make it out of this chamber alive."

"Nor will you, Farric," Vella seethed. "Whatever may happen, you will be the first to die. Your men cannot hope to prevail against the Holy Knights."

"First or last," Farric replied coolly, "it doesn't really matter. And I assure you, my Nizari are more than a match for your Knights. The Blades will remain independent, and… by attacking me, you forfeit your very sizable fee."

The Pentatarch's face paled—whether at the thought of forfeiting his fee or at the mention of the legendary assassins, Farric couldn't tell. Vella leaned back suddenly on his throne, his eyes searching the rafters above in vain.

"Apostasy!" Galea hissed, pointing an accusing finger at Farric.

"Perhaps," he replied evenly, his long black hair perfectly framing his high cheek bones and clean-shaven face. He glared at Galea, his dark eyes dancing with hungry anticipation. He gestured toward Vella and a crossbow bolt hammered into the arm of the throne beside the Pentatarch. The Knights urgently scanned the clerestory and balconies, trying to spot the hidden archers.

With an effort, Vella pulled his gaze from the bolt and looked down with a smile so false it would earn rotten vegetables were it produced by any mummer in a village square. "The Church has ever been your best client, no?"

"No," he replied, matter-of-factly. "No other client has ever sought to bring the Blades under their command. No other client has ever tried to bring spurious charges against the commander. No other client has ever dared to send troops in the night to ransack my private chambers and threaten my person. So, no, I would not consider the Church our best client." Then Farric looked disdainfully around at the Knights so openly threatening him. "Tell your dogs to sheath their swords and stand down, before this becomes an historical moment and a change in regime for both the Church and the Blades."

After a long, tense moment, the Pentatarch reluctantly gestured for the Knights to stand down and back away. A pregnant silence ensued in which he and Farric stared at one another. It seemed that Vella was trying to decide on the best means of extricating himself from this unfortunate situation. He glanced up to the rafters nervously before giving Farric a broad smile that failed to reach his eyes.

"We can still work together, Commander," Vella implored.

The young field marshal considered this possibility for a moment or two before speaking with a finality that surprised everyone in the chamber. "I think not," he replied flatly, then turned and stalked out, not even trying to mask the broad smile that blossomed on his face.

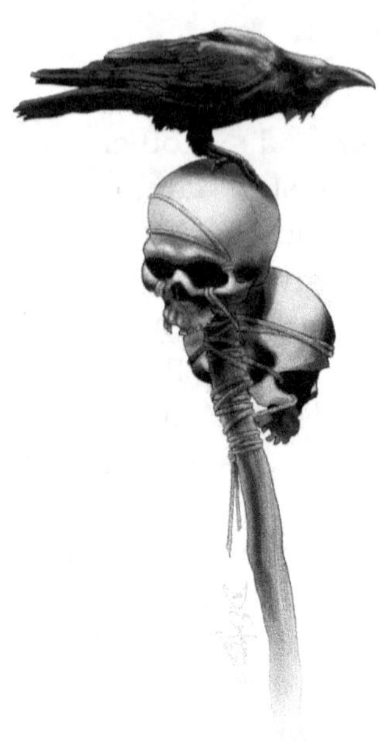

Chapter 16

Cruim was both the conscience and the cleverness of the Five. Wounded deeply by the betrayal of Duff, with whom he had been closest, Cruim dedicated himself to stopping his former comrade. While the others had power and compassion on their side, only Cruim was clever enough to parse Duff's stratagems, often anticipating his enemy's moves. For he and Duff had once been inseparable friends—the "Mischief Twins" Ilian had called them. And once Duff had betrayed them, Cruim bent every effort toward stopping his erstwhile brother, no matter the cost.

> *—"The Concordance of the Five," Eighth Edition, Raiden Oxbow III, Professor Emeritus, Academy of Cathonia*

One day before the Autumn Equinox
The Tor, Green Mount

Sangine

He hissed in frustration. His hand shot out and ripped a hunk of grey bark from the oak beneath which he was sheltering. *Damn the witch! The Nephellem were unbeatable!* His hands began shaking uncontrollably as he thought of Timor's wrath at yet another failure. He scowled. He would just have to see to this problem himself.

That execrable floating light the Raven had somehow invoked shone with a brilliance that he found unsettling and somewhat painful. He could endure it, though it was not pleasant. He puzzled, as he had for hours, over its provenance. It was clearly an artifact of some sort and, judging by the discomfort he felt beneath it, it must be an item blessed by the Golden One himself. But where would a simple Highland war chief come upon such a thing? Or… and this possibility made his skin crawl… perhaps the Five—or elements of the Five—had become directly involved. He shuddered at the thought. The fury of the princes would be extreme, never mind what he might expect once his master returned fully. But surely the Five couldn't have returned from their long inactivity. Though it might explain how the group atop the Tor had managed to resist so effectively… He played with the thought, as repugnant as it was, rolling the possibilities around. After a moment, he shrugged dismissively, concluding that he simply didn't have enough information yet.

However they've done it, they're resourceful, this Raven and his witch. I will not underestimate them again. A hungry smile played over his lips as he imagined this Corvus Corax kneeling before him, his skin blistering beneath Sangine's hands. *They are but a small company. No matter how much help they receive, they cannot stand against the Räubers and my magic!*

Dusk was near, though the roiling clouds above blocked any sight of the sun other than the fiery silhouette of the western mountains, visible beneath his summoned gloom. He would need to collect Vajk and enough of his rabble from further down the hill to finish the Raven once and for all. He winced in distaste as something in the shifting air currents suddenly brought the sound of the cursed music to his ear.

"A lovely melody, wouldn't you say?"

The voice startled him. With a snarl, he spun in a crouch, searching the stand of oaks for its source.

"Of course, I'm not surprised, as I taught it to him." The voice seemed to echo and rebound about him, without a clear source.

"Show yourself!" Sangine rasped.

A small bright-red ball bounced to a stop at his feet. Glancing up, he found a strange man with an unruly mop of hair, dressed in a motley vest and matching knee-length trews, lounging high on a branch above him with his back against the trunk. Beside him on the branch crouched a scraggly little dog, its teeth bared at Sangine as though the little beast might launch itself at him at any moment.

"Who are you?" the shaman growled, moving around the tree to get a better view of this unexpected visitor.

"Me?" the man replied with a carefree wave of his hand. "Oh, a messenger… a harbinger… a prestidigitator, though that's unrelated to the other two."

"A messenger? From whom?"

"From?" The motley man quirked his head, as if pondering the word. "No, no, no. *For* whom."

The shaman's eyes squinted in confusion.

"You see," the man continued, "I bring a message *for* someone… The *from* part is immaterial—or self-evident, you might say. Well, *you* wouldn't say that probably, but I might. In fact, I just did, didn't I?" He scratched his head thoughtfully, his eyes drifting upward.

Sangine circled slowly, trying to see a route up through the branches of the tree to the man. The lowest bough was over twenty feet above the ground, and the branch upon which the man reclined was another ten feet above that. The strange visitor continued.

"The message is for your master. You know, the scary fellow your princes chitchat with? Red eyes, hungry attitude, usually surrounded by black vapors—which could be from his diet. More vegetables might help. I knew a man once, had the worst flatu—"

"What is your message?" The shaman snapped, interrupting the foolish man.

"What's that?" The motley man looked down at him as if momentarily confused. "Oh, right, the message. Of course, if the big guy's still snoozing, we wouldn't want to wake him up. He's such a grouch when he first wakes. Maybe just tell the princelings, you know, Yip and Yap... Now, what was it?" He scratched his chin, pondering, then looked to his dog. "Do you remember?"

The dog barked once and wagged its stubby tail furiously.

"Of course, thank you!" He scratched the scruffy beast under the chin, slipping a small treat into its mouth. "You always know just what to say."

"What is it?!" Sangine's voice rose in irritation.

"Well, you needn't get snippy," the Fool responded, then rose to stand on the branch. Holding his arms out to his sides, he began skipping along the length of the limb like some acrobat balancing on a rope. "You are all," he said in a carefree voice as he leapt and cavorted with the grace of a dancer, "treading a dangerous path—precipitous, calamitous, even torturous, one might say." The Fool jumped and spun, reversing his direction on the swaying branch. The little dog yipped again, seemingly delighted by its owner's antics.

Sangine continued circling, moving directly beneath the Fool like a hungry wolf below a treed bear cub, waiting for his prey to drop.

"The message is this..." The Fool executed a perfect cartwheel along the narrow branch, then stood, hands on hips, his gaze suddenly serious as he glared down at the shaman. "We're back."

He turned and leapt down to a lower branch, disappearing from the shaman's view behind the trunk of the tree. Sangine shifted quickly around the bole, crouching, hands open, ready for battle. But the strange man was nowhere to be seen. He dashed around the nearest trees, searching both amongst the branches and along the ground for any sign of the strange visitor. Nothing. Only the distant tinkle of a bell sounded somewhere amongst the canopy. A cold breeze whisked in from the north, swirling the carpet of leaves about the shaman as he finally gave up his fruitless search.

Unsettled, he moved well away from the tree and quickly began to gather wood for the needed fire. He must commune with the princes at once, and he dreaded the ire he knew would greet him. But he had no choice. The Raven and his witch could wait a little longer. The princes must be informed at once.

Chapter 17

"It is the simple eloquence of soldiers in the field that astounds me. Poets, scholars, writers, and more may wax philosophical about the trials and the suffering of battle. But it is the soldiers, often simple, unlettered men and women, who find the most succinct way to express their grief, and the enormity of their experience. Simply amazing."

—King Mannon, Victory Feast, Esper, 569 HR

One day before the Autumn Equinox
Esper, The Royal Seat of the Glenfolk Region, Green Mount

Cailean

The blood-red rays of the setting sun found him crossing the short causeway to the gates of Esper. The bedraggled, yet victorious army of the Glenfolk marched behind him, their rough semblance of military order tightening into crisp lines and sure steps, sergeants hounding them to tighten up the closer they got to the gates. Behind the Glenfolk troops, a caisson draped in the purple and green of the Midlands preceded the soldiers of that region, their heads stooped in fatigue and grief. The caisson bore the body of the Lady Donella, who had fallen in the final battle, fighting bravely to the last. Beside the body walked a short woman with pale skin, and dark hair and eyes. It was Ciara, Donella's merry-begot daughter. Despite her estrangement from her mother these past years—since the arrival of Aengus—she would be the next in line to govern the Midlands. That was, unless Aengus challenged her ascension, which he very well might. *Bastard!* Cai shook his head in disgust, then silently upbraided himself. *You canna solve all the problems in the Green Mount, Cai.* He sighed and watched the rest of the procession.

Bringing up the rear of the three armies was what was left of the fyrd, close to four hundred citizen-soldiers led by Bradana, her spear hefted over her shoulder in a jaunty posture. Further back along the road stretched a train of wagons as far as the eye could see. At the battle's conclusion, Cailean's first order had been to send a rider back to Esper requesting as many carts and wagons as could be sent to shuttle those too wounded to march.

Despite their weariness, somewhere among the ranks of the fyrd, a song broke out. It was a well-known soldier's song, popular among the ranks and in the taverns. At first, it was but a lone female voice—Bradana, unless Cai missed his guess—but soon others joined her, and by the time they reached the gates of the walled city, the proud fyrd was singing lustily as the victorious warriors of the High Valley marched proudly into Esper.

> *For the road is long, and mickle's the chance,*
> *For the one who's gaun for adventure.*
> *And o'er the hill lies a heavin' dance,*
> *Of war, strife, and indenture.*
>
> *But wha' lies ahead, we ne'er can naw,*
> *Whether boon or baleful tide.*
> *Neath blisterin' sun or frosty thaw,*
> *All we can do is ride.*
>
> *Ride, me fellas, ride!*
> *While the sun is on yer back,*
> *There is no waitin' twixt time and tide,*

So pour me another jack, me lads!
Pour me another jack!

Cailean noted with sadness the black bunting and fabric that hung from every window, marking the passing of King Mannon. He would be sorely missed. A fair and generous monarch, gracious in peace and fierce in war. Though they had been notified days ago of the king's passing, seeing the black bunting hammered home the sad fact that King Mannon was dead. Cai knew Corvus would feel this loss sharply, as the two had a long history. The Raven had counted King Mannon among the very small circle of those he considered true friends.

Cai steered his mount along the broad thoroughfare, between the citizens of Esper who lined the streets solemnly, tears of pride and gratitude in every eye. The snap of the soldiers' boots as they marched echoed off the glass-fronted shops as they passed the merchant quarter and made their way up to the high street. Signaling the troops to halt behind him, he reined up before the King's Hall, where the entire council stood arrayed on the stairs before the building. Countess Derwhillie and Lady Stuart stood just ahead of the rest in matching postures, hands clasped before them, dutifully awaiting his official report. Though word of their victory had already spread, the populace of the town awaited the formal pronouncement. Then there would be a time for both celebration and mourning those lost, but the details must be observed. It was a ritual the people of the Glenfolk had gone through too many times over the past years. Yet, despite the solemnity of the moment, Cailean found it difficult to see anything beyond the blonde-red hair and piercing blue eyes of Lady Stuart—Brigit, she had said he should call her. He had only met her the once, and yet her luminous face, dusted with freckles and adorned with full lips and a strong chin, had filled his mind in every spare moment during the campaign. He realized he was staring, and with an awkward cough, tore his gaze away to survey the waiting townsfolk. Their silence was almost eerie, as the expectant faces in the crowd awaited his words. He stood in his stirrups so that more of the townsfolk might see and hear him.

"Members of the council and people of the Glenfolk," he croaked as loudly as his dust-choked throat would allow. "It grieves my heart to see the black banners, signifying the loss of so great a king. It is a loss that will be felt throughout all the lands of the Green Mount."

He paused with reverence for a moment before continuing. "As many of you may have heard, the people of the Midlands have suffered a similar loss in the death of the brave Lady Donella, who fell in battle, fighting bravely."

He gestured to young Ciara to lead the lady's caisson, and waited for it to be pulled up before the troops, only continuing once it had arrived.

"Yet even in the depth of these losses, which are felt dearly, there is cheer to be found. People of Esper, I present to you the victorious allied armies of the Green Mount. The enemies—the savage Barbárs who thought they could conquer the Green Mount—are vanquished to a man!"

The crowd erupted in cheers, and ribbons and flowers were cast into the air as the townsfolk embraced one another. Tears of relief and joy were shed as the shouts of triumph and pride rebounded through the city.

Cailean gestured to Captain Morag Fitzwalter to attend him. A stout, powerful woman with a perpetually serious expression stepped forward. Having been repeatedly honored by King Mannon for her bravery, Morag was a fearsome warrior and a solid, reliable officer who enjoyed the deep respect of the Glenfolk soldiers. Cailean had instantly recognized her competence and moved her into the critical logistics role. *An army is only as effective as its supply train,* his father was fond of saying. She had been his first appointment, and having watched how effectively she managed her new position, he was confident it had been a good move. She stepped up smartly beside him with a sharp salute.

"Sir!"

He turned to include the council as he spoke.

"Captain Fitzwalter," he said, "kindly arrange quarters for the soldiers of the Midlands and the fyrd. I'm sure the members of the council will be of assistance to you."

"At once, sir," she replied, and turned expectantly to the council.

"Of course," the countess said and, patting Brigit's arm affectionately, the older woman stepped forward to confer with the captain on the disposition of the visiting armies and their wounded.

"My Lord General..." Brigit spoke in a loud, clear voice, obviously intended for all to hear. "You have brought us a great victory, and we, the people of Esper, have a feast prepared for you and your brave troops."

"Right welcome, that is, milady," Cailean said as he dismounted and moved to stand in the road just below the step on which Brigit stood. Even with the advantage of the stair, he still stood some two inches taller than she. She smiled up at him and once again, he had to concentrate not to fall into those ice-blue eyes. He smiled, somewhat abashed, and continued, hoping those assembled did not note his blush. "Perhaps the feast could wait long enough for a wee bath? I doubt you'd want a guest like me at your table, that smells like a sheepfold." There was laughter among those gathered.

"Of course," she answered with an indulgent smile. "Let us gather in two hours' time to celebrate this victory and drink to the memory of those brave souls that helped secure it."

Cailean inclined his head crisply in acknowledgment.

"Sergeant Major?" he called over his shoulder.

"Sir!" Alasdair replied from his new position before the troops, having been promoted just days earlier.

"Dismiss the troops, and see to the wounded."

"Sir!" Alasdair turned sharply to the men behind him. "Well done, lads," he called out. "Get washed up and return in two hours for the feast. After that, you have four days to spend with your families and friends. Enjoy the time. Dismissed!"

Brigit looked confused at Alasdair's command.

"What happens in four days?" she asked Cailean in a more private voice.

"We march for Monarch's Pass, I'm afraid," he answered somberly.

"Are there more of the enemy coming?" She seemed horrified at the thought.

"We don't know, at this time," he replied matter-of-factly. "But should more of the bastards come, it makes sense to wait atop the switchbacks, rather than allow them to gain a foothold."

There were murmurs among the council members behind her, which she stilled with a raised hand. Cailean was surprised and pleased to note the air of authority this youngest town leader exuded.

"I understand," she said with a serious tone. "'Twould be folly to hope the enemy would not persist, and a greater folly not to prepare against it. Your plan is both wise and merciful to your men." Then, her face blossomed into a broad smile and she turned and gestured for him to follow her into the great hall. "Come, let's get you settled."

Cailean hesitated, confused. "Here? In the king's own hall?"

"I'm afraid every home within the town will be occupied, hosting soldiers and nursing the wounded. My own manor will be brimful of troops, and I've converted most of my yard to serving as a field hospital. The other members of the council have done no less. Besides, the King's Hall is vacant at the moment, and I canna think of a more worthy occupant than the Lord General who has brought so great a victory to us. The son of our king's greatest friend and ally. That is, if you dinna mind sharing the hall with the draped coffins of King Mannon and Lady Donella?"

"N-no," he stammered. "'Twould be a great honor, indeed."

"'Tis settled then," she said simply, and turning, led him into the building.

About an hour later, a washed and refreshed Cailean stood beneath a fast-growing blanket of stars on the balcony at the rear of the hall. He was partially dressed, wearing his trews and boots and a light linen shirt that did little to hold out the evening's chill. The last orange glow of sunset was dying over the western mountains, but his eyes gazed northwest—toward the distant flashes of lightning that he somehow knew were over the Tor.

Tomorrow's the Equinox, Da, he thought. *My thoughts are with you. Come home safe. You and Li. Come home.*

Though he didn't understand the significance of the deadline of the Equinox, he knew their fates would somehow be decided tomorrow. He longed to be there, sharing the dangers with his father and Ligulf, but knew his role was here, securing Esper and guarding Monarch's Pass against the possibility of further attacks.

A soft cough drew him from his reverie and he turned to find the Countess Derwhillie stepping out onto the balcony, carrying two cups of wine.

"Am I disturbing you?" the elderly woman asked as she stepped forward and handed him one of the cups.

"Not at all, Countess," Cailean said, accepting the goblet. "I'm pleased for the company. And thank you."

"I'm sure there's younger, more charming company you'd prefer," she said with a knowing grin.

"N-not at all, ma'am," he stammered, grateful that the night's dark hid his sudden blush as unbidden images of Brigit's radiant smile filled his mind.

She waved away his denial lightly and turned to gaze out over the raging river below for several moments before finally speaking again.

"Much has happened since the army marched forth."

Cai nodded. "You did a fine job organizing the people of Esper and putting them on a war footing. I imagine there was much turmoil on the council. How'd ye manage?"

"Brigit was a great help," the countess replied confidentially. "She'll make a fine queen, that one."

"Queen?" he blurted. "What have I missed?"

"The day before his death," she began, turning to him, her eyes serious, "King Mannon called the council to his chambers. He was so spent he could scarce speak. But he needed to express his wishes regarding the succession."

"I see," he responded. "And Brigit's his choice?"

"Not in so many words," the countess said. "He wished for the council to decide, but he made it quite clear that he did not want his nephew, Kevin, to inherit the throne."

"That must have come as a disappointment to him," Cai said.

"Aye," she replied with a wry smile. "He packed up and left that very night, still nursing the wounds your father gave him when he passed through."

"Me da?" Cailean laughed. "What wounds were those?"

The countess grinned at the memory. "A fair broken nose and a greater wound to his pride. Corvus cast the lad into a manure pile."

"He didn't!"

"Sure and he did," she answered with a conspiratorial grin. "I think he would have done much more to him had Fergus not intervened."

"Ach, me da." Cai shook his head. "Not one to suffer fools, I'd say."

"No, he's certainly not," she agreed, taking a sip from her cup.

"But you still haven't said how the election has fallen on Lady Stuart?"

"The council met the next day, right after the king passed," she said, turning once more to gaze over the river. "And, as you can imagine, there was much debate and discussion. Various names were put forth. However, at the end of it all, they selected Brigit—perhaps hearing my reasoning that the needs of our time were for a young, energetic monarch. One who could rule for years to come."

"Wise words," he acknowledged, sipping his wine thoughtfully. He allowed the silence to lengthen. The countess clearly had a point she was working toward, and he would let her arrive at it in her own time.

She sighed and turned to face him, her face serious and full of consequence. *Here it is,* he thought.

"But," she began, "Brigit, for all her gifts and intelligence, is no warrior like Donella was. She is not one to lead troops in battle like Mannon. She'll need someone upon whom she can rely to advance the banners of the Glenfolk when the need arises. Someone she can trust to support her rule and not undermine her."

"I see," he answered carefully. Was she asking that he stay on in Esper as Lord General? The thought hadn't occurred to him. His plan was to return to Dóchas with his father and brother once the battles were done and resume his life there.

"I doubt you do, lad," she said frankly. "The nation of the Glenfolk is riven by war and the mad scramble for power and influence that always follows the death of a king. 'Tis a precarious time for us, and we need sure hands to lead us forward in unity."

"Sure and I reckon Lady Stuart will be more than up to those challenges," he responded, still confused as to what the countess was driving at.

She sighed and rolled her eyes impatiently.

"I didna think Corvus raised a dullard," she said, patting his cheek sharply, "but sure and you're as thick as stone, lad. I'll speak plain. You should *marry* her. Become the consort of the queen, her strong right arm. The people trust you, and you've proven your worth on the field. Together, you'd make a formidable couple, and the Glenfolk would be in good hands."

"I, uh…" He was at a complete loss for words, so he changed tack. "Are you always so plain spoken?"

"When the walls are thick"—she tapped his forehead lightly with a finger—"you sometimes have to shout to be heard within the house."

He looked down and ran a hand through his short hair. "What does the lady say to this? I barely know her."

"Pish posh," she said with a wave of her hand. "I haven't broached the topic with her, but a blind man could see the way you two look at one another." She sighed wistfully, as though recalling the distant passions of her youth. "Now, you'd best fetch your doublet, the feast will begin presently and I've arranged for you to be seated next to the lady in the place of honor."

"Oh. I see." His mind was racing and he suddenly felt as skittish as an unbroken colt. "What should I say to her?"

"Just be your charming self, lad," she replied simply. "Let nature take its course."

With that, the countess downed the rest of her wine in one go, turned, and strode through the open door into the King's Hall, leaving Cailean's thoughts in turmoil as a sudden maelstrom of possibilities and a bright future—all unlooked for—swirled around him.

Let nature take its course, she says, he thought. *As simple as that.*

He had never courted a girl, though many in the village had shown interest over the years. Despite his love of his village and family, something had always told him that his future would take him away from Dóchas, and it wouldn't be right to leave a love behind. And, he reflected, the girls of his small village were as far removed as he could imagine from a self-possessed, sharp-witted woman like Brigit Stuart.

Oh, he chuckled ruefully, *this will be anything but simple.*

The feast was a grand affair, with trestle tables set end-to-end along the length of the high street, and torches in brackets and bright bonfires to counter the chill in the air as the people of Esper served and celebrated the brave warriors of the Green Mount. The head table, at which Brigit and the other members of the council sat with their spouses, was positioned on the elevated front porch of the King's Hall, where they could see down the full length of the feast. Cai caught Bradana's eye where she sat with the fyrd, and raised his cup in a silent toast to their victory. With a smile, she returned the gesture, then pointed across her table to

Yazid, pale and weak and bundled in blankets, but laughing and sharing stories with the troops nonetheless. The avuncular Aslene flashed a wink at Cai and inclined his head, a gesture of love and pride that touched Cai's heart and made his eyes sting with fondness. He spotted Alasdair sitting beside a tall woman with frizzy red hair that Cai assumed to be his wife. She was busy piling food onto his plate, a look of proud adoration in her eyes, then Alasdair said something and she slapped his shoulder, a look of mock outrage warring with amusement at his comment. He noted other officers and warriors from each region who had distinguished themselves during the campaign, raising an appreciative cup to each of them, the pride he felt bringing a lump to his throat. He imagined that this was but a glimmer of the pride, love, and appreciation his father felt after battle, having personally trained the fyrd and engineered so many victories with his clever stratagems. With a sigh, he turned his attention to the plate before him.

He had thought that sitting beside Brigit before the eyes of all would be nerve-racking, yet her easy manner and light laugh put him at ease soon enough. A young servant offered to refill his cup with more wine, but Cai waved him off with a smile of thanks, choosing to reach for his water instead. Brigit noticed his choice with an appraising, raised eyebrow.

"You do not indulge, General?" she asked.

"Best to keep my head about me, milady," he replied softly. "The troops are watching." She inclined her head in an appreciative nod. "So," he continued, setting down the cup, "the countess tells me that congratulations are in order, *Your Majesty*."

"No Majesty yet," she said with a self-effacing smile that nearly undid him. "But the members of the council were, indeed, kind enough to place their trust in me. Though I'm not sure they made the right choice."

"Why would you say that?"

"Och, Adaira would be a far better choice," she said, cutting a slice of the roast hen stuffed with apples and parsnips.

"Adaira?" He didn't recognize the name.

"Sorry, the Countess Derwhillie," she corrected herself. "She was the obvious choice and I spoke in her favor. The council would sure have chosen her, but she declined in the strongest terms."

"Did she now?" he responded, piecing together the countess' self-effacing version of events with this fuller picture painted by Brigit's words. The countess was clearly someone he needed to get to know better. "Turned it down, did she?"

"Aye," Brigit continued. "She insisted that the new monarch must be young and energetic. Then she put my name forward and spoke a bunch of blather about my worth and efforts to organize the town. In truth, I feel like the only contribution I made was in serving as apprentice to her. She's a marvel, that one."

"I suspect you did right more than that," he countered generously, scooping more colcannon onto his plate, making sure to get a choice crispy chunk of fried cabbage. "She speaks highly of you, and it's clear that you have the respect of the council."

"Perhaps," she said, thoughtfully. "But there will be trials ahead, and I fear I'll not be up to them."

Cai laughed at that, shaking his head and taking another sip of water.

She bridled, her brow furrowing in irritation. "Have I amused you, sir?"

"Forgive me, my lady," he answered, raising a hand to forestall her ire. "My da is a wise man, and he taught me early to judge the character of those I meet. He's always said that those who seek power rarely deserve it, and those of true worth doubt their own mettle. I laughed because I'm constantly amazed at how often that man's words are proven true. The very fact that you didna seek the crown speaks to your worth. That you might somehow doubt your own capabilities is further proof that you, above all, deserve the trust of these people. For that doubt will, I imagine, drive you to work tirelessly to serve your people and further earn their trust." He turned and looked at her sincerely before continuing. "Though I don't know her well, the Countess Derwhillie strikes me as a crafty and clever woman, with a keen eye that sees the true heart of a person. Further, I'd venture that at her age, she takes a long view and sees the future of the kingdom through the broad lens of the past. I'd be inclined to trust her instincts. Ye'll make a bonnie queen."

Brigit stared into his eyes a long moment, digesting his words. Her momentary pique mollified by his words, she now seemed thoughtful.

"And you, Lord General," she asked, "what does the future hold for the elder son of the Raven?"

"That is a grand question," he said, tearing his eyes from hers with difficulty to examine his plate. "I suspect that once these difficulties are passed, I'll find my way back home to the High Valley." He politely scooped a small bit of hen and roasted apple onto his fork, then abandoned his cutlery with a thought. "Though I suspect your army will need some time to reorganize and build, after the losses suffered. Many fine officers fell in the fighting, and the promotion and training of those worthy to step up will be a delicate matter. Many of these tasks would probably fall to Sergeant Major Alasdair to resolve, but really, you need a commander to oversee it. It might do well for me to remain for a short time to see to that. I wouldna want to leave things unsettled. That is, with your permission, of course."

"That would be a great comfort," she replied, placing her hand on his arm. "You have earned the respect of the people and the soldiers. I would be glad if you stayed on."

He looked down at the hand, its warmth somehow burning through the thick sleeve of his doublet. Despite the water he'd been drinking, his throat was suddenly dry. He reached for his cup.

With a smile that flustered him utterly, she picked up her own cup of wine and stood, raising her arms to silence the gathering. It took a moment for everyone to settle and give her their attention, but soon every eye was upon her as she spoke in a loud, clear voice.

"Friends, allies," she began, "since ancient times, the people of the Green Mount have lived together in harmony and friendship, each region pledged to fight for the common defense.

We thank and honor the brave soldiers of the Midlands for honoring that pledge and for their terrible sacrifice. Lady Donella's bravery shall long be remembered in song and story throughout the Green Mount!"

A cheer went up as the Midlands soldiers pounded their tables lustily, shouts of "Donella!" ringing through the gathering.

"We honor King Fergus and the soldiers of the White Cleft, who traveled so far to come to our aid, and even now strive against the foe somewhere near the Tor. We pray that the Five will protect them and see them victorious, and we hope to share a feast with them when next we meet."

Another cheer as all present pounded the tables in agreement.

"We honor the fearless fyrd of the High Valley, the men and women trained by Corvus himself, who left the comfort of their homes and hearths to travel uncertain roads and stand fiercely against the foe."

The fyrd pounded their tables and cheered with a wild abandon that took some time to settle. Bradana beamed and raised her glass to Yazid, who smiled sagely.

"And, of course," Brigit finished, "we honor the brave soldiers of our own Glenfolk, ever on the front line of danger. First to answer the call. First to stand against the foe, despite the loss of our own dear King Mannon. Know that you have made your people proud! We honor you! Indeed, warriors of the Green Mount and our fine Lord General Cailean, we honor you all!"

The loudest cheer of all erupted as every soldier that was able surged to their feet, cups and voices raised to one another and to Cailean, who stood and raised his own cup in answer. As the clamor subsided, Brigit encouraged him to say a few words. He set down his cup and gathered his thoughts.

"Friends," he said, his voice clear and strong. "This is a great day indeed, and you all have much to be proud of. I know that my father would have some great wisdom to share with you, were he here. But even now, he fights upon the Tor for the safety of us all. Let us take a wee moment of silence to stand in solidarity with our brothers and sisters who struggle on our behalf. This battle was won—and soundly—but I fear this war is not yet ended."

As one, the assembly lowered their eyes, their lusty cheers replaced by solemnity as their thoughts turned to those of their brethren who struggled on.

After a long moment, the silence was broken by a lone voice, singing an age-old song of concern for warriors far from home.

> Come home, come home,
> My Douglas come home.
> Where the hearth burns merry and bright.
> Your bairns and your lambs
> Have need of you still.
> Be safe, my Douglas tonight.
> Be safe, my Douglas tonight.

Chapter 18

As the day was done, I stood alone upon the battlefield, my fallen kin around me. I looked upon their lifeless eyes, now but food for crows, and felt the loss so keenly it was as a knife in my heart. I knelt to say the words over them, but my voice was stopped by grief, my tongue like a foreign, leather thing in my mouth. O forgive me, cousins, that I could not call forth your worthy deeds to the Valryim! Forgive me, Father! For your noble deeds outshone all, and I was mute!

> *—An excerpt from the tale of the Battle of Jelling,*
> *as told by Arne Fourfinger*

One day before the Autumn Equinox
The Tor, Green Mount

Corvus

Twilight had faded and the air had grown crisp with autumn's chill by the time Corvus and Mama crawled up the steep, final bend in the trail before the temple, the strange floating light overseeing their journey. Supporting one another, they stood panting, then staggered along the final stretch like two drunkards in halting steps, leaning on one another in their mutual exhaustion. The energy from the seeds long spent, Corvus was barely able to remain upright, while Mama gritted her teeth against the twin agonies of her dislocated shoulder and her grief.

Cuddy, MacLief, and the rest of the Adders rushed down out of the temple to help them, two immediately taking up a rear-guard position to watch the trail below while MacLief moved to slip his arm under Corvus' shoulder. Corvus waved him off, wearily.

"Lad," he said, his voice febrile and weak. "Lupe has fallen. Take the others down the trail, and gather her body. Bring her to the temple."

"Aye, and I will, Corvus," MacLief replied quickly, exchanging a stricken glance with Cuddy. Then with a curt command for the others to follow, he dashed down the trail.

Yadira and Amina rushed down the defile to Mama's side, their silent questions to her answered only by a tearful shake of her head. Yadira gasped softly and clutched her heart, her eyes suddenly world-weary, and her expression bleak and drawn. Amina looked down at her feet, shifting her weight from side to side. She adjusted her jimas nervously, and Corvus could hear the girl muttering something over and over in her quiet monotone as she tapped repeatedly at an eyebrow with her left hand. The four of them stood together for a moment, the ladies living in their moment of profound grief, and Corvus working hard to remain upright.

Yadira noted Mama's posture and discomfort, and before allowing her to attempt the final climb up into the temple, did a quick assessment of her shoulder, asking pertinent questions about the injury and the precise location of the pain. She nodded in a businesslike manner, clearly understanding what the injury was and moved to Mama's left side where she gripped her wrist in both hands. She instructed Amina to help hold Mama still, and with a deft jerk and a twist resettled the shoulder into its socket. Mama gasped in pain and shuddered, Amina staggering to hold her up. Yadira gently massaged the angry joint while Mama recovered herself, breathing deeply and chanting quietly.

Looking up, Corvus caught Ligulf's eye as the young man continued singing lustily, his voice interweaving with Rhona's so beautifully that it brought a lump to Corvus' throat. The three minstrels had found their purpose here and, despite the effort, had maintained this magical music for hours, holding the gloom at bay. Their faces were streaked with sweat despite the chill air, and their eyes showed their fatigue, but Piper continued playing the uplifting melody while the other two sang along as loudly as they were able. Li had a questioning look, no doubt noting the grief among the women and Lupe's absence. Corvus shook his head sadly in response. A look of fierce determination came over Ligulf as his voice grew louder still, his head leaning back as he sang to the sky with renewed and defiant fervor. Dallin had noted the silent exchange from where she was perched behind the pillar at the front corner of the temple. Corvus saw her shoulders slump and she covered her face with her hands.

Amina and Yadira assisted Mama and Corvus up the defile and into the temple, where the two finally collapsed against the fallen block nearest the small fire that Argant was tending. The boy seemed to already understand what had happened, and silently crawled over to nestle against Mama, his small arms clutching her girth. Mama stroked his head and once more gave in to her grief as silent sobs shook her.

A short while later, the Adders returned bearing Lupe's body. The care they showed, struggling to lift her gently up the rugged defile, spoke to the respect in which they held this fallen, foreign comrade. Anna, carrying the double-headed axe, brought up the rear. They laid Lupe gently on the far edge of the floor of the temple, folding her arms over the dreadful wound. Yadira, Amina, and Argant crossed and knelt beside her. Yadira clutched Lupe's limp hand and leaned over to whisper something to the fallen votary. Then she leaned her head back as if she were preparing to scream to the unjust heavens. Instead, she closed her eyes tightly, trying to stem the flow of tears. Amina knelt beside Yadira, absently stroking Lupe's shoulder and continuing to mutter in her soft monotone. Argant knelt by Lupe's feet, unable to tear his horrified eyes from the gaping, ragged wound in her chest. Finally, after several moments, he stood and rushed back to Mama, burying his face in her bosom.

Weariness unlike any he had ever known dragged on Corvus and he sagged against the stone block, struggling to keep his eyes open any longer. He looked around at this small, exhausted band of defenders and knew that the foe would come soon, in force. His resources now all spent, and the Adders' numbers so depleted, he could envision no scenario for survival. They would die here on the cusp of the Equinox, and he could see no remedy for it. Despite the defiant and joyful music, he felt nothing but bleak despair.

King Fergus

He moved his horse restlessly before his gathered men at the base of the Tor. His mount stumbled on a stone in the path, and he winced against the injury to his arm, still so very tender. They were weary from their long march, but he knew the enemy was ahead of them upon the Tor, and he also knew that the small force Corvus had ridden to join couldn't stand against that enemy for long. The Raven was crafty and the finest swordsman he had ever seen, but even the great Corvus Corax had his limits.

The strange black clouds swirled over the mount, blocking out all but a jagged line of fire as the sun set over the adumbration of the distant western peaks. The closer they drew to the Tor, the greater the sense of foreboding and hopelessness. Already, many of his men had broken ranks to collapse and sit, head in hands, as though defeated. Fergus glared at the nearest such soldier. Normally, he would have the sergeants scold or even flog the man back into the ranks for such a demonstration of cowardice, but he could feel the gloom from the unnatural clouds as heavily as they, and he knew his men. They weren't cowards. They were stalwart and hardy men, who had crossed the breadth of the Green Mount twice in ten days, and fought bravely both at

Eagle's Gate and at Ben Strath against the feared Räubers of the Barbár hordes. It wasn't their fault that the enemy's sorcery had undone their courage. They had never trained for this. He would proudly match his men against any warriors and feel confident in the outcome, but this black, unnatural gloom—which seemed to disjoint the courage of even the bravest among them—was beyond their experience or preparation.

Quany, his best scout, came staggering back toward the line, his hand on his head as he grimaced with the effort of bringing word to his king.

"What's the news, Quany?" Fergus barked. "Where are the other two?"

"They couldna bear it, my lord." The man's voice shook as he spoke. "They dropped along the trail in sobs. It was all I could do to continue on. Whate'er this ghastly gloom is, it o'ercame them both."

Fergus bit down hard in frustration. If he tried to storm the Tor under these clouds, only a fraction of his men would be battle-worthy. "What of the foe?"

"The enemy is entrenched upon the Tor as we feared, sire," the scout replied with great effort. "There's a chokepoint on the trail just upward of that great yew, yonder."

Fergus' gaze followed Quany's gesture up the Tor, where in the rapidly failing light, he thought he could just make out the silhouette of the tree in question.

"The trail is quite steep and narrow there," Quany continued. "And weaves between a stand of holly bushes. The enemy is encamped on the other side in force. 'Twould be suicide to brave that opening, sire. We canna go forward!" The scout dropped to his knees as ragged, despondent sobs racked his body.

Fergus was about to berate the man, when he noted more sobs and wails from behind him. Turning, he was horrified to note the majority of his army were now down. He glanced over to see that an equal number among the contingent from the fyrd was down too. Many were on their knees, others lay curled upon the ground. Scanning his forces, he reckoned maybe one in ten were still standing, and those were stooped, sagging beneath the unnatural despair. His hand gripped the horn of his saddle as his own body drooped forward at the sight.

It was hopeless, after all. All for naught, they had pushed and marched so long and hard. So many had died, and with a dread certainty, he knew that fate now awaited them all. He gritted his teeth against the knowledge, and forced himself upright in his saddle, panting at the effort. He lifted his head, tears streaming down his cheeks, and shouted in a battlefield voice trained over decades in dozens of conflicts.

"Stand up! Stand up, every one of you. Your King commands it!" He turned to face the fyrd element. "And you lot, is this how you would want Corvus t'see ye?" His voice faltered, and he paused to swallow heavily before continuing. "We may well die here today. But by Ilian's golden hand, I swear to you, I'll not die on my belly! We are the soldiers of the White Cleft and the fyrd of the High Valley! The last hope of all the people of the Green Mount, damn you! Now, stand up I say!"

He paused again, to see if his words had any effect. A few of his men staggered to their feet, gasping at the effort. Others stirred, but couldn't seem to rise. He continued.

"You are the bravest troops that I have ever had the pleasure to command!" he said, his voice growing stronger. "The courage of the fyrd is legendary, and the White Cleft has always stood forth in time of need. We have never shirked our duty, and we willna begin now! Regardless of our chances! Even though… Even *if* we face certain doom, we will stand and we will march together up that Tor! Your forebears marched and fought for the Green Mount! Their forebears did the same! Will we now be the ones who crawl into a hole in the ground and weep like fearful bairns? I say not! If we are to die this night, then so be it! But I will die with a curse of defiance on my lips and my sword in my hand, like a true Highlander! Stand with me now! Stand, I say!"

One by one, the troops rose, his words firing a defiant flame in their eyes, though it threatened to gutter and flicker out at any moment. Their faces were pale and drawn, yet the men of the White Cleft—proud, doughty men that they were—flanked by the stout members of the fyrd, managed to rise against the unnatural despair, lips trembling, tears streaming. Yet they stood, every man and woman.

"Draw swords!" Fergus barked, his voice thick with pride as he looked at these beloved, brave troops struggling against something so far out of their depth.

With a great shout, the weapons of his host were drawn, shields adjusted, and calls of encouragement sounded from amongst them. He dismounted from his horse, hefted his shield and drew his own blade, raising it high.

"Archers to the fore!" he called, then waited as over five score archers jogged to the front, lining up shoulder to shoulder. "Gather oil and light torches! The enemy thinks to hide behind some bushes! Let's burn the bastards out!" Then he turned toward the Tor as a fresh wave of despair hit him like an icy blast of winter. "Let the pipes sound!" He gritted his teeth, and held his sword aloft, as the skirl of bagpipes stirred the shadows of forgotten courage against the darkness. Despite the sure knowledge that he moved toward utter destruction and worse, abject failure, King Fergus strode forward, fueled by the majestic sound of the pipes and the indomitable courage of his troops — with steps unsure at first, but strengthening as they staggered into the teeth of the crepuscular wind that buffeted them. The army of the White Cleft, together with over three hundred members of the fyrd of the High Valley, advanced on the Tor, tears of forlorn defiance in every eye.

Sangine

The leader of the Angor Shamans reeled back from the flames through which he had communed once more with Prince Timor. He shuddered as the contact was broken and paused a long moment to gather together the flayed and torn fragments of his soul and mind. The prince was greatly unhappy with his news, and had lashed out with a fury unlike any Sangine had ever experienced. Urgency had been stressed. *Urgency!* They must seize the Tor quickly before the Five could stop them.

His hands trembled as he worked to still his breathing and gather strength to fulfill the new commands the prince had issued, the new gift he had been given. Carefully. He must tread carefully now. For the loyalty of the Räubers to the Shadow Lord was questionable. They followed Vajk, and their own towering pride, looking upon Sangine with perpetual disdain and wariness. But Timor's instructions had been unequivocal, and the shaman dared not vary from them in the slightest degree. He shuddered again at the memory of his recent torment and, swallowing heavily, he rose and moved to seek Vajk among his men.

He found the Grand Hadvezér seated with a group of his subordinates near a small fire on the sloping ground near where the trail wound up into the grove of pine trees. The commander glared at his approach, resentment and distrust chiseled into his handsome features. Sangine inclined his head obsequiously as he neared.

"Grand Hadvezér," he said in a silken tone, "may we speak?"

With a curt gesture, Vajk indicated that the chieftains should leave them. They rose and left the fire, their looks to Sangine ranging from surly to openly hostile. The shaman paused, absorbing their inimical glances, letting their hatred fuel his resolve for what must come, then sat by the fire, close enough to Vajk to speak in low tones.

"I have communed with Prince Timor," he began slowly. "He is… displeased." He infused that word with dark and portentous meaning.

"Is he?" Vajk spat. "Then perhaps he should come and fight for this hill himself."

Sangine recoiled at the commander's bold impertinence, fearful that the Prince of Fear and Punishment might somehow have overheard. "He instructs that you are to take fifty of your best men to storm the temple at once. We will put an end to this Raven and the witch, and seize the Key."

"So my men will once more do the dying?" Vajk snarled.

"Some, perhaps," Sangine allowed. "But He has sent another of his dark gifts, which I shall wield personally."

"Oh?" Vajk replied, eyes narrowed suspiciously as he glared at the shaman. "And who of my trusted men do you intend to sacrifice this time for your blood magic?"

"None of them, be assured," Sangine replied. "But His patience is no more. He will not tolerate any further failures."

The Grand Hadvezér grunted in disgust and stood, brushing off his trousers.

"Gather your men by the breach in the stone wall," Sangine added. "I will meet you there."

"What of the rest of my men?"

"They must hold here," the shaman replied. "The Highlander army advances, despite the storm."

With another grunt the commander turned and strode into the gathering night to issue his orders.

A quarter of an hour later, fifty restive Räubers stood gathered beneath the expansive branches of the oaks, just below the breach in the stone wall. The light from their torches flickered on the underside of the branches, making them appear more like the vaulted ceiling of some vast cathedral. In contrast to their normal garrulousness, the Räubers were hushed, speaking only in low, conspiratorial tones. Sangine passed among them, the massive warriors shrinking from the withered, pallid shaman, chary of his touch. He moved to the front, where he found Vajk conferring with two chieftains.

"The Raven and his band have retreated to the temple," he informed the commander. "There, no doubt, they hope to make a last stand."

Vajk received the shaman's intelligence with disdain, staring down at the greasy little man with distaste before finally speaking in a commanding voice for all to hear. "We will storm the top of this cursed mount," the Grand Hadvezér said. "Kill them all, as only Räubers can!" He raised his hooked sword above his head, and the men responded with a feral roar.

Sangine leaned forward and whispered to Vajk. "Send the men ahead. I have something to share with you that is for your ears alone." Vajk stepped back from the shaman, distrust and doubt written upon his face. "It pertains to what you are to do once the Key is seized and the temple is ours."

The commander's lip curled and his brow furrowed, but after a moment's hesitation, he stepped up onto the embankment below the breach in the wall to address his men.

"Take the temple," he instructed loudly. "Leave none alive, but save their belongings. They have something we need." Nods of acknowledgment rippled through the gathering. "Whoever kills the Raven will be Stone-Bearer, his family and tribe will walk in place of pride among our people!" There was a hungry cheer. "Now, go! Bring us victory!"

Vajk and Sangine waited as the fifty burly warriors rushed hungrily through the gap and up the trail, their torches a glowing serpent of bobbing lights winding its way up the steep mount.

"Now," the commander said, turning to the shaman, "what is it that you wish to tell me?"

Sangine rubbed his hands together, his eyes lowered as he approached. "My master has sent another gift."

"So you said. What is it?"

"A blood gem," Sangine replied under hooded eyes.

"What is that?" Vajk snapped. "Speak plainly. My patience with your riddles grows thin."

"Very well," the shaman answered.

Suddenly his left hand lashed out, the tips of his claw-like fingers penetrating the commander's bare muscular chest as easily as if he were tearing through old linen. Vajk's eyes went wide in horror as the shaman's hand slipped beneath his breastbone and closed about his heart. So sudden had the attack been, the commander did not cry out, only grunting in surprise as his heart was stopped. Acrid black smoke seeped from the wound as his face drained of all color, his eyes rolling up into his head, yet he did not collapse—the shaman's grip held the much larger man fast. The black smoke increased, now tinged with red as a magma-like substance oozed from the wound, steaming drops sizzling out beneath the shaman's wrist.

"You see, Vajk," the shaman said through teeth gritted with effort, his hand still buried within the commander's chest, "a blood gem is a rare gift of great power, but its might is directly related to the size and vitality of the heart from which it is crafted." A sheen of sweat covered Sangine's face, his eyes fixed on the wound and narrowed in manic concentration. "Your vitality outshines those around you. It's why they all follow you so loyally, like dogs."

A sudden rush of the glowing magma from the wound scorched its way down the commander's belly, filling the air with the smell of roasting flesh and hair.

"I'm afraid no other heart would be nearly as powerful. So, I'm sorry, Grand Hadvezér, but your reign ends today. Your dreams of personal glory are no more, though you will be a valuable weapon for my master." The shaman's face suddenly relaxed, and he withdrew his hand from the wound, accompanied by another gush of the glowing, molten scoria. No longer supported by the shaman's grip, Vajk crumpled to the ground, the strange glowing slag bubbling and hissing as it oozed from his chest down the embankment.

Sangine examined the fist-sized black-and-red gemstone he held clutched in his hand. Its edges were smoothed and rounded, yet it presented multiple facets. He stared at it in wonder, as within those facets there seemed to exist movement, as if he were viewing something alive through a deep, smoky mirror. Each flitting movement existed just beyond his ability to perceive it clearly, like something seen at the edge of one's eyesight just before drifting off to sleep. With a shake of his head, he tore his eyes from the enthralling facets. The almost gravitational pull the gem exerted on him was enticing and he found himself longing to study it, to plumb its mysteries. But he knew better. His long years of arcane study—so many lifetimes he had lost count—warned him of the risk of primal artifacts such as this. Though he had never encountered a blood gem before, somehow he knew and understood. This stone, so weighty and virtually humming with dark energy, was a juncture between the real world and some unfathomable dimension. A juncture, a doorway, that sought to pull him in. The glimmers of movement he perceived felt to him somehow like living beings, or at least those recently alive... Perhaps souls? *Are they in torment?* He risked further ensnarement and leaned closer, his eyes hungrily seeking answers. A movement within the gem pulled his attention and he rotated the stone to follow it. Something about it had seemed... A vague familiarity danced across his skin, raising gooseflesh. With an effort, he tore his eyes from the stone, its pull almost irresistible. He could easily become mesmerized by it, ensnared and lost within its mysteries. He closed his eyes tightly and shook his head until he felt himself return to the present.

He wasn't sure how much time had passed, but he looked around to find he was still standing alone, Vajk's corpse lying beside him. The snake of bobbing torches, however, so close but a moment earlier, was now barely visible higher up the Tor. He blinked and shook his head again to clear it. He turned his hand palm down, still clutching the stone, but blocking the artifact from his sight.

He could feel its energy humming through his skin, full of potential and unleashed might. Black smoke encircled his hand, its snake-like tendrils enveloping his arm, which soon began to shake with power—raw, unfiltered malice. He smiled a feral, hungry grin. His eyes slid up the Tor with a ravenous intensity.

"Now, witch," he said in a low, wet growl, "I come for you and the Raven. The Key will be mine."

Chapter 19

For though sailors and swordsmen turned to Feryn, hunters, farmers, and ranchers to Nuada, and Ilian and Manu were Father and Mother to us all, Cruim it was that kept our spirits light. God of music and dance, theatre and wine, he was the trickster god that reminded us all of the joy of living.

—"The Concordance of the Five," Eighth Edition, Raiden Oxbow III, Professor Emeritus, Academy of Cathonia

One day before the Autumn Equinox
The Tor, Green Mount

Argant

No sooner had he wrapped his arms around Mama, his eyes closed tightly against the horror of Lupe's body, than he found himself suddenly standing once more before the cobwebbed throne.

"There you are," the old man said with a weak smile. Athdar, he had said was his name. "Time is short, young one, and we have much yet to discuss."

"Lupe is dead," Argant said in a small voice, then wiped his nose.

"Yes, I know," Athdar replied sadly. "She was very brave to stand alone against the monsters."

"Why did she have to die?"

"Better to ask how many she may have saved with her courage," Athdar said wistfully. He tapped the dusty armrest of his throne with the fingers of his right hand. "You realize, Argant, that more of your friends may die before the morning comes?"

"What can we do?" the boy asked, worried. "Mama is hurt and Corvus looks sick or something."

"*You* must be ready when the time comes," the old man told him. "When the dawn breaks, you must act quickly."

The boy stamped his foot in frustration. "What do I do?"

"Listen carefully, and I'll tell you," Athdar said, leaning forward. His expression was more intent, less dreamy, than Argant could remember seeing before, and the boy listened as the man who had been the Gatekeeper of the slumbering Tor for the past five hundred years explained what needed to happen.

Dallin

"They're coming!" Cuddy called from his position at the first bend in the trail, pointing down at the rapidly approaching serpent of torches. "Could be fifty or more of the bastards!"

Dallin shifted the open kegs of arrows closer to where she stood at the front corner of the temple overlooking his position. From there, she'd have a clear line of sight down the steep, narrow trail. They'd have to come up single file, and she could rain arrows down upon them to slow them down. She nodded to Cuddy and Jack to be ready. The enemy would have to raise their shields to ward off her arrows as they climbed the final bend between the junipers. Hidden by the bushes, the two spearmen were poised on either side of the top of the rise where their spears would be able to snake in behind or beneath the Räubers' raised shields. It would be messy, but between the three of them, they should be able to take out a handful of the foe before the Adders were forced to retreat back to the temple.

She glanced over at Corvus. He'd been asleep since he returned with Mama. *The poor man,* she thought. *So much of this relies on his strength, and he's gone and spent it all on those two giants. We canna do this without him.*

She could see from the worry on Ligulf's face that he had reached a similar conclusion. His hand gripped the handle of his puntina as he continued singing, his voice now raw and hoarse, and his eyes hollow and weary. Piper grimaced in pain as he struggled to keep his wounded arm up in position to play the flute. *If that melody fails,* she thought, *we're finished.* Looking around at their small band, Dallin noted the fatigue and worry etched on every face, the shoulders slumped, the backs bent as though carrying a heavy burden. *Who am I foolin'? Fifty Räubers about to storm the temple… We're finished anyway.*

"You're playing that passage wrong."

Every head snapped around at the unexpected voice. Dallin's mouth fell open as she saw the strange man she had met in the village, Latrans, leaning against one of the rear pillars, a scratched, old wooden flute in his hands. His scraggly dog was perched on the fallen block near Lupe's body.

"Here, allow me," the Fool said and lifted the flute to his lips. Suddenly, the temple was filled with the most extraordinary soaring music. If Piper's playing was like a shield against the storm, Latrans' was a mighty bulwark, blocking out all sense of impending doom and lifting every heart with its transcendent melody. The minstrels finally stopped their music at the sound, sagging against one another in exhaustion. Piper's red-rimmed eyes brimmed with grateful tears as he raised a trembling hand to his mouth. Li wrapped his arms around both Piper and Rhona, hugging them tightly in silent acknowledgment of the crucible they had passed together.

Corvus

Corvus stirred, blinking away the heavy fatigue that had so weighted him since his return from battling the Nephellem. He looked about, eyes sharpening as his alertness returned. He rose to kneeling, scooping up Raven's Tooth as he did. He slowly pressed to his feet, gaining strength by the moment, somehow renewed by the Fool's music. He gripped his famous sword before him, a look of grim determination in his eyes. Mama gasped in wonder and worked her shoulder, seemingly now free of pain. The Adders looked to one another in wonder as every injury and the dread and exhaustion lifted from their bodies. Of everyone in the temple, Corvus alone seemed unsurprised by the inexplicable arrival of Latrans. He nodded his thanks to the Fool, who was busy capering about the temple, leaping from block to floor effortlessly as he played. There was more movement along the back edge of the temple platform too. Pherson touched the bandage on his breast, a look of wonder in his eyes, then pulled the dressing free to reveal pink restored flesh where a ragged wound had been. Yadira stepped back, her hand to her mouth in amazement. The dog yipped and wagged its stubby tail furiously. Pherson and Yadira exchanged a confused look, then both turned to stare in wonder at the strange man playing the flute.

"On your feet, Adders!" Corvus called, noting Pherson's restored state. "We have butcher's work ahead." He turned to Dallin. "Keep their shields high, Dal. We'll do the rest."

Once the spearmen were on their feet and armed, he positioned four by the top edge of the defile within the temple, two on each side of the opening. Turning to MacLief he said, "Place yourself in front of the boy and guard him wi' your life. Everythin' depends on him."

"I swear I will, Corvus," MacLief replied solemnly and placed himself by the stone block near the fire, gesturing for Argant to stay behind him.

"Anna, you're wi' me," Corvus said to the remaining Adder, then turned to address the rest of the group. "Be ready. The enemy will come fast and hard. We have to hold until dawn, still hours away." Then, switching to Aslene he added, "Mama, use that staff only as a last resort, we canna risk it getting lost or stolen in battle." She nodded grimly in response and gripped the staff tightly with both hands before her.

Corvus and Anna proceeded down the defile and over to the path to where Cuddy and Jack crouched on either side of the top of the last bend in the trail. Positioning Anna alongside Jack on his right, Corvus took up position in the middle of the path and watched the bobbing serpent of torches making its way up the Tor. Having tossed aside his shield when he faced the giants, he once more drew his long knife with his left hand.

He glanced up at the floating light, grateful for the silver beams that shone down and helped to hold the unnatural gloom at bay. Without it, they would need to rely on the enemy's torches to see. Many times over the years, he had fought by torchlight and knew how treacherous and difficult it was. *Five watch over us,* he prayed, and crouched in a ready stance.

The first of the Räubers growled as he spotted Corvus waiting atop the steep bend and redoubled his pace. Before he could set foot on the rise, however, an arrow took him in the face, snapping his head back. The Räuber dropped like a stone. The man behind him hopped adroitly over his fallen comrade, shield held high against the threat of another arrow. He charged up the steep trail, his barbed sword easily parrying Jack's thrust from his right as he crested the slope. He never saw Anna's thrust, however, which caught the back of his left leg, just above the knee. The tendon severed, he stumbled and fell suddenly, sweeping his shield to his left to block Cuddy's stab, but opening him to a quick thrust from Raven's Tooth in his chest. An arrow flashed past them, taking the next man in the groin, just below his raised shield. Then the charge of attackers stopped abruptly.

Corvus could hear discussion amongst them in their tongue just below and around the bend, out of reach of Dallin's aim. The serpent of torches bunched together further down the trail. Their attackers seemed content to wait. *But for what?* he wondered.

His answer came soon enough, when he detected a rustling in the junipers and other shrubbery between their position and the defile. The enemy was scaling the steep incline behind him, fifteen feet of sheer stone and overgrown bushes. Within a few moments he and the other defenders would be flanked and compromised.

"Back to the temple, now!" he shouted to Cuddy, Anna, and Jack, as a fresh assault up the main trail began. The three Adders scrambled back toward the defile as arrows lanced past them once more. With a savage snarl, Corvus kicked the shield of the next Räuber charging up the steep trail, overbalancing the man back onto his comrades below. The Raven then turned and followed the Adders, pausing to step off the trail into the junipers and slash at the eyes of an attacker who was just wrestling his way up through the prickly branches.

"Move!" he shouted to the Adders as Cuddy's foot slipped in the muddy stream and he stumbled, slowing them. Barclay rushed midway down the defile and grabbed the shoulders of Cuddy's jerkin, hauling him up and clearing the path. An Adder's hand reached down for Anna's and pulled her up quickly. Jack, a nimble hunter from the mountains east of Mallaig, dashed up the defile deftly, Corvus close behind him.

"Line the front!" Corvus barked, and the Highlanders prepared for their last stand.

Piper

He staggered to the rear of the temple and leaned heavily against a pillar there. He rolled his arm in surprise as the shoulder wound seemed somehow magically healed, restored by the magic in Latrans' music — much like Pherson and the others. He gaped in wonder at the strange, motley man.

He watched his comrades, as through a dreamlike slow-blinking haze, while Corvus and the Adders dashed back up into the temple and prepared for the assault. Yet, despite the imminent danger, his mind was swept away by the glorious and transcendent music from the Fool's flute. Piper was, after all, a minstrel who had spent his life immersed in music, yet never had he heard or experienced such a powerful, intricate, and moving melody as this. It felt as though a hole had ripped open the sky and through it, this celestial sound poured down, at once flawless, majestic, mournful, and inspiring. It filled his being and, strangely, he could almost see its effect on the others as spines straightened, color returned to pale cheeks, sinews stiffened, and the fear and nervousness that had plagued them these past hours melted away. He found it odd that the voices of the defenders were muted and indistinct, as though he were hearing them shout to one another from under water. Their movements were likewise slowed to his haze-filled eyes.

He saw Dallin launch another arrow, her scarred face pinched in a grimace of determination. Brochy crouched behind her, snarling his defiance at the oncoming attackers as they reached the defile and began battling to gain the temple. The spears of the Adders flashed with the lethal, exotic patterns drilled into them by Yazid. Corvus shouted something, then his blades blurred as he spun and leapt and two of the fierce attackers fell before him. Anna threw herself before a fearsome Räuber who had gained the temple and felled Jack with a thunderous blow from his shield. Time seemed to pause further as Piper watched this slip of a woman face off with a savage warrior from a distant land. The mythic and improbable tableau seared into his memory. The attacker easily outweighed her by ten stone, yet she straddled her fallen comrade fearlessly, the tip of her spear lancing in and out, gashing the Räuber's cheek and shoulder faster than he could parry. Time's normal flow resumed suddenly as Pherson joined the defense and the attacker fell, pierced in the side and belly by their spears. All the while, the soaring music underscored the action, seeming to emphasize particularly heroic acts or moments of distinct danger for the defenders. It was almost as if Latrans saw exactly the moments Piper witnessed and emphasized them, somehow, with his melody.

Piper was overcome with a sense of awe at this battle unfolding before him, so very mythic in scale. These common folk — farmers, shepherds, woodsmen, a stonemason — throwing their all into protecting their fellows with determination and unflagging bravery against these brutal attackers bent on destroying everything the defenders held dear. Upon this moment turned the very fate of the Green Mount, and he had a sense that far more than that hung in the balance. Latrans cavorted like a man possessed, the rapid-fire staccato of his flute matching the intensity of his antics. A lump formed in Piper's throat as he watched arrow after arrow lance forward from Dallin, the effort of drawing the great bow clear in the muscles of her back. He saw the lightning-quick stabs and thrusts from the Adders' spears and Corvus' deadly blades as the man leapt and spun with a martial grace that would be remarkable in a man half his age. There were shouts of warning, a body being dragged out of the fray by Rhona, a flash of needle-thin silver as Ligulf's puntina took the eyes of an attacker just cresting the edge of the temple at Dallin's feet. This was no common battle. He was witnessing a group of heroes as from legend, raised from humble origins, their lives ennobled by this act of holding the great foe at bay, against all odds.

He sighed with deep gratitude that it had come to him to witness this. Then, a golden light reflecting from the marble floor interrupted his thoughts. He glanced up through the missing roof of the temple where he beheld a sight that truly dumbfounded him. There, in the air above the Tor, he could just perceive the golden shimmering outline of a great castle sparkling like a mirage or dream. He stared in wonder, the chaos of the battle raging around him, as the fortress walls became clearer, more defined, and he realized that it was the music of the flute that was somehow building this — the strange motley man was creating this! Each note added a shimmering, translucent stone to the floating castle walls forming above them. He glanced in wonder at Latrans, whose eyes were now closed, his brow furrowed in concentration even as he continued to leap and dance about blindly.

Suddenly, there was a stunning flash of unearthly lightning, limned in blackness, that arced up from further down the hill. The silver floating light that had accompanied Corvus exploded into a shower of sparks, plunging them all into darkness. But even as the light was extinguished, Latrans finished his song with a triumphant, soaring conclusion and his luminous construct above them, now complete, descended. Its translucent, shimmering walls fit firmly about the temple. There was a great THOOM as the fortress settled, knocking the attackers back. The defenders lowered their weapons in surprise and wonder as they gazed in awe through the thick glistering walls before them.

A silence followed the bulwark's dramatic arrival, broken finally by Corvus.

"Fool, what magic is this?"

Before Latrans could respond, however, there was another flash of the strange, black-edged lightning from further down the Tor, the bolt scoring a shimmering rampart and leaving a blackened divot where it hit.

"I thought you could all use a break," Latrans said lightly.

Before Corvus could respond, the Räubers, as one, charged the temple anew. The defenders crouched in reflex, only to stand again in amazement as the Barbár warriors bounced back from the bulwark's diaphanous walls as though striking stone.

Another blast of black lightning came, leaving a long charcoal scar across the face of the fortress.

"It won't last forever," Latrans said. "But really, what is forever?"

Corvus shook his head. "You are truly a man of wonders."

"Oh, stop!" the Fool said with mock humility. "It is a brief respite only. A hiatus, some downtime, a lull, even…"

Before anyone could say anything more, however, their attention was pulled to Dallin, who groaned in pain and collapsed backward with a hand axe embedded in her left shoulder. Yadira and Rhona rushed to her side as her eyes rolled up and she fainted.

Chapter 20

For Destiny unfolds not as a flower, the bud opening suddenly to reveal beauty and a sweet aroma. No, it is much more like an onion, its layers revealed only with some effort and more than a few tears.

—Anonymous

The night before the Autumn Equinox
Wetheral Castle, Lachland

Darienne

The young queen couldn't sleep. She'd been tossing and turning for hours, occasionally dozing fitfully, then waking with a start, thinking someone—a woman—had called her name. Rolling over, she parted the gauzy curtains of her bed and gazed out the rippled glass of her bedchamber's windows. Though she couldn't see the slivered moon, the slight, luminous glow of the landscape suggested its presence. The stars blazed over the mere, reflected in its mirror-smooth surface. The Westron Mountains were a black, jagged shadow holding up the resplendent sky. Despite the glory before her, she was unsettled. She needed to attend to something, but whatever it was had slipped from her awareness like a skittish kitten, just beyond the edge of her thoughts, refusing to let her grasp it. A shooting star suddenly blazed from east to west with impossible speed, the bright streak of its tail mirrored in the lake. The two white lines — one in the sky, and its twin reflected in the water — defined for a brief moment the edges of a road or trail, receding into the distance, like some heavenly path hastily drawn, summoning her from the comfort of her bed.

She cast aside the warm coverlet, and the chill air greeted her with a wash that made her gasp. The fire in the hearth had withered, leaving only glowing coals that hissed their drowsy defiance to the cold darkness. She slipped on her fur-lined slippers and quickly donned the heavy, wool dressing gown beside the bed, its fur collar soft against her neck. Tying its belt tightly around her, she managed to light a candle from the dying coals and stepped to the great door, unsure of her destination but feeling she had to get out of this room.

Heaving the heavy portal open, she was greeted by the sharp snap of the guard outside coming to attention.

"Majesty," he said curiously. "Is something amiss?"

"No, Jacques," she replied softly. "I'm not sleeping well and thought I'd take a stroll."

"Of course, ma'am." Jacques had stood guard over her nighttime door for more years than she could remember, his weathered, clean-shaven features a comfortable and constant presence. As a girl, she recalled how he would accompany her on her occasional midnight jaunts to the kitchen in search of cakes and a glass of fresh milk. Aware of the clandestine nature of their missions, he would adopt a catlike stealth, dashing silently ahead of her, then waving her on, as though they were two thieves advancing upon the crown jewels. During her more rebellious years as an adolescent, her midnight sojourns were less about cake and milk, and more often involved taking a jug of wine from the cellar and finding a castle rampart on which to get drunk. But, like a faithful co-conspirator, Jacques had never tried to dissuade her from her activities. A raised eyebrow might suggest that he questioned the wisdom of her outings, but the ever-constant guard would still accompany her stealthily to the cellar door, which he would unlock quietly with a key on his ring.

Tonight, despite the fact that she was the Queen and no longer needed to sneak about, the two still progressed with a furtiveness, careful not to awaken any of the other denizens of the castle. Nighttime held an intrinsic solemnity, which, over the years, she had come to revere and was still loath to disturb. Jacques instinctively understood the mood of his charge and mirrored it. She was grateful for his customary sensitivity.

She wandered the long corridors aimlessly at first, the flickering candlelight turning the high-arched ceilings into looming figures like gods or giants observing their progress. At some point she became aware that her feet were taking her toward the Queen's Garden, as if of their own accord. She smiled softly, her curiosity aroused. She turned as she approached the tall oaken doors to the grand receiving hall, though that would be the most direct route to the garden. The thought of heaving open one of those massive doors and the attendant noise that would shatter the stillness of the night seemed wrong to her. Instead, her feet steered her the long way around, through the servants' wing, to a small side door that would lead to the northern edge of the garden, near the hill with the tree and her childhood swing. She flashed a smile of gratitude to Jacques as he dutifully opened the door, the gust of cold air extinguishing her candle and catching her breath. Her cheeks immediately reddened with the chill. Setting aside the dun candle, she gathered the fur collar more tightly about her neck. She forlornly regretted not taking the time to don her trousers before leaving her chambers.

"You needn't follow, Jacques," she said, knowing it a pointless gesture. A wry, raised eyebrow was his only response. He would accompany her into the cold, watching over her from a distance, ensuring her safety, for however long she decided to stay. Ever-constant Jacques. She touched his arm in gratitude as she stepped into the garden, gently illumined by the slivered moon. She paused a moment, drinking in its graceful arc and imagining that silver bow being the legendary lost bow of Nuada. A light frost had gilded the lawn, coating the drooping, bare branches of the great oak atop the hill. She took in the otherworldly sight. Everything sparkled in the dim, silver light.

The cold sky above her was awash with stars, like some mad painter had carelessly slashed her paint-laden brush over a black canvas, dashing droplets and globs of iridescence in its wake. The frosted grass crunched beneath her slippered feet as she stepped gingerly, the sound announcing her intrusion into this hoary landscape. A light breeze stirred as if inviting the tentative monarch to step further into this sparkling netherworld.

The swing atop the hill shifted in the breeze with a creak. She considered climbing up to it, but thought better of it given the slippery ground and her ill-advised footwear. Eschewing the pebbled path, she wandered the lawn, moving back toward a hedge of carefully manicured hawthorn. She smiled, remembering the many times as a child she had hidden from her tutors within that hedge. Poor Master Ducat, her long-suffering maths tutor. She could still hear his lisping voice calling for her with exasperation as she crouched beneath the hedge, giggling to herself. Her inattention and rambunctiousness had made his life miserable, no doubt. She wondered whatever became of him and made a mental note to inquire as to his health and whereabouts. She really should send him some token of appreciation and acknowledgment of the impossible task he had been given: to hammer sums and the principles of geometry into the head of a wayward and headstrong princess. She chuckled lightly, the smile causing her cheeks to burn and her eyes to water with the cold.

Rounding the hedge, she was surprised to find a bench nestled against the back of the hawthorn. She didn't recall that being there. It must have been a recent addition. Though the marble surface of the bench sparkled with the frost, it somehow seemed inviting to her. As she stepped toward it, Jacques advanced, unclasping his heavy cloak.

"Allow me, Majesty," he said softly, and before she could object, spread his cloak across the bench for her to sit upon.

"Won't you be cold?" she asked.

"Not at all, ma'am," he assured her, and moved off a discreet distance before she could thank him.

She sat on the cloak, the cold of the bench still reaching her, though she was grateful for the thick added layer. The garden was so still and pristine, its familiar contours reshaped by the frost and the moonlight into a crystalline, alien wonderland. She closed her eyes and inhaled deeply, the cold, fresh air biting at her nose. The sound of a gentle footfall on the pebbled path stirred her. It was unlike Jacques to move about when she sat in the garden; his normal pattern would be to watch her from a distance, as still as an additional statue added temporarily to the decorations. There was another step, just beyond her sight, around the far side of the ornate fountain—now drained for the winter—carved in the figure of Manu, the Mother, pouring water from a large pitcher beneath her arm. Another footstep.

There, at the base of the fountain, a feminine, slippered foot appeared, limned in a soft golden light. Darienne marveled at the otherworldly luminescence. Then a woman stepped into view, suffused with the same aureate glow. The velvet gown, high cheekbones, proud bearing, and silver circlet at her brow were all so familiar. Darienne gasped and tears of joy, not the cold, filled her eyes. Impossibly, it was her mother, Isador.

Darienne started to rise, but her legs refused, choosing instead to tremble beneath her robe, suddenly devoid of all vitality. Isador paused and regarded her daughter lovingly. Darienne returned the gaze, drinking in the welcome sight like a warm, delicious broth on a cold, winter's day.

"Mother," she attempted to say, though the tightness in her throat rendered the utterance voiceless.

"My little flower," Isador replied in a whisper that somehow seemed to echo.

Chills dashed up and down Darienne like playful frost-sprites chasing one another across a freezing pond, raising gooseflesh along the length of her arms and legs. Her mother hadn't called her that in years, not since her father had died. It had been their nickname for her. She began to tremble uncontrollably, and a tear defined a lone path down her reddened cheek. Isador swept forward and sat beside her, enfolding her in a warm embrace that somehow dispelled the cold entirely. The hole that had been ripped in Darienne's heart at her mother's death suddenly filled with the warm, glowing golden light that suffused Isador. She buried her head in her mother's shoulder, drinking in her familiar scent. A tide of emotions—gratitude, love, regret for her years of insolence and thanklessness—overcame her, and she wept there in the stillness of the frosty garden, beneath the observant stars, her mother's hand gently caressing her head. Memories washed over her— holiday celebrations, name day feasts, her father's funeral, public ceremonies full of pomp and import, as well as intimate, private moments, shared laughter, arguments, tears. Her mother was at the center of each recollection, constant, loving, stern, warm, encouraging, indulging, understanding. She perceived, in that moment, the fullness of their life together, and how complete her mother's presence had been.

"Mother, I..." She suddenly had so many things to say, so many apologies to make, so many questions to ask, so much love to express. Her words faltered at the enormity of it.

"I know, child," Isador responded gently, her words still bearing that ethereal echo. "Shush, now." Isador cupped her daughter's cheek in her hand. A deep, inchoate sense of ultimate understanding and unconditional love washed over Darienne, bringing with it an absolute and profound peace. She looked into her mother's eyes, so filled with love, and knew that to be a reflection of her own gaze.

"How...?" she finally asked, after what seemed a lifetime.

"The Mother has granted me a boon," Isador replied. "You carry great burdens, Dare, and I know you feel unready for the challenges you face."

"Yes," Darienne whispered, clenching her eyes shut as the dammed up self-doubt threatened to burst forth and leave her feeble and powerless in her nation's time of need, as it had done every day since learning of her mother's death.

"You are ready, my love," Isador said, lifting her daughter's chin and gazing into her eyes with an unyielding encouragement. "You have my blood, but so much more than that, you have your father's daring, your grandfather's cunning and grit, and the limitless compassion of your great-grandmother—the dearest woman I ever knew and she for whom I was named. Do not waste time worrying over what is expected of you, or trying not to disappoint me, or striving to live up to someone else's image of a queen. You must not try to do as I would do, or model your rule after one or another of your forebears. Instead, my willful, passionate child—ever so eager to take this life by the reins and ride it at a breakneck gallop wherever the road may lead—you must and will carve your own path forward. Your people love you, and they will follow you. Be the Moonflower, and know that no matter what may befall you or our country, you will forever have my love and pride."

"But I..." she began, but stalled as the overwhelming magnitude of her mother's words began to sink in. "You're not disappointed in me?"

"How could I be, Darienne?" Isador replied, her face rising in that familiar, indulgent smile. "You are everything you were meant to be, which is so much more than I ever was. You have somehow resisted my every effort to bridle you to some unnecessary sense of propriety, learning from it what you needed, but shucking the rest aside as unwanted chaff. There is so much more that I now understand. Had we a lifetime together in this garden, I might be able to share some of it, but that's unimportant now. What matters, and what I must impart to you in this brief moment, is that you bear every gift you need to succeed. Trust your heart, surround yourself with those you love, and as challenges arise—and your life will be filled with them, my sweet girl—make the best choice possible in the moment, then move ahead boldly. Ride, my sweet Darienne! Ride the wild stallion that is this life. Ride it with abandon and joy! And always know that you carry with you my love and pride."

Isador leaned forward and kissed Darienne's cheek for a long, tender moment then, rising, stepped away toward the fountain.

"Mother, wait," Darienne said, feeling suddenly bereft, the cold once more biting through her robe.

"Goodbye, love," Isador said, then suddenly closed her eyes, as if in concentration.

Her figure shifted and changed, like thin ice melting suddenly from a window pane. Another woman stood now in her place, shorter of stature, her figure more full, her long white hair hanging in a braid down her back. She was still limned, though, in that otherworldly golden light. The woman turned to face Darienne. She seemed younger than the white hair might suggest, almost ageless. Her complexion was darker than Isador's, her skin bearing an olive hue. Thick brows framed bright amber eyes. She wore a veil in the Aslene fashion, and just above the veil, on the cheek below her left eye, she bore a small tattoo of a crescent moon. She was somehow familiar, yet Darienne's confusion would not allow her to place the woman. Though she was veiled, her soft smile was obvious, the eyes shining with warm kindness.

"Your mother is no longer here," she said gently with the hint of an accent. "But I am glad you got to see her."

"Who are you, madam?" Darienne asked, confused. "What is this?"

"It is a moment," the woman replied simply, "nothing more."

"I don't understand."

"Darienne," the woman said, her brows lifting meaningfully. "This is a time of great change. It will fall to you to hold the many strands of a fraying weave together and somehow continue forward. You are at the heart of so much that is to come. But you are not alone. Others will stand with you to face the storm. Much will be asked of you—far beyond what you might expect—and much will be decided on this Equinox. By you, and others."

"But, I don't—" she began, but the woman cut her off, moving suddenly to her side and placing a hand on her recently healed shoulder, which suddenly tingled as though it were covered with biting ants.

"Your people have begun calling you the Moonflower," the woman said.

"Y-yes," Darienne managed to get out, despite her full attention being on her shoulder.

"She was a legendary woman, the first Moonflower," the glowing visitor said. "I loved her as a daughter."

"Wait." The young queen's attention snapped back to her visitor. "She was a *real* person?"

"Oh, yes," the woman answered. "Long ago. During the great struggles. I knew her well."

It took a moment for Darienne to register the meaning of those words, and when she did, a cold flush covered her and a stone dropped into her stomach carrying the weight of history. The woman smiled at Darienne's open-mouthed look of awe.

"Perhaps it is time for a new Moonflower to lead her people," the visitor said, and the tingling in Darienne's shoulder grew more fierce.

"What's happening?" she asked, no longer able to ignore the crawling, stinging sensation.

The woman smiled briefly and released her grip, then turned and disappeared around the fountain. Darienne quickly rose and followed her, dashing around the stone figure, only to find herself alone once more in the sparkling, frosted garden. As she stood, huddled against the cold and utterly flummoxed, Jacques rushed up to her.

"Majesty," he said, his hushed voice filled with concern. "Is everything alright?"

Rubbing her shoulder as the tingling faded, she turned to respond to him but her eyes fell upon the carving of Manu, the full figure, thick brows, long braid, and the crescent-moon tattoo upon her cheek. A profound sense of calming warmth washed over her. She relaxed her arms and stood straight and tall, the words of her two visitors replaying and reverberating in her soul.

"Yes, Jacques," she said, her eyes never leaving the statue. "Everything is quite alright, thank you."

Chapter 21

When the briny bastards charge, don't let me hear none of your wailin', weepin', and gnashin' o' teeth. We are the proud thirty-third regiment, and though we are outnumbered, and the enemy is prowlin' about the castle, just waitin' for their chance, we will make them pay for every sodding inch! We may well die here tonight, but we'll die knowin' we said a defiant "fuck you" to the enemy!

> *—Final speech of Sergeant Major Maxwell Fletcher*
> *to the doomed defenders of Buchey Castle.*
> *The final words are now carved into the stonework of the*
> *main gate.*

The night of the Autumn Equinox
The Tor, Green Mount

Corvus

"What are we witnessing, Fool?" he demanded again, though Latrans was unresponsive. Since somehow manifesting the shimmering fortress over the Tor, the Fool had plopped himself down against the fallen block of stone near the fire, crossed his legs, closed his eyes, and seemingly drifted into a deep sleep. Corvus stood over him debating whether to try to wake him or to let their enigmatic benefactor rest. Concluding it was best to let a sleeping fool lie, he turned back to assess their casualties. Dallin's shoulder looked painful, but the wound was not life-threatening, and given rest and care, she should recover, though she'd be firing no arrows anytime soon. He shuddered to think of what would happen once the battle resumed and they could no longer rely on the uncanny deadliness of her aim.

A thunderous screech ripped through the air, startling everyone, as yet another of the mysterious black-edged bolts gashed the front of the fortress. It seemed to be the only sound that fully penetrated the shimmering walls, the shouts of outrage from the frustrated Räubers only distant muffled voices.

"Where are those bolts coming from, Da?" Ligulf called, fear in his voice.

"I'm not sure, Li," he replied, striding to the front edge of the temple. "Whoever, or whatever, is wielding them must be hidden below the bend in the trail. But I suspect it's more of the shaman's blood magic."

The soft voice of Amina chanting behind him drew his attention. Turning, he saw that despite the Fool's magic, Jack had succumbed to his injuries and she was performing a death rite over his body. Nearby, Mama was tending to Barclay, who had a nasty gash in his leg near the groin and another on his brow over his left eye. Moving close, Corvus squatted to assess the injuries. The leg wound looked painful, but he was relieved to see that there didn't seem to be any arterial pumping of blood. The head wound would require careful stitching to reattach the flap of skin hanging down over his eye, but the exposed bone didn't look fractured. Anna's hand was apparently broken, though she bravely nodded to him, indicating her readiness to continue the fight. He turned back to Barclay.

"That scar will be a bonnie keepsake of your adventure here, eh, lad?"

"Aye, it will," the wounded man replied through gritted teeth, despite the steady flow of blood which covered his face in a gory sheen. "I hope my missus willna mind too much."

"Now, Barclay," Cuddy said with a mischievous wink, "you know the lasses love scars. They make a man look right dangerous."

Barclay chuckled in response, provoking a sharp intake of breath as the smile pulled at the wound. "Cuddy," he said, "when this is over, remind me to cuff you soundly."

"Will do, my friend," Cuddy replied, patting his wounded comrade gently on the shoulder. "Will do!"

"Use this turadh to get some rest," Corvus said gently. "I don't ken the nature of this Solasta magic protecting us, but we'd best take advantage of it while we can."

A screech ripped through the night as another black bolt struck the fortress, dissolving a glowing parapet into sparkling mist that drifted away on the breeze.

"Hard to sleep with that going on," Anna grumbled, masking her nerves with irritation.

"Och, Anna," MacLief replied from his spot by Argant, "just coorie in close to the fire. Y'look knackered."

"Dinna be a nyaff, MacLief," she responded testily. "I'm right as rain."

"Wheesht now, you two," Corvus scolded. "I said rest."

"Right, Corvus," MacLief replied, chastened, while Anna muttered a soft, "Sorry," under her breath and lay down.

With a nod to Li to join him, Corvus moved over to Dallin and the two knelt beside her. Her head lay in Rhona's lap, the bandages Yadira had applied to her shoulder were soaked through with blood, and her breathing was quick and shallow.

"Alright then, Dal?" Corvus asked softly, stroking her forehead.

"Alright," she replied, her voice quivering.

"You've done right well for us, lass," he reassured her. "We couldna have made it this far without you. Right proud of you, I am."

"Aye, Dal," Li added. "You've been amazing!"

She smiled weakly up at her childhood friend, then a tear slipped down her cheek, her lip quivering.

"Here now," Corvus said softly. "There's no need for that."

"Och, Li, Corvus," she said on the verge of sobs. "I'm lettin' you down. I'm lettin' you all down."

"Wheesht, now." Corvus spoke soothingly as he wiped the tear tracing a path back across her scarred cheek. "You're no' lettin' anyone down. You've done more than your share." He gently chucked her chin, as he had when she was a child. "Who would've ever guessed that wee Dallin should become such a warrior?"

"I don't want to fail you, Corvus," she replied with a quivering, brave attempt at a smile.

"Hush now," he said. "Rest." Leaning over, he kissed her forehead, then rose, gesturing to Li to follow. Together, they moved to the fountain, where they washed blood from their hands with the icy water spilling from the basin, careful not to pollute the clean water in the basin. Then they drank deeply. They stood together quietly for a moment, reflecting on the tumultuous and seemingly endless day.

"Solasta, Da?" Li asked softly. "That's a word I've ne'er heard you use."

In response, Corvus inclined his head in fond memory.

"A bedtime story my gram used to tell me," he replied after a moment. "Of a great, glowin' castle on a hill, that shimmered in the night, as though the very stones were lit from within."

"Did she, now?" Li said, encouragingly. It was exceedingly rare for his father to speak of his childhood.

"Aye," Corvus continued thoughtfully. "'Twas said the castle was summoned by Ilian himself as a grand home for him and his lady. It was filled with all sorts of wondrous magic—faeries and music, wine cups that ne'er would empty, great beds as soft as clouds. For some reason, I could see it so clearly in my mind and that image filled my boyish imagination... A golden, shining, enchanted castle with towers and shimmerin' flags flying. During my later travels, I saw many wonders, like the great Alcazar of the Shah of Oubane, and the spires of Tivat. Breathtaking, Li. But nothing I ever saw, not even the Palace of the Silken Emperor himself, could e'er match the image in my mind of Solasta. She used the word to both describe it and name it, y'see. When I asked her what it meant, she said it was an ancient word that meant something like 'luminous.' She said one day it would be rebuilt by the Five to save us from the darkness."

Li's eyes drifted up to the shimmering fortress above them, a look of reverent wonder on his face.

"Solasta," he said quietly.

"It was lovely." Latrans' voice startled them both, and they turned to find the Fool standing behind them. "Iridescent, luminescent… sparkly, even." He smiled impishly at them. "But this is not Solasta. It is inspired by it, based on it… After all, imitation is the purest form of… something. What was it?"

"You were there?" Ligulf asked in awe.

"Oh, sure," Latrans replied with a shrug as he pushed between them and stepped up to the fountain, plunging his shaggy head directly into the basin, heedless of the cold. He stayed like that, head submerged in the water, bubbles streaming from his mouth, until finally Corvus grew concerned and grabbed his shoulders, hauling the Fool back. Latrans spluttered and sniffed, then shook his head violently much like a dog fresh from a swim. The act showered Corvus and Li with the chilly water. Both now dripping, they glared at Latrans, who smiled innocently, heedless of their sudden sodden discomfort. It was even more infuriating that his face and hair were now completely dry.

"Where were we?" he asked Li. "Oh, right, Solasta. It was a pretty place. A bit gaudy, if you ask me. Garish, overdone. You know, *ungepachket*. But don't tell Him I said that."

Another horrid screech tore through the night, setting Corvus' teeth on edge and severing one of the remaining towers, which again faded into a sparkling mist and blew away into the night.

"What is that foulness?" Corvus snarled, his vexation at their helplessness momentarily getting the better of him.

"Nasty magic… Bad, very bad," Latrans replied, shaking his head disapprovingly, then added under his breath, "Very naughty, Duff."

"How long will this enchantment hold?" Corvus demanded of the Fool.

"Enchantment?" Latrans looked up at him with mild confusion, before looking at the shimmering fortress as if he'd forgotten it was there. "Oh! You mean this? A little longer. Not long enough, I think. I imagine. I suppose." He blinked innocently, as though heedless of the danger that awaited them when it broke.

"What happens when it falls?" Li asked fearfully.

"Oh," Latrans responded lightly, "blood, death, mayhem, screaming… There's always so much screaming."

"Fool." Corvus gripped Latrans' shoulder, turning him from Li to face him. "You've wrought a right miracle here. More than one, truth be told."

"Oh, well," Latrans said, looking down, and with a bashful wave of his hand. He kicked at a small piece of rubble with his toe.

"But," Corvus continued, leaning in close to the Fool's face, his eyes endeavoring to pierce the veil of jocularity, "it will be for naught if we canna hold this temple 'til the dawn."

Like a waxen mask suddenly melting away, the madness receded from Latrans and his sparkling blue eyes were filled with an intense clarity.

"You are not alone, Corvus Corax," he said, an uncustomary gravity to his voice. "Use the tools at hand. Doors of opportunity exist, resources still untapped."

He turned his head and looked meaningfully from Mama to Piper to Dallin to Argant before returning his gaze to the Raven. He winced, struggling to maintain his clarity as his madness threatened to return.

"You. Are. Not. Alone," he repeated, then he reached down, scooped up his dog, and with a leap, threw himself feet first down the rough defile and into the shimmering wall, where his body dissolved into a puff of glowing mist, just like the bits of the castle that were destroyed by the lightning blasts. The dog's final bark echoed in the night.

Corvus and Li stared after him, mouths agape, watching the eerie puff of golden mist float away on the night breeze.

"It was the Saga of Bearn," Rhona said, stepping up between them, her hoarse voice startling them.

"Sorry?" Corvus said, turning to her, though he was still deeply unsettled by what had just occurred. "Bairn, you say?"

"No, not bairn," she corrected. "Bearn. A great hero of the olden times."

"Never heard of him." Corvus looked to his son to see if he had any knowledge of Bearn. Li shrugged and shook his head.

"Bearn was sent by King Frode to battle the Fire Draig of Pelton Moss," Rhona said, as if trying to stir an old memory. "Have you not heard the tale?"

"No, never," Corvus replied. "Though if there's one thing you three have shown me, it's that vital details may be hidden in sagas and songs." He nodded a silent acknowledgment toward Piper. "Tell me."

Another screech, like metal scraping on glass, sundered the night as another black scar was blasted into the castle front.

Corvus winced, then added, "But do it quickly."

"Right, then," she replied, then paused a moment to gather her memories before telling the tale.

The Fire Draig was a fearsome creature, ten times the size of a warhorse, with claws and teeth like razors, and it belched flame in great gouts. For months, it terrorized the countryside, and the people begged the king for relief. One by one, he lent his sword to his greatest knights to battle the beast, for it was said the Draig could only be slain with the king's own sword, "Lysbringer." But the creature slew them all, and each time the sword magically reappeared in the king's sheath, letting him know the latest knight had also failed.

Finally, Bearn, the youngest of the knights, said that he would go. The king was loath to send him forth as Bearn was his favorite. Some even whispered that he was the king's own son—a merry-begot boy, conceived at the Festival of Midsummer. But, in his desperation, the king relented. Before he left, Bearn said a tearful farewell to his great friend and shield-bearer, Rowan. Rowan was a mighty warrior, chosen by the king to protect and train the boy from childhood. Faithful as a hound, the man had been a constant presence in Bearn's life, ever at his side. But the knight knew he must face the monster alone, so he prepared to ride forth to find the beast and do battle.

When the time came, the king handed the young knight his royal sword, as he had each of the other knights. But this time, the king's eyes were filled with tears at the thought of losing Bearn, his favorite. The king embraced him and reluctantly said the same words he had said to each knight upon their departure. "Return victorious, or not at all."

With a nod to the king, and a small wave and nervous smile to his friend and comrade, Rowan, the young knight mounted his steed and rode forth.

All too soon, misadventure struck, and Bearn found himself crawling in desperation into the fens. His brave steed was slain, his armor rent, and in his hand he clutched the grip of the shattered sword Lysbringer. His grand hopes of glory dashed, all he could hope for as he clawed his way into the cold water was to somehow survive. The monster pursued Bearn to the edge of the fens but would not enter the swamp. The knight dragged himself through the mire, ever further from the beast, and finally pulled his body up onto a small reed-covered hillock before he collapsed. In exhaustion, he slept, hidden among the reeds as the creature howled its frustration, gouts of fire blasting up into the night sky.

Soon, a glimmering light awoke the young knight, and he blinked awake to find a glittering, glowing, golden castle seeming to float upon the swamp. Despite his injuries, he was drawn to it. He rose and staggered to the magical walls. Touching them, he found them warm and solid, despite their shimmering translucence. He searched them and in time found a large wooden door set into one of them. He pushed it open and entered.

There, he found a great banquet table in a grand hall, with endless trays of steaming food stacked upon it. But there were no guests. Every bench was empty, and the great velvet-lined thrones at either end of the table were likewise unoccupied. Haunting music from harps and flutes echoed throughout the hall, though he could see no musicians. Famished, he set to, though not before speaking his thanks aloud to his unseen hosts, and begging their leave, for Rowan had always taught him that to be a true knight was to be courteous in all things—and everyone knows you don't just eat the food of the otherworld, at least not without giving thanks.

The meat was roasted venison, wild boar, and beef so rare it melted in his mouth. It was unlike any he had ever tasted, delicately spiced and roasted to perfection, and swimming in melted butter. It was so delicious he ate like a starved man, the juices running down his chin. The blood-red wine tasted of blackberries and currants, and despite him refilling his cup several times, he remained clearheaded. The bread was soft and nutty, still warm from the oven, with slabs of honeyed butter melting upon it. Truth be told, he had never eaten food so fair and knew this was a rare gift. The meal restored his health and strength and filled him with a vitality unlike any he had known. A great silver cup, adorned with jewels and intricate carvings was set by the head of the table, clearly the cup of a monarch. But Bearn knew better than to drink from a king's cup unbidden, and he left it untouched, though the swirling, cloudy mead within beckoned with an enticing aroma of honey and wildflowers.

Having eaten his fill, he rose from the table, again speaking his thanks aloud to his unseen and unknown hosts. He then began to rove about the castle, exploring. Many rooms he discovered, each filled with treasures unknown. Rare silks, sparkling diadems, golden jewelry cascading from chests overflowing with riches. But he touched nothing, took nothing, merely gazing into each chamber in wonder at the wealth. Then, speaking aloud, he would say, "By your leave," and close each door carefully.

In time, he stumbled upon a long corridor, its entrance draped in a rich velvet that shimmered, its color defying description. There were a series of three doors in the hallway. Moving to the first, he found an inscription on the lintel. "Glory Past" it said. He eased it open to discover a great room, filled with men in armor—the first people he had seen in the castle. He greeted them cautiously, and when they turned to him, he realized that he recognized them all. Here were gathered all the knights slain by the Draig, their armor and weapons refreshed and polished, their cheeks flush with life. He couldn't understand how it was that they lived, but he rejoiced in it, greeting each man with a warm embrace. He told them of his quest, and the strange, enchanted palace. With visages grim and determined, each man swore to follow him and aid in his battle with the monster. Each of them, himself included, had failed individually against the beast. But perhaps, working together, they might overcome it.

Moving on, he stepped to the next door in the corridor. On the lintel of this one was carved "Glory Present." Opening the door, he found but one man sitting alone with his back to the door, in a room adorned with weaponry and armor. Bearn greeted the unknown man, who turned upon hearing his voice. It was Rowan, his stalwart shield man and greatest friend. The two greeted each other with tears and words of wonder at how this had come to pass. But Bearn knew that his friend was meant to join him in this fight.

Leaving Rowan to don armor and gather weapons, Bearn moved to the last door in the hallway, on the lintel of which was carved "Glory To Come." Opening it, he found an empty room, in which stood but a grand looking glass, taller than a man, in a carved golden frame. Stepping up to the mirror, he gazed upon his own image, and there he beheld himself not as he stood then, but some years forward—grey in his beard, a royal circlet upon his brow, jewels on his fingers, a rich velvet cape trimmed in golden lace that reached the floor behind him, a restored Lysbringer at his side. This was an image of him as king. But not like the humble and rough-hewn monarch he had left behind. No, this was a regal image of the king of a prosperous land. He stared at the mirror in wonder for a moment, and then, without warning, the reflection moved of its own accord, drawing Lysbringer from its jeweled scabbard. King Bearn's arm reached forward from the mirror, impossibly handing young Bearn the restored royal sword. In awe, he accepted the weapon, and with that, the image of the king faded away, leaving but the reflection of the young knight staring at the shining and bejeweled sword in his fist.

Understanding his purpose now, the young knight returned to the room with Rowan, donned fresh armor, then he gathered his comrades together in the great hall, where the knights ate their fill. Each then spoke his thanks aloud, at Bearn's urging, and though many eyed the king's cup, wanting to drink from it, Bearn would not allow it.

Together, the company left the enchanted palace. They strode forth through the fens and did battle with the fearsome beast. Many of the knights were slain anew. Rowan, in a selfless act of bravery, leapt in front of Bearn, shielding him from a merciless gout of flame. The loyal man suffered grievously, spurring Bearn to rush forward and strike the Draig a mortal blow with Lysbringer, finally putting an end to the terror.

"The saga goes on," Rhona added, having finished her tale, "as sagas do. The monster slain, the knights who had passed drifted into mist, leaving only Bearn and the wounded Rowan to make their way back home. He returns to find the old king has died of worry, and the people unanimously select him to be their new monarch. He rules for many years to come, becoming a wise and gracious king."

Corvus' brow creased as he pondered the meaning of the tale, trying to tease out anything that might be of strategic value. There were still some three hours until dawn, and the rate of collapse of the fortress indicated it wouldn't last that long.

"Da, look," Li said softly, indicating the rear wall of the fortress, near Argant's fire. Following his son's gaze, Corvus could see the shimmering outline of a door forming. Looking along the length of the wall, he realized there were actually three doors coming into focus, each of a different design. The one nearest the fire had a pointed arch, in the style of Aslene architecture. The door in the middle had stones of alternating colors set all along its perimeter, like the great castles he had seen in Lachland or Sudland. The third door was more rough-hewn and looked familiar to him, though he couldn't place it.

Mama stirred from her rest, seeming to sense something was happening. She rose from her place by the fire, a look of wonder in her eyes as she approached the Aslene-style door, her hand raised, trying to understand the magic at play.

"'You are not alone,' he said." Corvus repeated the Fool's words with quiet awe then looked meaningfully to his son just as another horrid screech sounded behind them, tearing a small hole in the fortification. The sounds of the ravenous warriors on the other side suddenly flooded the temple. It wouldn't be long now until the fortress was breached.

"Should we try the doors?" Li asked.

"Aye, lad," Corvus responded grimly. "That we should."

Chapter 22

"I bow and accept your words as punishment from the gods, but believe me, I do not forgive."

—*"The Tragedy of Madame Consodine," Act IV, Sc. 7*

The night before the Autumn Equinox
Wetheral Castle, Lachland

Pietr

The doorway at the far end of the dungeon corridor creaked open, the jangle of keys echoing down the empty hallway. Pietr was instantly awake, sitting up on the edge of his cot. He knew what this was. He'd been waiting for it. No one came down here except the guard that brought him food—if you could call it that—and occasionally removed his slops. When his cousin, Darienne, had sentenced him to this cell, he had doubted her sincerity. Surely she did not mean to let him live, after what he'd done? A relative of the Queen who had plotted against her? Wisdom and prudence suggested that she see to it that he never leave this cell alive. Every breath he drew was a potential rebellion waiting to happen. Of course, he understood that she couldn't be seen to start her reign in blood—a public show of mercy to assuage the nobles, then a knife in the dark.

He was surprised to hear the swish of a woman's skirts and the soft scrape of a slippered foot. It sounded completely out of place in the dark of night. He stood up. *So, she's coming to face me herself instead of sending her assassin alone? She's got stones, I'll give her that.*

Given the pattern of the guard rotations, he knew that no one should be in these corridors until the dawn bell, and that was hours away. Then, he heard the telltale sound of a man's boots accompanying the woman, the sharp ting of spurs suggesting the man was a cavalryman—perhaps a Lake Jack. He prepared himself for a fight as the woman's footsteps paused outside his cell. The man's boots came to a halt a moment later, and keys sounded in the lock. With a squeal, the door opened inward and he beheld the silhouette of a slender woman in a lady's gown and a large, broad-shouldered form behind her.

"Viscount," the woman said, in a tremulous voice.

"Who are you?" Pietr replied, his eyes slowly adjusting to the light. He thought he recognized the blonde woman's face, but at first he was unable to place her. Then, like a thunderclap, he remembered. She was the woman that Ormond had abducted and tortured—*at his behest*. A lump of dread dropped into his stomach and he leaned back against the stone wall, striving to distance himself as far as possible from the door.

"What do you want?" he demanded, panic beginning to vibrate in his chest.

She stepped into the cell, followed by the hulking and proudly mustachioed man behind her. Pietr's eyes scanned both their faces frantically. *This is not good! Not good at all!*

"Why are you here in the dead of night?" he asked, his voice rising in fright, the flutter in his chest moving up to his throat.

The woman stepped aside to allow the large man forward. With two powerful strides he crossed the cell and grabbed Pietr roughly. With almost no effort, he hoisted the viscount to his feet and slammed him against the wall. Stars exploded in his vision as his head bounced off the stone. The large man leaned closed to

Pietr's face and scowled pure contempt at him before once more slamming him against the wall. Pietr cried out as something in his shoulder cracked and blood streamed down the side of his head.

"What do you want?" he cried in frustration.

The man said nothing, but simply hoisted the viscount with one burly arm and buried the other fist in Pietr's stomach. Air exploded from him as the man released him. He collapsed in a fetal position on the floor, gasping like a newly caught fish.

The man began to reach for him again, when the woman spoke. "Jules, wait."

She stepped toward Pietr and knelt down beside him. She had a fresh, lightly perfumed scent. *Quite nice,* he thought absurdly. He lay there still gasping and utterly terrified as she carefully removed the glove on her left hand. Up to that moment, he hadn't noticed that she was wearing gloves.

"You did this to me," she said, holding her disfigured hand before his face. "This, and so much more."

"I… I didn't," he stammered before a powerful kick to his stomach set him back to gasping desperately for air.

"Oh, but you did," she said. "I was starved for weeks, fed only a thin broth every other day and a small heel of stale bread. The guards beat me and… and groped me like a common whore."

This comment evoked a growl from Jules, who looked like he would surge forward despite the woman's request holding him back.

"Then," she continued, "she ordered them to take my finger, and when I cried for mercy, they beat me. Then… they laughed." This last was said with a dark, vengeful tone, a muscle in her cheek twitching uncontrollably. "The woman I was—dutiful, polite, gentle—died in that cell, Viscount. You destroyed so much with your callous scheming. But now…" She paused to rise from her crouch before continuing. "*You* are alone here in *this* cell. No one will hear you scream, and Jules and I plan to become regular visitors. We'll be fast friends, you and I, and I look forward to hearing you weep and cry for mercy."

Loeiza

An hour or so later, she stood in the courtyard, the slivered moon low over the mountains. A frosty breeze blew up, causing her eyes to tear. She wiped them with a gloved hand and noted that the glove came away with blood on it. She wiped her face with the other hand and found a few small smears of blood on that one too.

Oh dear, she thought. *I'll have to tidy up before Zach wakes.*

She heard the door to the bailey close, and Jules' booted steps descending the few stairs to stand behind her.

"All locked back up?" she asked.

"Tight as a drum," he said softly, his deep voice rumbling as he stood close, his mouth nuzzling her hair. She closed her eyes and leaned back against him, reveling for just a moment in his solidity. *Dear Jules. Safe Jules. My rescuer. My protector.* He had been there that night at the hunting lodge when she'd been rescued, the world a dark swirl of pain, fever, and dizziness from hunger and infection. When the door had burst open, she had at first believed it to be the knights returning to inflict some new torment upon her, but instead of the cruelty in their eyes, she looked into the compassionate and protective eyes of this bear of a man. Horrified at what had been done to her, he'd scooped her up in his arms, carrying her outside. Not waiting for orders, he had ridden all the way back to Wetheral with her sharing his mount, his strong arm clutched about her protectively. Once there, he had dismounted behind her, then gently lowered her once more into his arms, carrying her into the castle and—after conferring briefly with the brigadier—he had taken her to the chamber of Carmine Lavalle, one of the midwives. Only when he saw that she was in safe, caring hands did he finally release his grip on her, promising to return in a few hours, once she'd had a chance to bathe, eat, and sleep.

Another frosty breeze swirled past, stealing her breath. She shivered, and Jules' strong arms wrapped around her protectively. Part of her felt horribly guilty taking such comfort in another man's arms. Zach had struggled so mightily with the impossible dilemma they had given him, and she loved Zach, she did. But Jules had entered the cellar in which she had been tortured, the cellar in which they had stripped away her former life, changing her forever. He had rescued her, taking her from that hellish torment. He had protected her. Yes, her clear mind—the daytime part of her—loved and needed Zach. She needed the normalcy, the safe, public face. But her damaged mind—the nighttime part of her—*needed* Jules, and tonight they had together crossed a boundary. A terrifying and exhilarating boundary in her soul. She trembled at the thought of what they had done to Pietr, and what they had promised to continue to do. A part of her mind recoiled at the blood, pain, and terror, while another part, perhaps the greater part, swelled with newfound agency. As though she finally were taking charge of her life. no more would she be a victim. No more would others, even dear Zach, control or direct her. She would bathe in the viscount's blood and tears if it meant reclaiming herself—her soul. And Zach? She sighed and shook her head regretfully. Poor, kind Zach. Perhaps once she had exorcized the demons that her ordeal had birthed in her heart, she could find her way back to him and be, truly, his wife again.

Jules squeezed her tightly, his breath warm and inviting against her ear.

Perhaps. She wanted that to be true. But for now, she *needed* Jules, and to be perfectly honest, she *needed* to visit the viscount's cell again… and again.

Chapter 23

Beware the bargains made in the shadows, for regardless of the gain, the price will always be too steep.

—Anonymous

The night of the Autumn Equinox
Hall of Convening, Atalaya de Locus, Cantabria

Bishop Galea

For the fifth time in fifteen minutes, Ecclesiarch Salucia washed his hands, scrubbing them as if they were soiled with filth, though no stains were evident. He carefully dried them once again on the soft white linen towel offered by Bishop Galea.

"The creature in the cell is missing, you say?" he demanded. "How?"

"How did he escape, you mean?" Galea clarified.

"Yes, dammit!" Salucia snapped irritably. "Or was he abducted? What do we know?"

"Only that the heretic's cell was empty this morning when the servant arrived with his breakfast. There was no sign of a breach, nor did the guards hear or see anything amiss." Galea blinked and looked down to hide a silent slithering movement he suddenly felt behind his right eye, crossing toward his left. He had no idea if it was perceptible to others, but examining the floor before his feet seemed a wise choice nonetheless.

Stop moving around! he scolded the creature silently. *You risk discovery.*

I'm hungry, Geminus replied. *It has been long since I have fed.*

Galea suppressed a shiver as he understood somehow that the shaman spirit now abiding within him was not referring to normal food and drink, but something more sanguinary.

Not now! the bishop snapped inwardly. *After this meeting we'll discuss… things.*

I'm HUNGRY, Galea!

The bishop clenched his eyes shut and rubbed his brow with a trembling hand.

You will feed me, or I will find another.

NO! He was surprised by the intensity of his own response. But for some reason the thought of Geminus leaving him was terrifying. Why?

A soft chuckle vibrated along the back of his skull. *You have so much to learn.*

"Gone," Salucia continued, oblivious to Galea's soft gasp as the Ecclesiarch's voice pulled him from his distraction. "And four of his brethren have now fallen?"

"That we are aware of, Your Grace," the bishop replied with an outward calm he didn't feel. "With the shaman now absent, we no longer have information on the remaining two."

"We have to tell the Pentatarch." The ecclesiarch's voice nearly broke at the thought. It was well known that Vella had a notoriously sharp temper and a very low tolerance for failure. While each of the Watchtowers had specific areas of responsibility within the Church's structure, Salucia's Locus Watchtower was responsible for governance and the security of their ecclesiastical campus. As the Ecclesiarch of Locus Watchtower, the blame for any lapse in security — like a strategically important prisoner escaping — would ultimately fall on him. To have allowed such a critical asset to escape would be an unforgivable oversight. Since the time of Vella's ascension to

Pentatarch, no fewer than eight archbishops and two ecclesiarchs had "disappeared" suspiciously. It was whispered in the blind corridors that each had committed some grievous error or had failed Vella in some unforgivable way. No one dared search the dungeons beneath the palace to find out the truth. The bishop waited quietly some moments for Salucia's slow mind to grasp the gravity of the situation.

"Perhaps," Galea offered thoughtfully, "a time of retirement is near."

"What do you mean?" Salucia's eyes narrowed at the bishop, his cheek twitching slightly.

"There is a fast ship with a black-striped sail anchored in the harbor."

"A ship? What…?"

"I came to you as a courtesy, to inform you before I relate this terrible news to my master," Galea said with a generous gap-toothed smile.

"Yes?" The ecclesiarch's mind slowly came to grasp the enormity of the situation and the bishop's words.

"This conversation is not so that we might present the bad tidings to him together." The bishop shook his head with a rueful smile. "But, instead, to give you—as I have heard it called in the pits—a head start."

A self-satisfied smirk danced across Galea's lips as he exited the ecclesiarch's tower and crossed the nighttime cobbled cuadrado, circling the enormous marble fountain in the center that depicted the vengeful Father fighting the three demons, Amentia, Insipientia, and Stultitia—the three faces of ignorance. He hugged the fountain's edge so closely that flecks of water from it dotted the side of his face and threatened to moisten his robes to an unacceptable degree. But he didn't care. Salucia was gone. A light chuckle escaped his lips at the thought.

Why does the removal of this one please you? Geminus asked curiously. *I had thought your goal was to remove the Pentatarch.*

Oh, it is, ultimately, the bishop replied, finding a rare buoyancy in his stride. *But by convincing Salucia to run, the blame for your disappearance will conveniently fall on him, and the Pentatarch will never suspect that I had anything to do with it.*

But why arrange the ship for his escape? the shaman asked.

Oh, rest assured, Galea told him, smiling to himself, *he will never set foot on that ship.*

You will tell the Pentatarch of his intended flight? Duplicitous.

Galea grinned as he turned down the Avenida del Ciprés toward the Pentatarch's palace, the towering cypress trees creating a dark shadowed colonnade against the stars. *Duplicitous, yes.*

And… the vacancy he leaves? Geminus asked.

Creates chaos, and chaos brings unknown opportunity.

I'm confused, the shaman said. *The webs of this intrigue are so foreign to me.*

As you said to me, "You have so much to learn."

Apparently so, Geminus replied. Galea once more felt the movement behind his eyes. *I'm hungry. You promised.*

Quite so, the bishop replied calmly. *It's just up ahead.*

The shaman's mind vibrated with anticipation.

Farric

The field marshal slipped inconspicuously across the cuadrado and past the fountain, pulling the hood of the academic robe forward until his face disappeared into its shadowed folds. He smiled a predator's grin. His assassins had performed brilliantly against the Pentatarch and his Knights. No one had seen or heard them enter, and once he had left, they had removed themselves with equal stealth. He had recruited these killers—known through legend as the Nizari—years before, from the shadowed mountains of the Free Territories, and they had proven their worth again and again. Wrapped in dark robes, their faces obscured, their stealth was unparalleled, they were skilled with a dizzying assortment of deadly weapons, and they were utterly loyal, just so long as he continued sending funds each month to their clan chief in his remote mountain monastery. And the cost was truly excessive.

Over the years, he had argued with his Executive Officer, his Sergeant of the Exchequer and his council over the need to pay the exorbitant sums to secure the services of the assassins. There were times when he feared that the monthly fee would beggar the Blades of Sebastian, and on several occasions it nearly had. But time and again, when all other methods of persuasion or negotiation had failed, his Nizari would go in silently and solve whatever problem he was dealing with, leaving only mysterious death in their wake — and always only one witness, usually a child or some wizened elder, left to spout what seemed like fantastical nonsense about shadows, blood, and death. Indeed, such was the mystique that had grown around them that often, merely letting slip a hint that perhaps the rumors of the Nizari working for him were true was enough to persuade recalcitrant warlords or local governors to submit.

He smiled to himself once more as he descended the stone stairs behind the tomb of a forgotten Cantabrian war hero from ages past. He paused as he lifted a hand toward the hidden lever in the stonework. Something was wrong. There was a scent in the air. Blood. He lifted his left foot, feeling stickiness beneath his boot. In an instant, his tomahawk was in his right hand and his long knife in his left. He leaned lightly against the hidden portal and it swung wide on well-oiled hinges to reveal a long, familiar corridor, though its lanterns were all extinguished. *It was unlatched.* The portal was never unlatched. There was another smell — burnt flesh — lingering in the air. A stone of dread dropped into his stomach.

A raven croaked from the top of the stairs behind him. He spun, expecting an attack, only to find the raven perched on the railing looking down at him. Somehow he was certain it was the same bird that had come to his chambers the night of the raid. Its intelligent eyes peered at him knowingly.

He was about to speak to it when a figure stepped out from behind the plinth of the monument to join the raven looking down at him. He squinted against the gloom and could just discern that it was the scribe, Briguglio.

"Scribe?" he asked softly.

"Farric," came the reply as the man began to descend the stairs.

The field marshal tightened his grip on his weapons and readied his stance.

"You have nothing to fear from me," the scribe said with a light wave of his hand. "Unless you fear the truth." The raven croaked again and fluttered down into the stairwell, alighting on the railing some two strides from the field marshal.

"You sent the raven to warn me the night of the raid," he said, gesturing at the bird with his knife.

"You misconstrue our relationship," the scribe said, indicating the raven and himself. "My friend here does not work for me… Quite the contrary."

"What do you mean?" the field marshal demanded, confused.

"Another time," the scribe responded as he reached the bottom stair and peered down the open corridor. "I suspect that we have horrors to discover."

"What happened here?" Farric asked, a note of panic creeping into his voice.

"In a word — evil."

Farric's heart sank at the answer, then he wheeled about, his knife suddenly at the scribe's throat.

"This place was secret," he hissed. "How do you know of it?"

Unfazed by the threat of the blade, the scribe answered calmly, "We have known for some time of your Nizari and their secret lair."

"We meaning who?" He pressed the knife forward with immediate menace. "What have you done?"

"What we will find within are not the actions of the Ludicra," the scribe replied with remarkable equanimity. "I am not your enemy, Farric. You are in grave danger. I have come to help you escape. But first" — the scribe gestured toward the corridor — "we must see what is within."

Farric stared at the shadowed figure of the other man a moment longer, trying to discern the truth of what he said. Then, startled by another harsh croak of the raven, he turned to once more face the darkened passageway. There was a flare of light from behind him as he stepped inside and he spun to find that Briguglio had relit one of the lanterns and was holding it aloft. As Farric's eyes adjusted to the light, he could see the entirety of the marble floor was painted in blood, seemingly rivers of it.

"What in the seven depths?!" He swore softly and continued forward, his body trembling with battle readiness and an inchoate terror.

His every step stuck to and slipped on the gory floor until he reached the end of the hallway. He paused near the archway on his left and waited for the scribe's lantern to draw near and illuminate the chamber within.

As it did, he stared in horrified awe at the sight before him. Bodies and furniture lay broken and strewn about. Knives, axes, and throwing stars stuck out from every surface — walls, doors, cupboards, the clock, the paintings. It looked for all the world as though the Nizari had fallen upon one another in a fit of madness of some kind. Nearest the entrance lay Auraq, one of the leaders of the squad, his throat nearly severed by one of their silver garrotes. Some few feet away, Yureed, the strongest of them, was pinned to the wall with a spear. Farric began moving around the chamber in horrified fascination. Here was a decapitated man draped over the back of a couch, his turbaned head several feet away on the floor. There was another slumped against a wooden pillar, several daggers buried in his torso.

With every step, the stench of burnt flesh grew stronger, becoming a cloying itch in the back of Farric's throat. As he rounded another divan, he found the source of the reek. There, piled atop one another, were some six or seven bodies — all Nizari by the look of their clothes, though their faces were utterly unrecognizable. The skin was a mixture of horrific burns and still-oozing blood blisters. Their eyes had melted from their heads and a rank black smoke seeped from their open mouths, which were frozen in a rictus of agony.

"What devilry is this?" Farric whispered, aghast.

"An appropriate choice of words, my friend," Briguglio said softly.

Just then the raven flew into the chamber, croaking urgently.

"They return!" the scribe said, pointing to a doorway at the rear of the chamber. "We must hide."

"I'll not hide," Farric replied, hefting his tomahawk in readiness. The raven croaked twice more, flapping its wings in agitation.

"Farric," Briguglio urged, moving toward the door, "this is the work of demons! Fel's own creatures. You are mortal and cannot stand against them. We must hide and wait for them to leave."

"We have already given ourselves away," he said with a wry look, pointing at the floor by their feet. Their bloody footprints were obvious and would lead whoever was coming directly after them.

Briguglio blanched at the sight, his hand beginning to tremble.

"Follow me," the field marshal ordered curtly, and ran through the doorway into a blood-splashed corridor that zigged and zagged its way further back into the windowless structure, past a kitchen, several sleeping chambers, and a tiled bathing suite in which were heaped more bodies, until they finally came to a small, circular reading room with no exit.

"We're trapped," Briguglio gasped, his face white and sweaty.

"Not quite," Farric replied, pulling the scribe onto an ornate round carpet in the middle of the room. "Remember, these were the chambers of assassins. Warriors who would never allow themselves to be cornered without an exit."

The raven flew into the small chamber and perched on the scribe's shoulder without a croak, its uncustomary silence more worrisome than its obvious urgency. They could now hear footsteps approaching in the gallery beyond, accompanied by a man's voice, humming. The voice was familiar, though Farric couldn't place it.

"I hope you can swim," was all Farric said before he reached into a nearby bookshelf and triggered a hidden lever. A trapdoor beneath the circular carpet suddenly opened and they plunged into darkness.

Briguglio

"Swim?" he said as the floor beneath him opened and he fell into the dark. But what came out ended in a scream, the raven clutching his shoulder and flapping against the fall. The shock of cold water silenced him and he lost any sense of up or down. He struggled in the inky blackness to find the surface. He was no swimmer. He was no fighter. In fact, he regularly wondered how he, of all people, had been selected for this mission. Suddenly, his flailing arms broke the surface, followed quickly by his gaping mouth as he gasped for breath. The water, the air, all was pitch black — were it not for his head being above the surface, he would have no sense of direction whatsoever. But he could feel movement. The water was moving, carrying him along... somewhere.

"Farric?" he called out.

"Quiet, you fool!" the field marshal hissed from nearby. A moment later, he was heartened to feel a strong hand grasp his robe as the two men floated along with the current toward an ominous roaring.

"What's that?" Briguglio asked.

"Things are about to get interesting," the field marshal replied, pulling the scribe even closer. The current quickened, as though the chamber in which they floated had begun to narrow toward a roaring exit.

"Oh, this can't be good." The scribe tried in vain to swim against the current.

"Relax, and enjoy the ride," Farric admonished, and suddenly they were in a tunnel of some sort, the water moving at breakneck speed as they sluiced through the blackness, bumping and banging their way from stone wall to stone wall, all of which had been worn smooth by the water's journey over untold years. They careened, pell mell, carried along by the rushing current, until up and down had no meaning other than the constant awareness that they were falling ever faster down this course.

Moments later, the blackness became starlight as they turned a corner and once more experienced the nauseating feeling of freefall. They were spat out from a tunnel mouth, like bitter morsels disgorged by some giant, and fell over a waterfall toward the ocean surface some fifty feet below.

"Oh, really?" the scribe demanded of the universe as he began his plummet.

Daylight found Briguglio lying face down in the sand, the waves of the surf toying with his feet like a playful dog wanting her master to awaken. A raven's croak nearby, and he began trying to blink his encrusted eyes clear to see his surroundings.

"You live." Farric's laconic voice came from nearby. "Good. You have much to explain."

Briguglio smacked his parched lips and ran a thick tongue over his teeth, spitting out sand and pushing himself up to sit and survey their surroundings. They were on the narrow beach of a stony, cliff-faced bay. The crystal-clear waters reflected the sun mercilessly. Shading his eyes, he glanced at his companion.

"And to think," he croaked, his voice not unlike that of the raven, "I came to rescue you."

"Rescue?" Farric snapped. "From what? What was that thing up there? What slaughtered my Nizari?"

"That," Briguglio began slowly as he arched his back and stretched his limbs, grimacing at the soreness, "I believe, was the missing Angor Shaman."

"The creature from the cell?" Farric asked, and Briguglio only nodded. "But how could it possibly have…?"

"They have rare, arcane gifts, foul and…" He spat sand from his teeth before finishing, "Bloody."

"I don't care how arcane the gift," Farric replied acerbically, "nothing could dispatch my Nizari so completely. Their talents are legendary."

"We believe the shaman in question has the ability to possess the mind," Briguglio said as he removed his robe and began ringing the water from it. "To the Nizari, it would be as if one of their own had turned on them. Based on what I saw back there, it would seem the shaman can inhabit more than one mind at a time."

"How do you know about all this?" Farric asked. "And why didn't you warn me?"

"I told you," the scribe replied, holding up a hand, "I am a member of the Ludicra Veritas, we… *know* things."

"Who do you mean by "we"?" demanded Farric, his temper fraying.

"The society," Briguglio replied weakly. He was having trouble forming coherent thoughts, and given the events of the past few hours, did not feel up to an interrogation. Perhaps sensing his weakness, the field marshal threw up his hands in frustration, his eyes searching the sand before him for answers.

"I'll return to my barracks and gather my men," he began, but paused as the scribe raised his hand and shook his head mutely. "What?"

"You will never return to your barracks, field marshal," Briguglio said softly. "This was a coup, planned and organized behind your back. Your Executive Officer—Colonel Franco, if I'm not mistaken—colluded with Bishop Galea to bring this about. It was the backup plan, should the Pentatarch's effort to arrest and convict you fail."

"Franco?" Farric said, a wounded horror in his eyes. "But I made him what he is. I trained him. I brought him up."

"Betrayal is never easy," the scribe replied, tilting his head to the side and tapping it to get the water out of his ear. "But I assure you, you have no future with the Blades of Sebastian. Indeed, you have no future in Cantabria."

The raven croaked again and hopped from one ocean-sculpted boulder to another, all the while staring at Farric, who looked from the sodden scribe to the bird and back again, seeming utterly adrift.

"Where shall I go?" he muttered. "What shall I do?"

The raven croaked loudly once more, then hopped onto another rock, larger than the last. From here, the bird peered down intently at the fallen commander, an intensity in its black eyes.

"You are needed, Farric," the scribe said, looking at the field marshal with a piercing gaze. "You are very much needed."

Chapter 24

The ionnsaigh board is filled with pieces. Stones of two colors—white and black. To the unschooled eye, the game can look like a chaotic mix with no discernible pattern. But to the players, all the world is on that board.

—"Ionnsaigh, the Master's Game"
by Matron Edith LePugh

The night of the Autumn Equinox
Wetheral Castle, Lachland

Darienne

She stayed in the garden, once more seated on the cold bench, mulling over the words of her unexpected visitors, until the chill became too much. Trembling from both the encounters and the cold, she rose to head back in. Jacques quickly retrieved his cloak from the bench, and wrapped it about her shoulders, despite her weak protest. She nodded her thanks to him, then walked carefully over the frosted grass back to the door to the servants' wing. Knowing that her agitated mind would find no rest, she turned her steps toward the kitchen, rather than return immediately to her chambers. The room was redolent with the smells of fresh baked breads and pastries and the great ovens produced a sweltering heat, which she was grateful for, chilled as she was. The three startled kitchen attendants on night duty stopped their work kneading the pastry dough and bobbed in frantic curtsies, their floured faces and arms resembling the frosted statuary in the garden. Two of them then rushed to prepare food and drink for the Queen, while the third urgently wiped off the flour that dusted the servants' table. Darienne had interrupted the making of the breakfast loaves and pastries. *Well, I won't stay long,* she thought. *Just long enough to break this chill.*

Jacques pulled the bench out for her and, once she was seated at the humble table, moved to position himself between the doorway and the welcome warmth of the blazing hearth. Within a few moments, a steaming mug of mulled wine was set before her, along with a silver pot filled with more, vapor slipping from its spigot. As the wine was still too hot to drink, she clutched the mug with numbed hands and deeply inhaled its tart, heady aroma, scents of cinnamon, nutmeg, and cloves swirling about her. One of the cooks set down a platter with five of the crisp shortbread biscuits that she had loved since childhood. Her mouth instantly watered, and she was suddenly aware of how hungry she was. Just as she was reaching for one, another hand slipped in front of hers and stole it away. She looked up in alarm to find Latrans straddling the bench beside her, facing her, and chewing noisily. His elbow was on the table and his head rested on his fist, while his other hand held the stolen, now half-eaten biscuit.

"Fool!" she exclaimed. "Oh, you gave me a start."

She heard Jacques stir and partially draw his sword in alarm. She raised a placating hand to him. With a crisp click, the sword snapped back into its sheath, though Jacques was clearly disturbed by Latrans' presence.

"That's why I'm here," the Fool replied, still chewing, and smacking his lips loudly in appreciation. "To give you a start."

Sensing from his tone that the strangeness of this night was somehow not over, Darienne took a sip of the wine and instantly regretted it, scalding her lips and tongue.

"What do you mean?" she asked with a wince.

"Well… you've had a big night," he said knowingly. "Visitors in the garden." His eyebrows waggled conspiratorially.

"How do you…?" She faltered, not entirely sure how to describe what had happened, nor question how the Fool was aware of it.

"Yes, indeed, a big night. And it's only going to get bigger," he said with a dismissive shake of his head, then dunked his shortbread in Darienne's wine and popped it into his mouth.

"Fool!" she exclaimed, shocked at his forwardness, yet unable to repress a grin. Despite her newfound status, a part of her would forever be the uncouth Darienne that took joy in breaking the stilted expectations and behaviors at court. She found his impertinence refreshing and a welcome reminder of her own social daring.

Latrans' face slowly registered distaste, as he smacked his lips in disgust. "Never dunk shortbread in wine," he said, sitting up and shaking his head. "Tea? Absolutely. Warm milk? Grand. Wine? Not so much." He smacked his lips again.

A small yip sounded from behind him, and he turned and pulled his dog onto his lap, where it immediately began sniffing along the edge of the table for food or crumbs. Without asking, the Fool plucked up another biscuit and set it in front of the dog, who promptly and noisily devoured it. Not sure where this was going, Darienne resignedly slid the plate of biscuits closer to Latrans.

"Please, help yourself," she said, taking a more careful sip of her wine.

"Oh, I couldn't," he replied with a theatrical refusal, his hand over his heart. "Those are for you… Oh, well, if you insist." He helped himself to another biscuit, though not without casting baleful looks at the kitchen staff and muttering under his breath. "I mean, who would serve shortbread with hot wine? Who would *do* that?"

"Is there something you wanted to tell me, Fool?" Darienne asked, attempting to pull Latrans' fleeting focus back to her.

"Yes, there is!" he said with sudden urgency, his head snapping back toward her. She waited for him to continue, but he just stared at her.

"And that is…?" she prompted after an awkward pause.

"What? Oh, right," he replied, with a flourish of his hand that finished with him holding up two fingers. "Two things… both very important. Very, very important." He emphasized his words by shaking his two fingers each time he said the word "very."

"Very well," she said. "And… what are they?"

"First," he said, dividing the rest of the shortbread and giving half to his dog before popping the remainder in his own mouth, "you should never, ever serve shortbread with hot wine. Never. And you should seriously examine your hiring practices if your servants do that." He shot another venomous glance in the direction of the short, round cook, who rolled her eyes and stifled a giggle at his animated behavior.

"I'll take that under advisement," Darienne replied, turning her attention back to her wine and hoping the Fool would soon get to his point.

"And second…" There was a decided shift in his tone that caused her to look back at him. All sense of levity had left him, and he stared at her with a burning clarity in his eyes. "Tonight is the night that much will be decided and discovered." His voice was grim and serious.

"So I've been told," she answered slowly, recalling the words of the otherworldly visitor in the garden. *Could it actually have been Manu herself?*

"Another visitor will be here shortly," he continued, his brow furrowing with the effort of maintaining his focus. "You, Maddie, and Kaiso *must* go with him."

"What? Who? Go with him where? It's the middle of the night!"

The Fool's face contorted as he struggled for clarity. "Be… dressed… for action." With a shake of his head, all intensity disappeared from his gaze, and he looked down at his dog. "Did you say something?" The beast yipped an answer and rose to lick his face eagerly.

"What do you mean, Fool?" she pressed, setting down her mug and turning to him. "A visitor?"

"A visitor?" Latrans echoed, looking about. "At this hour? Preposterous!"

"But you just said…"

"I said," the Fool replied, standing and dusting the shortbread crumbs from his motley vest and exposed chest, "that one should never, ever serve shortbread with mulled wine!" His voice rose in indignation and his eyes narrowed at the plump cook, who stuck her tongue out at him in response. He returned the gesture petulantly.

"But…" Darienne began, but before she could say more, Latrans turned and cartwheeled away toward the door, his dog yipping and following him on its hind legs. When he reached Jacques at the door, he tapped him on the chest and pointed accusingly at the giggling cook.

"Watch that one," he said, before slipping out.

Jacques looked at Darienne with a confused, almost helpless look.

"Never mind, Jacques," she said, forestalling his questions. "Perhaps you would be so good as to wake Maddie and Captain Kaiso and have them meet me in my chambers, dressed for expedition, at once."

"Of course, Majesty," the perplexed guard replied with a nod, and exited.

She then spoke to the cooks and requested a tray of food be sent to her chambers. "Enough for three of us," she started, then paused, remembering that Latrans had said a visitor would be coming. "Best make that service for four."

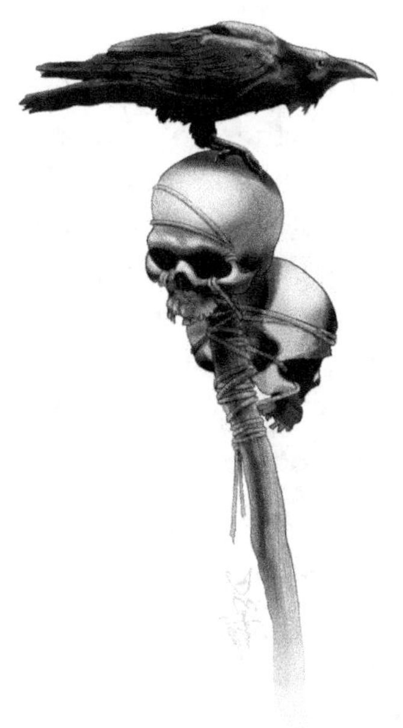

Chapter 25

"...and from the midst of the swirling shadows, a strange lightning flashed, all black, as though conjured from some nightmare. Instead of thunder, the report of the bolts sounded more like the tormented screech of some great creature. As though the wrongness of these bolts did offend the very air."

—*Signor Antonio Delacruz, Mayor of Vipazia, Excerpt from testimony before the Emperor Horatius II*

*The night of the Autumn Equinox
The Tor, Green Mount*

Sangine

The shaman crouched, panting, behind the rise in the trail and stared at his blistered arm in horror. Each time he summoned the black lightning from the blood gem, he paid an agonizing price. The energy that coursed through his body with each bolt was overwhelming and left him gasping. Excruciating blisters appeared along his arm, neck, and chest, many of which ruptured, leaving runnels of black fluid striping his pale skin. Each streak of blood leeched away his vitality. He had lived for hundreds of years in the service of the Shadow Lord, his thirst for his master's blessings driving him ever further to levels of depravity that shocked even his fellow shamans. But his willingness to go to any length, steep himself in any degree of vileness to try to please Fel had earned the approval of Prince Umbral, and gradually Sangine had risen in power, surpassing his fellows and finally becoming first among them. He had never actually been in the presence of Fel, but earning the trust and praise of Prince Umbral, and even the grudging acceptance of Prince Timor, had been honor enough.

Often the explorations directed by Umbral had involved painful, even torturous ordeals. To serve the Shadow Lord was to embrace pain, as he was constantly reminded. But this agony was unlike anything he had ever endured. He looked once more at his blistered and bloody arm. His throat clenched and he shuddered at the thought of continuing the effort. Despite his need to destroy the unearthly, glowing fortress and finally unleash his warriors upon the paltry few defenders, he knew he simply couldn't sustain the effort. *Forgive me, my lord. I am unworthy.* Drops of sweat mixed with the blood that dripped from his nose and chin, and he trembled at the thought of unleashing another bolt. *Such agony! There must be another way.*

His breathing was ragged and rapid, and his eyes flashed from side to side, searching for a solution. Suddenly, he froze, an idea birthing in his frantic mind. He rose unsteadily and moved shakily back down the trail. Perhaps it was inspiration from his master that guided him, perhaps it was merely terror driving him to seek any possible alternative to the torment of unleashing another bolt, but his desperate mind would have grasped at any possible solution at this point. His feet shuffled down the steep, winding trail, and he staggered into a large rock at the bend of the path. Leaning against it, he paused to gather his strength. He couldn't remember the last time he had let himself become this weak. With a trembling hand, he wiped his eyes, and his hand came away bloody. Blinking, he looked about to get his bearings. Nearby, he could see the figure of one of the fallen Nephellem, and the idea that drove him down the Tor came into sharper focus. A febrile grin spread upon his face, his cheek twitching. *This might work.*

Pushing himself off the rock, he staggered further down the trail, leaving the fallen giant behind as the sounds of battle below were now clearly audible. So, the army of the White Cleft was attacking, despite the gloom. He had to hurry. These Highlanders were doughty indeed. Or… perhaps some other aid was being given to them. He silently cursed the Five and the Tor's hidden Gatekeeper. *I will overcome you all and this land will be awash in blood! I, Sangine, First of the Angor Shamans, swear it!*

Increasing his pace, he careened unsteadily down the trail until he stopped suddenly and stood panting over the corpse of Vajk. His strength and focus were faltering. He needed blood to rejuvenate, but there was no time to find another victim. He could feel Prince Timor's impatience like an acidic black cloud burning and pressing on his addled mind. He blinked and struggled to clear his thoughts, shaking his head violently, producing a shower of bloody droplets that painted the corpse at his feet. With an effort, he knelt beside the body of the Grand Hadvezér. Slowly, he reached forward with the blood gem, his sclerotic left hand dripping blood and shaking so violently he feared he might lose his grip upon the stone. His brow furrowed in concentration as he inserted the dark stone once more into the hole that gaped in the corpse's chest. He hoped this effort wouldn't be as costly as the black lightning had been. He ran his thumb over the stone's smooth and irregular facets as he inched it deeper into the fallen warlord's body. He could feel the gem pulling his arm further, like the tug of a lodestone. Dreading what was next, he grimaced and shut his eyes tightly. With the last of his waning strength, he willed the stone forward, seating it once more in its place. A surge of agony shrieked through him. His eyes shot open, his face a rictus of torment as he howled a silent scream to the heavens. There was a blast of black energy, which hurled him onto his back, leaving him heaving great wracking, shuddering breaths. The world spun into darkness.

King Fergus

The combined White Cleft and fyrd warriors were making progress, though it was a meat grinder. The bodies of the dead and wounded — both Räuber and Highlander — piled high before them. The king's jaw ached from the constant clench required to struggle against the unnatural gloom that weighed upon them all. Despite their sobs of despair, his men had hacked their way through the holly trees that bordered the narrow path, and though that meant they had a broader approach, still they faced a determined defense by the Räubers, who had formed a shield wall on the uphill slope. The White Cleft troops had formed their own wall, gathering some small encouragement from the close presence of their fellows, and pressed their way forward.

"Stand firm, lads!" Fergus shouted, though he was unsure if any heard him over the din of battle. His voice was raw from screaming repeated encouragement to his troops and from the near constant growling he found necessary to remain standing against the damnable gloom.

He ducked his head as an axe splintered the shield of the man next to him. His left arm was still injured and he could not hold a shield himself. Nonetheless, the king stood in the front rank of his men, being seen to fight, and shouting continuously to hold up their flagging spirits — as though he alone bore the weight of their despair. His seax lashed out beneath the shield of his opponent, finding meat and glancing off a hip bone. The Räuber before him grimaced in surprise and pain, and Fergus' blade lashed out twice more, felling the man. He took no joy in the kill, however. Under this gloom there was no joy to be found, only grim determination, constant defiance, and attention to the grisly task at hand.

He saw movement to his left, and stealing a quick glance, noted that enough of his men had finally pushed through the gap to extend their wall and begin wrapping around the south flank of the enemy defense — despite the ground being littered with boulders, logs, and corpses. *It won't be long now,* he thought.

A horn blew from somewhere within the enemy ranks and the Räubers, as one, shoved forward a pace, momentarily staggering the surprised Highlanders. Then the Räuber wall dissolved as they broke formation and sprinted up the trail in retreat. The White Cleft soldiers would typically give chase to a broken enemy, but instead they watched their foes flee, each man drained with the effort of fighting both with sword and spirit. Fergus himself resisted the temptation to collapse to the ground and began shouting orders to form up and prepare to pursue in an orderly fashion. The trail ahead wound through a stand of tall pine trees, then climbed steeply and doubled back. No real chance for a shield wall ahead. Their progress now would rely on the individual grit and courage of each man.

We'll all die here, this day. The thought came unbidden to his mind and, despite knowing it to be the product of the gloom, he couldn't disagree.

Sangine

When his eyes opened, he was aware of movement around him. Time had passed, but he had no idea how long he had been unconscious. It was not yet the break of day, but the chill in the air suggested the dawn of the Equinox was fast approaching. He had to hurry, but he was weak, so weak. He needed blood, and quickly.

The Räubers were filing noisily through the breach in the stone wall. Many were wounded, the iron tang of their blood filling the air. He became aware of someone standing beside him in the darkness. Squinting, he could just make out the form of Vajk looming above him, silently staring as though waiting for something.

Sangine rose unsteadily to his feet and wiped bloody sweat from his brow, despite the chill air. Fresh blisters covered his face and throat, many having ruptured, draining still more of his dwindling vitality. He swayed and reached a hand out to Vajk to steady himself. The man didn't move, and he noted the commander's skin was cold, smooth, and mottled like marble, as though Vajk had transformed to become like the blood gem itself. A faint light seemed to limn the Grand Hadvezér's form, as though energy surged just beneath the skin.

"I need blood," Sangine muttered, though it hadn't been his intention to speak aloud. Without hesitation Vajk turned and, moving with startling speed, dashed silently amongst the wounded Räubers. The pre-dawn dark prevented Sangine from seeing what transpired, but there was a grunt and a few shouts, and then Vajk was standing before him again, the limp form of a wounded Räuber dangling from his outstretched arm. Without hesitation, Sangine reached up and placed a hand on the man's face. Immediately, the boiling began beneath his fingers as the blood within the wounded warrior surged to Sangine's touch. The man was too badly injured to do more than grimace in agony as the shaman felt the familiar surge of strength. Typically he would need no more than to place his hand on the man to feed but his strength was so depleted, his need so great, he bared his jagged teeth and with a feral fervor, bit deeply into the man's broad chest, drinking the blood directly. His head shook back and forth, worrying the wound like a hound with a hare. Vitality streamed into him and down his throat as newfound strength coursed through his body. The flesh tore and he came away with a mouthful of meat. He chewed it sloppily, great gobs of flesh and sinew dropping to the ground before him. Then, with a smile of anticipation, he fixed his mouth once more on the wound and drained the man completely, blood dripping from his chin.

Replenished, but just barely, he finally pulled back from the husk and sighed, chewing and savoring another morsel of meat he had torn from his victim. Vajk silently cast the carcass over the precipice that edged the south bend of the trail. Sangine needed still more blood, but a stiff pre-dawn breeze warned him that time was fleeting. He dared not wait any longer.

"Destroy that fortress and bring me the Raven's head," he commanded Vajk, pointing up the Tor.

Without hesitation, the former Grand Hadvezér turned and dashed up the hill, faster than a man could possibly sprint on level ground. Flashes of blackened power sparked in his thighs as he ran.

"Follow your commander!" Sangine shouted to the hundred or so remaining Räubers, who had formed up in the darkness to repel the slowly approaching White Cleft soldiers. His voice echoed with reinvigorated, preternatural power. "Never mind the Highlanders! Take the temple, now!"

Chapter 26

Gather your friends and meet at the appointed place. There, we shall face the foe. Whether victory be ours this day, or we fall and die, we shall do it together—as comrades.

—Qatae Tariq, "Tales of the Mountain Bandit"

Just before the dawn of the Autumn Equinox
Green Mount, The Tor

Corvus

"It's the three of us should go through," Corvus said softly to Mama and Ligulf. They had each been drawn instinctively toward the doors. Mama nodded and Ligulf swallowed nervously.

"But Da," Li said, fighting to keep the quaver from his voice. "What if we're gone and the fortress falls? What if we canna return? What if…?"

"I canna believe that Latrans would endanger our mission here," Corvus said reassuringly. "Nor would he do anything that might risk our lives. He's helped us along, every step."

"But the man is daft!" Li protested.

"He's Cruim, lad," Corvus replied. "He's one of the Five, I'm quite sure of that now."

After a moment's surprised consideration, Li conceded, "Alright, Da." The feathering of his jaw told of his uncertainty, but Corvus knew his son wouldn't challenge his decision further.

"Sister," Corvus said to Mama in Aslene. "It's fairly obvious which door you should enter."

"Yes, Corvus Corax," she replied, staring at the door with the Aslene-style arch. "It is very strange, but the portal beckons me somehow. I feel it, in my heart."

"I feel the same way about this one, on the left," he replied. "It's like a tug behind my breastbone."

"Yes, exactly!" She turned back to him, her dark eyes shimmering with anticipation. "It feels urgent."

"I agree," he replied. "We must not tarry."

He then indicated that the three of them should move toward their respective doors, and with a nod to synchronize their passage, they each reached out a hand and opened them.

Argant

When Mama had risen to examine the shimmering door, Argant had stirred awake. His eyes widened at the marvel before him and a frisson of "other" washed over the boy as he watched Mama, Corvus, and Ligulf each raise a hand to open the doors before them. The portal before Mama opened, blinding Argant with a brilliant golden light and a blast of dry, warm air. He raised a hand to shield his eyes, trying to peer through to what might lie beyond, but he could make out nothing beyond the threshold. Mama stepped through the doorway cautiously, then the shimmering door closed behind her with an audible click. By the time his eyes cleared, Corvus and Ligulf were also gone.

"What if they don't come back?" he softly asked the silence.

Amina stepped next to him and gently hugged him to her side. Her quiet presence was the only reassurance she could offer.

A stiff, pre-dawn breeze blew through the temple and Argant suddenly recalled the words of Athdar, Gatekeeper of the Tor. *When the dawn comes, you must be ready.*

It was almost time! Stepping away from Amina, he knelt beside the ornate tile he had spent time cleaning earlier. This was the one. It had to be. He pushed on its edges and the tile shifted slightly, but the centuries of caked mud along its edges seemed to block any further movement.

"What are you doing, Argant?" Amina asked in her soft monotone.

"I have to be ready for the dawn," he replied, once more scratching furiously at the tile's perimeter with a stick. Rather than question him further, Amina knelt beside him and took out her small knife to quietly join him in his efforts. After a few moments of scratching that seemed to make no discernible progress, Argant grew frustrated, his efforts verging on frantic as tears of frustration filled his eyes. He was aware of movement behind him, and then, quietly, Yadira knelt down between the two of them, a simmering pot in her hand.

"Here," she offered. "This may help. Lean back."

Amina and Argant leaned away from their toil to watch Yadira slowly pour a pot of steaming water onto the tile. The hot water broke up the encrustation far more effectively than their tools, and then drained rapidly through the gaps around the tile. Argant looked up at her with gratitude and resumed his efforts, the tile now shifting more easily beneath his fingers.

"I'll fetch more water," Yadira said, rising.

"I think it worked," Amina said as her thin blade pushed deep along the edge of the tile, shifting it. Argant's tiny fingers were able to slip beneath its edge and, pulling with all his might, he slowly lifted the tile. The opposite side slid slightly down into the hole beneath, as if it was hinged. Once he had raised the edge enough, Amina was able to add her strength, and together they heaved until, with a crunching sound, the tile suddenly slid down into the side of the square hole, revealing an irregularly shaped recessed metal cup that was securely connected to some hidden structure below.

"What is that?" Argant asked, staring at the strangely shaped object.

"I don't know," Amina answered slowly, then added, "but that shape is somehow familiar."

Ligulf

He stepped cautiously through the door, the golden light blinding him at first, before the aureate glow dimmed to reveal the pre-dawn interior of what seemed to be a castle. The air was warmer here and there was a distinct smell of fresh-baked bread that instantly made his mouth water. It had been many days on marching rations, venison, and hare, so the smell of the loaves seemed luxurious and tantalizing. He had to remind himself to focus on his immediate task. He found himself walking along a high, arched stone corridor with a plush carpet runner that spanned the entire length. He couldn't see anyone moving about the castle, though ahead of him, near the end of the hallway, a lone guard stood vigil across from a doorway. The sentry turned to face him as he approached, his hand moving to the hilt of his sword in a threatening manner. The man wore a thick cloak over a polished metal cuirass. His clean-shaven face was rugged, yet handsome, and though the ginger hair that escaped the base of his equally polished helmet was sprinkled with grey, he did not look old. Despite the hour, the guard's eyes showed no sign of fatigue. This man was clearly accustomed to night duty.

"Keep the heid, mon," Li said, his hands up and open in a peaceful gesture. The guard's brows furrowed in confusion, as though Li had spoken in a foreign tongue.

"Who are you, and what business have you here?" the guard demanded, his accent strange to Li's ears.

"My name's Ligulf," he replied with a friendly smile. "I mean no harm to any here."

The guard's posture remained threatening as he examined Li up and down. Then, apparently satisfied that the strange visitor was no threat, he relaxed and his hand dropped from his weapon. "So, you're the visitor she said would come?"

"I s'pose I am," Ligulf responded with a bemused smile. "Though whoever *she* might be, and how in the great wide world she knew I was coming, is beyond my ken."

"*She* is Queen Darienne of Lachland," the guard replied with a hint of indignation. "You stand outside her chambers." He nodded to the great oaken door across the corridor from his post.

"Ach, you don't say!" Ligulf muttered under his breath. He was utterly nonplussed. "Lachland, eh? Sure and this is some great magic indeed."

"She told me to show you in upon your arrival," the guard continued. "Your weapon stays here."

"Of course, of course," Li replied, shaking his head in wonder. He unbuckled his sword belt and handed his puntina to the guard, who raised an eyebrow in surprise at the unusual needle,-like blade. The guard then stepped to the door and knocked softly. The door opened, and the face of a shorter man with a darker complexion peered out. He had short black hair, and a neatly trimmed beard just beginning to streak with silver, but what caught Li's eye was the long scar down the man's left cheek.

"He's here," the guard said simply, indicating Li.

The shorter man's piercing dark eyes examined Li carefully, before nodding curtly and opening the door more widely to invite him in. Li stepped forward cautiously to find himself entering a luxurious, candlelit sitting room with a fire blazing in the hearth and a small trestle table set with a platter of breads, meats, cheeses, and wine that set his mouth watering again. A young woman, dressed in leather breeches and riding boots sat in a grand, upholstered chair facing the door. The deferential bow the scarred man gave her as Li entered suggested that this was the Queen.

She's the Queen? She was certainly no older than Li himself. She had fair skin dusted with freckles, sharp crystal-blue eyes, and her fiery red hair was tied up in a high ponytail, from which an abundance of ringlets cascaded about her shoulders. She wore a long leather vest, open over a practical white shirt—a man's shirt to Li's eyes—bloused and tucked into her trousers. She looked as though she were dressed for a riding jaunt in the countryside. Indeed, her appearance was so at odds with any expectation he might have had of what the Queen of Lachland would look like that Li glanced about confusedly, wondering if perhaps he was mistaken and this wasn't the monarch at all. The only other person in the chamber was a tall, striking woman, who stood behind the Queen's chair. She had skin darker than Li had ever imagined possible, and almost glowing green eyes. A fountain of loose black curls framed a face with smooth skin, high cheekbones, and a sharp nose. She wore black trousers and boots similar in style and cut to the Queen's, with a long-sleeved shirt tucked into them, its collar and sleeves frilled.

Li looked questioningly back to the scarred man, who gestured with his head toward the Queen, eyebrows raised in obvious expectation. Yet his meaning was unclear. Then, suddenly, Li realized his mistake and knelt, bowing his head.

"Your Majesty, forgive my confusion," he said quickly. "It is a rare and strange magic that has brought me here, and I am at a bit of a loss for words."

"Stand, please," the young monarch replied simply. Her accent was similar to the guard's, and her manner forthright. "State your name and how you came to be here."

Li rose and looked again at each of the room's occupants. "'Tis a wondrous tale," he began, aware of the nervous tremor in his voice. "And I am afraid that time presses, milady, so I'll need to be brief."

"We were forewarned of your arrival," she replied bluntly. "Though we do not understand the circumstances, we trust you are a new friend, whose need is great. Please be seated by the fire, eat, and tell us your tale."

Relief washed over him at her words, and he moved to a cushioned chair by the hearth. When he was comfortably seated, he leaned forward, elbows on his knees, to begin.

"What do you know of the Tor of the Green Mount?" he asked.

Corvus

He found himself standing in the Great Hall of Esper — King Mannon's seat, though he knew his friend had passed. The darkened interior was only dimly lit by the embers of the central fire pit, the blaze having been allowed to die down in the night. There was movement from beyond the far wall that separated the hall from the king's chambers. With a pang of regret, Corvus recalled his last meeting in that chamber with his old friend.

He heard the soft slide of steel as a sword was eased from its scabbard. In a flash, his own blade was out as he spun quickly to the center of the room, facing the unknown threat.

"Show yourselves!" he barked. "I'm a friend to the Glenfolk."

"More than a friend, I think," replied a familiar Aslene-accented voice from the dark as the bulky form of Yazid eased from the shadows, spear in hand. Despite the dim light, Corvus could tell the Aslene was weak, leaning on his spear uncharacteristically.

"My friend!" Corvus said with relief, sheathing his weapon and crossing quickly toward him. "Right glad I am to see you!" Before he could embrace his oldest friend, however, another voice called out.

"Da?" Cailean rushed out from behind the wall. He sheathed his sword and rushed to wrap his father in a fierce embrace. As the two men hugged warmly, he noted a third figure stepping out from hiding.

"Alasdair?" he asked. "You should be home in bed."

"Aye, Corvus," the man replied with a broad grin and a wink. "At our age, we need our beauty sleep. Though I dare say you need a right bit more than I."

Corvus pulled back from Cai, though he kept a hand on his son's shoulder, needing the reassurance that all this was real. He grinned broadly and placed his other hand on Yazid's shoulder, causing his friend to flinch in pain. The Aslene had clearly lost weight since he last saw him and was favoring his left side.

"Are you well, my friend?" Corvus asked him earnestly.

"A scratch, a scratch," the Aslene murmured dismissively. "The Ancestors were not quite ready for me to join them, I think."

Corvus searched Yazid's face, though in the dim light, it was difficult to read.

"Is there some light, and a place to sit?" he asked Cailean. "I have a tale to tell and I must be quick about it. Your help is needed."

"Sure, Da," Cai replied quickly. "Come in here, and have a seat and a cup of tea."

Corvus followed his son into the candlelight of the king's bed chamber, where he found Lady Brigit Stuart pouring cups of tea for them.

"Lady Stuart," he greeted her bemusedly. "I'm surprised to find you here."

A sudden blush painted her cheeks and she flashed a quick look at Cailean, who cleared his throat and turned away to reposition a chair for his father. Corvus suppressed a grin and accepted the steaming cup she offered him. His brows furrowed in concern as Yazid eased himself into a chair with difficulty. The Aslene flashed him a reassuring, though unconvincing, smile as he set his spear on the floor beside him. Then Corvus realized that the five chairs and small table they now sat around had been brought into the chamber before he arrived.

"Were you expecting me?" he asked.

"Aye. That scunner fella in motley breeks," Cai said.

"Latrans?"

His son nodded. "Aye, that's the one. He came by in the wee hours and told me to gather Yazid and Alasdair, don our kit, and to expect a visitor, but I ne'er imagined it'd be you! He's a right sleekit type, that one!"

"Ye have no idea, son," Corvus replied with a wry chuckle. He sipped his tea, the warm drink welcome after the cold of the Tor and the struggles of the recent days.

"What's doin', Corvus?" Alasdair asked. "How'd ye come to be here? Shouldn't ye be at the Tor?"

"Aye, I am… or I was. And I suspect I will be again, shortly," he replied, struggling to find words to encompass the strangeness of the night.

"Whatever you need, Da," Cai said, leaning forward in his chair. "You know we're with you."

"Perhaps it is best," Yazid said slowly, gauging his friend's confusion, "if you take a moment to tell us your tale."

Corvus nodded gratefully to the Aslene, took another sip of his tea, then set the cup aside and looked at each of the four occupants of the room before speaking.

"Great, rare things are afoot," he began. "The Tor, it turns out, is a rare source of power. A power that Fel, himself, covets. Even now, he moves on the Tor with Räubers and foul sorcery. The Five stand against him, through us and blessings they've given us." The gravity in his voice and the import of his words silenced them all as every mouth fell open. "We defend the Tor and rare magic protects us for a short time, but our strength and our numbers dwindle, and our situation is dire indeed."

"Da, that's madness," Cai interjected. "Sure and you're days travel from the Tor!"

"I know, Cai." He shook his head resignedly. "And I dinna ken the power that brought me here, but I need your aid. *We* need your aid, and time is too pressing for me to explain properly."

"You need say no more, I think," Yazid said, setting down his tea and reaching for his spear. "It is enough that Corvus needs us. No more need be said nor explained. We follow you wherever you might lead."

"Right, then let's be about it," Alasdair said, standing and pulling on his gloves.

Chapter 27

"For I tell you, my children, the days of darkness threaten from lands far across the sea. We must be ready, for the faithful will not be spared in this reckoning."

—Hayim, the Wanderer

Just before the dawn of the Autumn Equinox
Green Mount, The Tor

Corvus

Corvus was relieved to see that nothing had changed as he returned to the temple on the Tor through the golden door. The shimmering walls still stood, holding the Räubers at bay. Yadira gasped in surprise as he stepped out of the portal, drawing the attention of the others. The Adders rose from their various resting places, gripping their spears, looks of relief on their faces as they saw Cai, Alasdair, and finally their mentor Yazid step through behind Corvus. . Rhona, who was crouched at Dallin's side with Piper, tending the wounded archer, flashed a knowing smile at Corvus as she saw the other men. He nodded gratefully to them both in turn. Piper's words had proven true. The knowledge of ancient lore possessed by the three bards had been invaluable on this adventure, and they had indeed had a significant role to play.

The three newcomers each had a look of wonder on their faces as they stepped into the ruins atop the Tor. Barclay gave a shout of welcome at the sight of Yazid, and the Adders quickly surrounded their teacher, smiles of gratitude and welcome shifting quickly to concern at his obvious frailty. Yazid greeted them as heartily as he was able, his wan smile fading first to concern, then to grief as he was apprised of the names of the fallen Adders. He had trained each and every one, and loved them as his own.

"Come, sit," Yadira said to Yazid, pushing in between the crowded Adders. "You are wounded." She flashed a reproving glance at Corvus as she guided Yazid to a place by the fire.

Cai's eyes searched over the defenders, nodding to each of the Adders as he made a mental tally. His hand moved to the hilt of his sword when he spotted the ravenous Barbárs shouting beyond the shimmering walls, though their cries were muted by the barrier.

"Da?" Cai asked, nodding toward the throng.

"They canna cross for now," Corvus replied, indicating the golden fortress around them. "But the walls willna hold much longer."

"And when they fall…" Cai mused.

"It'll be a right donnybrook," his father answered.

Corvus could see his son was thinking strategically — calculating lines of attack, the number of defenders, weaponry, the approximate size of the attacking force. *He thinks like a commander*, he observed proudly.

Alasdair walked the perimeter of the temple, assessing the quality of weaponry, the amount of food remaining, the source of their water. He was, after all, a quartermaster and command sergeant.

After a few moments of greetings and introductions, where necessary, Cai moved to Dallin's side.

"Alright, Dal?" he asked softly as her eyes opened, her shocked look at seeing him on the Tor almost comical.

"Cai," she murmured. "How?"

"Not sure, luv. 'Tis braw magic indeed, eh?"

"Och, aye," she answered, blinking.

He nodded to her wound. "How's it?"

"I've been through worse," she offered bravely after a moment, then winced at the memory that provoked.

"I know you have, luv." He stroked her cheek gently. "You rest here. Help has arrived. We'll get you home."

"Cai," she said with sudden urgency, reaching for his hand. "I canna just lie here while others fight and die! I'm lettin' em all down, d'ye hear?"

"From what my da says," Cai responded softly, "they ne'er woulda made it this far without you. You've been a right hero, lass. Comes a time for rest, Dal. You've done your share. Lie back. Rest now." He removed his woolen cloak and handed it to Rhona. "Keep her warm and safe. She's dear to us."

"I will," Rhona replied, covering Dallin's shivering form with the cloak. "My thanks."

The Adders returned to their positions, heads down, worry written on their brows.

"…too frail for a scrap," Corvus overheard Barclay say softly to Anna, who nodded grimly.

They were right. He looked to his friend, who sat by the fire, nursing a cup of tea while Yadira fussed over him. Yazid's skin was ashen, his eyes sunken. He had no business bringing him here. The man belonged in bed. He had been so pleased to see his friend, and so desperate for the help, that he hadn't thought clearly. Yes, the man was a devil in a scrap, but not like this. So weakened.

Thinking perhaps to undo his error and send Yazid back, he glanced toward the golden door through which he had passed, only to find it missing.

Well, that answers that, he thought grimly. *Nothing for it then.*

He gestured to Alasdair and Cai to join him by the fire as he moved toward Yazid to discuss their situation.

"You can see our situation is dire indeed," he began. "The enemy has a shaman as well, who has remained hidden, but hurls fearsome bolts of Fel's own magic at us." He indicated the scoring and damage on the fortress.

"How long must we hold this ground?" Cai asked.

"Come the dawn," Corvus replied, "I understand some grand transformation will occur, and the lad will become the new Gatekeeper of the Tor — provided we hold this temple and protect the boy. The shaman will push to stop that at all costs. If the enemy takes the Tor before the renewal… At best there'll be no Gatekeeper, and at worst, the shaman will assume that position and a dark age will fall upon the Green Mount indeed."

"This is an outcome we must prevent, I think," Yazid offered wryly.

"I'd say so." Corvus grinned, his smile fading into a determined grimace. He glanced over at Dallin and her bow that had proven so vital in their efforts thus far. "Alasdair, how's your archery?" he asked, stooping to pick up the intricately carved bow. He handed it the sergeant, who shrugged and tried a test pull on the string only to find that the draw was beyond him. He shot a confused look at Corvus, then tried to pull the string again, but succeeded only in moving it a hairsbreadth. He turned to Corvus in wonder, but before the sergeant could speak, the middle door opened, bathing them all in golden light.

Darienne

"Majesty," Kaiso repeated for the third time, "you cannot put yourself in such danger. There are others more suited to the task."

"Yes," Darienne replied with irritation. "So you have said."

"You hired me to ensure your safety," he replied sharply. "I cannot do so if you insist on stepping through that door into untold peril." He pointed to the shimmering golden portal that had formed in the castle corridor before them.

"Maddie, your thoughts?" Darienne asked, turning to her attendant.

"If the gods have so ordained—" Maddie began before Kaiso cut her off.

"Gods, pfah!"

"If the gods have so ordained," she repeated in her richly accented voice, her voice rising in volume, "then you must follow your destined path."

Darienne hesitated, ice down her spine. For the first time that she could remember, she was truly afraid. Had the gods ordained this? Or was this some mad fancy? Perhaps Kaiso was right. While her skills with the blade had developed nicely under his tutelage, there were certainly more potent and versatile warriors that could be sent to help defend the Tor. Why her? She was likely to get herself killed, and then where would the people of Lachland be? She was the Queen, she had responsibilities. It was foolhardy and reckless to consider dashing away into a far-off battle without her soldiers about her. She was no great hero from the legends. She was a monarch, tied to her people and her land. Why would she be chosen to go? Was it the fact that she *was* Queen? Could that possibly have some bearing? Was the purpose for her to meet Ligulf's father, the renowned Raven—whose daring exploits and strategic genius were known even in Lachland—perhaps to form an alliance? Was there some mystical need for a queen to be present? Or perhaps there was some other intent to her involvement, as yet unclear to her.

No, this is folly. I cannot be so reckless. What was I thinking to even consider following him through that door?

Her eyes met Ligulf's, who stood by the portal, ready to pull it open, his expression raw and full of genuine need. His urgency was clear and difficult to deny. He had spoken of the situation in his Highlander accent with clear, poetic eloquence, told them of his father's battle with the Barbár horde and subsequent, enchanted ride across an impossible distance to reach the Tor. He had mentioned the arduous and dangerous journey undertaken by Mama Warad and her votaries in order to bring the Tor's Key from far-off Asland. He told them of the Nephellem, diabolically enchanted giants against whom his father had fought with such courage and whose enchantment could only be undone by the mystical skills of Mama Warad, how one of the votaries — a fierce young warrior maiden — had fallen against the giants, protecting the rest of them. He spoke of divine gifts bestowed upon various members of their troupe—the bow and the floating star that banished the unnatural gloom. He spoke of the boy with the mismatched eyes, whose destiny, it seemed, was to become the new Gatekeeper. Indeed, Ligulf had spoken for what seemed hours, yet the night had not progressed noticeably; the position of the moon and stars seemingly unchanged from his arrival. It was all so very fantastical.

It was a tale she would never have believed were it not for the fact that Ligulf's arrival had been foretold and that he had been transported via *magic* to meet her in the dead of night. Indeed, before this night's remarkable events—the visitations by her mother and the golden-limned woman she assumed to be Manu herself—she would have dismissed it all outright. But so much had happened recently to open her mind to the supernatural: Maddie's talent, the unnerving enchantments of the Holy Knights, and the tales from the battle of Autun of the strange wizard's dark, blood magic that had slain her mother. Perhaps Ligulf's story was true, and this was indeed a struggle between the very gods themselves. If so, how could she deny the call to join such a battle? She was, after all, a Queen and—perhaps—the Moonflower herself, whatever that meant. The young Highlander's visit had been foretold by Latrans. *Is he one of the gods? The Fool? How can that be? One of the gods is mad?*

And yet, somehow Latrans *knew* of the visitation, and continued to display talents and knowledge that simply couldn't be explained. *Maddie certainly trusts him and believes wholeheartedly in his divinity. But… the people of Lachland need me. Should I really be dashing off on a dangerous, midnight escapade just because a madman — a mad god — told me to? And yet… Manu said that much would be decided this night. Did she mean this battle? Did she intend for me to participate? Aargh! My thoughts crash together without mercy! Mother! This is too much!*

Kaiso had positioned himself between her and Ligulf, his arms crossed as if he intended to be a physical barrier against her going through the door. His brow was furrowed and his jaw clenched and feathered with unspoken emotions. His eyes were narrowed, dark, and angry, but behind the anger, she could see something more: a pleading, as if he were silently begging her not to do this.

She turned to Maddie, whose tall figure stood reassuringly behind her. Maddie had no skill in combat. Why had Latrans insisted on her going? Of course, her healing skill would be useful in a battle, but in tight confines such as Ligulf had described, she would be in mortal peril the moment the fighting began.

As if in answer to Darienne's concerns, Maddie smiled warmly and placed a reassuring hand on her shoulder. "We each have a role to play in this drama. And if it is our time, then so be it. We must resist the Dark One and rise to this challenge. Trust that there is a greater purpose."

"Majesty," Kaiso interjected urgently, "this is dangerous folly!"

Darienne stared up into Maddie's eyes, imagining the horrors her friend had undergone on her long journey to find and serve her. Latrans had sent her, somehow, from her faraway land. Just as he was now sending them to the Tor. Latrans, who always seemed to arrive at critical junctures in her life, offering wisdom and clarity in his foolish and obscure antics. Latrans, who—according to Ligulf—had somehow conjured a magical fortress with this shimmering portal. Latrans, who seemed to travel vast distances with impossible speed, having apparently been at the Tor in the far-off Green Mount mere moments before stealing her biscuits in the castle kitchen and abjuring her to go on this journey.

Maddie nodded, as if following Darienne's thoughts and silently urging her to their obvious conclusion.

"He is one of them, isn't he?" Darienne asked softly. "One of the Five."

Maddie smiled, as if proud of her friend's realization. She gently squeezed Darienne's shoulder and nodded again.

A frisson shivered through the young Queen's body and the corridor seemed to shift. When the dizziness passed, she found herself calm and resolute, her decision made.

"I'm sorry, Captain," she said, turning back to Kaiso, "but I am needed by the Five."

Kaiso bit back a derisive comment and opened his mouth to argue.

"You need not accompany me," Darienne told him, forestalling his retort with a raised hand. "I release you from your service to me. But know that Maddie and I are going to follow Master Ligulf through that door."

Cailean

The situation atop the Tor was dire indeed. Cai could see dozens of ravenous Räubers through the translucent, shimmering walls now. *Gods, but the bastards are huge!* Somehow, these Räubers were even bigger than the ones he had just battled on the road to Esper. This must be the royal guard or the Barbár equivalent.

He glanced about the interior of the temple ruins. Besides Alasdair, Corvus, and himself, he saw five Adders; Yazid—still weak, clutching to his cup of tea as though it held that last warmth in the world; three bards—or there would be, once Ligulf returned; one gravely wounded archer; the two remaining votaries and the child; and, of course, Mama Warad, once she returned. Not a terribly impressive fighting force to pit against the howling savages outside the temple. He caught Alasdair's eyes as the sergeant seemed to arrive at the same conclusion.

Corvus asked Alasdair how his archery was, interrupting their silent conference. Alasdair shrugged and picked up the ornate bow. Cai and Corvus watched in wonder as the veteran soldier struggled with all his might to draw the string, without success. The bemused Alasdair tried again with no luck, then with a shrug and a confused shake of his head, he returned the bow to Dallin's side and turned back to Corvus just as the center portal opened, bathing them all in the flickering light of torches.

Ligulf stepped through the door, a sheepish smile on his face as though he'd been sent to the kitchen to fetch a platter of steaming roast venison, and had returned with naught but cold bangers and mash. Behind him, a short, dark, and scarred man in an unfamiliar military uniform stepped out, hands on the hilts of his blades. Cai could sense an immediate shift in Corvus' posture, and Yazid rose, with difficulty, to stand by his friend's side, his eyes never leaving the newcomer. But before his father could say anything, a young woman—barely twenty, if Cai was any judge—dressed in buckskin trousers, riding boots, a leather vest, and a long overcoat stepped through the door behind the scarred man. Her hair was a cascade of auburn ringlets that splashed over her shoulders and framed an attractive, intelligent face that was dusted with freckles. She wore a saber on her belt, and her hand hovered near its hilt, ready to draw. He noted her left hand had disappeared under her long coat, no doubt clutching the handle of a hidden dagger.

The third member of the party stepped through behind the redhead. She was as tall as Cai, with fine, chiseled features and velvety dark, smooth skin. Her piercing green eyes shone, as though lit from within. Her hair was as black as midnight, some of the generous loose curls were bound up in a makeshift ponytail. She was dressed in a similar fashion to the woman who had preceded her, but to his eye, she was unused to these clothes. From the timid manner in which she stepped through the door, toe-heel rather than a warrior's heel-toe stride, Cai could tell she was no fighter. The redhead, however, moved with a feline grace and balance that bespoke martial training.

"Everyone," Ligulf said in his clear tenor. "Allow me to introduce Queen Darienne of Lachland." He indicated the redheaded woman, who seemed far too young to bear such a title.

"Your Majesty," Corvus said in response with a slight bow. "I am Corvus Corax. Right welcome you are, though I wonder if you understand the danger into which you step."

As Corvus was speaking, Cai noted Yazid shifting his spear into a ready stance, his look full of hostility toward the man with the scar. There was obviously some history here. Cai couldn't recall ever seeing the jovial Yazid respond with such clear animosity to anyone before. He looked to his father for any clue as to Yazid's posture and noted Corvus' hand resting upon the buckle of his sword belt. From a very young age, his father had drilled into his sons the etiquette and unspoken language of the sword, the subtle hand positions on or near the sword belt that indicated the level of threat and one's willingness to face that danger. The hand upon the buckle indicated an above-average readiness to draw at a moment's notice. Despite his father's respectful tone to the Queen, his weight had shifted to a seemingly casual wide stance that Cai knew to be the preparatory posture for Badger form. *What's going on here?*

"You are, I assume, the famous Raven, Warden of the Green Mount?" The young Queen spoke with an unfamiliar accent and more grit in her tone than Cai would have expected. He sensed movement from the far end of the temple and, glancing over, noted Rhona rising from Dallin's side, her eyes transfixed by the young monarch.

"I am," Corvus responded, "though the title of Warden is one with which I am unfamiliar. I'm simply a man trying to protect that which is dear to him. And so I must ask you"—he turned to face the scarred newcomer even as he continued to address the Queen—"why is it you are accompanied by an officer of the murderous Blades of Sebastian?"

"This is Captain Kaiso," she replied, her brow furrowing in confusion. "He is my trusted bodyguard."

"Trusted, you say?" Yazid interjected. "No member of that company could ever be trusted, I think."

Kaiso's posture shifted into a battle crouch, his lip curling in a sneer as his eyes darted between Corvus and Yazid like a threatened animal.

"Gentlemen!" the Queen scolded. "I do not believe we were summoned to this mount by the very gods to fight amongst ourselves. If I am not mistaken, there is the enemy." She gestured to the Räubers crowding beyond the shimmering wall. "Whatever your personal history with Captain Kaiso's company, surely every blade will be needed in the coming struggle?"

Corvus' jaw clenched and his brow furrowed and worked as he stared with open malice at the scarred stranger. Cai couldn't remember the last time he had seen his father so clearly upset and ready for slaughter. Whatever history he had with this group, the Blades of Sebastian, it was an open, raw wound that had never healed.

"Da..." Ligulf stepped between Corvus and Kaiso. Cai tensed. It would be all too easy for the captain to seize Li and use him to hold Corvus and Yazid at bay. Cai caught the captain's eye and with a subtle shake of his head, warned against any hostile action. Kaiso's eyes narrowed in response, measuring the distance to Ligulf. Cai's body coiled in readiness matching his father's. The tension grew, becoming palpable, every hand hovering on or near the hilt of a weapon.

"This is ridiculous!" The tall woman with the black hair stepped forward to stand beside Ligulf, her voice accented and rich, slicing through the tense air with scorn. "We have come to help defend the Tor, not to settle old scores. There will be time enough for this later, assuming we are victorious."

Something about the woman's tone dispelled the tension, and with a collective but reluctant sigh everyone's posture eased — though his da continued to eye the captain warily.

"You are correct, ladies," Corvus acknowledged. "There will be time enough after the scrap for your captain here to answer for the crimes of his company."

"I don't answer to you," Kaiso spat back disdainfully.

"Oh, you will," Corvus replied grimly. "That's a promise."

Kaiso snarled in response, his crouch once more deepening.

"Kaiso, stand down!" the young Queen barked sharply, startling all present with the force of her command. "Now, Raven, I believe you have wounded that need tending? Maddie here is a gifted healer."

Corvus blinked and tore his eyes from Kaiso. "Aye," he responded, gesturing toward Dallin. Maddie nodded curtly to Darienne and moved with purpose toward the stricken woman.

Just then, the third door opened with a gust of hot, dry air and a wash of golden light.

Corvus

Corvus half expected Mama Warad to return alone, as this fight was so far removed from the concerns of the desert dwellers. Given the unexpected company that Ligulf had collected, he also thought it was entirely possible that Mama might return with a string of other young votaries in tow. Either way, he expected to see Mama Warad step through the portal first, leading whomever she might have gathered from Asland to join them on the Tor. The last thing in the world he expected was the single short, lithe, and aged—but still graceful—figure that stepped cautiously through the portal before Mama. Dressed head to foot in the grey-white cotton of the Mudiya, the Illuminated Ones, and carrying a slender staff, the older man stepped forward into the temple and cocked his head as if listening. Despite the years since he had last seen him, Corvus would have known that stormy brow anywhere, though there was something about his eyes… *Wind on the mountain! He's been blinded!* He looked in horror at the milky-white orbs and telltale scarring that spoke of Ashahl's disgrace and punishment.

"Master," Corvus said in Aslene, his voice suddenly thick with emotion as he pushed past Ligulf and Kaiso to kneel before the newcomer. "The moon has gazed upon me too many times since last we met, thrice-honored Ashahl." The formal phrase for a long absence came awkwardly to him, but he was pleased he remembered it.

And yet, she has brought us once more together. That was the expected and traditional response. Instead, the older man's shoulders stiffened at the sound of Corvus' voice and his hand floated forward, seeking to touch the face of his long-lost protégé. Corvus gripped Ashahl's hand tightly with both of his and brought it to his face, allowing the fingertips to trace the contours of it, finding wrinkles and scars where none had been and baldness where hair had once flourished.

"Is it possible, Coinneach?" the grandmaster asked, his resonant voice, always so powerful, now quavering a little. Ashahl's lip quivered ever so slightly, but to Corvus, it was a glaring and atypical loss of control for the little master with the outsized presence. He knew Ashahl must be quite moved indeed to have neglected to make the formal reply to his greeting. Corvus had only once seen emotion crack Ashahl's stone-like reserve, and that was at their parting when the master had turned away lest Corvus see the tears that gathered in his eyes.

"Yes, Master," Corvus replied, rising but still gripping his master's hand. "Though I must remind you, my name is now Corvus Corax—you gave me that."

Ashahl nodded. "Nothing was given," he replied sagely. "All was earned and paid for in blood." He raised his other hand and gently patted Corvus'.

"But Master," Corvus asked, confused, "why have you come here? This isn't your battle, and, forgive me, but…"

"Yes, I am blind," Ashahl answered before Corvus could finish his thought. "But do not presume to tell me what is and what is not *my* battle. Remember, I was the one to ask Nabila to travel these many miles to bring the Key to you. I have toiled many a sleepless night, striving to understand the machinations of the Shadow Lord's minions. Despite my blindness, I see much, thanks to my many friends."

"Ashahl!" Mama exclaimed. "You should not speak of this."

"Nabila," he soothed. "We are halfway across the world, atop a distant tor. I cannot imagine hostile ears can hear me here."

"But the Blessed Attendants…"

"The *Blessed* Attendants did this to me!" he said, gesturing to his eyes, his voice insistent. "As a punishment for stealing the Key from the temple. They have forgotten their purpose and have become lost, wandering aimlessly in a maze of futile tradition and meaningless ceremony. They were to lead us to greater understanding, prepare us for the days of trial. They were to help us fulfill the destiny set forth by Hayim — the Wanderer — not circle endlessly in mindless rote repetition of forms and practices that bring us no closer to enlightenment. No, I will no longer follow the Attendants, nor their edicts."

"Lord Raven," Darienne interjected, "we should be most happy to meet your friend."

Corvus looked over his shoulder at the young Queen, surprised at the resentment he felt at her interruption. She was but a bairn — how could she understand the depth of importance, the magnitude that Ashahl's presence represented? He noted the sneer of disapproval on Kaiso's scarred face and made a silent promise to himself to wipe away that sneer. The muted, yet ever-present roar of the Räubers reasserted itself as a cheer inexplicably arose among the rabble outside the fortress' walls. Corvus shook his head and reminded himself of the situation. Those shimmering walls were going to come tumbling down at some point soon, and they would find themselves beset by scores of the barbarous bastards. He'd kill many, as would Cai, Yazid, and even Ligulf, but they'd all likely die in the ensuing attack. The reminder allowed him to refocus.

"Queen Darienne of Lachland," he said, with a formal bow to her, "allow me to present Master Ashahl, sword master to the Silken Emperor of Asland and my own teacher." He gestured to Ashahl, who seemed to understand the Sudlandic words and offered a graceful incline of his head, drawing the palm of his hand to his mouth, then his forehead, then sweeping it elegantly toward the young Queen.

"Master Ashahl," she responded, "we are pleased to make your acquaintance."

"The blessings of the Ancestors protect you," replied Ashahl in Aslene.

Another roar from the horde without drew their attention, and there was movement near the last bend in the path. Corvus couldn't quite see what it was, but glanced about to remind himself once more of his assets: five Adders, three bards, a child, two votaries who knew little of combat, a young Queen—who looked so green as to be worthless in a scrap, her "bodyguard"—a faithless mercenary, her lady-in-waiting—the healer, a wounded archer, the doughty Mama, and a blind, elderly martial arts master. How could they ever hope to survive?

A tearing screech echoed all along the front of the shimmering wall as a black bolt of lightning methodically tore the face of the fortress, leaving a smoking, jagged scar behind. A Räuber—taller than most with a great mane of shaggy white-blonde hair decorated with far more beads, bones, and feathers than his fellows—had stepped around the final curve of the path, his smoking hand extended toward the fortress front. His skin seemed unnaturally smooth and somewhat darkened, almost purple, and mottled with striations that resembled stone or marble, and his eyes were black like those of the Nephellem. *Possessed*, Corvus thought, then watched as the man lifted his hand again and another bolt of the black lightning lanced forward, gashing the damaged fortress still further.

"The time approaches," Ashahl said calmly, crouching into his ready stance, his hands gripping his staff.

"I told you this was a bad idea," Kaiso muttered to the young Queen.

Chapter 28

In the night, I listen to the burbling brook,
The wind soughing through the trees,
The call of owl and corncrake,
And wonder, my love, if you are near.
—Verse 29, "Love Poems of the Highlands"

Dawn, the Autumn Equinox
Esper, Glenfolk Region, Green Mount

Brigit

Brigit Stuart was still standing in the royal chamber at the rear of the great hall. She was still in the same place, staring at the blank section of wall where, some minutes before, she had witnessed Cailean, his father Corvus, Yazid, and a veteran Glenfolk soldier named Alasdair step through a shimmering, magical portal and disappear. *What have I just seen?!* They had all been so businesslike in their decision to follow Corvus through the golden door—none had really even remarked on the profound and, to her, unnerving manner of their transport.

That Corvus is a marvel, indeed! Sure and if he'd arrived floating on a great bubble blown by the moon, and told them he needed them to dance a jig naked while eating honeycomb tripe and cabbie claw, their kit would have come off faster than they could say "pass the ginger!" She sniffed at the thought, suppressing a wry grin. *And why shouldn't they trust him? Aye and he's earned the blind loyalty of every Highlander throughout the Green Mount.* She shouldn't be surprised by it, nor envious of such devotion from those who knew him best. Envy… Was that what she was feeling? Why should she feel envious, she wondered, raising her hand to her heart as the identification of the emotion hit home. Sure and she *was* envious of him. Of both of them — Corvus and Cailean — if she were being honest. *Brigit Stuart!* she berated herself silently. *This is well beneath you! Those two are the greatest blessing the Green Mount has seen in generations! How could you begin to be envious of them?* Her brow furrowed in response to her own remonstration.

"I know," she whispered to herself as she gathered the tea cups. "But I'll ne'er command such dedication… such blind loyalty. And here I'm supposed to be Queen of the Glenfolk!" She sighed in exasperation and worry, her right fist punching into her left hand in frustration.

Fair enough, her inner voice continued chiding her. *So a good monarch surrounds herself with those whose strengths supplement hers. You canna be all things, you simple lavvy heid!*

"I know, I know," she said aloud again with quiet frustration. "They are great men, true, and I'm lucky to have the likes of them supporting me. But is it wrong to feel diminished in the presence of a legendary warrior and his son, the dashing, conquering general? Is it wrong to feel as though my opinion matters little, though I am to be Queen?"

Your opinion! her inner voice huffed. *And what would you have advised contrary to what they did, you silly feartie?*

"I don't know!" Her whispered tone rose in her frustration. "It was just a matter of days hence that my life was quite predictable and normal! I tended to my lands, my people, and planned ahead for the next harvest. Like every year before. Suddenly, the King is dead and I'm to be Queen, I think I'm falling in love with a man I just met that's ten years my junior, and… I just watched him step through a magical doorway into untold danger. I think it's fair to say that I'm right unsettled at the moment. So forgive me if I'm feeling and saying things that are a bit beneath me!"

A wind brushed against the doorway to the balcony, rattling it gently in its frame, the sound pulling her from her thoughts. She felt suddenly embarrassed, as if she'd been overheard, standing here arguing with herself out loud like a numpty. *No, she thought with a sigh. I'm not envious or resentful of Corvus and Cailean. Just aware of how far I need to rise to truly be a Queen.*

She and the other monarchs might manage the banal day-to-day concerns of their people, but it was the spirit, grit, and vision of Corvus that breathed life and pride into the Highlanders. Even more so for her people, in that his son would be the consort of their Queen — if their mutual activities earlier that evening were any indication. She was beginning to understand what the other rulers had probably understood for years: that despite his protestations that he held no ambitions to be High King, all of them existed in the long shadow cast by Corvus Corax, and she would have to come to terms with that if she was to govern the Glenfolk effectively.

"Well, you didna waste any time, didja?" The rasp of the nasal voice shocked her from her reverie and she spun to find Kevin, King Mannon's ill-favored nephew, standing in the doorway behind her. He was holding a dirk in his left hand, and his right rested on the pommel of his sword. He looked about, confused. "I heard voices, are you alone?"

The shadows from the flickering candlelight exaggerated the savage crook of his recently broken nose. Corvus had given him that before running him out of town.

What's he doing here? If Corvus catches wind of this…. Then it struck her. *Of course!* He had hidden near the town, biding his time and licking his wounds, no doubt sheltered by one of his allies — Griogair MacLennan most likely. He'd must have heard the news of her elevation and impending coronation and sneaked back in to put a knife in her heart. *But why did he come here? Everyone thinks I'm at my own manor house.*

Her mind raced, trying to imagine if she had been indiscreet in her tryst with Cai. No, she was sure of it. She quickly retraced her steps that evening. After the feast, he had walked her back to her manor, during which time they had quietly plotted their assignation carefully—Cai applying his remarkably gifted tactical mind—so that no one might know, no eyebrows would be raised, and no taint of scandal could attach to her impending elevation. Shortly after midnight, she had slipped back out of her sleeping household and met him in the barn. There, he had wrapped them both in dark cloaks and led them back into town and to the rear of the great hall, where the ground dropped away down to the roaring Gomul River. He had placed a short ladder up to the edge of the balcony on the back of the building, securing it with a rope, and they had scaled it as silently as an owl in flight—whatever noise they might have made was utterly drowned by the roaring river. From there, they'd slipped like two flitting shadows into his chambers and then… into his bed.

No, there's no chance Kevin could have known that I'd be here. A wave of cold washed down her neck as she suddenly realized, *Cailean! He's come to slaughter Cai in his sleep, and is surprised to find me here.*

She affected a nonchalance that she didn't feel, turning to stack the tea dishes as she spoke. "I dinna ken what you mean, and you should know you're not welcome here, Kevin."

"Is that any way for a hoor to speak to a king?" He stepped forward with a stagger. He was drunk. "Where's your laddie-buck? Stepped out to the privy, did he? Leaving you all alone."

She set the stack of cups on the side table, spotting a carving knife on a cutting board nearby. Before her hand could drift three inches toward the knife, Kevin leapt forward, his dirk stabbing violently and loudly into the wood. She jumped back with a cry of alarm.

"None of that, now," he growled.

"W-Why are you here?" she stammered as she backed away, ashamed at the new tremor in her voice.

"Well," he said with a sly grin, "I thought I might catch yer chavie nappin' and tickle his ribs with this." He waved the dirk menacingly. "But lo and behold, I find you here in his bedchambers instead, and him nowhere to be found. You, the Queen-elect of the Glenfolk, sneaking about like a wanton trollop. Whatever would the council say to that?"

Infuriated by this, she lifted her head, threw her shoulders back, and glared at him with utter contempt. "You are foul," she spat. "Cailean is a thousand times more a man than you might ever aspire to be!"

"Oh, is he now?" Kevin snapped back at her. "And where is this man of yours, eh? Seems like he got what he wanted and toddled off to sleep somewhere else. Leaving you all alone, *Your Majesty.*"

He stepped toward her menacingly, the dirk raised, pressing her back into the corner of the room. Panic loomed within her and she glanced about fearfully, desperately seeking some escape. It was hours yet until the attendants of the great hall would arrive to stoke the main fire and prepare for the day's events. She could cry out, but the roaring of the river would surely mask the sound. Her heart hammered like a blacksmith at the forge. She glanced around the room, desperately looking for something to use as a weapon. *Think, woman, think!*

"Now," he said with undisguised hunger, "let's see what hochmagandy you've given so willingly to the young general." His left hand suddenly lashed out and grabbed her breast, squeezing painfully as he leaned forward and panted his sour, milky breath in her face. His loathsome smile revealed stained and crooked teeth. The point of the dirk slipped beneath the ribbon that tied the shoulder of her gown, the blade pressing against her skin and lifting the tie. Somehow, in spite of the terror and disgust of the moment, she found herself focusing on the fact that the break in his nose caused his breath to whistle with each exhalation, and as his excitement rose, the tempo of the whistling increased. Despite herself, despite his loathsome, sweaty palm groping her, despite the cold steel of the dirk tracing along her shoulder and neck, she began to giggle. It all seemed suddenly comical and absurd to her. The grotesquely misshapen nose, the piping whistle with every breath, even his drunken fumbling at her breast. He was pathetic. The giggle rose to become a silent chuckle. She covered her mouth with her hand, aware that the inappropriate laughter might rise still further and become an open guffaw.

The whistling paused as Kevin pulled back, his hand still gripping her breast painfully. His eyes lit with sudden fury, but somehow the jagged crook in his nose beneath those owl-wide eyes just made her laughter increase. Releasing her, he stepped back, incredulous, the dirk wavering threateningly before her face. But she was lost to her mirth, and even the waggle of the deadly blade was now hilarious to her. She pointed to it as another irresistible guffaw spluttered forth. He just seemed so utterly ridiculous and pathetic.

"You don't laugh at me, hoor!" Kevin snapped, his face turning red. "You don't laugh at—"

There was a resounding crack, and Kevin's head jerked to the left violently. Someone behind him had struck him with something, though his frame still blocked her from seeing who it was. He staggered, confused for a moment, but a moment was all Brigit needed. Reaching up quickly, she wrestled the dirk from his now limp grasp, and pointed it at him threateningly. He seemed dazed and unaware of her disarming him. Blood streamed down the side of his head from a gash opened over his ear. His eyes were unfocused as he ignored her and turned to face his assailant. Brigit could see her now. It was a woman—the commander of the fyrd, if she wasn't mistaken. What was her name? Bradana, yes that was it. *What's she doing here?*

"Ow! You bitch!" he yelled at Bradana, who still held the butt end of her spear out toward him. He started to move toward her, perhaps not yet realizing that he no longer held the dirk. Bradana placed the end of the spear firmly on his chest and pushed him back a step.

"Easy now, fella," Bradana cautioned, her voice firm. "Or I'll flip this stick about and gi' ye a jab with the sharp end."

Kevin's only response was to bend at the waist and roar, his hand clutching the wound on the side of his head where she'd hit him. Brigit couldn't tell if the cry was one of pain or frustration, but assumed the latter—for as he rose back to full height, he strode purposefully toward Bradana. The fyrd commander pushed him away twice more with the butt of her spear, prompting growls of drunken rage from him, but he kept pressing her back toward the far wall. Finally, in desperation, Bradana lashed out with another fierce blow with the butt end across his face that nearly dropped him. While he wobbled on his feet in reaction, she placed her boot on his chest and shoved him back once more—this time with much greater effort. Kevin fell backward into Brigit, impaling himself on the dirk in her hand as the two crashed into the wall. She screamed in horror at the realization of what had just happened, and pushed him forward, extricating the blade from his back. He turned slowly to face her. Veins bulged in his neck and forehead as he bore down on the pain, blood streamed from a new gash on his cheek, while his whistling breath came in gasps and pulses. His brow furrowed in consternation as he struggled to remain standing. Then, with a groan, his legs gave out and he crashed to the floor, striking his head on a wooden stool as he fell. There was an unmistakable crack as his neck broke, then his bowels released and the room was suddenly filled with a remarkably foul odor. Bile rose in her throat, threatening to burst forth.

"Here, now." Bradana took her arm firmly and guided her out the door onto the balcony, where fresh air and the mist from the river below might help her recover her equanimity.

"Why…? What…?" Brigit gasped, unable to form a cogent question.

"Cailean asked me to look after you," the veteran responded. "And I'm right glad he did."

"As am I," Brigit replied gratefully. "Hang on. Cailean asked you?" She blinked in confusion. "When?"

"Not two hours hence," Bradana replied.

"But…" she began, then she recalled. In the small hours of the night, after their lovemaking had concluded, Brigit and Cai had been awakened by a laughter, a manic-voiced stranger in their chamber. Cai had leapt, naked, from the bed to confront the motley man, only to relax once he recognized him. *Fool,* he had called him with irritation in his voice. The man had told them of the imminent arrival of a visitor and that he needed to gather Yazid and Alasdair to his side to join them. They should dress for battle and be ready to depart with the visitor. Then the Fool had pranced beyond the privacy screen that separated the royal chamber from the great hall, and disappeared into the night. Brigit had been quite flummoxed by it all, but Cai had reassured her that the Fool was one to be trusted, and his advice — however irksome — was to be followed. While she dressed and prepared tea, Cai had thrown on his breeches and headed out into the night to find and awaken Yazid and Alasdair.

While he was out, she realized, *he must have found Bradana and given her instructions as well.*

"How did he know?" Brigit said, finally finishing her question.

"Of Kevin?" Bradana asked. "He didna. At least, not that he told me. He just said he had to leave Esper for a time, and that danger was imminent. I was to watch over you and keep you safe. Of course, he could have mentioned that you were here," the veteran added with irritation. "Would have saved me a right bit of tracking. First I headed o'er to yer manor house, only to find you'd slipped out."

"You woke the servants, then?" Brigit asked resignedly. She'd have to face the scandal head-on. Not the way she'd hoped to start her reign, but not the worst of calamities. An indulgence. Once they were wed, it would merit no more than a naughty snicker. Still… it was just the sort of inauspicious beginning to her reign that they had been hoping to avoid.

"Well," Bradana replied, "I guessed that as you seemed to have gone to some lengths to sneak out unseen, you probably had good cause, and who was I to upset that apple cart?" She winked at Brigit, who sighed with profound relief.

"I followed your tracks to the barn," she continued, "Where I saw Cai's prints join with yours — he wears a distinctive boot, you see—confirming my suspicions. Then, I followed your tracks back to town to the back of the hall where I found the ladder affixed to the balcony. O'er the roar of the Gomul, I could just make out voices within and decided that since they sounded close to the balcony door, I might enter unseen through the front. That proved true. Glad I wasna too late."

"Your timing was perfect," Brigit answered with a grateful smile, and placed a hand on Bradana's arm warmly. Then, glancing back toward the bed chamber, she said "'Tis a right shame. To begin my rule in the blood of a rival for the crown. 'Twill set many against me from the start."

"And how exactly are they to know anything about this?" Bradana asked, leaning against her spear with a casual air and a mischievous grin.

"What do you mean?" Brigit asked, confused. "When the watch arrive, we'll have to explain what happened. We'll need to…" Her voice trailed off as Bradana's raised eyebrow moved higher still. "Surely, you dinna mean…" she began, her voice shocked.

The veteran merely shrugged and looked meaningfully over the railing at the raging whitewater below.

"Oh," Brigit replied softly, her eyes searching the furious, foaming water below. "Right." Then with a sigh and a playful grin that matched Bradana's, she added, "Well, let's to it, then."

And the two women moved to fetch the body.

Chapter 29

"'Tis the calm before the storm, lad," the aged sea captain said with a wry smile. "The morrow will prove most challenging indeed."

"But how can you tell?" the boy asked, tucking his scarf more firmly about his neck.

"I feel it in my bones. Deep in my bones. Tomorrow brings woe."

—"Pirates Of the Isthmus," from "Tales of the Red Hand"

Dawn, the Autumn Equinox
The Tor

Dallin

She had never felt such bliss. The woman's touch had been gentle at first, then her fingers probed the wound more deeply — painfully. Dallin had borne it for as long as she could, just gritting her teeth and enduring yet another wave of nauseating pain and weakness. Since getting injured, it had been one wave of agony after another, each moment filled with pain so sharp, so raw, she never would have imagined that she could endure it. But endure it she did — for hours that seemed like days upon the ice-cold stone floor of the temple. So this stranger's touch had merely ignited but one more wave of her torment.

Once more, she had ground her teeth and tensed against the soul-shredding pain she knew would come, but then… the light happened, and with it came the bliss. She didn't know how to describe it any other way. It felt like a glorious sunrise under her skin, accompanied, impossibly, with the scent of summer flowers and ocean breezes. The throbbing, fiery ache was replaced by a soothing comfort so soft and warm, she felt she had been wrapped in a down coverlet. A swirl of pleasant heat coalesced around her injured shoulder. She felt movement beneath the bandage, as though her flesh were moving of its own accord—which was so alarming that she almost cried out and wanted to rip away the bandage to see what was happening. But the subsequent wave of warmth was so calming that her alarm —so very elevated just a moment before—evaporated, leaving only mild curiosity in its place. Her eyebrows raised as the last of the residual pain and tenderness in her injury attenuated to nothing, leaving a renewed vigor in its place.

But the light's work was not done, as she felt it spread now throughout her entire body. The resulting wave of euphoria that overcame her was beyond description, and she stretched and sighed in ecstasy. She could feel the warmth tickling the backs of her hands and fingers where countless small scars crisscrossed her skin from years of sheepshearing. The knob on her right knee, that she had earned falling from the loft in the barn when she was but a girl of ten summers, suddenly bubbled and fizzed away to nothing. The crooked toe on her left foot—broken when their cow had spooked and trod on her—tingled, grew quite warm, and straightened. Injuries she carried from a lifetime of tending livestock melted away like sugar in warm tea. She marveled at the sense of wholeness and vitality that filled her. But when the glowing tide washed against the emotional trauma of her assault… that night when Brodie and Smitty and the others… She felt her spine stiffen and her soul rose up in panic to refuse the light, to turn it away from *that* place. *Anything but that!* The light paused as it lapped against the stone walls of her mind that surrounded the ordeal, respectful of her pain, yet continuous in its desire to wash it away, to purge her of this agony. That thought terrified her more than she could express or understand. That pain, that torment, those violent memories, had burrowed so deeply into her being that their thorns and barbs raked and pierced the tender flesh of her spirit. The anguish had become such a constant companion that she couldn't imagine existing without it anymore. Her spirit had grown defensive callouses around those thorns. Parts of her soul had calcified, annealing and thickening, becoming necessarily tough and coarse like old, thick leather. That pain was her constant companion—and, on some inchoate level, she felt like she deserved it, though that had never been a thought she had articulated. The idea of removing the chancre terrified her. What would happen to her defenses, her habitual torment, her identity? Could she live with such vulnerability? What if the thorns returned and the callouses were all removed? She couldn't bear the thought of going through the toughening again. *Not again!*

No, I beg you, her inner voice pleaded with the light. *You canna reach there. Just leave it, please!*

The woman with the dark skin leaned forward over Dallin. Her eyes were more than gentle, they were…loving.

"Dallin," she said softly. "I won't proceed if you don't want me to, but please, think about it. Kely and I can remove the trauma, the hurt and all of the pain. It will be but a distant memory, and you will have the chance to be more of your old self again."

Dallin shuddered, the terror bringing on a wave of nausea. "But…I'm scared."

"I know," the healer replied, the tone of her voice reminding Dallin of Kamdyn, her mother, despite the accent. "But think back to the carefree days before the attack. Remember who you were, then. Running and playing silly games with Ligulf, laughing at the festival dance, singing your songs when you thought no one was listening."

That brought a smile to Dallin's lips.

"Och, and that's caterwauling, sure."

"Wouldn't you welcome the chance to put all of that ugliness behind you?"

"But…"

"It will not hurt, I promise." The healer's luminous green eyes held such gentleness.

"Alright," she said with a quaver. "If you think you can get it all."

With that, Maddie smiled and stroked Dallin's cheek gently.

"Close your eyes, child," the healer said. Dallin did as she was bid, then Maddie closed hers and Dallin felt the light, the life, the healing begin again.

Probing fingers of light pushed gently at first, but then with more force, firmly and irresistibly forward, until the defensive walls of Dallin's heart began to crumble. She sobbed in fear, her hand clutching Maddie's tightly. Dallin heard the tall woman inhale deeply, as though fortifying her spirit against some greater effort. Then, like the sun breaking out from behind hazy clouds, the light intensified and brightened. The warmth flowing through Dallin exploded with newfound power, euphoric and overwhelming. The constricted muscles in her back, arms, and fists released suddenly, and she heard herself sigh loudly. As promised, there was no pain — only the memory of pain and a warm, persistent pressure.

All at once she felt the last of the internal stone walls — the calcification of her spirit and the foul barbed pustule of venomous memories and pain — burst, dissolve, and wash away in a great, irresistible tide of light. The place where the pain had been remained tender, vulnerable, but Maddie sent wave after wave of glowing, gentle warmth that soothed her spirit, healed it, strengthened it, stitching new healthy layers over the tenderness until that injured area of her soul gleamed with a newfound resilience — all the former toughness and the fragility at its core was being replaced by a joyful and durable strength. She could see it, now. She could visualize the powerful, joyful woman she could become — free of shame and trauma. A woman strong enough in spirit to truly stand beside Corvus Corax and his sons. She wanted that. *Needed* that.

The light swirled once more through her spirit, chasing off fears and worries like stray cats. She found herself smiling, a broad, joyous grin — like her old self.

She wept with relief. Disbelief and gratitude struggled for primacy in her thoughts. It couldn't be gone. The trauma, the self-loathing, the guilt, the hatred that she had carried these past months. It couldn't be gone. Yet... it was. Miraculously, undeniably, impossibly. It was gone. Her spirit bore no malice, her heart no shame. Somehow, the light had erased it all, like it was but a distant memory from a nightmare she had once experienced.

She felt as though she were floating, rhapsodic at the sudden absence and corresponding wholeness. The light shone so brightly beneath her skin, she was sure that if she opened her eyes, she would find herself incandescent. Her eyelids fluttered open tentatively, ready to wince against the brightness she knew would be there. But instead of blinding brilliance, she saw only the gentle, loving, and now bone-weary eyes of the tall, green-eyed woman who smiled down at her — Ambinintsoa, Ambini, though her friends called her Maddie. Somehow Dallin knew the woman's name, yet it was so much more than merely knowing her name. She *knew* her. Deeply. As closely as she knew Ligulf or her own mam. Memories of Ambini's childhood, the great ordeal of her journey to be at Queen Darienne's side, her love of and recent separation from the dashing Major Justiniere. All this she knew as intimately as if the women had shared a lifetime together and were as close as sisters. And with that knowledge came a soul-deep trust and affection. She reached a quivering hand upward toward her healer, who clasped it with both of hers.

"Welcome back, Dallin," Ambinintsoa said in her mellifluous voice.

"I am back, aren't I?" Dallin replied in wonder as she sat up, pain free, and assessed the renewed state of her body and spirit. Brochy snuffled and licked her hand eagerly. She stroked his head and clucked in wonder as her tongue traced newly repaired teeth. She lifted a hand to her cheek and found no scar. She looked to the healer, silently seeking affirmation that this wasn't a dream. Ambini smiled wearily, a tear cresting from an emerald eye and coursing down her velvety-smooth cheek.

A horrible rending sound pulled Dallin's attention to the front of the temple as another bolt of the infernal, black lightning ripped a gaping rupture in the shimmering fortress.

She sprang to her feet with a lightness she hadn't felt since her childhood. She smiled at Ambini and, scooping up her bow, said, "Time for me to quit lollygaggin' about and get back to work!"

Mama Warad

She saw what everyone could see: that the golden fortress would soon fall, and the slavering, savage Räubers would then be upon them. Glancing about the temple, she could see the trepidation in the eyes of every defender... save Corvus and Ashahl, who both seemed possessed of a similar practiced calm. Ashahl, her lost love. How was it possible that he still radiated such power and grace in his seventies, despite the years, and the ravages of torture and blinding? She allowed herself to drink in the sight of him for one more precious moment, then, with a sigh, she scolded herself. They were about to die here on this hilltop, so very distant from her homeland, and she was mooning like some adolescent girl!

Another shriek rattled them as yet another bolt of the dark lightning ripped another gash across the face of the fortress. *Not long now.* She heard a soft whimper and her eyes followed the sound. The three bards were standing in a clutch near the rear of the temple, holding one another. Rhona and Piper trembled with terror and Ligulf had his thin blade out, though she doubted it would do much good against the monstrous foes. She beckoned to the three to come stand with her, and they gratefully shuffled over, crowding around the small fire in the temple's corner alongside Yadira, Amina, and Argant.

"When wall falls," she instructed sharply, "no move."

"What d'ye suppose she means by that?" Piper whispered to Ligulf. Before the younger minstrel could reply with his best guess, Yadira answered.

"She means to hide us from their sight," the older votary said. "Stillness will help the illusion."

"Illusion, is it? Och, aye," Piper responded, grasping the plan. "As still as stane, I'll be, if it'll scouk us fae that lot!"

Mama's brow furrowed as she concentrated on the lead Räuber, who was casting the bolts of lightning. His latest attack had left a rent in the wall through which she could see him more clearly. His skin was unusually smooth and almost purple in color, with striations and mottling not unlike marble. His eyes were pure black, just like those of the Nephellem, though his did not seem to drip the vile ichor. He was clearly possessed of some evil spirit, as they had been. The Canon of Release would once again be needed. But she would be too busy with the Canon of Perception, hiding those behind her. The effort and concentration that would be required to obscure the three bards, her votaries, herself, and Argant would be significantly more than she had ever attempted—there would be no way she could also approach the possessed man and release the demon within him.

She tried to think of alternatives but decided that obscuring the noncombatants and keeping them huddled near the back, out of the way of the warriors, was the best option.

"Be ready, dear ones!" Mama warned.

Corvus

His brows raised in wonder as Dallin stood and scooped up her bow, a renewed buoyancy in her stance. He squinted and looked more closely. In the dim half-light of dawn, and from this distance, he could swear the scar on Dallin's face was gone. *That canna be. Just a trick of the light, but… there's no denyin' that Dallin is up, on her feet, gripping her bow with a divil's own smile on her face.* He shook his head in wonder and flashed an approving glance at the young Queen, who smiled proudly back at him.

He turned his gaze to Cailean, who was adjusting the strap on his shield. His son seemed to sense his father's eyes upon him, and he turned, giving Corvus a sparkling smile. *Cai, my boy,* Corvus thought proudly. *Never worried afore a fight. A born leader, that one.* Corvus returned the smile and looked over his shoulder at Ligulf, who was standing with the other bards by the rear of the temple. Rhona and Piper looked worried, and Ligulf had a hand, protectively, on Piper's shoulder. In his other, he held his puntina. Corvus knew the lad could defend himself but neither that slender weapon, nor his younger son's slight frame, were built for the storm that was about to break upon them. Corvus gestured to Alasdair to step close.

"Aye, Corvus?" the grizzled veteran asked as he approached.

"When the scratch begins," Corvus said softly, "keep those three behind ye."

"I assumed as much," Alasdair said with a wink. "I'll watch yer boy."

"I'm obliged," Corvus replied, and patted the veteran's shoulder. Then he turned his attention to Yazid. "Alright, old man?"

Yazid's weary grin turned into a grimace as the act of facing Corvus stretched the skin of his wound. "I am fine, I think," his friend answered, though the lie was all too apparent.

He wouldn't be much help in this state, and Corvus' concern for his friend would prove a liability. He looked to the tall healer who had returned to the Queen's side and nodded toward Yazid. "Any chance you have some of your gift left to help that one?"

"Healing leaves her quite drained," Darienne said protectively. "I don't think it would be…"

"It's alright, Majesty," the tall woman interrupted. "I'll see to him."

Though as she moved toward Yazid, her knees buckled. Corvus caught her and made sure she was able to steady herself.

"Are you certain, lass?"

She insisted she was fine and continued over toward Yazid — the Queen's glare shooting daggers at Corvus.

"There will be others to heal," Darienne said with irritation. "She should save her gifts."

"Fair enough," Corvus replied. "But that man, healthy, is worth any five others in a scrap."

The Queen sniffed in response. Her eyes kept darting from one enemy to another, and she was shifting her weight from side to side, clearly nervous. Corvus turned to Kaiso.

"When it begins," he said brusquely, "you and Her Majesty pull back to the corner, yonder. Our archer will need protecting."

The captain nodded, clearly understanding that Corvus was placing the Queen in the most defensible position.

"Badger or Eagle?" Ashahl asked in Aslene, causing Corvus to turn to him.

"Well," he pondered, "I had considered Mountain, but I suspect I'll begin with Badger. And how will you fight, Master?"

"You mean, how will I fight without vision?"

"Exactly," Corvus answered simply. Despite the decades gone, he could feel them each falling into their old rhythms. Master and student. Ashahl always leading every exchange, challenges in his every question, wisdom in every answer.

"Do you recall observing the blind fighting trials of the young masters?" Ashahl asked.

"I heard word of them, Master," Corvus replied, thoughtfully. "But I was never invited to observe."

"Ah, yes." Ashahl nodded. "The Prince forbade your attendance. I had forgotten."

"Forbade?"

"Yes," Ashahl said. "You had earned your position, training among us. But nonetheless, you were still considered an outsider and therefore a possible enemy of the Silken Throne. Certain secrets were simply not to be shared."

"That would explain much," Corvus said, then added, "You pushed those boundaries on my behalf repeatedly, did you not?"

"You were the most gifted student I ever trained," Ashahl said with a wistful smile. "I wanted to test your limits, to teach you everything I could, to see you truly master the breadth of our practices. But I was restricted in so many ways."

"What you taught me, Master," Corvus replied gravely, "has served to protect me and mine for a lifetime. It was through your teachings I was able to keep my people free and safe all these years."

A screech interrupted their remembrances as another bolt ripped across the front of the fortress, carving off yet another chunk of the front wall to dissipate into golden mist. The gap it left was now almost big enough for the Räubers to squeeze through.

Corvus shifted his stance, Raven's Tooth held low before him.

"Stand behind me, Master," he said. "The wall will fall with the next bolt."

"Behind you?" Ashahl replied with a chuckle. "Why ever would I do that?"

With that, the aged master dropped into a low crouch, his left leg extended to the side. He held his staff in his right hand, horizontal, some inches from the floor, while his left arm curled behind his back like the bent leg of an arachnid. Corvus' skin suddenly tingled and at the edges of his vision he perceived a strange sparkling around Ashahl. Something was happening that was beyond human sight. He eased his mind from conscious thought, as with the opening movements of Eagle form, and as he felt the familiar vertigo of the Sight coming over him, he could see faintly luminous lines extending from his master like the strands of a spider's web. Each line extended to one of the defenders in the temple. Ashahl swung his head slowly from side to side, as though hearing or feeling something from each strand—or, perhaps, *seeing* something? That was it. He had no idea how he understood this, but he knew it to be true nonetheless. His master was somehow seeing through the eyes of the other defenders, the lines of energy like a spider's webbing.

"Form of Sabat?" Corvus whispered, awestruck, using the Aslene word for spider. It was one of the most mysterious and most difficult forms, reputedly only mastered after a lifetime of study by the most gifted and powerful practitioners — so difficult and subtle, its secrets were thought to have been lost to antiquity as no one had mastered it in generations, if ever. The only knowledge of it came in rumors and tall tales told in the dormitory after hours. Corvus had never truly believed it to be a real thing, the tales seemed so exaggerated. He had always assumed it to be a myth, relegated in his mind to the children's stories of dragons, Al Anqa'a, or djinn. But here it was before him, being performed by his own master.

"Though she spins her web in the dark," Ashahl intoned quietly, "it is perfect and strong, each strand telling her a tale."

A final screech sounded and the golden walls protecting them came apart completely, dissolving into a great cloud of golden mist that rose toward the glowering black clouds that had covered the Tor these past hours. As the golden mist encountered the stygian clouds above, the two canceled each other out like some solute added to a colored liquid causing an alchemical reaction that suddenly turns the elixir clear. The black clouds and their attendant unnatural gloom dissipated leaving behind a glorious, rose-colored dawn that spread over the Tor and the lands surrounding it. The Equinox had arrived.

And with a savage cry, the Räubers attacked.

Chapter 30

No greater bond exists than that between brothers of blood and steel.
—*Anonymous*

Dawn, the Autumn Equinox
The Tor

Maddie

As Maddie turned her attention toward the burly Aslene man—had they said his name was Yazder? or Azid? Yazid, perhaps?—she swooned. But this was not exhaustion — though she hovered dangerously close to overextending — but connection, perhaps. It was as though she were in two places at once. She still felt the cold solidity of the temple floor beneath her, but somehow also a wooden floor, slick with moisture, that moved and swayed… like the deck of a ship.

Pierrick, some part of her spirit told her. Justiniere's warm presence filled her mind for a moment, before slipping away into a gust of cold, wet air. *Pierrick! By the mountain's grace, it is Pierrick!*

He was on a ship sailing to Autun. She closed her eyes and concentrated on him, and suddenly she could perceive the cold waters of the Claws beyond him, practically feeling the icy wind. She marveled at the feeling—it was so strong, so real! The few times she had ever bonded with someone she had healed, she had afterward been able to sense their presence if they were nearby. Sometimes she could sense their emotions, or get a sense of their immediate surroundings. But nothing like this. Pierrick was over a hundred leagues distant in a vessel on the Claws, while she stood upon the Tor in the Green Mount. She had never imagined connecting with someone over that distance.

Knowing that time was pressing, she paused for only a moment longer to try to get a sense of his emotional state. He was worried… about her. Somehow he knew she'd stepped into danger, but he didn't know what or where. She smiled and tried to send loving reassurance to him, but she was uncertain whether he perceived it.

Opening her eyes, she found the heroic young man — Cailean? — standing before her, his strong hands holding her arms and worry on his face. He must have caught her when she swooned. With a shy smile, she pulled away from him. The warrior's brows were knit with obvious concern for her. She placed a hand briefly on his arm until he was reassured. Then, with careful steps, she finished crossing to Yazid and, taking a deep breath, laid her hands on his shoulders. He looked at her quite confused but allowed the touch. Despite her fatigue, she called upon her fanahy to rise and begin healing him. The childlike spirit was slow to stir, as though waking from slumber. But after a moment she felt the familiar warmth in her hands as they began to glow.

Then, with a shriek and a crash, another black bolt of lightning struck the shimmering wall and, with that, the fortress about them fell.

"You must step back, I think," Yazid said, gently pushing her away and turning his wobbly stance to face the onrushing Räubers.

Maddie staggered back from him, suddenly realizing the immediacy of the danger. Giant men, slavering with bloodlust, were scrabbling up the short defile that led to the temple. Others were leaping the scrubbed thicket in the gap between the path and the temple's raised front. Defenders' spears lashed out, opening chests and taking eyes or teeth, and arrows flew from Dallin with deadly accuracy. The heroic-looking young man with the sword and shield gave a challenging shout and rushed forward to defend the defile. Corvus too rushed forward with surprising agility and power, his curved blade dealing death and flashing in the rose-hued light of dawn. Yazid stepped up next to his comrade, spear moving with surgical accuracy. But she could tell his strength was limited. Even as she watched, he sagged against a pillar next to Corvus, allowing the marble to bear his weight, so that more of his waning strength could go into his efforts with his weapon. However, despite his weakness, she watched as he dispatched one of the huge enemies with his deft and precise spear work.

To her right, she heard a triumphant shout as one Räuber scrabbled over the dead body of another and gained the temple floor unchallenged, the defenders all occupied elsewhere. He bared his teeth and pointed at Dallin, his black tongue waggling hungrily as he brandished short axes in each hand. There was an answering shout from behind Maddie and suddenly Darienne leapt in front of the archer, her saber slashing furiously at the intruder.

A sense of incredulity flickered in her mind. Worry for the Queen. Justiniere couldn't believe what he was perceiving across their bond. Was it possible that he could see some of this through her eyes?

She felt a burning urgency to pull the Queen back, to get her out of there.

I cannot, Pierrick, she thought, her weary eyes crinkling in pride as she watched Darienne bravely engage a warrior twice her size. *It is why she is here.*

As if it were a planned joint attack, Kaiso slid along the marble floor to Darienne's right, his blade hacking into the

Räuber's shin. One of the enemy's axes chopped downward at the Queen, while the other narrowly missed Kaiso's prone form. Darienne pivoted, her blade redirecting the axe, then—spinning and dropping to a knee—she slashed furiously at the man's belly, opening it and spilling his intestines. More quickly than the Queen's face could register the fact that she had prevailed and killed the Räuber, two more took his place, and she moved in response. Maddie blinked in surprise and awe. Darienne was quite good with her blade. Quite good indeed! *So… sand and blood in her clothes. She had been training!*

She watched as Darienne deftly avoided a wicked backhand slash, spun gracefully, and stabbed the back of her opponent's thigh with her dagger. Before the man could turn to strike back, she knelt suddenly, all her weight riding on the dagger handle. The blade sliced down the length of the man's leg, opening the artery and slicing tendons. The Räuber collapsed to the ground, where Kaiso dispatched him with a quick thrust to the chest.

A white blur drew Maddie's eye to her left. The blind old man with the staff was spinning, whirling, moving with a smooth power that defied his age. There was an economy to his movements, using only the force and speed necessary to affect the goal. And such grace! She had never seen anyone move like that. How he could see his opponents was beyond her understanding, but she watched in awe as he spun and slid along the floor, his staff shattering bones, blocking weapons, spearing into groins, eyes, armpits and throats with preternatural accuracy. All the while, a gentle smile played upon his lips, and his milky white eyes seemed to be focused inwardly.

Three of the enemy gained the temple floor on the far left, and the grizzled soldier—Alasdair?—rushed to meet them alone. He kicked the smallest of the three in the chest, backing him up, then the Highlander crashed into the largest, their swords tangling. The Räuber was a huge, scarred beast with black feathers tied into his wild, white hair. An arrow from Dallin pierced the spine of the third man, felling him before his sword could hit Alasdair's unprotected side. Maddie watched in horror as—with a roar—the feathered Räuber lifted Alasdair from his feet and slammed him down on his back. The shorter Barbár that he had previously kicked recovered himself and, stepping around, raised a bulbous war club for a killing blow. Instinctively, Maddie screamed and rushed to Alasdair's aid.

She was no warrior. She had never trained a single day in martial skills, yet somehow — perhaps through her connection to Pierrick — she avoided the hazards of nearby battles and slipped up behind War Club as he reared his arm back, gripped his weapon arm at the elbow, and instinctively spun the huge man, using leverage she didn't know she had.

If she had held a weapon, she could easily have buried it in the man's chest in the moment he spun, his surprise mirroring her own at what she'd done. Instead, she stood dumbly, staring up at him, not sure what to do next. Her indecision was short-lived as War Club slapped her away with a vicious forehand blow that sent her tumbling back across the temple toward Darienne, the taste of copper flooding her mouth.

A sense of alarm flared in her mind from Pierrick.

Blinking away stars, she watched as War Club then turned back toward Alasdair with a hungry smile, raising his weapon once more for the killing blow — only to find Ligulf now standing astride the fallen veteran, the minstrel's puntina naked before him.

"That'll be enough from you," Li said softly, before unleashing a lightning-fast, withering series of four slashes with his feather-light blade, culminating with a thrust to the man's groin. The Räuber dropped his war club as blood suddenly spurted from the various injuries. His twitching eyes drifted down toward his groin, where the needle-like blade still impaled him. With a jerk and a kick to the man's bleeding chest, Ligulf withdrew his puntina from the wound — which spouted black blood — and, pivoting, quickly slashed it down across the face of Black Feathers, who was still choking the rapidly fading Alasdair. The Räuber's cheek opened and he released the veteran with a scream of outrage, then turned and surged into Ligulf, tackling him to the ground. A meaty hand gripped the young man's sword arm and a barbed dagger was instantly in Black

Feathers' other fist. Ligulf twisted and struggled to try to avoid the hacking chops raining down, but held as he was, his mobility was limited. He hissed in pain as the dagger opened a line of fire down his left side along the ribs.

It was then that Piper threw himself upon Black Feathers' back, despite having no weapon, and wrapped his arms around the attacker's throat, his teeth ripping at the man's ear. With a shout, Rhona, despite her injured wrist, leapt to join him. Grimacing with pain, she wrapped herself around the dagger arm. MacLief appeared, and his spear stabbed into the Räuber's side, blood splashing onto Ligulf. The brute dropped his dagger and seized the spear haft. With a mighty jerk he yanked the weapon from his body and shoved the Adder away. MacLief staggered back and tripped, his feet fouling on the stone block by the fire. With a roar that seemed equal parts pain and frustration, Black Feathers cast Rhona off. She cried out as she fell, her injured wrist beneath her. Then, with Piper still clenched about his neck, the Räuber grabbed his dagger, not bothering to switch from reverse grip, and clubbed upward at Piper's skull with the bone handle. The bard's body went instantly limp. Battered and bloody, Black Feathers' hungry eyes returned to Ligulf, but a ragged shout pulled them up just as a dazed Alasdair arrived and plunged his sword into the man's chest.

"Tough bastard, that," he muttered.

"Thanks," Ligulf said with a grimace as he rose, holding his ribs.

"Not quite as fancy as your rare moves," Alasdair replied, his voice raspy and raw. "But at least I let him die with his manhood."

Li grinned and moved to check on Piper and Rhona.

Maddie just stood, her hand covering the rapid swelling on the side of her face, when Kaiso slammed into her back. He was exchanging blows with a one-eyed brute who was already bleeding from at least two serious wounds, though the Räuber seemed undaunted by the injuries. Darienne, meanwhile, was locked in a fierce exchange with a bare-breasted female Räuber, who stood at least a head taller than the young Queen.

An impulse to duck was suddenly hammered into Maddie's mind.

Without thinking, she complied just as Darienne's sword sliced over her head, winding up for powerful attack.

Thank you, Pierrick, she thought.

She turned and stumbled from the violence only to find herself trapped at the southern edge of the temple. Despite her best efforts to stay clear of the fighting, she increasingly found herself underfoot. Darienne backed into her again. This time, the Queen's sweeping sword arm caught Maddie in the stomach, the elbow doubling her over, forcing her to take a knee. She found herself clutching a pillar desperately to keep from falling off the edge. Her vision swam and she felt a strange tingling sensation in her fingers—as though she were sending her fanahy forth for a healing.

Kely, what is happening? she asked of her child spirit.

I'm not sure, Ambini, the girl's voice answered immediately. *It is Darienne. She is calling me.*

Calling you? How?

I'm not sure, but she needs me.

As Maddie tried to make sense of things, the Räuber fighting Darienne pressed forward, his sword pounding down like a blacksmith's hammer. The Queen staggered back, bumping once more into Maddie. Just then, Kaiso crowded into them, his sword held high. Suddenly, the tingling in Maddie's fingers became a full roar as her fanahy rushed out. The Queen's sword flared with a luminous silver light, its movements leaving a tail of light behind it, as though a long, luminous silver scarf were attached along the length of the blade. Darienne was so stunned, she nearly dropped the weapon. Instead she froze, staring at it. The attacking Räuber paused her own next attack as well, her eyes wide at the magic before her. Kaiso took the opportunity to plunge his sword into the Räuber's naked chest. As the woman collapsed, Kaiso turned back to Darienne, his face going pale at the sight of the still-glowing weapon. He stepped back, clearly unsettled by the magic. As he moved away, the sword's glowing light extinguished.

By the blade! Maddie exclaimed, echoing Pierrick's customary phrase.

"What was that?" Darienne demanded. She looked to Maddie, her eyes wide with shock and surprise. Maddie shrugged helplessly and looked to Kaiso, whose bloodless face told of some unspoken dread.

Then a scream drew her attention away from the Queen to the front edge of the temple. She gasped in horror as a huge attacker lifted Barclay's limp body and cast it down into the surging mass of enemy warriors, who fell upon it with a savage ferocity, chopping and stomping him into the ground. It had been Anna's scream she had heard. The female Adder had been knocked to her back, her spear broken. Apparently Barclay had rushed to her aid and died for his gallantry. Now, with a vengeful cry, Anna launched herself onto the back of the attacker, her left arm clinging to his throat as her right plunged the broken spear head repeatedly into his chest. The Räuber spun and slammed his back into the nearby pillar, and Anna's head cracked against the marble audibly. Her arms went limp and she crumpled from his back, the spearhead still protruding from his chest as he turned and raised his axe over her. There was a sudden white blur as Ashahl leapt across the front of the Räuber, slapping a rigid open hand down onto the protruding spearhead and plunging the blade fully into the man's heart. The Räuber stood momentarily still, seemingly confused by the old blind man. Then he collapsed backward out of the temple.

"What just happened?" Darienne demanded, still staring awestruck at her blade, apparently oblivious to the unfolding crisis involving Anna, Barclay, and Ashahl.

Yazid had now limped over in response to Anna's scream and positioned himself protectively over her prone form, spitting defiance in the faces of the Räubers. However, as he stepped into position, his left foot fouled on the fallen Adder's body and he almost fell, barely catching himself with a hiss and a visible grimace of pain.

Maddie rushed forward, ducking to avoid Ashahl's spinning staff on her left and Yazid's flashing spear on her right. She grasped Anna's limp arm and, grunting with effort, dragged her back toward Dallin at the rear of the temple. She propped the wounded Adder against a pillar with a quick promise to return once the Queen was out of danger. She paused and looked in confusion at her hands. The involuntary tingling in her fingers had ceased once she moved away from Darienne.

A cry from Yazid pulled her attention back to the battle. He had apparently taken a blow and sagged to a knee against the pillar on the southern edge of the temple, his fragile strength all but gone.

"Yazid!" Corvus shouted from where he was positioned at the mouth of the defile, the fountain to his back. The Raven's singing blade was holding a crush of the enemy at bay, despite their numbers. She could see a sheen of sweat on his bald pate as he glanced over with concern in their direction. There was a pile of corpses and gravely wounded Räubers at Corvus' feet. Yet, despite all the tumult, he had still heard and recognized his friend's cry.

With a shout, Darienne jumped forward, engaging the nearest Räuber. Three of the brutes now faced off with Ashahl, the Queen, Kaiso, and the kneeling Yazid. Blades, fists, and feet flashed mercilessly and despite Kaiso's skill, Ashahl's grace, and the wild abandon with which Darienne fought, it was clear the Räubers would soon overwhelm them. Maddie watched the rhythm of Darienne's sword arm, trying to gauge a good moment to move to her lady's support, though she had no idea what she might do once there. She made two or three false starts, but her courage failed when she didn't see a clear opening.

She felt a strong sense of fear flood through her bond.

I must be near her! she thought. *If she gets injured, I have to be ready.*

Strong disagreement and more fear.

She was about to yield to Justiniere's wisdom when she saw her moment. The combination of a wild slash from the Queen and a weak thrust to the face from Yazid drove the center Räuber back into the other two, fouling their attacks for a precious moment. She leapt forward, placing a supporting hand on Darienne's back as the Queen took a brief moment to breathe, her eyes flashing among the enemies, gauging their recovery time. As she touched the Queen's back, Maddie's fingers suddenly starting burning again as her fanahy was being pulled into Darienne.

"Kaiso!" Maddie shouted, startling the mercenary. His dark eyes flashed at her questioningly. "Come close to Darienne!"

"What?" he snapped peevishly as he traded blows with the center Räuber.

"Just do it!" she yelled, and the irritated captain adjusted his fighting stance, shuffling over to stand closer to Darienne while still trading blows with the scarred brute, who sported a long earring of human finger bones.

As he stepped near, several things seemed to happen at once. Darienne gasped as her blade ignited with the same pearlescent illumination as it had earlier. The Räuber on their right, who wore a golden nose ring, launched a vicious attack at the kneeling Yazid, the look of resignation on the pallid Aslene's face making clear that his resistance was gone and he had no defense against this. Ashahl slid to his left, engaging the man on that side and drawing him away from the Queen, while the center Räuber screamed a ululating cry and raised his sword above his head, preparing for a crushing blow to Darienne's skull. The Queen's sword flew up to parry that attack, passing in front of Yazid as it rose, leaving a ghostly trail of argent light behind it. When Nose Ring's blade, which was striking out toward Yazid, encountered the light tail, his sword shattered with a screech, leaving the weakened Aslene untouched and the Räuber mutely staring at the metal stump in his hand.

Darienne's sword easily parried the blow descending toward her from the screaming center foe, his weapon likewise shattered. Without hesitation, the Queen completed the movement of her blade, sweeping the sword down past her left shoulder, narrowly missing a surprised Kaiso, and slashing across the midsection of all three Räubers in an attempt to dust them back and give her some breathing room. But this was no mere dusting back. As she slashed, a razor thin line of silver light flashed forward from her blade, actually cutting the Räubers in half, their torsos falling back upon their fellows below the lip of the temple.

"What devilry is this?" Kaiso shouted, and once more pulled away from Darienne, her sword's light immediately extinguishing as he stepped away.

"The prophecy!" Maddie whispered in awe. "She is the Moonflower!"

Darienne spun on her. "What? What are you saying?"

"The legend. The flower only blossoms between sorcery and steel, yes?" Maddie pointed to herself and Kaiso. The sword only seemed to ignite when Maddie and Kaiso were both close to Darienne—Kaiso steel, and Maddie sorcery. "It is your birthright, Majesty! Your blood!"

Kaiso's face was a mask of distaste and fear, but a scream from their left caused the bodyguard to spin, putting his back instinctively against Darienne. A furious Räuber was storming toward them, a war hammer held lightly in his grip. Darienne's sword once more ignited, and with a surge of newfound strength, she spun toward the oncoming brute, her rising sword cleaving the air with a glowing tail that whipped forward like a silken scarf, slashing the Räuber's face. The brute dropped his weapon and fell to a knee screaming, clutching a ruined eye with both hands. Kaiso's sword flashed and the Räuber's head fell from his shoulders.

Amazing! Maddie stepped back, in awe. *The legend speaks of one who would wield the very light of the moon, but I never thought it was real. Such magic!*

Not magic, she corrected herself. *It is her legacy—her blessing from the Goddess.*

"You are indeed the Moonflower, Majesty," Maddie said to the Queen, who met her gaze with dawning realization.

Darienne looked at her glowing blade then whipped the tip of it in the direction of a scarred Räuber just climbing past the lip of the temple. Faster than an arrow in flight, a small silver ball of energy leapt from her sword and flew at the man's face. The Räuber snarled as it hit him, his nose spouting blood. But the man did not fall backward. Apparently, the energy summoned by such a quick flick was minimal, or else perhaps the gesture was not expertly done. Still, Darienne shouted a shrill yip of joy and flicked her weapon once more at the brute. As before, a small ball of energy flew at him, just as he was shaking off the effect of the first one. This time, the energy struck the side of the man's head, turning him and causing him to lose his balance. With a shout, the Räuber fell backward into the seething mass of his companions.

Before the Moonflower trio could discuss this latest experiment in her newfound power, they heard a cry of warning from Yazid. Maddie turned and saw the Aslene surge unsteadily to his feet, his eyes filled with horror at something across and below the temple front, directly before Corvus. Following his gaze, Maddie saw the strange, tall Räuber with the marbled skin. He had been casting the bolts of lightning from his hands and had now stepped directly in front of the defile, his eyes on Corvus and his arm crackling with imminent energy. Corvus was either unaware of the danger or unwilling to yield his position despite it. An arrow from Dallin flew past Yazid's head, striking the strange man in his cheek, but the arrow shattered on impact as though he really were made of marble, leaving no mark. At almost the same instant, with a burst of speed that Maddie would have thought impossible for one in such a weakened state, Yazid hurled his spear at the man and pitched his body at Corvus, knocking his friend out of the way just as a bolt of the black lightning detonated like a bomb.

Yazid's smoking body was hurled backward, up and over the fountain, where he crashed to the floor and slid toward the back edge of the temple. Ligulf and Rhona ignored their own wounds and threw themselves onto Yazid to stop him before he slid off the sheer drop on the westward side of the platform. They managed to arrest his movement, but then recoiled in horror from the blackened, smoking hole that gaped in his chest. His glazed eyes stared at nothing.

Yazid was gone.

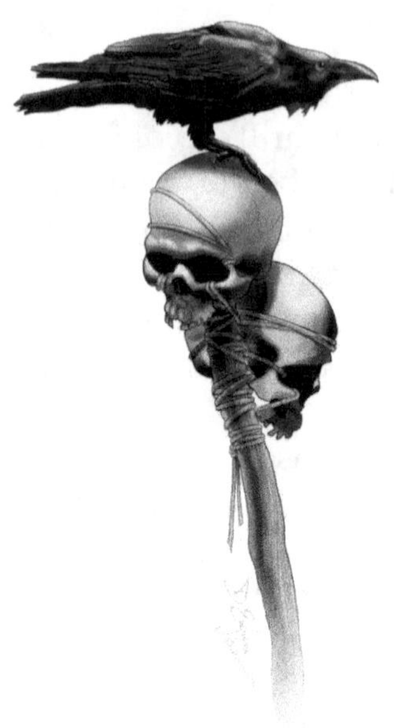

Chapter 31

Early in the practitioner's journey, each step of their learning is laid out and prescribed. The path before them is simple and obvious. The metaphoric stepping stones are spaced evenly and at understandable distances, so the practitioner need only focus on learning the predetermined next step. However, with advancement, the steps become further and further apart, their spacing irregular. Sometimes there are multiple possible paths forward, and frequently it will be unclear as to which stone represents the correct next step. This is the time of choosing, when the practitioner begins to shape their mastery. At the highest levels of enlightenment, the practitioner has moved beyond any given path and instead stands within a constellation of possible paths. Now, the practitioner begins to discern and truly develop their own tariq alruwh, the Path of the Spirit. At this level, the practitioner is discovering the endless possibilities and choosing what will constitute their personal journey.

—*Most Elevated Samal bin Malik*

Dawn, the Autumn Equinox
The Tor

Sangine

Dawn was upon them. There was no time to waste. Sangine struggled to shove his way through the massed Räubers at the top of the trail. He shoved into the press near the final rise, eager to get past them all and lay eyes on the temple. A snarling brute with a scar that ran vertically through his lips and corresponding missing teeth turned and shoved back.

"Back off, little man!"

Sangine shoved again, trying to squeeze between the bodies and press his way up the rise, but he was still weakened from the agony of the blood gem and the Räuber was having none of his efforts. With a violent shove, Sangine was tossed backward, down the trail, landing roughly on the steeply slanted stones and tumbling down the path until he crashed into the rock outcropping at the switchback below. A trickle of blood streamed from a gash above his temple and he sat blinking for a moment, waiting for the world to stop spinning. He didn't have time for this. The Equinox was upon them, and the dissolution of the gloom meant that the blasted White Cleft troops would be approaching more quickly now, unhindered by the dread. Soon the Räubers would find themselves pressed between two enemies. He cared not a jot for the health and well-being of Vajk's warriors — they were a means to an end — but they had to kill the defenders and he *had* to get into that temple before the boy assumed the mantle of Gatekeeper of the Tor.

With shaking hands, he pushed himself up to standing. The exertions of the past hours were once again weighing upon him. He *needed* more blood. He *needed* to be in that temple! On wobbly legs he climbed the path, his eyes locked on the back of the brute that had hurled him down the trail. Precious blood streamed and dripped from the side of his head. The crack of lightning sounded from above, followed by a brief lull in the hubbub. He tried to picture what was happening up there as the urgency of the moment pressed him onward.

He clutched at the arm of the offending man, who spun, snarling. Faster than he could react, however, Sangine's other hand clamped onto his face, the Räuber's knees immediately buckling as his eyes rolled upward in sudden agony. Black blisters bubbled up on the barbarian's face and blood streamed from his eyes and nose. Before the screaming could even begin, Sangine felt the swelling of his sinews, might and vitality burgeoning within him. By the time the man did howl in agony, alerting his fellows to his distress, Sangine's strength had returned. With a slap of his hand, he easily deflected their efforts to dislodge him from his victim, his eyes flashing a murderous warning to them to stay back—a warning that was reinforced by the horror of his victim's disfigurement and obvious torment. They watched in revulsion as Sangine's victim collapsed, mewling in agony, while the shaman's muscles swelled, veins bulging, threatening to burst through his paper-like skin.

Finally! He was whole again, the hours of depletion and the agonizing hunger that accompanied such weakness were now but a memory. Energy coursed through his veins and his clawed hands closed and opened rhythmically.

Just then, the skirl of bagpipes sounded from behind and below them. The damned White Cleft troops were nearing. With a snarl and a sigh, he lifted the shriveled remains of the Räuber effortlessly and cast it down the Tor at the Highlander troops. He spun back to face the massed Räubers, his eyes searching for a path upward through the scrum of bodies. Then, deciding against pressing his way up the trail, he instead turned and leapt up the steep slope, easily clearing the fifteen feet and landing in a feral crouch among a mass of Räubers. The warriors recoiled from his sudden presence among them. Quickly scanning the temple's confines, he picked out the cursed Raven, his son, and an old blind man in white silk wielding a staff. There was a woman with a sword that he hadn't seen before, the damned archer bitch near the back of the temple, and a tall black-skinned woman also near the rear.

Where are the rest of them? Where are the boy and the witch? He scanned the temple furiously, unable to find them. The tingle in his skin told him that magic was being used, but where? How?

"Find the boy!" he screamed to the massed Räubers, his enhanced voice shocking them out of their momentary confusion. The Highlander army was fast approaching their rear, the damnable bagpipes screeching their approach. In response to Sangine's shout, the former Grand Hadvezér lifted his still smoking hand and reached toward the temple. Another bolt of the black lightning arced forward. One of the defenders tackled the Raven in the split second before the lightning struck, saving the warlord but sacrificing himself in the process. The Räubers charged the temple, seeking to capitalize on the defenders' momentary disarray.

Corvus

"No!" Corvus screamed, though his voice sounded faint and remote.

His entire world seemed to dissolve around him. The sounds of battle suddenly became muted and distant, replaced by a steady ringing. The movement of the Adders nearby slowed down, even as they tried desperately to stem the tide of maddened Räubers rushing the defile. All he could see was the body of his oldest friend lying in smoking ruin at the back of the temple, and Ligulf's hollow eyes staring at his father in mute despair from where he crouched beside Yazid's body.

Faster than Corvus could catalogue the memories, his mind flashed through countless moments with his friend who had been an ever-present and balancing force in his life. So many memories, so many important moments in the boys' lives... It felt like too much for Corvus to grasp all at once—the enormity and totality of this loss. He had somehow always known that Yazid had come into his life for a purpose. The gods, the Five, the Ancestors, *someone* had guided this gentle, jovial, intelligent, and skilled man to his side for a reason. Clearly, there had been vital lessons he had to learn from Yazid in order to complete his journey, and his friend's affable, solid presence had come to be so ubiquitous, so constant, that he had never imagined what life would be without his comrade there beside him. Too many were the recollections of long, laughter-filled conversations late into the night, baring his hopes and dreams, fears and frustrations, to his Aslene friend.

A yawning pit opened in his soul and, still prone after being shoved aside by Yazid, Corvus closed his eyes against the despair and felt his forehead touch the floor. The sounds of battle around him receded, replaced by a great roaring. He clenched his eyes shut more tightly and slowly rolled his head from side to side.

Cailean

From where he fought near the middle of the temple, Cai had watched as Yazid barreled into his father, shoving him aside just before the black lightning struck. And despite seeing Yazid — this man that was like a dear uncle — get blasted over the fountain, Cai's mind stupidly hung on the last burst of energy the injured Aslene had shown.

How did he do that? He could barely walk, much less run, throw a spear, and tackle a man. How did he…?

His thoughts were interrupted when the nearest Räuber slashed at his face with a barbed dagger. Cai's shield came up instinctively, but then the enemy suddenly redoubled his attacks, demanding Cai's full attention.

He scolded himself for letting his focus get drawn away during a scrap. It could easily have cost him his life. Thankfully, his father and Yazid had drilled him mercilessly over the years to sharpen his reflexes.

Yazid. *Oh, sweet Manu, no!*

He blinked back tears and forced himself to channel his blossoming grief into rage. He launched a vicious attack series against his opponent, which clearly surprised the man. Within three strokes, the Räuber's dismembered arm slapped against the marble floor, still clutching its dagger. As its owner staggered back, eyes wide with horror at his severed limb, Cai spun into a low foot sweep, putting the man on his back. Cai pounced, his knee driving down into the warrior's throat as he pounded the hilt of his sword repeatedly into the man's face with rhythmic, powerful blows. His muscles, honed by years of daily martial practice, drove the weapon down with the force of a sledgehammer. Another Räuber rushed to the fallen man's defense, but a disdainful rising stroke from Cai's sword opened the would-be rescuer from groin to chin without even causing the pummeling to break rhythm.

After a moment, he stood, blood-spattered and gory, looking about for another target for his boundless rage. To his left, a trio of Räubers gained entrance to the temple up through the defile. He looked about in confusion. His da was covering that area… Where was Corvus? Then his eyes fell upon his father, lying motionless on the ground.

Cai's heart stopped. *No, it's too much! Not both of them!*

Then he noticed Corvus' head moving back and forth in a rocking motion, his forehead against the floor, as if he was voicing his denial to the very Tor itself. Cai breathed a sigh of relief, though it would be short-lived if those three reached the Raven.

"Da!" he shouted over the din, but his father didn't seem to hear him. "Da, get up!"

The three Räubers closed on Corvus' prone form. This was their chance to end the dreaded Raven once and for all. The three strode forward, weapons raised, their hungry focus on the fallen man before them.

In a panic, Cai launched a sweeping cut at the nearest man's back. But he knew that it wouldn't be enough. He couldn't possibly reach the other two before their blades fell upon his father. The world seemed to slow as his sword arced toward the Räuber's neck and his mind raced to try to think of a solution.

Suddenly, to his left, he saw Ashahl execute a dramatic flying kick toward the center Räuber. The kick and Cai's sword arrived at their respective targets as one. The head of Cai's opponent flipped through the air, while Ashahl's attack on his struck the nerve cluster located in the rib cage, just below the left pectoral muscle. The Räuber froze, stunned, his left side suddenly immobilized. As Ashahl rebounded and landed lightly from his flying kick, his right hand lashed out to tag two more specific points on the Räuber's right arm. Cai knew these targets to be other nerve clusters, and across the center line of the body — known as the Governor's Vessel — from where the kick had landed. While Cai's instruction in nerve point attacks was limited, one of the key elements that had been hammered into him was that striking points across the Governor's Vessel from one another could, and usually did, have a profound effect.

The Räuber dropped, slack-jawed, to his knees, his weapon falling from limp fingers. His eyes dilated and he looked confused. Cai recognized that look — the man was about to vomit all over Master Ashahl, whose attention had now turned to the third Räuber. Just as the first heave pulsed up the Räuber's throat, Cai thrust his shield between the man and Ashahl, ducking his own head behind it. A fountain of foulness erupted against the shield, splashing all around them. With a nod of thanks and a grimace of disgust, Ashahl pushed the shield aside and placed a foot on the unfortunate man's chest. With a heave that belied his small stature, the sword master shoved the Räuber violently back, out of the temple and back down the defile. Knowing they were too late, Cai looked at the third Räuber that had been threatening Corvus. Surprisingly, the man stood facing away from all of them, his weapon hanging from limp fingers while his body jerked from side to side. Behind him, Cai could hear Ligulf's unmistakable tenor, screaming defiance and rage. Splashes of blood arced through the air as Li's puntina savaged the man. After a moment, the Räuber turned away, whimpering. The flesh of his face, throat, arms, and chest hung in ribbons, both eyes were missing, and his nose clung to his face by only a thin strip of skin. Arterial blood pulsed from the side of his neck, while deep, black pulses oozed from multiple thrust wounds on his torso. The man took one staggering step, then collapsed in a heap atop Corvus' form. Ligulf stood panting, his eyes crazed with protective fury.

Cai waited until the sense returned to his brother's eyes before speaking. "A bit much, don't ye think, Li?"

The younger brother sniffed, cuffed a drop of blood from his nose, and flashed a rueful grin.

In all the years that Cai had watched Li train with the thin sword, he had never known his brother to strike a foe more than once.

"Ye have'ta follow up, Li," he used to argue. "One stab or slash from that wee thing willna stop a big man. They'll just keep coming."

"It's nae a thresher, Cai," Li would respond. "This is a blade of finesse and strategy."

Looking at the bloody ruin of this Räuber's face and chest, he thought, *Finesse, eh?*

He was about to say something more when Li's eyes widened in sudden alarm. Cai spun just in time to see another of the brutes rushing at his back, his axe already in motion in a horizontal swing at Cai's face. Without thinking, he dropped immediately into the Shepherd's Crook, a powerful and somewhat cheeky defensive sequence he had developed in his teenage years, in which he would crouch suddenly to duck under an offending swing. The key to this sequence was to leave the sword point up—in the path of the attacking weapon—as he crouched beneath its arc. He had never used the sequence in real battle, only sparring, so he was amazed when it worked perfectly.

The Räuber's axe hit the blade of his sword, the force of which rolled the weapon around the back of Cai's hand, flipping it into an inverted grip, so his right hand was now holding the forte of the blade. He deftly slipped the handle of the inverted weapon over the shoulder of his foe, the cross guard hooking behind the Räuber's neck like a shepherd's crook to a wayward ewe. With a heave, he yanked the man's head forward into a mighty, smashing punch with the edge of his shield. Teeth, bone, and blood erupted, then Cai yanked him in again for another. To his surprise, the front of the man's skull gave way after only two hits. Cai shoved the corpse away angrily as he casually flipped the sword back to his standard grip and looked about for another foe.

With a roar of disgust, Corvus shoved his way out from under the large corpse and was quickly on his feet, eyes full of murder as blobs of the other Räuber's vomit dripped from his beard.

"Alright then, Da?" Cai asked carefully. In truth, he couldn't remember ever seeing such fury in his father. The death of Yazid, coupled with the indignity of being vomited upon, seemed to have pushed the mighty Raven to a new level of rage. Murder was in his eyes. Cold, unrelenting murder.

Argant

Argant had been crouched behind Mama, his left shoulder tucked against Amina's leg, eyes wide with terror as the big men attacked. Their waggling, black tongues and huge, scary weapons brought back terrible memories of the day his family was killed. The screams of his mother and sister that had haunted him for so long came crashing back now, overlaying the sounds of the melee about him. He closed his eyes tightly and tucked his face into Amina's robes, hoping to block out the awful images and sounds. He could feel a vague tingling on his arms and neck, and knew that Mama's magic was obscuring their little group from the Räubers. He tried his best to remain still like Mama had told him, but the violence around them was so extreme he couldn't help but recoil, shudder, and gasp.

He knew he shouldn't be hiding. He had to do something.

The old man had told him that when the Equinox came, he needed to be ready. Well, the Equinox was here, and Argant didn't know exactly what to do. The man had explained it all to him, but his words were suddenly like trying to recall a dream. He looked at the open tile on the floor and the strangely shaped cup within. *Why does that shape seem so familiar?*

And then his eyes drifted to the head of Mama's staff. She was holding it across her body while she concentrated on chanting. This put the head of the staff directly in front of his gaze, and he suddenly understood. He had heard her, and others, refer to the staff as "The Key to the Gate," but that hadn't made any sense to him until now. He looked from the staff's strange, crooked, driftwood-like head to the cup seated within the floor tile. The carve-outs and crenelations within the cup exactly matched the irregular shape of the staff's head. It was an actual key—and the cup in the floor was the keyhole! Athdar's words came back to him now. He had told him to place the key in the slot, but that had confused Argant at the time. Now, he understood.

Dawn is here, young one. He heard Athdar's voice in his head. *You know what to do. Fetch the Key! You must turn it thrice around and thrice around again. Now, Argant!*

Cailean

Cai's father shook the vomit from his head like a dog coming in from the rain. Then, his da roared defiance, channeling his loss into a white-hot rage as five more of the Räubers fought past the defenders and gained the temple.

Cai watched in awe as his father unleashed a martial flurry of attacks so rapid, so surgical, and so lethal as to leave Cai breathless. He had seen his father fight many times over the years, watched his peerless bladework with admiration. He recalled the battle of Esper years before. Then he had watched his father rush at an entire company of Barbárs and Räubers, slaying them with fearless abandon. But in that fight, his father had been calculating and dispassionate. This fight, against the five in the temple, was anything but. Corvus' fury was a force of nature, his blade a thresher, and the giant warriors pressing forward fell so rapidly, Cai had trouble following his father's attacks.

"Come at me, you bastards!" Corvus roared at the rest of the enemy milling before the temple once the five had fallen.

In response, Cai noted the shaman move suddenly to the side of the tall, marbled Räuber and whisper something.

Cai's heart sank, for he knew what was coming.

Chapter 32

And even as the monster's great clawed foot crushed down upon the people, Sylvie's small form ducked and danced between its legs, rushing the potion of health to her mother as the wyrm snarled and snapped after her. She was like a squirrel leaping and dashing 'neath branch and brush, avoiding the gaping jaws of a wolf.

—The tale of Sylvie and the Draig of Autumnvale

Dawn, the Autumn Equinox
The Tor

Argant

Now Argant! Athdar's voice rang in his head. *You mustn't delay a moment longer!*

Argant jumped up onto the fallen stone block by Mama and grabbed the staff. Mama's concentration on her chanting faltered for an instant, then she released her grip with a slight nod and once more resumed her concentration. He leapt down from the block, the awkwardly shaped staff dragging behind him as he moved toward the open tile. He ducked beneath the backswing of a Räuber who was engaged with MacLief, dragging the staff between the man's legs. With a grin, the Adder saw the opportunity and planted the butt of his spear on the floor, vaulted up, and kicked the warrior backward, where he tripped over the staff and fell. Before the Räuber could regain his feet, MacLief was upon him, burying his spear head in the man's chest.

Argant gasped and bit his lip in concentration, pressing on toward the open tile. He struggled to hold the long staff over the hole as he lowered it to insert the head into the oddly shaped cup, and he couldn't quite get it to line up. The length and weight of it was hard for his little hands to manage and it slipped, jamming his fingers painfully against the side of the opening. He breathed against the pain and shook his hand out.

Hurry child!

Tears threatened to burst forth. He was just a little boy. Why was he here trying to solve such big problems? He kicked at the staff in frustration, causing it to shift. It slipped down into the cup. He quickly bent to try to fit it the rest of the way in, when he heard a commotion behind him. Turning, he saw a furious, scarred Räuber near the front of the temple knock Alasdair aside and stride purposefully straight toward him. MacLief moved to intercept the warrior, his spear threatening the Räuber's belly.

Not waiting to see the outcome of the struggle, Argant returned his attention to trying to fit the staff the rest of the way into the hole. He almost had it. It was moving in. A flash of movement drew his eyes as MacLief tumbled past, his spear haft broken.

He looked back to the hole, but before he could make any progress, a meaty hand plucked him up like an errant puppy. He was suddenly face to scarred face with the Räuber, whose sour breath was hot on his cheek.

"No!" he yelled, his little voice shrill in its defiance.

The man's mouth pulled up into a foul, hungry grin. It reminded Argant of the Barbár that had killed his sister—the hungry grin, the foul smell.

All at once, a cold rage overtook the boy. He was tired of being scared! Tired of being hurt and hungry! There were too many scary men; too many big problems; too much blood and death; and Amina, Mama, and the rest of his friends were all going to die just like his family had! He would be all alone because of men just like this big, scarred monster. He was sick and tired of it all!

"No more!" he shouted, his eyes closed in fury and his hands clenching in the curls of the Räuber's sheepskin vest.

When he closed his eyes in frustration, he saw something familiar. It was a tiny dot of light, like the one he had seen when he lit the campfire earlier. But this time, it wasn't the wood waiting to burn, it was the vest. He concentrated on the dot as he felt the Räuber turning and holding him aloft like a trophy.

"Come on," he beckoned to the dot, as he became aware of the telltale tingling in his fingers. Then the man's sheepskin vest burst into flame beneath his hands. His eyes sprung open in surprise as the lanolin in the wool caught and the flame quickly spread. The Räuber shrieked in surprise and dropped him, furiously slapping at his chest. Just then, MacLief came staggering back, shaking his head as if to clear it, blood flowing from his nose and mouth. The Adder planted the broken end of the spear haft in the Räuber's gut and shoved the brute back. Off-balance and furiously stripping off the flaming vest, the Räuber only staggered a few steps before an arrow from Dallin's bow buried itself in his back and he collapsed.

"No more!" Argant whispered to himself, as he stared at the fallen Räuber. He knew he should feel something for the man, or for the deed. He had been instrumental in the killing of a Barbár. He—Argant—had helped to kill a man! He folded his arms and hugged himself, trying to still the trembling that was coming over him. No time for that now. He took a deep breath and let it out slowly, like Mama had taught him, then he turned back to the staff still resting in the slot. His hand shook as he wiped away a tear of frustration, then bent to his previous task. He grasped and wiggled the staff, allowing the head to slip the last few inches into place with a satisfying thunk.

Now, which way to turn it?

His mind whirled with momentary confusion, until he latched onto something he remembered Mama telling him soon after he had joined the ladies' company. It was something about the moving meditation—the altaamuli. Mama had told him that depending on his needs, he should proceed either the direction of ruh or the direction of lahm. Clockwise or anticlockwise, Yadira had translated for him. Though he had never seen a clock, he nonetheless understood clockwise to be circling to the right. What did Mama say about the directions? He stamped his foot in frustration. He couldn't remember.

Clockwise, the direction of creation, Athdar's voice quietly suggested. Clutching the body of the staff with both hands, Argant started turning the key to the right. He grunted with the effort of turning the mechanism, his small feet pushing one in front of the other.

Click.

"One," he said quietly. As he finished his first rotation, he wiped the sweat from his brow and glanced up to judge his safety. There, below the temple's defile, he spotted the figure of the shaman conferring with the purple-skinned Räuber. Even as the boy's gaze fell on him, the shaman turned and their eyes met across the distance. With a triumphant cry, the bald creature pointed at Argant and shrieked something. Terrified, Argant returned to his task, his feet slipping as he fervently struggled to continue turning the huge key.

Zsoka

The Empress was sitting with her back against a pillar behind the embers of the little fire that Yadira had been using to make tea and hot water for sterilization. Zsoka's knees were pulled up to her chin despite the lingering soreness in her back. When the shaman had thrown her against the tree, something had broken, and she had found breathing increasingly difficult in the hours since. However, once the music from the strange man in motley clothes had roused everyone, she had found that both her breathing and the commensurate panic she'd felt had eased. But her body was still sore from days of privation and exertion.

She was also terrified.

She knew she would die here in this ruined temple. Her former lover, Vajk, the Grand Hadvezér of the Barbárs himself, was here—though changed. The strange marble striations on his skin, the solid black eyes, and the incessant sorcerous lightning he wielded… This wasn't the Vajk she knew. This wasn't the father of her son. More than once he had looked directly at her, and he had not acknowledged her in the slightest. Not the faintest whisper of recognition on his face. No, this was not the Vajk she knew, so full of life and intelligence and always ready with a plan. It was clear that Vajk was under some kind of spell or possession, and she knew the source of it must be the shaman—Blood-Tooth's kin.

She saw the shaman spot the boy as he struggled with whatever he was doing, and she saw the corresponding terror in the child's face. Much was happening around her that she didn't understand. Why was this Tor so important? Why was Vajk here? Surely the Grand Hadvezér had better things to do than to lead a raid behind enemy lines with only a few hundred Räubers. This was a man capable of summoning legions of Barbárs; tens of thousands waited upon his every word. Why was he here with so few? She had heard Blood-Tooth speak of the "Gatekeeper" and the "Transference," but he had never explained the terms or what was happening, only that there was tremendous urgency for him to prevent the boy from using the key.

The key!

She watched Argant struggling with the huge staff, then quickly looked back to the foul shaman, who seemed to be giving Vajk some directions. Yes, he was the puppet master here. She wasn't sure what it all meant, but she somehow knew that this little boy had to be helped and the shaman had to be stopped.

With a gasp of effort she surged to her feet and, circling the small fire, she climbed over the fallen stone block. Bending down, she set her hands beside Argant's as he struggled to turn the key.

The boy glanced up in surprise, his jewel-like eyes sparkling in the morning light. She smiled and helped him push the staff in its rotation.

Corvus

As Raven's Tooth punched through the armpit and into the lung of a barbarian who had rushed forward in answer to his challenge, Corvus suddenly became aware of a movement by the marbled Räuber. The shaman was beside him, pointing toward the back of the temple with great agitation. The purple-skinned behemoth raised his arm, electricity dancing along its length. Corvus followed the creature's black-eyed gaze and saw Argant and the Empress struggling with something. Dropping Raven's Tooth, he quickly reached down and lifted the nearest Räuber corpse. Spinning to gain momentum, he flung it at the marbled giant just as a bolt of black lightning arced from the creature's hand. The body was incinerated in mid-air, the brow of the marbled man furrowing in surprise, and his black eyes then fixing once more on Corvus like the implacable and unreadable eyes of Fate.

Click. The sound was followed by Argant's wavering voice. "Two."

The marbled man raised his hand once more, this time pointing toward Corvus, but even as the electricity began to build along the length of its arm, an arc of argent power slashed out from the temple, striking both the Räuber and the shaman, and sending them both staggering back toward the drop-off above the path below.

Corvus quickly nodded his thanks across the temple to the young Queen, who stood closely surrounded by the mercenary and the healer.

Click. "Three."

The boy was picking up speed, perhaps due to the assistance of the Empress. That was good, they might just have a chance. But even as that thought crossed his mind, the shaman screamed instructions again in his preternaturally amplified voice, and the milling Räubers—even those struggling against the advancing Highlander army—responded. The temple's defenders were hard-pressed by a sudden refreshed assault by dozens of enemies.

Corvus lost track of time then, as his entire world became blood and killing.

Click. "Four."

Blades flashed. Warriors on both sides screamed in either defiance or death. Corvus keened his battle song and Raven's Tooth tracked its merciless path through flesh and bone.

Click. "Five."

The shaman's voice once more cut through the tumult, its tone rising with urgency and panic. Then the marbled man, with only the slightest flex of his legs, leapt over the heads of the surging Räubers, crashing into the temple's defenders with a sound like the breaking of a thick, wooden door.

Cai went flying back, his shield burst into tatters as he crashed into a pillar on the far side of the temple, unconscious.

"No!" Corvus screamed, and leapt at the monster at the same moment Ashahl did from the opposite side. Almost faster than thought, the marbled man swatted Ashahl from the air. Ashahl— the greatest martial artist in generations—batted aside like some annoying insect. Then, with astonishing speed, the monster pivoted to Corvus, Raven's Tooth skating harmlessly across the stone-like skin of the creature's chest. A massive hand lashed out and struck him in the chest.

He heard two things as he flew backward. A distinctive "pop" in his body as something broke, and the boy's voice, somehow louder than would be natural.

Click. "Six."

Chapter 33

For though the Key had allowed the Transference, so caught up in the dream was he that Athdar left it aside, unclaimed for its greater purpose. Centuries passed, the Gatekeeper dozing perpetually in the chimeric dream of the Tor. The Key was lost and the secrets of the Gates submerged still further beneath the inky waters of Time.

—"The Histories of the Latter Age,"
as translated by Cyrus of Visivia

The moment of the Transference
The Tor

Argant

The click was the last sound he heard clearly. A great roaring filled his ears, subsuming the clash and clangor of battle, and the screams of agony. His arms and legs tickled like ants were crawling all over him. He looked down to find them glowing, an aureate, flame-like light coruscating from his fingertips, sparks leaping several inches from his hands. His mouth fell open in wonder as a brighter golden glow began emanating from his chest. His body lifted from the ground, as though suspended from a rope attached to his breastbone, but there was no pain. On the contrary, a soothing, comfortable warmth seemed to emanate from his heart, flowing outward to his entire body. He heard a scraping beneath him, like stone on stone, and then he was lowered gently into a little chair, the back and arms of which looked like woven branches that were actually made of stone. It was just like a much smaller version of Athdar's throne. As his body touched it, his mind suddenly filled with awareness of all the life on the Tor — every bird, bug, animal, bush, tree, and vine. All of it at once. It was overwhelming. It was beyond overwhelming, and he cried out in alarm.

He could feel the breeze ruffling the feathers of a tawny owl tucked high among the branches of a fir, while nearby a pine marten nibbled on the edge of a shelf mushroom and kept a wary eye focused on the owl's back. The needles of an ancient yew tree danced in the wind while a black fly tacked noisily about the corpse of a fallen Räuber further down the Tor, choosing its landing spot. The sensations were staggering. Were he not seated, he would have fallen to the ground, unsure of what physical impressions were his and what belonged to the flora and fauna of the Tor. It felt amazing and euphoric, and he devoured each new sense, somehow binding it somewhere deep within him. As though the knowledge of the creature or plant were like a putty or plaster that adhered to his very spine, sculpting and building what he would become out of the very life around him. It felt good, and a great, wondrous grin split his little face as his jewel eyes danced about blindly, his focus entirely within.

He stretched his senses further, reaching hungrily beyond the Tor, absorbing the flight of a hen harrier tracking chickens in a farmer's field, some miles from the base of the mount. On a farmstead near a lake at the base of a mountain peak, a donkey joyfully brayed its full-throated greeting to the woman coming to feed it. A salmon leapt upstream, deftly slipping over the rock that was its obstacle and continuing its journey against the current. A bear, sighing with satisfaction after his nocturnal hunt, licked the blood from his lips as he settled in for a morning nap.

All this and infinitely more washed over and through him. So overwhelming was it that he could easily have been lost forever in that great subsumption, but for a voice that tickled the back of his awareness. *Who was that? What did he say? Is he calling my name?*

"Argant," Athdar's voice repeated, more firmly now. He realized the old man had been calling him for some time. "Argant! Awake now, boy! The Transference isn't finished."

Argant blinked and came slowly—oh so slowly—back to his body, seated on the little throne in the temple atop the Tor, with the sounds of fighting, the skirl of bagpipes, and the moans of the injured still around him. But he couldn't see much of what was happening now as Athdar stood before him, blocking his view. Athdar—standing before him!

"Athdar!" he cried in surprise as another wave of euphoria washed over him, threatening to whisk him once more into the dream. "You're not on your throne…" he murmured.

The old man's ancient form was so fragile and wispy, Argant was amazed his legs could bear him up and that he didn't collapse. The man's robe, once fine and majestic, was now so dusty and ancient it had faded to a threadbare grey and seemed ready to resolve to dust. His long, white beard, wispy like spider silk, masked grey lips and yellowed teeth, and cheeks the color of chalk. But those jewel-like eyes, the mirror of Argant's—one ice-blue and the other the rich, warm brown of almonds—burned with an intensity the boy had heretofore not seen in the old man.

"You must hold the Key now, boy," he said, indicating Mama's staff, the head of which was still in the hole in the tiles. "Else you'll repeat my error and not awaken the Tor."

"But I am the Gatekeeper now," Argant answered with a laconic smile. "I can feel it all. Everything! It's wonderful!" And with that, he closed his eyes and began to slip once more into the fast current of life that swirled about and through him.

"You are *connected,* true." Athdar's voice was sharp now, insistent, but his strength seemed to be waning and the stridency of his tone wavered. "But the Tor slumbers still. You must take the key, and slot it there." He pointed to another new hole that had appeared in the floor by Argant's right foot. "This was my error, boy! Do not repeat it! It will be five hundred years before the chance comes again to awaken the Tor."

Argant struggled through the waves of euphoria cascading over him to try to understand Athdar's meaning. Something about the Key. He had to get out of the chair and retrieve Mama's staff. But... he didn't want to leave the throne. He suddenly found himself experiencing the exultation of flight as his mind entered that of a kestrel banking on a stiff breeze, searching the landscape below for prey. It felt so good. It was so amazing. *Why do I need the Key? What does it matter?*

"No." The boy shook his head slowly, his eyelids closing dreamily. "This is too nice."

"Argant! You must!" Athdar's voice was losing strength, the frailty of his age catching up with him. Vaguely, the boy was aware of other people suddenly surrounding the throne. Was that Ligulf? And Rhona and Piper, as well as the lady with the silver streak in her hair? She had helped him turn the Key.

Gentle hands eased the old man down to sit upon the fallen block of marble, while someone else — Piper, he thought — fetched the staff and brought it to the chair to slot the narrow tip of the butt end into the newly formed hole in the tile at the boy's feet.

"Li, help me!" Argant heard Piper say, as he seemed to struggle with the insertion of the staff into the new smaller hole. The boy's eyes dipped dreamily as another wave of awareness washed over him — gulls floating on the updrafts by the western cliffs of the High Valley. There was a scurry of activity near him as Piper and Li, each wounded and working with one hand, worked to fit the staff into the slot by his feet. There was a loud click, followed by a deep thrumming in the Tor beneath them. Argant's hand reached out in instinctive alarm and grasped the staff.

Clarity returned immediately as his awareness suddenly rose above — or outside — the rhapsodic waves washing over him. He felt like a swimmer who had been tossed by the turbulent tide, but was then lifted out and set safely upon the deck of a vessel calmly traversing the tumult. He looked with lucidity at those around him. Piper and Ligulf stood leaning together over the collapsed form of Athdar as Rhona knelt and tried to comfort the ancient man. Zsoka, meanwhile, had resumed her place sitting against the pillar, her knees pulled up to her chin, eyes wide with terror.

Corvus

With a grimace, Corvus struggled to his feet. Raven's Tooth hung limp in his right hand as he gritted his teeth against the pain. His left collar bone was clearly broken—the bulge under the skin near his neck was unmistakable and excruciating. With a quiet hiss, he used his right hand to tuck his left thumb in his belt, minimizing his left arm's movement. Not as good as a sling, but it would do until he could get it looked to by the healers.

The marbled Räuber towered over him, its fathomless black eyes staring unblinking at the Raven, who stood shakily before him.

"Da," Li called from behind him. "Get back!"

Sweat stung his eyes, despite the chill in the air. He took a long, steadying breath, and flexed his sword hand. Raven's Tooth danced in his grip, lethal as ever, despite his injury—at least it would be lethal, were he facing a mortal man. But this was no mortal. This was some possessed Räuber with skin as tough as stone. And it had already devastated their defenses. Cai, Corvus, and Ashahl had all already fallen before the monster, and Corvus knew when the stone man next attacked, he would have very few options. He was in far too much pain to concentrate on the forms effectively. He suspected that, like the Nephellem, Mountain form would be the only one that was any use against this creature, but it required the greatest concentration. And his injury would prevent that. Without Mountain form, he would be crushed. Wisdom suggested that he mind his son's advice and step back… but could he?

He glanced around at the rest of his small company. Mama stood, hunched and panting, over Ashahl's prone form. The aged sword master was, like Corvus, injured and likely in too much pain to resume the forms. Without Spider form, the aged master was blind, and would be of minimal help. Ligulf stood with his back to the little throne, blood seeping from his side as he faced the marbled monster. The young man held his puntina before him in a defiant low guard. Sadly, the puntina would be of little use against this creature. Cailean lay against a pillar near Dallin, his eyes fluttering as he struggled to regain consciousness. His left arm and shoulder were mangled and useless, and his face was ashen and wan as blood seeped from his wounds. Dallin crouched nearby, her face a mask of fear and helplessness. Her arrows had already proven useless against this monster. Behind Li, Argant sat on his little throne, his mismatched eyes glazed as though his mind were turned inward. The boy was clearly unaware of his peril. Corvus feared his time as Gatekeeper of the Tor was about to be cut tragically short, and there was nothing he could do to stop it.

MacLief, honoring his promise to Corvus, positioned himself to stand between the marbled man and the boy, standing just in front of Li, the haft of his broken spear clutched defiantly in his grip like a quarterstaff. Beside him, blood dripping from mouth and nose, Alasdair stepped up, his shield raised and a string of quiet curses on his bloody lips.

This was the calm before the inevitable, and no doubt final, tumult. Any second the marbled man would attack, and in all likelihood, they would all die. The creature seemed to be choosing its first victim. It turned its head away from Corvus, its black eyes locking on the boy. Everyone tensed. The speed the creature had shown after leaping into the temple was breathtaking. In a matter of seconds it had devastated Cailean, overwhelmed Ashahl, and beat down Corvus. He couldn't let the creature move on the boy. He had to do something!

"Here, monster!" Corvus yelled at the demon's back. "I'm here for you."

The marbled creature ignored him, shifting its body to fully face the child.

"No!" Mama yelled, her voice full of fury and command as she moved to join Alasdair and MacLief in shielding Li and Argant with their bodies. She was trying to chant something, but exhaustion slowed her lips.

"Here!" Corvus screamed and lashed out, Raven's Tooth glancing harmlessly off the stone-like skin on the creature's back. A mottled hand flashed back toward Corvus' head. He barely managed to avoid being struck with a painful twist of his shoulders that stressed his injury and sent a wave of weakness and nausea through him, dropping him to his knees instantly.

"Da!" Cailean's weak voice called.

A shuddering breath escaped Corvus as he struggled once more to his feet.

"Right, ya foul stoatin' beastie," he muttered as he circled the temple, moving to stand beside Alasdair. "I canna stop ye, but I'll die afore I let ye harm the boy."

"As will I," Alasdair echoed.

"Me as well, ya bastard creature!" MacLief shouted.

"And I," Li said in his clear tenor.

"And I," Rhona and Piper echoed.

"Me, too," Amina added in her soft monotone as she joined the others standing before Argant.

Maddie

This was bad. This was terrible. That creature was unstoppable, felling their three strongest warriors in a matter of seconds. So far, the only thing that seemed to have any effect on it whatsoever was the silver light from the Moonflower's blade, and in Maddie's current state of exhaustion, she had no more fanahy to feed to Darienne, so the blade's shimmering power had extinguished. From where she knelt, she glanced at the Queen, who cursed colorfully in impotent rage while staring at her blade, which was decidedly *not* glowing.

"I'm so sorry, Majesty," Maddie said, the lassitude of fanahy depletion creeping over her. "I have nothing left to give you."

She had overspent. The signs were clear. She looked at her hands, the skin chalky and grey. Kely was silent. Her vitality was gone, yet she could not regret anything she had done. Healing Dallin had been critical — without her, they had no hope. Yes, she could have stopped the healing earlier, before tending to the trauma, but when she was there, Dallin's spirit had been so damaged, she simply had to offer Dallin the chance of wholeness. A wave of feebleness washed over her, further collapsing her. A silent sob slipped from her lips as she felt the depth of her failure. She would now slip into a drowsy state and drift away, leaving Darienne, Kaiso, and all the others to die. All because she had overspent.

Impulsive fool! Talé Naissa's harsh words echoed in her memory. *Never one to imagine the consequences of your actions. Never think, just rush forward. Then regret! Fool!*

"Fool…" Maddie repeated the word softly, the world going dark as the last of her strength ebbed from her.

Calloused, feminine hands caressed her cheeks. She struggled to open her eyes. Finally, she was able to wedge them open just enough to see it was the tall, thin votary, her jimas askew. She was saying something, but Maddie couldn't hear or understand her. Her eyes closed once more as she drifted down toward oblivion.

But her descent was interrupted by an unexpected sound. There was a clapping, soft at first, then gaining in volume and frequency. She became vaguely aware that her head was moving with each clap. *No, not clap… slap!* Someone was slapping her repeatedly. Her dulled senses and mind tried to make sense of what was happening. Someone was speaking again, whispering with urgency alongside each slap. Like a swimmer who had dived too deep, she struggled toward the surface, each moment weighing on her like an anchor about her waist. *Slap! Slap!*

Finally, with a loud gasp, she managed to open one eye , only to discover she was laying on her back on the marble floor. *How did that happen?* Crouched over her was the tall votary, concern evident in her eyes above the jimas. The woman was still slapping Maddie repeatedly. The blows were sharp and rhythmic, but not violent. Maddie blinked and rolled her eyes, struggling to bring the world into focus. Seeing her eyes open, the woman pressed something into Maddie's mouth. It was small and dry, like a… seed of some kind.

"Chew this," the votary said, her eyes darting nervously toward the marbled giant about to strike at Argant. "Quickly."

Maddie bit down on the seed obediently, and that was all the energy she had. Her eyes closed and darkness took her.

"Ambini, Ambini!" the child's voice cried, interrupting her descent. The voice was accompanied by a roaring of some kind. Kely rushed into her mind's eye with such energy and fervor, the ribbons in her hair flounced uncontrollably as the girl spirit giggled and twirled joyfully.

"What is it, my love?" Maddie somehow had the energy to ask. "What is that sound?"

"That's me, Ambini!" the child squealed joyfully. "*I* am the roaring you hear!"

And then it struck her — energy, health, power, and a raging tingle in her fingers that almost felt like burning. Her eyes shot open, and she sat up suddenly, looking in shock into the eyes of the votary, who nodded sagely and sat back onto her heels, muttering something — a prayer of thanks, perhaps. There was a flash of silver nearby, accompanied by a triumphant shout from Darienne.

Then chaos erupted.

Ligulf

When the creature attacked, it moved with a breathtaking quickness. The marbled man's right hand lashed out, grasping for Argant. It moved faster than the flight of an arrow, but those arrayed before him — Mama, Corvus, Alasdair, and MacLief — were ready. As one, the four of them surged forward, Alasdair's shield shifting quickly to block access to the boy, while MacLief and Corvus raised their weapons to ward the blow, and Mama used her weight and considerable strength to crash into the creature's torso. There was a clack and a clang, Alasdair grunted with effort, and Corvus staggered away grimacing, Raven's Tooth dangling from one finger as he struggled to regain his grip. Mama was thrown to the ground in front of Li and fresh blood ran from MacLief's mouth where his staff had slammed back into his face. They had managed to block the first effort at reaching Argant, but now they were all out of position. The second rank between the boy and the monster — Li, Amina, Rhona, and Piper — prepared for the worst.

The creature stepped toward them, looming over Mama's prone form, its hand crackling once more with surging electricity as it reached toward Argant.

"Vajk!" a woman's voice yelled, filled with authority and command.

The creature ignored the call and, baring its teeth, leaned toward the child.

"Vajk, hear me!" The Empress stepped up onto the fallen block before the little throne, putting her at eye level with the marbled Räuber.

The creature's head turned to her, its brows furrowing with some confusion… Was that recognition? It lowered its arm, still crackling with electricity.

"Kill the boy!" shrieked a preternaturally loud and heavily accented voice from outside the temple. Like a recalcitrant mule touched by a whip, the creature's eyes snapped back toward the boy and its arm raised once more.

"Stop this!" the Empress interjected again, touching the creature's chest with a tentative hand. "If ever you loved me, Vajk, stop."

The creature's brows furrowed in confusion as it turned once more to the Empress, and Ligulf would forever after swear the look on the creature's face had been one of regret.

Just then, a flash of silver light arced into its back from across the temple, sizzling as it struck.

The marbled monster grimaced in pain and flailed its arms, knocking the Empress violently off her perch. She fell to the ground beside the boy's little throne. The creature's head snapped around toward Queen Darienne, its face contorted with pain. It hissed at her, not unlike a mountain cat, then it gestured toward her with its right hand. The air crackled and Ligulf's hair stood on end as a flash of black lightning tore across the temple at the young Queen — and it would have struck her, had she not raised her sword instinctively at the last moment, the trailing silver light somehow stopping the bolt and defusing its fury. For an instant, the Queen stood still, the red curls of her hair lifted by the residual charge in the air, the surprise on her features mirrored by the shock on the creature's. Then the marbled Räuber leapt toward her, its hand raised to strike.

"Look out!" Li shouted, though his cry was unnecessary. Faster than thought, she staggered back away from the sudden assault, her sword flashing instinctively again to ward the blow, gossamer silver light trailing the blade. As the monster's fist encountered the passing light, it rebounded as if it had struck a solid wall or shield. There was another sizzling sound, and Ligulf was amazed to see the creature's knuckles were smoking after the contact. A chill scampered up Li's spine and across the top of his scalp. *She can do this!* It was the first glimmer of hope they'd had since the creature had leapt into the temple.

What magic is this that she wields? he wondered. But before he could puzzle over it any further, the Queen responded with a series of slashes and cuts, each sending a silver razor slicing into the demon. It hissed and spun, trying to avoid the light. Leaping to clear a low arc of her power, the creature vaulted high over the

Queen, its body twisting acrobatically above her. Ligulf was amazed when her bodyguard, Kaiso, shouted suddenly, "Ballestra—passato!" Without hesitation, the Queen leapt gracefully forward just as the monster landed behind her. Finishing her move, she dropped suddenly into a deep, coiled sideways lunge, her left leg curling under the other and extended out to her right, and her torso nearly touching the ground. Even as she dropped, the monster's fist swung with lethal speed and force, missing her by a finger's breadth.

"Inversa!" Kaiso called. "Capo mandritti!"

The Queen responded immediately, her body uncoiling and pivoting to face the beast even as her sword circled her head and sliced from the right at the creature's midsection. Once more, the silver light flashed and the creature backed away a step, hissing and clutching its side where the light had scored a deep burn mark in its stone skin.

"Montanto!" Kaiso cried. The Queen dropped once more into another deep lunge, similarly twisted as before, and even as her left hand found the floor, her sword was rising in a vertical cut as the creature's grasping hands passed harmlessly overhead once more.

There was another sizzle as the glowing blade struck the monster's abdomen, the silver radiance that trailed the sword creating a long, blackened gash up its torso. The Räuber spun in an effort to escape the silver light, but it had run out of room. Even as one of its feet stepped out over the precipice on the southern edge of the structure, it desperately reached out to grasp the nearest pillar, spinning around it like a child might dance round the ribboned pole on May Day. But this was no child; it was a seven-foot-tall Räuber, possessed by gods only knew what kind of demon. Ligulf gasped as the creature finished its spin about the pillar, its brows creased in hatred and rage, and it used the momentum of the maneuver to once more launch itself toward the Queen as she tried to stand.

It was too fast. Her sword flew up defensively as—with a cry of surprise—she fell backward. The monster's open hand once more struck the light, but this time, the creature bore his weight forward, slamming into the barrier. The force of its collision knocked the already off-balance Queen from her feet, and she fell hard, her head bouncing off the marble floor. The light on her blade extinguished.

The marbled Räuber loomed over her, rage and homicide twisting its features.

Corvus

Corvus surged toward the fallen Queen, intent on putting his damaged body between her and the Räuber, but the mercenary was faster.

"I think not," Kaiso said, his sword held in the traditional backsword high guard as he placed himself athwart the Queen and stared defiantly up at the marble-skinned monster.

The creature's brow furrowed, and faster than should have been possible, its hand lashed out at the mercenary to bat him aside. The captain's blade flashed as his torso twisted and rotated, just avoiding the grasping hand. In the space of but a breath, he managed to parry and counterstrike the hand twice in rapid succession, though his blade did no damage to the monster's limb. Nonetheless, as the creature drew back to reconsider this irritating opponent, Kaiso was still unhurt and unmoved, standing protectively over the fallen Queen. Corvus nodded in grudging approval. There was no way the mercenary could keep that up, but still, it was impressive.

Suddenly, both of the monster's hands lashed out together, catching and lifting the bodyguard like a child's toy. There was a collective shout of alarm from the defenders, which was interrupted by a flash of silver from the Queen. Corvus was shocked to see the dazed monarch suddenly upon her knees, blood streaming from behind her left ear and a look of fury on her face.

The creature hissed as the silver burned black lines across its ankles, Kaiso momentarily forgotten in its hands.

"Release that man," the Queen rasped, her voice raw. The coruscating energy on her sword crackled with leashed potential that drew and fixed the eyes of the Räuber.

"Never mind them!" the shaman screamed from among the Räubers outside the temple. "Kill the boy!"

Corvus searched the mass, trying to locate the shaman, then he spotted the ill-favored man huddled near the back of the milling Räubers, back hunched, veins and muscles bulging unnaturally.

"Dallin!" he shouted, pointing him out.

"On it," she responded, an arrow flying quickly into the midst of the throng. As chance would have it, a thick-necked warrior leapt into the arrow's path before it could find its mark. The man crumpled, but before he even hit the ground, Dallin had sent three more arrows at the shaman. Two buried themselves in Räubers, as the first had done, while the third found the shaman's right arm, blasting a hole directly through its inflated bicep. The foul creature shrieked and ducked down, disappearing from view behind the milling warriors.

Back inside the temple there was another flash of silver and the marbled Räuber shrieked in agony, dropping Kaiso and staggering back from the Queen. A new black line scored the purple skin of its abdomen.

Sangine

His breath came in shudders as he clenched his wounded arm, blood streaming from his fingertips, his vitality, his strength, flowing away and pouring onto the trampled shrubbery. He was running out of time, and he knew it. Once the umbral despair has dispersed, the cursed Highlander army had advanced quickly up the Tor, and now there remained fewer than fifty Räubers to oppose and slow them. Vajk had failed to seize the child, and was now staggering back from the strange silver light the redheaded woman wielded.

It's all too late, he thought. *The little bastard has assumed the Gatekeeper's post. The only hope is in killing the boy before he learns to master his powers.*

A scream from among the attacking Highlanders drew his attention. One of the Räubers holding the top of the trail against the White Cleft troops had been tackled in a suicidal assault. The Räuber was tipped off the summit of the trail, his attacker clinging to him in a deadly embrace as they both fell to their deaths.

"Just moments left before they overwhelm us," Sangine muttered through his chattering teeth, his muscles deflating as he considered his options. He shifted his position, peering around a cluster of Räubers to glimpse Vajk, careful to keep out of sight of the archer. More damage had been done to the Räuber leader, and the erstwhile Grand Hadvezér of the Barbárs was about to fall to the cursed woman with the silver sword. *Who is she?!* Numerous black stripes marked Vajk's body where the silver magic had burned him. His legs quivered as though he were about to collapse, while the battered defenders clustered together like a human wall in front of the child. The redheaded sorceress had moved to stand in front of the defenders, slashing her glowing sword and its pearlescent trailing light like some magical whip. Each slash produced a corresponding howl of agony from Vajk.

Sangine. Prince Umbral's disembodied voice rang in his head, startling the shaman almost to paralysis. But one must respond to the princes.

"Y-yes, my lord?" he muttered, dropping to his knees, his arm throbbing as more vital blood sluiced away.

You have failed again, the shadow prince said flatly, in a tone that conveyed weary disappointment. *You have no idea how blisteringly angry Timor is. But there's nothing for it. Summon a portal and return to us, and bring your creation lest he be destroyed and the dark gift lost.*

"We can still—" the shaman started to respond, the trembling of his failing body undermining his purpose.

I'm afraid not, old man. Prince Umbral's response silenced the shaman. *This battle is over. Much has been lost. Recover the blood gem and return to us at once.*

"But—"

At once, Sangine. The Prince's tone brooked no disagreement.

"Yes, my lord." He looked at his withered, trembling hands, dripping with gore. He was too weak at the moment to summon an umbral portal, and his injury was such that any new vitality he might gain through subsumption would quickly leak away. Another hiss and shriek of pain from Vajk. He would have to act quickly. He knew that torments awaited him for this failure, but those punishments would pale in comparison to what would be unleashed upon him should he allow Vajk and the gem to be lost. A blood gem was a rare and difficult magic—even for the princes. They would have expended a significant portion of their still gathering power creating it for Sangine to use and should Vajk fall, as looked imminent, the gem would be lost and the power used to create it wasted.

Another flash of silver, and Vajk's corresponding cry of agony sounded like the mewling of an injured and dying dog.

No time to waste, he thought, and reaching out to seize the ankle of a nearby Räuber. The shrieking was immediate and startling for the nearby warriors. As quickly as the man's vitality flooded Sangine, he could feel a portion siphoning off through his injury, which was startling. The wound should have closed and healed the moment he began to feed. It must be those damned engraved arrows. There must be some sorcery there that prevented his body from healing. He shook his head. A mystery for another day.

Closing his eyes, he named the sigils of might in the correct order, the combination prescribed by Prince Umbral during his communing the night before. There was a vast and deep thrum that overtook him and the world around him fell silent as a cone of living shadow suddenly surrounded him, steaming darkness pouring off its edges like water.

"Vajk, come!" he called to the former Grand Hadvezér, like he would to a dog, his enhanced voice the only sound he could hear beyond the deep thrum of the cone. The marbled Räuber's black eyes snapped toward him, his brow furrowed in agony.

More arrows flew at Sangine from the archer, but the cone seemed to protect him, though he couldn't worry about that right now. His mind was too occupied with holding the portal open and summoning Vajk. He clung to the wound in his arm with desperation, trying to stanch his once more rapidly draining vitality.

"Strike again, Your Majesty!"

The Raven's voice somehow penetrated the silence of the cone, and he could see the man gesticulating toward the Queen, urging her to lash Vajk with more of her power before he could escape. The woman looked fatigued and it took a moment for her to summon her silvery light again. That moment was all he needed. With what remaining strength the marbled creature had, Vajk leapt from the temple toward him. A flash of silver and more arrows chased him toward the cone of darkness. Sangine's strength was fading quickly, and as Vajk tumbled into the portal, Sangine's grip failed and the cone collapsed, plunging the two into a silent darkness.

Argant

Vaguely, he became aware of the continuing sounds of battle outside the temple. Looking beyond Corvus and Ligulf, he could see there were still Räubers fighting. Dallin's mercilessly accurate arrows dropped man after man, keeping the Räubers from trying to gain the ruin. They were being driven back by the White Cleft army and those of the fyrd whose unfailing advance had brought their front ranks to the last bend in the path before the temple. Though the Räuber numbers were rapidly dwindling—somehow he knew there were exactly forty-two of them still alive and fighting—they were exacting a bloody toll on the White Cleft soldiers.

He closed his eyes. The fighting *hurt* him, in a way he could not explain. Unlike the struggles of the fauna in his mind—who fought to eat and to maintain balance in the natural world—this was wrong. This was unnecessary and cruel.

There was a shriek of pain as another White Cleft soldier was felled brutally.

Argant's eyes flashed to Mama, rising groggily from where she had hit the floor. Then he looked to Amina, who was facing him, worry and terror on her brow… Her expression was so like his sister's on the day she died. His heart broke as images of his family flashed before him. All of them killed so cruelly by these Räubers, these savage, evil, mindless warriors. Who would be next? Corvus? Mama? Amina?! It had to stop. They kept taking those he loved from him! He had to stop it all! *They can't keep doing this!*

A red rage was building inside him. He began punching his leg, harder and harder, as memory upon memory washed over him. With each blow, the rage built, perhaps fed by the enormous potential of the lifestream all around him. Perhaps it was the dam of his long-sequestered grief finally bursting.

Punch! The tentative and careful moment Amina had crawled beneath the hawthorn to rescue him from his ordeal and draw him out to meet Mama, Yadira, and Lupe. *Punch!* His sister laughing and squirting him with goat's milk from the animal's teat. *Punch!* Yazid's indulgent smile as he gave Argant that amazing cheese. *Punch!* His mother telling him a bedtime story and stroking his cheek. *Punch!* His father carrying him on his shoulders as they hiked to market. *Punch!* Yadira making the multicolored pants for him. *Punch!* Lupe handing him the sticky honeycomb. *Punch! Punch! Punch!* Each memory carried a sweetness with it that caught in his throat before transforming to bitter bile and rage.

"Stop fighting!" He shook his head, tears streaming down his cheeks as he could not tear his eyes from Amina's terrified face. "Stop, stop!"

No one listened.

"Stop!" he called again, but the fighting just continued, despite his cries.

"STOP IT!" Argant shouted, his right hand instinctively clutching the staff. His voice was suddenly, impossibly amplified. He noted his hand upon the staff as his voice continued to echo from the Tor, reverberating across the surrounding countryside. All fighting upon the Tor ceased abruptly, and the combatants looked about, some of their weapons mid-swing as though they had momentarily forgotten what they were doing.

Argant's shout had reverberated with echoes of other voices swirling about his—voices that somehow felt ancient and imbued with an inchoate puissance. It was as though every Gatekeeper of the Tor, from ages long past, had joined in his cry, all exerting their wills. But as the last of the whispering echoes dwindled away, a Räuber near the defile entrance to the temple shook his shaggy mane, freeing himself of the effect. While the others struggled their way to clarity, the Räuber turned and pointed an accusing finger directly at Argant. The man's black tongue extended and waggled terrifyingly at the child.

The boy's perceptions shifted at the sight, and he was unable to separate reality from memory. In place of this Räuber, he saw the leader of the Barbárs that had murdered his family, taunting his restrained father with that same waggling black tongue. The warrior had laughed at his father's pleading before turning his cruel attentions to Argant's mother. Her screams echoed anew in his mind, turning the entire flow of the current of life around him blood-red, its progression and eddies growing, flaring, cresting, and crashing in response to his bottomless grief and rage. His eyes fixed once more on the warrior's gloating face and faster than the beat of a hummingbird's wing, he plunged down into that current, its power and reflected rage inescapable and self-feeding. He felt himself swell with unimaginable might. It was as if his rage had become so towering, so huge, that all of this lifestream, this tide of life, could not feed it. With a paroxysm of fury, he directed the agitated red current at the space before the temple, and *pushed* the swirling energies toward the taunting Räuber and his fellows.

Corvus

In the years that followed, Corvus would struggle to understand and explain what happened next. But somehow his mind shifted to the slow-motion perception of Badger form and perhaps because of his skills manipulating extraordinary energies, he was able to perceive the wave of force that roiled from the boy in remarkable and sequential detail. To Corvus' eye, he saw a curling, moving wave of force made up of dozens of red ribbons, each vibrating with unique characteristics and energy, but somehow all bent in this moment toward harmonious purpose. He watched as it swept past him and Ligulf and Piper. It washed past the mysterious and frail wizened old man. The wave flashed past the defenders, who were largely oblivious to it. But its effect upon the remaining Räubers was a sight that would haunt the defenders and every member of the fyrd and the White Cleft forces that beheld it.

Without exception, every Barbár on the crest of the Tor suddenly turned to look in Argant's direction, their eyes wide with an unnamed terror, as though they knew something horrible was about to happen. Faster than any could break and run, vines, branches, and grass snaked forward and suddenly wrapped about their arms and legs, seizing them where they stood. The shoots of plants bound arms and legs, sought open mouths, nostrils, eyes, and ears, and pulled the warriors irresistibly down onto their backs before the temple, where more plants wrapped across throats and foreheads, tying the warriors tightly to the ground. The soldiers of the White Cleft and the fyrd stepped back from the suddenly bound Räubers as a chitinous wall of sound grew ever closer to them. Movement in the surrounding trees and leaves made them all recoil, and they watched in horror as a black wave of countless insects—ants, termites, beetles, roaches, clouds of black flies, spiders, and more—crawled, flew, and buzzed up the face of the Tor, washing like a black tide over each of the Räubers. The hungry creatures then set to, devouring the savage warriors held motionless by the plants. The screams were sudden and severe, a dramatic crescendo that rose in pitch as the insects found tender, hidden flesh. Streams of blood flowed from a thousand tiny wounds. The insects entered mouths, eyes, ears—any opening they could find—devouring the warriors' bodies both from within and without. The shrieks of agony rose to a maddening crest, but then, as the Räubers succumbed to the insects one by one, the cries tapered to whimpers and eventually ceased altogether until the only sound remained was the chitinous clicking of the insects as they finished their grisly meal.

One by one, the defenders shared looks of disgust commingled with horror as the smallest residents of the Tor finished devouring the large invaders. After a time that seemed to last far too long, the Tor fell quiet under the caress of a soft morning breeze.

Soon the Räubers' corpses and even their clothing were gone, leaving no trace—not even bones—to mark their passing. Indeed, had it not been for the multitude of barbed weapons scattered about, one might think it had all been a horrible dream. All of them were gone, completely.

Then, like sand over the dunes in a desert wind, the carpet of insects slowly dispersed back into the surrounding flora, disappearing back into the trees and bushes that covered the Tor. All stood still, staring in wonder and revulsion at what they had just witnessed, the silence only broken by the sobs of a little boy who had been forced to grow up too quickly.

Chapter 34

Who built the temple atop the Tor of the Green Mount? What was its purpose? How long ago was it created? We may never know the answers to these questions.

> *—Hortensia Celestina, "The Traveler's Guide to the Green Mount, Expurgated Version*

Moments after the Transference
The Tor

Corvus

As the last of the insects finally disappeared, a great weariness descended upon Corvus. He looked from the boy on the little throne to the mysterious old man dead before him, then to Ashahl and Mama Warad. He looked to both of his sons, nodding to them in heartfelt relief that they lived, though it was clear that Cai was in terrible pain. Then he crossed to Yazid's body and gingerly knelt beside his longtime friend.

"We did it, old man," he said softly, placing his right hand on Yazid's cold shoulder, smiling ruefully down at his fallen friend.

Friend.

A friendship like no other he had ever known or seen. A trusted partner, co-conspirator, comrade… *yes… friend!* Yazid had been the epitome of that word, and for thirty years, he had been there to support Corvus every step of the way, sharing triumphs and defeats, proudly watching the boys grow into fine men and contributing richly to that cause. So steady and constant had their bond been that even now Corvus expected to hear his friend's voice offering some Aslene wisdom or a pithy comment to put a humorous button on the day. But that sonorous voice was forever stilled. And now, he must carry on alone.

Ach, Yazid. I'll miss ye something fierce.

He stood and started to stretch, arching his back, but was immediately reminded of his broken collarbone. With a hiss, he adjusted his left arm, once more tucking the hand inside his belt to stabilize the limb. The Aslene would have teased him about his injury, no doubt saying something about Corvus getting old and slow.

"Aye, dinna start wi'me," he said under his breath, answering the imagined jibe from his friend. He stood for a moment, staring out westward over the verdant fields of the Green Mount as the rose-hued morning light spread. He wiped his eyes against a wave of almost overwhelming fatigue. He suddenly felt terribly, terribly old.

There were unsteady footsteps on the marble behind him, then Cailean lay his hand upon his father's uninjured shoulder.

"A great heart stilled," Cai said softly, staring down at the body of the man who had helped to raise him since the age of seven. Yazid had been like an ever-present, loving uncle—wise, patient, kind. Corvus smiled gratefully to his son, only to notice the pallor of his complexion.

Ligulf stepped over, holding his cittern, which looked incongruous given the gore that painted the young man's face and body. He began to softly strum "Merrick's Lament," an ancient song that bade farewell to a beloved wise man. Corvus and Cailean knelt silently and each laid a hand on Yazid's form as Ligulf's voice filled the temple.

Ne'er will we know your like again,
Ne'er will we see your kind
From an t-earrach to am fogharadh
The last of the harvest is in.
Your sails you now unwind.
To the sunset you sail, my friend.

As the last notes of Ligulf's song echoed softly within the temple, Corvus bowed his head and whispered an Aslene invocation from the Path of the Divine Halls.

"May you walk forever in the cool breezes of twilight. May your path be redolent with jasmine and eucalyptus. Drink now from the cool waters of the oasis, O Traveler. For your journey has been long, and your rest well deserved. Sleep now in the bosom of your Ancestors, their loving arms enfold you. Bi'iiradat al'ajdad!"

" Bi'iiradat al'ajdad!" Mama, Amina, and Yadira echoed respectfully behind him. They had approached quietly during the song and stood on either side of Corvus and Cailean.

With a sigh that promised more grieving at a later date, Corvus cuffed a tear from his cheek and stood gingerly. There was much to which he must attend.

He offered an appreciative wink to Li, then reached out to Mama, took her hand, and squeezed it gratefully, nodding to Yadira. He would thank them more formally later, but at the moment, he needed to find Fergus. As he turned to seek out the White Cleft monarch, Yadira stopped him.

"No, Corvus Corax," she said firmly. "Your wound…"

"'Twill keep, Yadira," he responded. Then, with a nod to Cai's broken arm, he said, "See what you can do for him. I have things to do."

She gave him a look that left no question as to her opinion of his decision to put off care. Then, muttering a string of sharp deprecations in Aslene about the foolish pride of men, she led Cai off to have his arm tended to.

As Corvus turned once more to try to find King Fergus, his eye fell upon the form of the tall healer that had accompanied the young Queen. The woman was curled up against one of the fallen blocks that had at one time made up the roof. Asleep? Unconscious? He flashed a questioning look at Mama, who nodded reassuringly to him.

"She sleeps," she told him in Aslene. "When the seed wore off, she was spent."

"Ah," he replied with understanding, grateful that the woman was not injured, or worse. Then, with a quick smile to Mama, he turned and crossed the temple. Across the defile along the path, the soldiers of the White Cleft and the contingent of the fyrd were busy tending to the wounded among them, of which there were far too many. He climbed down carefully and, walking through the soldiers, moved to the bend at the top of the trail. Here he had a less obstructed view of the path below, and the many Highlander corpses that littered the ground.

"We lost a right many," Fergus' rough voice said over his shoulder.

"Aye," Corvus replied sadly, staring down the Tor at the dozens of bodies, "but you came, nonetheless." He turned to meet his friend's eyes. "Despite dark sorcery and long miles and sheer exhaustion, the soldiers of the White Cleft fought on and saved us, Fergus."

"Wheesht, now," the King answered, glancing down. "'Twas what needed to be, nothing more."

"Nay, my friend," Corvus put a hand on Fergus' good arm. "The bravery shown here this day by you and your lot will be remembered in song and story for generations."

Cheeks reddening, Fergus scratched his neck and nodded silently, then after a moment added, "Well, let's not forget that many of the fyrd marched with us."

"Aye, they did," Corvus answered. "But they were led by King Fergus of the White Cleft." Corvus knew the deep shame Fergus' people still felt over the fact that five years prior, at the battle of Esper, the White Cleft forces had broken and nearly cost the Highlanders the victory. This monumental effort in the face of black sorcery, and taking the Tor despite horrible losses, would go a long ways toward erasing that stain on their reputation.

"Ach, well…" The King's eyes searched Corvus' face for a moment, as though pausing to memorize Corvus' praise. Then a warm smile lifted his beard. "I'm just glad we arrived in time."

Kaiso

The mercenary was seated at the south edge of the temple, his legs dangling over the edge as he cleaned his weapons, lost in thought. Somehow, he and the Queen and Maddie had survived, and more than that, Darienne had become the Moonflower. *Whatever that means.* He suppressed a shudder. His world had turned upside down. He had a deep revulsion for all things supernatural. Indeed, for years, he had convinced himself that magic didn't exist. It was all tales told to frighten children and gullible adults. But now…

He looked up as Darienne approached. Without a word, she sat beside him, dangling her feet over the edge next to his and staring out over the landscape below.

"How's your head?" he asked, nodding to the dried blood behind her left ear.

"I've had worse," she answered absently, and they lapsed into silence.

A mourning dove called from a nearby treetop. The tree was rooted further down the Tor, which placed the bird at eye level to them.

"My mother loved those birds," she said, nodding toward the tree. "After my father died, she would take long morning walks in the garden. Any time she heard a mourning dove, she would stop and stand transfixed, as though the cry of the bird was speaking directly to her."

They sat together in silence for a while longer, considering the enormity of the day's events.

"You fought well."

Corvus' voice surprised them. The two looked up to find the Raven standing over them. Kaiso was unsure as to whether the compliment was intended for the Queen or for him.

"You as well," he said in answer, once more focusing on cleaning his sword.

"We have unfinished business, you and I," Corvus said flatly and Kaiso sighed resignedly, his hands pausing in their work.

The Queen started to rise, irritation on her face, but Corvus held up a hand forestalling any response.

"But that," Corvus said, "will have to wait for another day."

Kaiso frowned in confusion and sheathed his sword, standing to face the Raven. "I thought you said I would have to answer for the crimes of the Blades," he said, hands on hips defiantly, his lips curled into a sneer.

"You fought well," Corvus replied. "And bravely, you protected those I love, and your Queen, and together with her, you gave us victory here today. I'll not sully that with the settling of old scores."

Darienne nodded approvingly and Kaiso grunted in surprise. Before he could find an appropriate response, Corvus turned and walked away. After a moment spent staring at his receding back, Kaiso sat once more beside Darienne in companionable silence. The call of the mourning dove underscored their thoughts.

"So," he said after a long moment, "you are the Moonflower, and Maddie and I…?"

She nodded again, her brow furrowed, but said nothing.

"What do you think it means?" he asked after another pause.

"I think…" she said, choosing her words carefully, a look of determination blossoming on her face. "I think it means King Serastin is going to rue the day he attacked Lachland."

Alasdair

Once the Räubers were all dead and gone, the grizzled veteran walked unsteadily over to the fountain, shedding his shirt and weapons belt, until he stood at the edge of the basin, his bare chest steaming in the morning chill. Careful to not dirty the clean water in the basin, he ducked his head beneath the stream of water flowing from the broken stone lip until his head ached from the cold. He then proceeded to scrub the blood from his arms and chest, the icy water raising gooseflesh up and down his torso. It was invigorating. He slipped his shirt and belt back on and strolled out of the temple, where he found Corvus moving among the wounded, offering encouragement and help where he could.

"You know there's others will tend to that, eh?" he asked the Raven.

"Aye," Corvus responded, not looking up from where he knelt beside a wounded member of the fyrd. "But it eases my conscience to help where I can."

Alasdair shook his head but said nothing. He had known and fought alongside Corvus Corax for more years than he could remember. The man always carried guilt for his dead and wounded soldiers after a battle, as if his own actions had killed or injured them.

Well, Alasdair thought. *I suppose that's why we all follow him and trust him so. He's never careless with our lives.*

"Where to now?" he asked after a moment's pause. "What's next, d'ye suppose?"

The Raven took a deep breath before answering. "There's still so much we dinna understand. The boy is now the Gatekeeper of the Tor. But what exactly does that mean and how will it affect the Green Mount? We defeated the enemy today," he said with an affirming nod, "yet I fear this was but a single battle in what will prove to be a long, bloody, and very ugly war. Two hundred and fifty Barbárs died here today. But in their camps, there are tens of thousands, eager to try their luck at the Green Mount. I suspect we'll be fightin' this war a long, long time."

"Where will it take us, d'ye suppose?" Alasdair asked.

"There's no telling," Corvus said, then turned to the veteran with a wry smile. "But I suspect we'll find out soon enough."

Corvus

With a grimace of pain, Corvus rose and placed his hand on Alasdair's shoulder, where he paused beside the veteran soldier long enough for the lightheadedness to pass. After a moment, he felt ready to proceed, and flashing a brief smile at Alasdair and patting his shoulder in gratitude, he made his way back up into the temple. Carefully stepping over the wounded soldiers that now covered the marble floor, he made his way over to where Argant sat. Seeing Corvus moving toward the throne, Mama likewise rose and joined him. The boy's eyes were unfocused, his thoughts turned inward. Corvus knelt beside him and carefully placed a hand on his knee. Argant's eyes fluttered open and with an inhalation he brought his focus onto Corvus.

"Hello," the child Gatekeeper said, looking from one to the other. His eyes fell on Corvus' broken clavicle. "You're hurt."

"Aye, a bit," Corvus responded with a small smile. "How fare you, lad? Are you well?"

"I'm fine," the boy replied simply. "Oh, you mean the Tor?"

"Aye," the Raven responded, searching the child's face for any sign of discomfort or confusion. It was all so very much to ask of a wee child, and Corvus was already feeling guilty for the carefree days and all the joys of youth that this little boy would never know.

"Don't worry," Argant said, placing his little hand on Corvus'. "The Tor is awake now."

"Aye, but—" Corvus started, but Argant cut him off.

"It's wonderful." He smiled dreamily. "So much love."

"Are you hungry?" Mama asked in Aslene as she reached out and gently stroked the boy's cheek.

"No, Mama," he reassured her with a radiant smile. "The Tor takes care of me." Then he turned to Corvus and added, "Don't worry. I'm fine." He paused to reflect for a moment, his little hand on his chin in a very adult gesture. "I think I'm beginning to understand it all."

Epilogue

"This place, these books, they have a sort of magic, you see. For between their covers, or wound within a scroll, you'll find adventures, breathtaking sights, journeys to faraway, exotic lands filled with mystery and wonder—all to be discovered in the comfort of your sitting room. One need only turn the page to begin a new sojourn, meet new friends, discover new oddities, and unlock the very mysteries of the ages. Yes, these books are a magical thing indeed."

> —Zacharias Malmat
> *Last Archbibliognost of the Great Library in Tabith*

Corvus

He paused in the open doorway, stamping his feet on the small mat to shake the snow from his boots before setting his armload of firewood in the stand beside the hearth.

For years, this stone house that he had built for Greer had been filled with laughter and song, Yazid's rich voice telling tales by the fireside as wonderful smells emanated from the kitchen—exotic spices and roasted meats. Corvus looked to the padded stool by the hearth that was Li's customary spot, where he would sit and pluck at his cittern for hours, learning a song or creating a harmony. The stool was unoccupied now, as was the house, except for Corvus. He stoked the fire and adjusted a pot of water hanging from a hook over the flame. Within a short time, the water was boiling and he made himself a cup of tea, adding a generous dollop of honey to the steaming mixture. It wasn't the fine brew that Yazid would make, or the even more heavenly brew that Yadira managed, but it would have to do.

Settling himself in his armchair beside the fire, he sighed and looked around the quiet house. It had been three months since the battle on the Tor, and all their lives had changed. Cai lived in Esper now, where he and the new Queen of the Glenfolk, Brigit Stuart, were planning a spring wedding. It would be a grand affair, and gods knew the people of Esper were due some joy after the harrowing days of the autumn and their losses suffered.

"They'll make a fine..." he started, only to pause mid-sentence when he found himself addressing Yazid's empty chair . It was a great padded armchair with silken throw pillows trying to fill the space left behind by its former occupant. *Again.* He sighed. He had lost count of how many times he had turned to share something with his friend, only to be once more reminded that Yazid was no longer with him.

The familiar stone of loss once more dropped into his stomach. He sipped his tea and recalled once more the events that had immediately followed those dangerous days upon the Tor.

The day after the battle, Maddie the healer had finally awoken, groggy but recovered from her overexertion. She had immediately tended to Cai's broken arm in a wondrous manner, repairing his shattered shoulder and mangled limb. Then she had healed Corvus' collarbone with what seemed to be very little effort. Afterward, she had turned her attention to Ashahl, despite his weak protestations. The sword master, ever noble of heart, kept insisting that given his advanced age, she should tend to those more youthful and let him pass. But none of the defenders would hear of that and insisted that she look to him. After an effort that nearly undid her again, she was able to repair his internal bleeding and broken ribs, and save the aged master's life.

She stopped short, however, of healing his blindness, both due to a concern that the effort would overtax her and in honor of Ashahl's desire not to have his eyesight restored—he said he somehow found greater clarity in the solitude of his blindness. That made little sense to Corvus, but he knew better than to argue. By the end of the day, all three men stood refreshed and healthy thanks to Maddie's exertions.

It was then that the next big question arose, first voiced by the mercenary Kaiso. How were they to get home? The golden fortress with its magical doors was no more, having been destroyed and dissolved into the gloom.

No one knew the answer, and the Queen and her group were less than thrilled at the notion of having to travel back to Lachland by mundane means, which would take weeks or even months, depending upon weather and any hardships and dangers along the way. No one knew the answer, and a foul mood descended upon the party as they settled in for yet another cold night on the Tor.

The next morning, with the hubbub of the soldiers of the White Cleft gathering their wounded and preparing to march home as a backdrop, Corvus noted a figure seated on the fallen block by Argant's throne. He didn't recognize the person as they were wrapped in a hooded cloak and hunched forward, facing the boy. Curiosity getting the better of him, he strode over, his fingers absently trailing in the cold water of the fountain as he passed it. He was about to greet the figure when he heard the telltale yip of a small dog.

"I wondered if you'd return to us, Latrans," he said to the hooded figure's back, relief coloring his voice.

"There's no fooling you," the Fool said, turning with a sly grin. He was holding his dog in his lap, tucked under the cloak. With a laugh, the odd man leapt up and shucked off the cloak, revealing his characteristic motley garb.

"Fool!" The young Queen shouted from across the temple, rushing over to speak to him.

"Majesty." The Fool greeted her with a bow. "So glad you survived this ordeal. Tell me, did you learn anything? About your friends? Or perhaps yourself? Hmmm?"

"One might say so," she replied, her voice and words a case study in regal understatement as the other defenders began to gather around them.

"Fool," Corvus said, drawing Latrans' attention, "we are deeply grateful for all your assistance and… wisdom. As you can see, the boy is now the Gatekeeper of the Tor, though I must confess I'm less than clear as to the meaning of that."

"Yes!" he cried, leaping down from the block with his characteristic animation. "You did well!" As he said this, he poked Corvus in the chest. "And so did you… and you… and you!" Each of these was said with an accompanying poke into the chest or arm of one of the bemused defenders. Cai, Alasdair, Darienne, Maddie, Mama, Piper, and so on. When he finished, he swept once more into the middle of their ad hoc gathering and spun himself in a circle. "You all did so well!"

"Never mind that," Kaiso interrupted, a sour look on his face. "How are we to get home? The nation of Lachland has been invaded and has need of her Queen."

"Yes," the Fool said, scratching his chin thoughtfully. "There is that. Hmmm. Well, I'm sure you'll find a way."

"Wait," the Queen demanded. "Don't you have magic to return us?"

The Fool's mouth opened and closed several times in consternation, not unlike a landed fish.

"Fool?" she persisted. "Answer me."

"Well," he started, then shrugged. "Not really, no."

"You mean we're stranded here?!" She exploded, her voice becoming shrill in disbelief. Many other voices quickly joined in and were soon speaking at once.

"No." A high voice somehow penetrated the din, silencing them all.

With a knowing smile and a bow—like the maître des cérémonies of a street play turning the audience's attention to a new actor just entering the stage—Latrans directed the group's attention to Argant.

"You're not stranded," Argant said as all eyes turned toward him, a look of unfolding wonder on his little face.

"Argant?" Corvus said gently. "What d'ye say?"

The boy looked up at him, those jewel-like eyes sparkling in the morning's light. "The Tor can get you home," he said, the slight frown on his face suggesting he was discovering this at the same time they all were. "I think."

The defenders looked back and forth to one another, to see if anyone understood what was being said.

"How, Argant?" Mama asked.

"The Tor has always been a Gate," the boy said distractedly. "But it has been sleeping, and now… it's awake." He smiled up at the surrounding adults as though that explained everything.

There was some discussion as people moved to gather their belongings and prepare for a journey. At some point, Corvus became aware of a great thrumming sound emanating from the Tor beneath them. He had lost track of Latrans and after searching the temple and surrounding area, concluded the Fool had slipped away, as was his habit.

The thrumming in the Tor grew in intensity. Just as Corvus had witnessed the red ribbons of power during the battle, he now saw multicolored ribbons flow from Argant's staff. The ribbons moved like a river over the heads of the soldiers preparing to march, then began weaving a path or road out into the air, the near edge anchored at the eastern edge of the Tor, high above the path below. Corvus watched as the magical trail of ribbons rapidly wove and bound itself together into a substantial and glowing road that stretched into the distance, far beyond sight.

Mama clutched Ashahl's shoulder excitedly as she watched the path—clearly a gift from the Ancestors—form before their eyes.

"It is the *tariq qaws qazah*!" she whispered, in a voice that conveyed equal parts excitement and awe.

Ashahl nodded sagely before replying, "Yes, the legendary Rainbow Path. Its mysteries were lost to us centuries ago." The sword master then turned toward Corvus, an uncharacteristic grin splitting the old man's face. "We are living in a time of legend, Corvus Corax. I am eager to see what other mysteries our young Gatekeeper unlocks as he learns to manage the Tor."

"Aye, Master," Corvus responded. "These are rare times indeed."

Mama clucked her tongue in wonder at the sight of the bridge, then crossed back into the temple to once more embrace Argant. Corvus couldn't hear what was said, but both Mama and the boy had to wipe their eyes several times. They hugged once more, and Mama kissed Argant's cheeks and held his face tightly, leaning her forehead against his. She whispered something that Corvus assumed to be prayers, then finally, with much difficulty, she turned away from the boy and made her way back to Ashahl's side.

Yadira then bent down to Argant, handing him a small, cloth-wrapped bundle. His bejeweled eyes examined it in confusion for a moment, then lit up with delight. He pulled one edge of the cloth back to reveal a large chunk of honeycomb. He thanked her and gave her a hug, which she returned more warmly than she had in the past. Then, wiping her eyes, she joined Mama and Ashahl. Finally, Amina stood before him. Argant did his best to keep from crying, but when she spoke quiet words to him, his resolve failed and he threw his arms around her, sobbing aloud. She returned his hug, holding him until the worst of his tears had passed. Then, she placed a hand awkwardly on his head and turned away to join Mama, her eyes downcast.

Ashahl had then hugged Corvus and quiet, meaningful words were spoken between them. They did not speak long, nor overmuch, as was the way of these warriors. But the few words exchanged were clearly profound, as both were soon wiping away tears. Mama had embraced the Raven in one of her powerful hugs, once more gripping his face in her hands and clucking her delight.

"I am enriched by having met you," she said to Corvus, clutching his face.

"I suspect this won't be the last we see of each other, Mama," Corvus replied with a wink, taking her hands and kissing them in the Aslene tradition for departing family. "Sure and the Five will no doubt have need of your wisdom and strength once more."

Yadira and Amina were next, after each bidding farewell in their own way: Yadira with a chaste and careful handshake and Amina with an awkward, non-contact curtsy before him.

Ashahl turned to face the rainbow trail, as though he too could see it. A broad grin lit his face.

"That will do nicely," he said, as though this all made sense to him. Then, the blind sword master of the Silken Emperor took the hand of his long-lost love, Mama Warad, and led their party onto the magical trail. Just before their feet touched the multicolored path, they paused to wave one last time, and then they were gone—though the trail remained, the ribbons writhing and shifting, as though the path were remaking itself.

The Queen stepped forward, a question on her face.

"Yes, you are next," Argant said softly, his free hand drawing invisible designs in the air.

"One moment, if you please," the Queen said to Argant, before turning to Zsoka. "Empress, we have not had the opportunity to speak much. But I wonder if you would do us the honor of accepting an invitation to join us in Lachland. There is someone there we would very much like to introduce to you."

"Of course we accept your kind invitation," the Empress responded, surprise and a hint of suspicion in her voice, "though Lachland is further from my homeland."

"Yes," the Queen responded. "I assure you that at the earliest convenience, I will see you aboard a ship bound for Orense."

"Then by all means," the Empress said with a shallow tilt of her head.

Goodbyes were said all around, though Corvus and Kaiso limited their exchange to wary but respectful nods. Then the Queen, Maddie, Kaiso, and Empress Zsoka stepped up to the path, over the trampled junipers, and paused at the edge of the mystical roadway. It took Corvus a moment to realize it was

Kaiso that was hesitant to step onto it. The Queen, after urging him on, laughed lightly and shook her head, stepping out and disappearing from view. Maddie and Zsoka followed, leaving Kaiso alone and flummoxed. Looking around, embarrassed, he cursed and then stepped onto the magical path. And then he too was gone.

"D'ye suppose that trail might carry me and my men back home to the White Cleft, as well?" King Fergus asked as he stepped gingerly forward, his arm wrapped once more in a blood-spotted sling.

"Oh, yes," Argant said easily, and began drawing more invisible sigils in the air with his free hand.

Corvus turned and wrapped his arms around his old friend, careful not to aggravate the King's wound.

"You and your soldiers have proven the valor of the White Cleft in a way that can never be denied," he said to King Fergus, holding him at arm's length and staring into his eyes. "This will not be forgotten."

"Wheesht, now," Fergus answered, pressing a medallion into Corvus' hand. "This is my vote."

Corvus looked down to find it was an enameled and intricately carved brooch showing a crown floating above mountains, with a river cutting through them. This was one of four High King brooches! Each of the three monarchs of the Green Mount, as well as Corvus—representing the High Valley— possessed one of them. Should the time ever arise when a High King was needed to unite the Green Mount, each leader would give their brooch to their nominee. Anyone that held three of the four would then be elevated to become the High King of the Green Mount. This was a rare and unlooked for honor.

Corvus shook his head and started to give the brooch back, but Fergus would have none of it.

"We all know you're the man for the job, Corvus," Fergus said, squeezing his friend's fist. "You prove it with every battle, every stratagem, and every victory. And I suspect the dangers of the time are only going to increase. We need you, as High King, to keep us all safe."

Corvus stared at the brooch in his hand, dumbfounded and at a loss for words.

With a chuckle, Fergus patted his shoulder and added, "'Til next time, old friend."

The King of the White Cleft turned and called to his soldiers to follow him. Corvus watched as each of them disappeared when their foot touched the multicolored path floating in the air.

Once they were all gone, it suddenly felt very quiet—only the murmurs of wonder from the members of the fyrd could be heard, along with a lone mourning dove calling to the blossoming day.

"Right," Corvus said with a sigh, turning to his sons, "time we should be heading along as well."

"Da, wait," Ligulf said.

"Aye?"

"We've been talking, Piper, Rhona, and me," his younger son said.

"What's doin', Li?" Corvus asked, confusion in his voice.

"Right sorry we are, sir," Piper interjected. "Bit thir's a seendle ancient ballad that speaks o' th' sleeping bourach o' th' north."

"Sorry?" In his tired state, Piper's dialect was nigh incomprehensible even to Corvus.

"Piper recalled the words to another ancient ballad last night," Li explained. "It tells of a 'sleeping mount' somewhere in the north sea."

"Och, aye?" Corvus affirmed. "What of it?"

"The ballad says this mount can awaken," Li said haltingly, as though breaking worrisome news, "once that of the autumn stirs."

"Ye don't say?" Cai exclaimed in wonder.

"Aye," Li told his brother. "It seems clear enough. That's one of the four Gates."

"But what's that to do with you?" Corvus asked.

"The ballad calls for minstrels three to 'light the fire that wakens the Tor.'"

"Li, you canna mean…" Corvus began.

"Sir," Piper interrupted. "Ye didnae hawp me afore. Hear me noo. We hae a part tae speil in this saga. We're aff tae fin' th' northern Tor 'n' wake it up."

These three minstrels—Piper, Rhona and his younger son, Ligulf—planned to go on an adventure seeking the northern Tor? Corvus looked in horror from one to another.

"No, Li, Piper, hear me—" Corvus began.

"The ballad's clear, Corvus." Rhona cut him off. "Only minstrels three have a chance to light the flame and awaken the northern Tor."

"Sure you're not remembering clearly," Corvus pleaded, turning to Cai for support only to find his older son's eyes alight with pride. "At least let me send some troops with you for protection."

"They've all done enough," Li said, shaking his head. "And long for nothin' but to be home with their loved ones. We'll be fine, Da."

"This is your time, Li," Cai said with a broadening smile. "I only wish I could go wi' you, to watch yer back!"

"Cai, Li, no, you're no' minding me," Corvus said helplessly as his sons embraced in a fond farewell.

Then suddenly all was hugs and tearful leave-taking as the minstrels gathered their bundled belongings and Li's cittern and puntina.

"I love ye, Da," Li said with tears in his eyes, then the three were off, disappearing the moment their feet touched the floating path. Corvus stared at the empty, mystical trail for a long moment, his throat thick with emotion.

"Where didja send 'em?" Corvus finally asked Argant when he felt like he could trust his voice again.

"As close to the northern Tor as I could," the boy replied enigmatically.

"Wait, what d'ye mean as close as you could? Canna ya send them anywhere you like?"

"No. There is something around each Tor, like an invisible wall..." Argant's little brow furrowed as he tried to perceive and understand what he was feeling. "I can't send them directly there for some reason, so I sent them as close as I could."

"Now, you listen here..." Corvus began, a father's worry bubbling up.

"Da," Cai said, resting a hand on his father's shoulder. "They'll be fine. 'Tis Li's time. This is what he's been after all along. A purpose."

"He's too young to be—" he started.

"If I recall correctly," Cai interrupted, "you weren't much older than Li is now when you went on your grand adventure halfway around the world, eh?"

Corvus started to object, but relented in the face of his son's knowing smile.

"Well," he finally said, turning to face the mystical path once more, "Five keep them safe."

"Aye," Cai agreed. "Five keep them."

"Your turn," Argant said to Cai and Alasdair, his free hand continuing to draw sigils in the air.

"He'll be fine, Da," Cai reassured his father. "He's a rare one, our Li."

"What of you?" Corvus asked. "Will ye be comin' home?"

"I think the new Queen of the Glenfolk has other plans for me," the young general said with a wink. "But I hope you'll come to Esper for Beltane, if not sooner."

Then, with a smile and light punch to his father's shoulder, Cai led Alasdair to the edge of the trail. He turned and nodded once more, then they too were gone.

After that, Corvus had rounded up the few remaining Adders and Dallin. He had watched as the members of the fyrd that had marched with Fergus disappeared one by one on the multicolored road, and then the Adders had followed. Finally, Corvus and Dallin stood on the trail head facing the temple.

The boy sat in his small, unimposing throne near the rear of the temple. In his lap, a bundle of fur that Corvus recognized to be Brochy snuggled happily, Argant's hand absently stroking him.

"C'mon, ya wee beastie!" Dallin called impatiently.

With a grunt of irritation, the young badger crawled out of Argant's lap and trundled across the temple floor. With a hop and a slide, he descended the defile and crossed to join Dallin and Corvus.

"The temple looks a might empty now, eh?" Dallin commented with a wistful smile.

"Hmmm," Argant responded noncommittally.

"You'll be alright, then?" Corvus asked, his every fatherly instinct rebelling at the thought of leaving the child alone on a mountaintop.

"Better than alright, sir," the boy answered with a grin and a wave of his hand.

With that gesture, a flood of multicolored ribbons flowed from the staff, swirling throughout the temple. Structures sprang into being as the temple suddenly rebuilt itself, somehow recalling a shape and structure that hadn't been seen in millenia. The new walls and ceiling decorated with elaborate painted patterns and swirls of color. Ancient stonework, scarred and marred by centuries of wind and weather, was suddenly polished to a mirror reflection both inside and outside. Torches burst to life in sconces that hadn't existed a moment earlier. A great roaring hearth came into being on the northern wall of the temple and lush woven carpets covered the clean and polished marble floor. The little chair on which the boy had been sitting was suddenly positioned in the center of the temple, and had grown to become quite magnificent in size. Great cushions padded the stone seat, and the boy was wrapped in velvet robes and the softest of blankets. Dallin gasped as a great brown bear suddenly appeared from the curve in the trail to their left. The creature padded past them and climbed the new marble steps that led to a great iron-banded wooden door, which now stood open at the front of the temple. The bear entered and curled up at Argant's feet protectively.

Then, the boy's sparkling, mismatched eyes caught Corvus' — and for an instant, he saw what the boy was seeing, felt the disorienting sensations. Argant was somehow sharing his mind with Corvus. The boy was soaring, seeing through the eyes of a bird… a raven… as it soared down from the slopes of the High Valley. There, the smoke fires from Stilling could just be seen in the distance. The bird banked sharply and dove down, making Corvus' stomach fall. He struggled to gain his bearings even as the bird alighted on the branch of a tree above a small campfire where a mop-headed man in motley clothes sat tossing treats to his scraggly little dog. The man looked up briefly and smiled.

Then the vision ended and Corvus' hand shot out to Dallin's shoulder to steady himself.

"You see," Argant said. "I'm not alone. I'll never be alone again. I'll be fine."

"Aye, I suppose you will," Corvus said unsteadily. He sensed almost no limit to the child's power and reach, but more than that, he felt a sense of balance had returned. Argant was no longer the innocent child, but somehow his innocence, his inherent goodness, had bonded with the Tor. He had no idea what this would mean for the land or his people, but looking into that cherubic face with those sparkling eyes filled with wonder, hope, and peace, he wasn't worried. The Green Mount was in good hands.

With a tilt of his head to Dallin, the two of them stepped onto the ribboned path and found themselves back in the High Valley, a short walk from the village of Dóchas.

Three months had passed since then. The Winter Solstice approached with all of the attendant gaiety in the village. Decorations adorned every house, save his. Each market stall had garlands, pomanders, ribbons, and bells hanging from the rafters. But the stone house perched atop the snow-covered hill at the eastern edge of the moor was unadorned and lit only by the firelight from the hearth within. No candles, no lamps, just a gloomy dimness that mirrored the spirit of its lonely occupant.

He sipped his tea and stared into the flames, wrapping a woolen blanket more tightly around him as the winter's chill seemed to ignore the blazing hearth and penetrate the air.

There was a knock at the door, and with a slight frown of confusion, he set aside his tea, rose, and answered it.

"Corvus!" Dallin cried, bursting into the room followed by Brochy—now a full-grown badger—who promptly shook the dusting of snow from his fur.

"Dal?" he asked, surprised. "What's doin?"

"Didja forget then?"

"Sorry?" His mind raced, trying to think of what she could mean.

"The Yule party," Dallin said with an exasperated roll of her eyes. "I told me ma you'd forget."

"Oh, right," Corvus said, shaking his head. "Listen, Dal, I think I'd best..."

"Don't even think about making some excuse, Corvus Corax," she said, stopping him with her hands on hips. "The whole village is there waiting for you."

"For me?"

"Aye, ya numpty! For the love of the Five, Corvus, yer the guest of honor! Now go get changed, man. Brochy and I'll warm by yer fire while we wait."

The rest of the evening was a blur of laughter, hearty hugs and slaps on the back, the warmth of community and even family, he might say. Slowly, Corvus' icy shell of sadness melted and he warmed to the love and joy of those around him. Songs were sung, dances were danced, and it was entirely possible that too much holiday cider was drunk. There were heartfelt toasts to the memories of Toren and Yazid, and all those lost in battle. Shanna, the healer, served the drinks, taking it upon herself to gradually add more water to them as the groups became more inebriated throughout the night. Despite many requests, Corvus begged off telling tales of the battle. That would have been Yazid's role. However, Dallin joyfully jumped right in and shared their stories—embellished so colorfully that his Aslene friend would have been impressed. She told of Corvus arriving in the night, both he and his mount glowing with golden magic and accompanied by a floating star that illuminated his way, like Ilian himself. She told of the battle for the Tor, the bravery of the Adders, and the desperation they felt as the gloom overtook them. Inspired, perhaps, by her long years of friendship with Ligulf and his rare gift of storytelling, Dallin dramatically recounted the battle, giving each person that fought on the Tor a moment of glory. Prayers were offered for those that had passed, and congratulatory hands clapped the backs of all who were still with them.

Hours passed, and finally the party wound down. Corvus wished everyone a happy Yule, then managed to walk a bit unsteadily back home under the cold, clear sky, still humming a tune and chuckling at the punchline from a joke Maclan's older boy, Damhan, had told.

The croak of a raven surprised him as he climbed the small hill toward his front door, and he looked up to find the bird perched upon the outside sill of the large window, its black beak tapping the glass.

The bird flew off as he reached his house, and he stood for a moment on the threshold, watching it disappear into the night. Lifting the latch, he opened the door to be greeted by a gust of wind carrying the unexpected and quite impossible scents of the kitchen spices favored by Greer. A frisson of "other" washed over him as a chill crab-walked its way down his spine. He stepped into the darkened room, closing the door quietly behind him. The embers in the hearth crackled softly. Then a voice, *her* voice, spoke in his… mind? His memory? It was Greer wishing him a happy Yule, as she had done for so many years. He almost felt her warm lips on his cheek, and the clean scent of her skin was so present it brought tears to his eyes.

"Greer," he said softly.

"My heart," the voice seemed to answer, and a warm sensation, not unlike the embrace of his dearest love, enveloped him.

Cast of Characters:

<u>High Valley Region of the Green Mount:</u>

Bradana – Senior leader of the fyrd and highest ranking female. Trained by Yazid in Aslene spear technique.

Cailean MacRaven – Elder son of Corvus and brother to Ligulf. Expert in all forms of bladed combat.

Corvus Corax – The Raven. Legendary swordsman and untitled warden of the Green Mount. Born Coinneach MacLir. Father of Cailean and Ligulf, and best friend and longtime comrade of Yazid.

Dallin – Childhood best friend of Ligulf. Her family and Corvus' have been very close for many years. Dallin was attacked and assaulted by a gang of itinerant traders, prompting Corvus to seek justice in the Circle of Grievance. Despite her experience, she has a huge spirit and great courage. She has a pet badger named Brochy and carries an enchanted bow.

Davonna – Matriarch of the village of Dóchas. Village elder. Married to Toren, the hunter.

Ligulf MacRaven – Younger son of Corvus and brother to Cailean. A gifted minstrel. Best friend to Dallin, and Piper's committed lover.

Piper – Highly skilled minstrel from the town of Mallaig, over the mountain from Dóchas. Has a vast knowledge of ancient lore, legend, and song. Ligulf's lover.

Shanna – Village healer for Dóchas and the lead healer for all the fyrd.

Toren – Village hunter and elder. A man of painfully few words and surprisingly deep knowledge and wisdom about bushcraft, forest lore, and hunting. Davonna's husband.

Yazid – Best friend and longtime comrade of Corvus, originally from Asland. A burly, likable raconteur, he is Corvus' most trusted ally in all things.

Midlands Region of the Green Mount

Lady Donella – The Lady of the Midlands, ruling from her great house in Stilling.

Rhona – Highly talented and popular minstrel. Friends with Ligulf and Piper. Niece to Donella.

Glenfolk Region of the Green Mount

Alasdair – A valued veteran soldier among the Glenfolk and longtime friend of Corvus.

Brigit Stuart – Daughter and heir to the lands of the late Lord Stuart. Upon King Mannon's death, she is elected Queen of the Glenfolk.

Countess Derwhillie – Elderly leader of the King's council, and one of the wealthiest nobles in the Glenfolk region.

Kevin McKay – Nephew to King Mannon. Lives in the White Cleft region.

King Mannon – Recently deceased King of the Glenfolk. Close friend to Corvus.

White Cleft Region of the Green Mount

King Fergus – Wry, brave, and dependable monarch of the White Cleft. A longtime friend and ally of Corvus.

Lady Yvaine – King Fergus' niece and military advisor.

Mama's Group

Mama Nabila Warad – Aslene priestess of the Path of the Divine Halls of the Ancestors. After traveling with her votaries from the far-off desert kingdom of Asland, Mama has succeeded in finding Corvus Corax and presenting him with one of the lost Keys. Fiercely loyal, mystically powerful, and deeply loving.

Yadira – Mama's eldest votary. Superb skills with herbs and spices, which makes her cooking memorable. Those same skills translate to a variety of poisons, powders, medicines, and tinctures.

Lupe – The middle votary. A solid young woman with a natural affinity for martial skills. Highly talented practitioner of mulakima, she serves as the huntress and guardian of their group.

Amina – The youngest votary, gifted with an amazing facility to remember, word for word, anything she has ever read or seen. A fragile, waif-like, young woman, she speaks in a monotone and recoils from any physical contact, except that of young Argant.

Argant – The young boy found and adopted by Mama's group after his family's settlement was burned and everyone in it slain. Mystically trained by Athdar, the Gatekeeper of the Tor, to be his successor.

Ashahl ben Qadir – Sword Master to the Silken Emperor. The most highly skilled sword master in recorded history. He was the teacher for a young man named Coinneach MacLir, whom Ashahl renamed Corvus Corax, the Raven. Ashahl also secretly courted Nabila Warad in their youth, until his father put an end to that.

The Stray

Empress Zsoka — Empress of the Orensian Steppes. Born to be Úrasszony — War Queen — of the Orensian people, by the age of twenty, she had more than doubled her nation's territories. At an infamous rendezvous with the belligerent neighbors of Orense, the Barbárs, she had crafted a lasting peace between them, and much to the horror of those at court, she arranged for Lord Vajk, the Grand Hadvezér to father a child on her. Talon, the 'bastard heir.' Shortly after the birth of her son, she was deposed by her cousin — with the aid of the Church of the Five — and sent to exile on the forbidding and frozen island of Vas. Seven years later, again with the Church's involvement, she was able to convince Vajk to free her, but at a steep cost. Against her will, she was compelled to aid and follow the Angor Shaman Blood Tooth as he and a small band of assassins made their way to the Tor.

The Adders

Anna – Prickly and bossy. Excellent skills with a spear and fiercely brave.

Barclay – Quiet and very much a follower. Tends to do whatever Anna says.

Cuddy – Stonemason with a warm heart. Beloved by his fellows for his stalwart nature.

Jack – Large, but nimble hunter from the mountains east of Mallaig.

MacLief – A quiet leader. A builder from the village of Applecross, he is respected for his engineering skills.

Pherson – Dependable.

Una – Soft-spoken, but fierce in battle.

Lachland

Brigadier St. Fiacre – Commander of Horse for all of Lachland, including the Lake Jacks of Wetheral Castle.

Darienne – Darienne I, Queen of Lachland, Duchess of Chambrun, Defender of the Marches. Referred to by her people as "the Moonflower." Assumed the throne after her mother, Queen Isador IV, died defending Autun. Served closely by Maddie and Captain Kaiso.

Kaiso – Mercenary captain with the notorious Blades of Sebastian. He serves as Darienne's personal bodyguard, sword trainer, and aide-de-camp.

Loeiza Zachar – Wife of Zachar ben Zachar. She was abducted by the Lady Ormond and tortured as a means of forcing Zach to kill Queen Isador. Now freed, she has been elevated to the position of a lady-in-waiting for the Queen.

Maddie – Darienne's attendant and close friend. Rumored to possess some form of sorcery.

Major Pierrick Justiniere – Second in command of the Lake Jacks at Wetheral Castle. Was elevated to Knight Commander following the inauguration of the young Queen and sent to replace Sir Reginald Bleiz.

Sir Reginald Bleiz – Knight Commander. Responsible for the defense of Autun.

Talon fia Vajk – Eight-year-old son of Empress Zsoka and the Grand Hadvezér of the Barbárs, Lord Vajk. Taken from Zsoka as an infant, he was raised for a time by her usurping cousin. He was then traded to Archbishop Mormand as part of a political deal between the Church and the Empire of Orense. Currently living in Lachland, in the care of Sir Zachar and his wife Loeiza.

Viscount Pietr van den Berg – Disgraced cousin to Queen Darienne. Plotted to murder both his cousin and her mother Isador. Was the cause of Loeiza's capture and torture. Currently serving a life sentence in the dungeons of Wetheral castle.

Zachar ben Zachar – A humble junior officer, elevated to high rank due to his steadfast bravery and loyalty. Upon the death of Queen Isador in the battle for Autun, Captain Zachar's actions rallied the town to defeat the Barbár invaders. Subsequently promoted to Major and then elevated by the new Queen to knighthood.

Cantabria

Bishop Xosep Galea – Personal secretary and aide-de-camp to the Pentatarch.

Field Marshal Farric – Young and arrogant commander of the Blades of Sebastian.

Pentatarch Vella II of the House Oscuridad – Supreme leader of the Church of the Five.

Scribe Briguglio – The senior scribe assigned to the Office of the Exchequer of the Church.

Angor Shamans

Blood-Tooth – Shaman with the gift of Farspeak, sent to liberate Empress Zsoka from exile on the Isle of Vas and take her up the Hidden Stair to the Tor.

Bone-Eye – *Deceased*. Shaman whose blood magic was triggered by the scent of fear. Killed by Corvus at Eagle's Gate.

Geminus – Shaman with bizarre gifts of possession and suggestion. Mind-shares with the other shamans and is therefore able to report on casualties in real time to his keepers in Cantabria.

Philaenus – *Deceased*. Shaman with the gift of unbelievable leaps. Killed by Dallin at Dóchas.

Singer – *Deceased*. Shaman with the gift of sonic attacks. Killed Queen Isador at Autun, and was then killed by Zach.

Torn Claw – Shaman with a unique ability to observe while unseen. Strong connection to Prince Umbral and his shadow magic. Chief spy among the shamans that follow Sangine.

Sangine – Leader of the faction of shamans working with the Barbárs. Able to commune and draw strength from other shamans. Also able to commune with Fel's princes, Umbral and Timor.

Barbárs

Bence – Sub-commander of the Räubers invading the Green Mount.

Barnat – First Stone Bearer to the Grand Hadvezér.

Farkas – Second Stone Bearer to the Grand Hadvezér.

Lord Vajk – Grand Hadvezér of the Barbárs and commander of their armies. He fathered a boy named Talon with Empress Zsoka years earlier.

The Five Divinities

Ilian of the Golden Hand – Patriarch and leader of the Five. Most noted for his endless generosity and calm leadership. Golden beard and gold-flecked amber eyes.

Manu, the Mother – Wife of Ilian, Mother Goddess, and Matriarch of the Five. Noted for her endless love of all her children. A crescent tattoo on her cheek.

Nuada, the Archer – Cheerful hunter and provider, patron of archers, warriors, and hunters. Noted for his unerring skill with bow, spear, knife, or sword. When not hunting, he was known to wear colorful clothing that contrasted his black skin.

Feryn, the Lucky – Fearless patroness of gamblers, sailors, adventurers, and risk-takers. Noted for her love of games of chance. Always wears a sapphire bindi.

Cruim, the Clever – Smartest of the Five. Patron of scholars, secret societies, monarchs, spies, and fools. Noted for his understanding of languages and ability to communicate with animals. Among his many other blessings, Cruim celebrated wine, song, and mirth.

The Forces of the Shadow

Fel, the Reaper – Originally known as Duff, the Delver, until his research broached the cosmic secrets of life and death. Also known as the Shadow Lord, sponsor of all dark deeds and cruelties. His appearance remains unknown, as all who look upon him are corrupted or die.

Umbral – One of the Shadow Lord's two princes. Umbral is pitch black in appearance—including his eyes and teeth—and is continuously surrounded by a swirling mass of shadows, which he can command to do his bidding. Rumored to possess enormous and baleful powers, Umbral's presence is a harbinger of his master's return.

Timor – The other of the Shadow Lord's two princes. Skeletal in appearance, with worm-ridden flesh clinging to the bones, Timor wields fear and dread and is said to be able to enter the dreamscape at will. Timor's presence is a harbinger of his master's return.

Sample chapter from

the
hIGh KING

The Chronicles of the Raven
Book IV

# Chapter 1

The rhythms and cycles of life—of this world—are immutable and keep us connected to the eternal. They are unchanging... until they change.

—Erdene, Id Shidiin of the People of the Marmot

Summer Settlements, The Frosted Lands

Sukh, a Tribesman of the Tümen

Sukh paused, his two-handed axe in mid-swing above his head, frowning at what his younger brother had just said.

"What are you saying, Shuvuu?" the burly tribesman demanded, using an affectionate nickname for his brother. He knew Timicin hated it, but like all big brothers the world over and throughout time, Sukh enjoyed tweaking him—never mind that Timicin had recently passed his thirty-second summer, and their days of childishness were long past. Timicin had been elevated to the position of Id Shidiin, tribal mystic of their people, those of the Corsac Fox. It was a position of great authority and respect, though Sukh had trouble believing his brother actually heard the voices of the spirits or could actually read the bones. A big part of him believed—or wanted to believe—his brother to be a fraud.

"The bones don't lie, Sukh." Timicin absently fingered one of the beads tied into his long, black hair as he answered. "The time approaches."

Sukh shook his head in disgust. How he had come to hate those bones! The way his brother stroked them, named them, and spoke to them like they were his children. *Foolishness and nonsense!* He chuffed in frustration, hoisting his axe once more for another swing.

A loud clatter interrupted them. But it turned out to be just one of the yaks knocking an empty bucket over in search of extra feed.

"Sorry, Mico," Sukh called out to it. "No more for now." Then he turned to a ten-year-old girl who sat by the entrance to their yurt, churning the butter. "Bayarmaa, fetch the pale from Mico before he breaks it."

"Yes, Father," the girl's clear voice answered. He watched her progress, lost in thought.

The summer had been extraordinarily wet, flooding the migratory plains the tribe followed. It hadn't hampered their spring movement, following the herds north, but the flooding had begun when they were in their summer camp, driving the herds and their tribal followers to seek higher elevation to try to escape the suddenly impassible bogs as the tundra transformed to muck. Now, the Autumnal Balance neared. In a typical year, they would be departing any day to follow the herds on their southward trek, back toward their winter homes near Hobur, a trading post. This year, however, they would delay their departure until the last possible day, trying to salvage a summer of poor hunting and wild harvest. He grimaced at their bad luck. It would be a bitter winter. The rains meant the tribe would have precious little with which to barter for their winter stores. They would need oil for their lamps, kumis—the fermented milk that made the long, winter nights bearable—cloth, beads, metal arrowheads, and tubers and vegetables grown by the Gazar, the people of the lowlands. The lowlanders would eagerly trade for the dried meats, furs, and bearskins Sukh's own people typically harvested during their summers in the north. *There will be precious little trading this winter,* he thought bitterly.

He turned back to his brother, only to find Timicin's eyes closed and his lips moving in near silent chanting, his fingers caressing a mountain cat's carved leg bone. With a sigh, Sukh returned to his woodchopping. He shook his head in disgust. *Spirits! Bones! Pfah!* He had no use for any of it. Would the spirits heat his yurt, or feed his livestock? He swung the long-handled axe, deftly splitting the thick branch he was working on.

"I know you doubt me," Timicin said quietly, eyes still closed.

The fall of Sukh's axe onto the branch was his only response.

Timicin held up the bone, showing it to his brother. "Khuvirgalt, Sukh," he said, meaningfully. "In the position it fell, it signifies great change. The *greatest* change. But it shouldn't be here."

The axe fell once more with a resounding chop.

"Don't you see?" The mystic rose, stepping closer to his brother, his sealskin cloak dragging on the soggy turf. "It *shouldn't* be here. And that means this is the time. It is upon us, as our mothers and grandmothers foretold."

Sukh paused in his labors and planted the axe head in the spongy ground, resting his hands on the handle as he caught his breath. "You expect us to upend our lives and change our movement, because one bone fell from your hand differently than you expected?"

"Sukh," the mystic said with unaccustomed intensity. "That bone wasn't in my set or my hand!" He paused to let that fact settle. "I swear to you, I didn't bring it north! There are thirteen bones in a set when casting. Always. I had removed Khuvirgalt, along with many others, as this is the first Year of the Leopard and the bones rotate with the totems."

"So?"

"Barilga is rotated in during the years of the Leopard, and Khuvirgalt is one of those that are rotated out."

"Oh," Sukh said, his voice rising in frustration. "So you were mistaken and accidentally brought this bone along in place of the other one. Everyone makes mistakes, Shuvuu."

"Just a fortnight past, here in the pass, I did a casting in which Barilga came in the throne position," Timicin said, a slight quaver in his voice. "Ask Nimci! It was a reading for her!"

"What of it?" Sukh demanded.

"Barilga is gone," he said angrily, indicating his set of thirteen bones. "It was here, in my hand, when I cast this set today. But now it's gone!"

The older brother scowled in disbelief but said nothing.

"Sukh," Timicin said, holding the bone up for closer inspection. "I examine and greet each bone before casting. It is part of the ceremony. Khuvirgalt *wasn't* in my hand. It was back in Hobur, locked in my chest."

"Then how is it here?" Sukh demanded, waving away a cloud of black flies.

"I… I don't know," Timicin replied, a look of awe in his eyes as he stared at the offending object.

"Alright, Shuvuu," the older brother said, relenting, "tell me what it means, exactly."

Timicin met his brother's gaze as worry and fear blossomed on the younger man's face. He paused before speaking, gathering the tale before beginning, as if he wanted to make sure he got it right.

He told his brother of the legend of the time of change. He told him of the three riders and what their arrival would mean. He told him of the great enemy and the upending of the seasons. He told him of the war of the gods, the coming of the khümüüs — the hungry ones. He told him how they would presage the end of all time. He told the full story, and for once, Sukh *listened*.

When he finished, they stood in silence for a time, each lost in their own thoughts, weighing the implications of the tale. Implications that, if true, would forever change their lives and the lives of all their people. Implications that suggested they were in great danger indeed.

The croak of a raven stirred them from their reverie. It was perched on the lowest branch of a stunted larch nearby. Sukh set his axe aside and, turning back toward the yurt, shouted for his daughter to go fetch her mother. He turned back once more to meet his brother's intense gaze.

"We need to be moving," Sukh said, gesturing with his chin to the southeast, not the migratory path his people had journeyed each year since time immemorial. Instead, it was the pass down toward the Free Territories. The path toward the coast and the Iron People. "We need to be moving, now. Sound the horn, call the tsuglarat. I will speak to the chieftains."

As the brothers strode off urgently in opposite directions, the raven croaked once more and lifted from its branch, flying westward with a carved bone — Barilga — carried in its beak.

About the Author

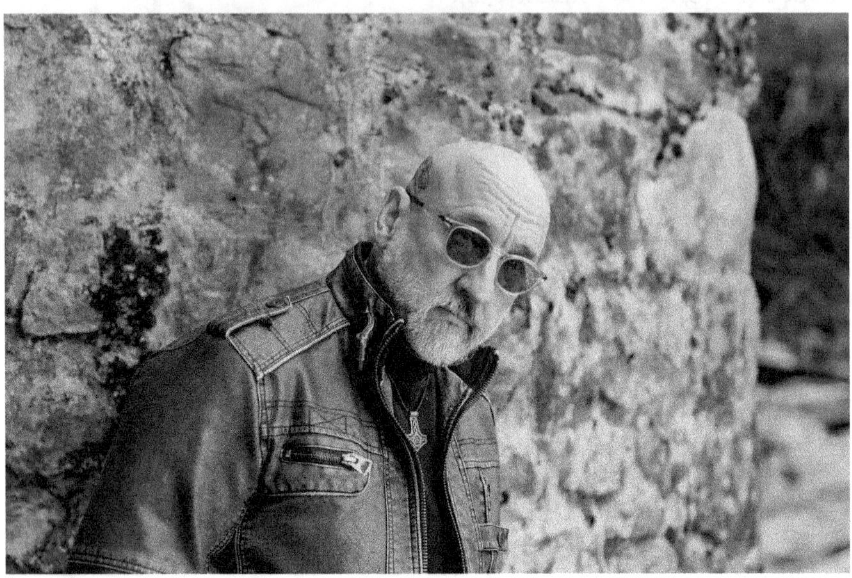

David Doersch lives in the mountains of North Carolina with his wife, Cathy, and their two cats, Harriet and Winifred. Ensconced in his living room, writing, surrounded by the unrivaled beauty of the Smoky Mountains, one would imagine it to be a quiet life. But in addition to being an author, David is a fight director and stunt coordinator for live action spectacles, a touring musician playing bagpipes with his Celtic Rock band, and a theatrical director, specializing in the works of Shakespeare. All of these competing interests try to pull him away from Daffyd and the adventures of Corvus. But then Winifred curls up on his lap, purring, and he simply surrenders once again to the call of the Green Mount.

On the web, David can be found at:

www.daviddoersch.com